BOOK THREE OF AURAGOLE'S JOURNEY

auragole
of
mattelmead

shirley latessa

LINDISFARNE BOOKS

acknowledgments

I would like to thank the many people — friends and family — who have encouraged me to keep at this long and sometimes overwhelming project. In particular, I'd like to thank Jane Lincoln Taylor for her enthusiastic and meticulous editing, Susan Handman for her beautiful covers and book design, and Bob and Nancy's Services for agreeing to distribute the Auragole Quartet, of which this is the third book.

ISBN: 978-1-58420-077-2

Published by Lindisfarne Books
www.lindisfarne.org

dedication

This book is dedicated to all the young women and men
who have graduated or will graduate from
the Waldorf Schools worldwide.

And to my granddaughter, Madeline Latessa Ortiz,
who I hope will someday read this quartet
and remember me.

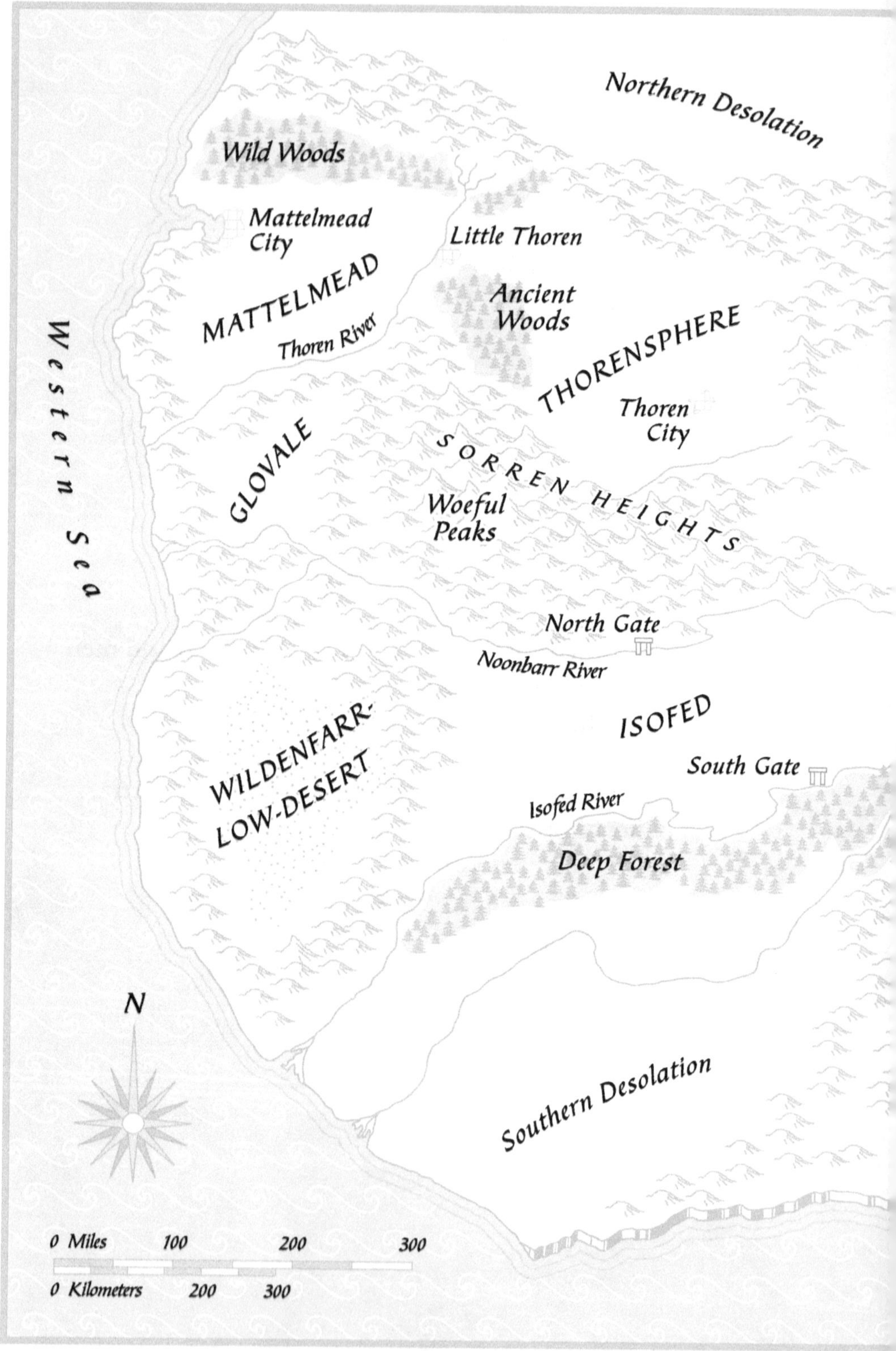

Northern Desolation

Wild Woods

Mattelmead
City

Little Thoren

MATTELMEAD

Ancient
Woods

Thoren River

THORENSPHERE

Thoren
City

GLOVALE

S O R R E N   H E I G H T S

Woeful
Peaks

W
e
s
t
e
r
n

S
e
a

North Gate

Noonbarr River

ISOFED

South Gate

WILDENFARR-
LOW-DESERT

Isofed River

Deep Forest

N

Southern Desolation

| 0 Miles | 100 | 200 | 300 |
| 0 Kilometers | 200 | 300 | |

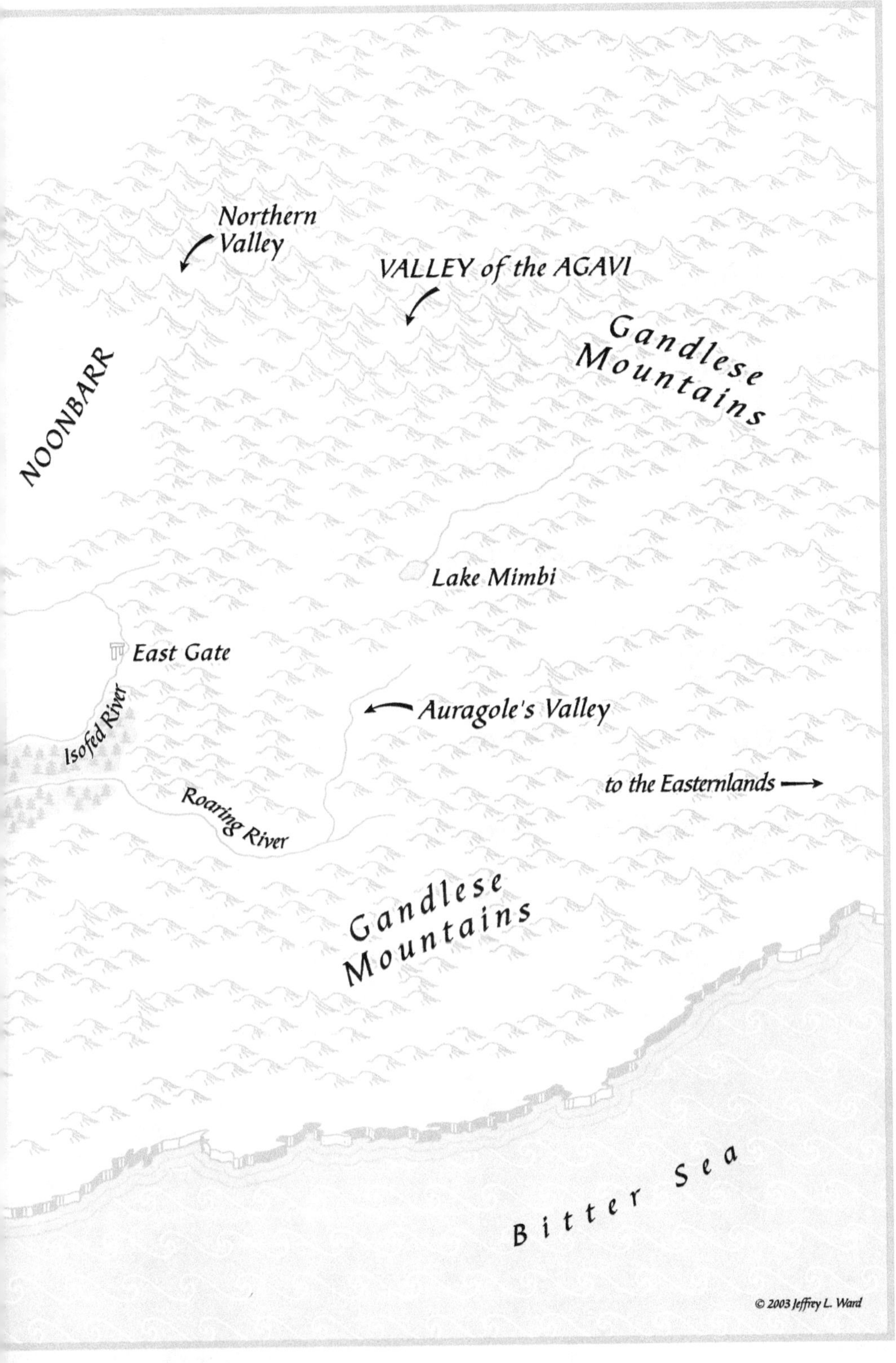

Northern
Valley

VALLEY of the AGAVI

Gandlese
Mountains

NOONBARR

Lake Mimbi

East Gate

Isofed River

Auragole's Valley

Roaring River

to the Easternlands →

Gandlese
Mountains

Bitter Sea

© 2003 Jeffrey L. Ward

There is an orientation of the spirit,

an orientation of the heart.

It is not the conviction

that something will turn out well,

but the certainty

that something makes sense,

regardless of how it turns out.

— VACLAV HAVEL

N

prologue

THE MORNING AFTER Auragole left the camp of the Companions of the Way in the Doldarr Valley, Meekelorr felt restless. When the morning training of his soldiers was over, he saddled his horse, Sunflight, and rode up into the snow-covered hills of the Woeful Peaks. The Woefuls were the highest mountains in that country known as the Sorren Heights and as a consequence were sparsely settled. The Doldarr Valley made a good hideout; therefore it had been chosen as the headquarters for the Companions in the Westernlands. However, Meekelorr's mind was not on the Doldarr, the Woefuls, or the Sorren Heights. It was on the country of Thorensphere to the north, recently conquered by Ormahn of Mattelmead.

With every land in the west that Ormahn subjugated, the time drew near when the Companions would have to leave the Westernlands and retreat east to the Gandlese Mountains and the Valley of the Agavi. It was there they would prepare for the

Last Battle against the Adversary God incarnate. It would not be many years from now—if one read the signs correctly. So the call had gone out to the Companions wherever they were stationed in the west to leave their posts and to assemble in the Doldarr Valley as soon as they were able. Come spring, Meekelorr would send most of these soldiers out of the Sorren Heights to Agavia, led by his second in command, Elarr.

Meekelorr then turned his mind to Auragole.

Though the young man had been with him many times during these past two years, Meekelorr had deliberately kept his distance. The longest period Auragole had spent in the Doldarr had been that half year waiting and hoping to get word of his lost comrades, Sylvane, Donnadorr, Glenelle, and Glenorr, from the Companions who came to bring their reports. But Auragole had also been waiting for Lorenwile.

Lorenwile had come back from his journeys in the east in early spring. It was now November.

That spring, that summer, and into the fall, Lorenwile had traveled with Auragole throughout the Woeful Peaks, teaching him the art of True-singing. During each visit back to the camp the two singers had given concerts, and Meekelorr had to admit he was amazed at the changes in Auragole. He had grown physically and was singing superbly.

Though Auragole was to leave the Doldarr for Mattelmead with Lorenwile, Auragole refused to go until he had news of his friend Elarr. Elarr had gone with a contingent of Companions into Thorensphere to bring his fiancée and others out of the children's community in the Ancient Woods. So Lorenwile had gone on to Mattelmead City without Auragole, but had given Auragole a safe-pass signed by Ormahn himself. Once Auragole reached the borders of Mattelmead the pass should serve him well.

At last Elarr had brought his charges out of Thorensphere, and with him a large contingent of Companions. A few days later Auragole had left to join Lorenwile in Mattelmead City.

It wasn't Auragole's journey to Mattelmead that troubled Meekelorr. Auragole's fighting skills were admirable and his hearing had been made keener by True-singing. What made Meekelorr uneasy was that he had not told Auragole, nor had he allowed others to tell him, that Auragole had a crucial role to play in the Last Battle—that battle that would be fought against the Nethergod, as the Agavians called him, fought by the Companions of the Way and the Agavians in the Valley of the Agavi in the faraway Gandlese Mountains. Auragole had to be free of any coercion. Free to choose either good or evil. Free to fight against or with the Nethergod. Without any manipulation, no matter how high the stakes.

Well, there was nothing at present that Meekelorr could do; Auragole was now in the hands of Lorenwile, or soon would be. Meekelorr turned Sunflight and headed back down to the Doldarr Valley. Destiny would take its course. In that he must trust.

POHL WAS LYING sleepless in his bed at the Last School in the hills just above the Valley of the Agavi. Once again he was thinking about Auragole. He knew from Lorenwile's last visit that Auragole and his friends from the Easternlands had made it as far as the southern border of Glovale on their way to Mattelmead. It was there, on the Noonbarr River, that Auragole had become separated from his comrades. All save Auragole had been attacked and abducted; that much Lorenwile had been able to tell him. Whether the four missing youths were dead or alive, Lorenwile hadn't known. Pohl was saddened by that. He had a fondness for the Easterners—especially for Donnadorr, who had been heart-parented by Pohl's old friend, Aiku, before he died.

Am I culpable? Pohl wondered. Yes and no, he decided.

After he and Galavi had guided Auragole and the Easterners out of Agavia into the Westernlands, Pohl had left them to find their own way, by a harsh and mostly unknown route, to

Mattelmead City. All the known roads had become unsafe. Should he have traveled farther with them?

No, the decision to send them on their way alone had been the right one.

Meekelorr had promised to guide Auragole and the others as far as the borders of Mattelmead, but Meekelorr hadn't shown up at the rendezvous spot. Therefore, it had been necessary for Galavi and Pohl to return as quickly as possible to the Valley of the Agavi. If something dire had befallen Meekelorr, then he, Galavi, and the Lady Claregole would be the ones responsible for the preparations for the Last Battle.

Thank all the Gods in the Agavian pantheon that Lorenwile, on his last visit, had told them that Meekelorr was safe. That had brought a lightness to the Lady Claregole's heart.

And as destiny would have it, Lorenwile had found Auragole wandering the hills of Glovale in search of his lost friends and had brought Auragole to Meekelorr. Pohl wondered if Auragole had become Lorenwile's pupil.

The Gods are endlessly creative, Pohl told himself. Trust in them. With that thought, he drifted into sleep.

LORENWILE WAS NOW riding openly and in the daytime on his pony, Surefoot, having finally entered the safe, and peaceful, country of Mattelmead. After leaving the Doldarr Valley Lorenwile had traveled mostly at night, and it had been no easy task. What had slowed his progress was that Gazber— a pompous man who called himself a duke—and his soldiers in the northwestern part of the Sorren Heights were jittery. It had been widely rumored that Ormahn of Mattelmead, who had marched into Thorensphere in the spring on his relentless conquest of the Westernlands, was now returning by the southern route to Mattelmead. Even though it was November, Gazber apparently was afraid that Ormahn might decide to attack the part of the Sorren Heights Gazber tentatively held. It seemed to Lorenwile that Gazber had his ragtag army out in full force, so Lorenwile, once out of the safe Woeful Peaks, had traveled with the utmost caution.

While riding, Lorenwile thought often of Auragole, with whom he had spent the spring and summer leisurely journeying through the Woeful Peaks. In those beautiful wilds, Lorenwile had taught his new apprentice the rudiments of True-singing— a rare kind of singing that few knew existed, and even fewer could accomplish. Auragole had been an apt pupil. Should time permit, Auragole would someday be a fine True-singer.

Lorenwile had been away from his home in Mattelmead City much longer than he had anticipated. He had to get back before he was forgotten and while he could still reclaim his job at the Blue Heron as its premier singer. But Auragole would not come away from Meekelorr's camp until his friend Elarr returned from war-torn Thorensphere. So Lorenwile left Auragole to find his own way to Mattelmead City. Somehow Lorenwile sensed he would see Auragole in the not-too-distant future.

There was another mission Lorenwile had to attend to—one he had set aside for far too long. He hoped to determine if the Adversary God, the Nethergod of the Agavians, was someone at the court of Ormahn.

WIHL, THE STARMASTER, was standing on the plateau behind his cottage, observing the ever-changing drama of the stars. At his feet sat Beya, the wolf. He was stroking her head and talking to her.

"A very clear sky," he said, "for a November night. Just see how much activity there is in that portion of the sky." And he pointed west.

Beya stood up, and her intelligent eyes followed where Wihl's finger pointed.

"The Gods are having quite a conversation." Wihl continued to stare at the western sky. "Now that's very interesting," he said, and reached for Beya's head again to stroke it. "There's a configuration up there that has something to do with Auragole. You remember Auragole, Beya. He visited us with Lorenwile last summer. He is about to meet someone the world calls great. So, another beginning. And each beginning brings us closer to that decisive conflict. Who knows, Beya, as old as we both are, we may yet live to see the end of this story—and the start of a new one. Come, my friend. I need to draw this on my chart. This configuration is precious and we must preserve it."

HE WHO, ALONE, knew himself to be the Nethergod sat staring out at a vast expanse of land from on top of his horse. But his mind was elsewhere. So, he thought, the young man is making his way north. Good. It is time he walked into the net. In a few years I will draw the net in, tighten it, and then pluck him out like a caught fish. He should not be too difficult to devour.

finding
and losing

PART SEVEN OF AURAGOLE'S JOURNEY
AURAGOLE OF MATTELMEAD

N

preface

WHILE ON THE road to Mattelmead, Auragole had a dream. He was young, perhaps eight. He was a girl, but that seemed perfectly acceptable in his dream. A woman, who was his mother, and the child in the dream were walking up a steep, winding mountain road. He—that is, the girl—was dressed in a rough garment and was barefoot. She clung to her mother's hand and was afraid. The mother didn't speak to the child, nor did she look at her. It seemed hours that they walked. The child wanted to cry, but knew she mustn't. She wanted to ask questions, but knew she mustn't. Finally they came to their destination. They stood in front of a small hut that sat on a ledge against the side of the mountain.

The mother called out, "Master?"

The door was flung open and light from a fireplace almost blinded the child. A large figure stood there, blocking their way. Then a deep voice said, "Come in."

They entered a room whose walls were covered with shelves

of books and scrolls. The center of the room was neat, the furnishings simple—a bed, a table, a chest of drawers, a rug, flowers.

"Master." The mother's voice, merely a whisper, shook as she spoke. "I bring you my youngest daughter. She. . .she. . .sees."

The Master nodded.

"In the village the elders told me I must bring her to you," the mother said, regaining her composure.

The man squatted down until his eyes were level with the girl's. He looked at her with such kindness that the child's heart was suddenly filled with joy. She ran toward him and he took her in his embrace.

When Auragole awoke, still safe in the Woeful Peaks, he felt a sense of well-being. He knew it had something to do with his dream, but try as he would, he could not recall it.

N

chapter one

THE SOUND OF a horse, crashing through the underbrush not far from where Auragole slept, startled him awake. Auragole was instantly on his feet, bow in hand, heart pounding. It was late morning in mid-November. Auragole had ridden most of the night before taking refuge, and had been asleep only a few hours. He had thought himself quite safe here. The small glade he had chosen to camp in was surrounded by brush and trees, far from any road—far, or so he had thought, from the march of armies. He parted the bushes and peered into the small, secluded clearing where his horse, Starwanderer, had been grazing. At that moment a magnificent black charger galloped into view. Its rider was bent low over a sweat-drenched horse.

How hard the beast must have been ridden to have caused it to perspire so in the cold of November, Auragole thought.

Once inside the clearing the horse stumbled to its knees. As the horse collapsed, the man astride it was pitched forward over the beast's neck. He landed, chest down, and slid forward on the ground. There was an arrow embedded high in the back of his left arm near his shoulder.

Auragole ran out into the open toward the man just as Starwanderer whinnied loudly. Auragole dove to the ground as an arrow whistled past his ear to hit the fallen man in his left thigh. The man, twisting to lie on his side, groaned and opened his eyes. They were wide with pain and shock. Quickly Auragole rose to his knees and fired an arrow into the trees in the direction from which the assailant's arrow had come. Auragole could hear him but could not see him. But a horse was circling the clearing, keeping to the protective bushes and trees.

Auragole crept on his belly away from the wounded man. The second arrow, this one aimed at Auragole, went wide. Auragole caught a glimpse of the pursuer then. He was enveloped from head to foot in a black cloak and hood. To Auragole, barely out of dream, barely out of the dark images of sleep and filled suddenly with the tension of unexpected battle, the shadowlike figure seemed the personification of death. Auragole shuddered. He crouched and shot again but his arrow struck a tree. How could one kill Death?

Nonsense. Auragole shook his head to clear the cobwebs away. That rider is merely a man. And it is difficult to bring anyone down in dense woods.

Perhaps Auragole could drive him off. He shot again, but by now the man and his bay mount were riding away from them, out of sight, clumsily maneuvering their way through the bushes. No wraith that. Just before he retreated into the far trees, the assailant loosed another arrow, again aimed at the fallen man. It too was far off its mark. Auragole shot one more precious arrow at a sound, the sound of the would-be killer's horse beating its way back through the underbrush and away from the glade. Auragole rose to his feet, leaned against a tree, bow ready, and waited several moments to see if the man would return.

When the sound of his retreat faded into silence, Auragole turned his attention to the one who had been injured. The man was half sitting, shaking uncontrollably, but trying to hold himself up with his right hand. His left arm was bleeding from the arrow that was deeply embedded there just below his shoulder, but bleeding not so profusely as the wound on the man's temple. His face was bruised, no doubt from his fall, and his trousers were torn. There was an arrow sticking out of his thigh. Lying near his right hand was a beautifully wrought sword.

The wounded man was richly dressed in pale-gray wool trousers, a white shirt, a tunic of light-blue silk, and a velvet cloak, all showing the hard wear and tear of an arduous ride and of his precipitous fall from the horse. The man's leather boots were finely tooled. It was not the attire one expected to find in the northern hills of the embattled Sorren Heights, so close to recently conquered Thorensphere.

All this Auragole took in as he ran from where he had been standing to kneel at the wounded man's side. The man's large hazel eyes saw him, then glazed over slightly, but he didn't lose consciousness.

"Man," Auragole said, his heart still pounding wildly, "are you mad to be running about the countryside unprotected and dressed as if you were going to a festive dinner? Everyone knows these hills are overrun with soldiers." Auragole untied the man's cloak and loosened his scarf and his shirt collar, but the words tumbled out of Auragole in a torrent of emotions, the battle heat still on him. "What can you be thinking? Duke Gazber's men are everywhere around us, ready for a fight. Haven't you heard that Ormahn's army is marching this way on its return to Mattelmead after conquering Thorensphere? They say he will sweep through the northern Sorren Heights—what with the weather still so fine—and attempt to conquer that too. Haven't you heard that either? Stars in the heavens, man, this is no time to be traveling alone and in full light of day."

These last miles on the way to Mattelmead had been as hard for Auragole to traverse as his friend Elarr had told him they would be. Luckily, there had been no snow in the lower hills to add to the difficulty of traveling. But the safety of the Woeful Peaks, in the heart of the Sorren Heights, was many days behind him.

The man ignored Auragole's barbed questions. He was in his early forties with short brown hair peppered with gray, streaked now with blood and dirt. He was tall and broad shouldered. His face, though ashen and bruised, was handsome, with well-defined lips, high cheekbones, and a firm chin.

Auragole's breathing slowed. Without touching the man, he carefully assessed his wounds. An arrow, sticking into the man's upper left arm from the back, had likely pierced the bone. It would have to be cut out. His right side had been grazed, but there was no arrow there. Though the wound was bleeding, it was probably superficial. With luck, it might not have cracked his ribs. And the arrow in the man's well-muscled thigh was deep, but it did not look as if it had struck a bone. Auragole would have to get that one out also. The man's slightly graying temple had been grazed by an arrow, too, and was bleeding heavily. Someone had certainly been intent on killing him. He had been hit four times. Auragole pulled the man's scarf from around his neck.

"Lie down as best you can, and hold this scarf to your head with your good arm while I examine you." The man acquiesced. He had fallen hard from his horse, but Auragole, his hands moving gently up and down the man's body, feeling carefully for broken bones, could find none, other than the one in his arm that still held the arrow.

"What happened to you?" Auragole asked, after his assessment of the man's wounds was done. "Soldiers? Or did some thief covet your finery?"

"The horse, what's his condition?" His words cost the man much.

He doesn't look like a fool, Auragole thought, and regretted his accusatory questioning. But he had, after all, been pulled out of a much-needed sleep into danger and battle. Still, it spoke well of the man that he had asked first about his horse.

"Go look at the horse," the man urged in a weak but commanding voice.

A man used to giving orders, Auragole thought. He reluctantly left the man's side and hurried to where the horse lay several feet away, panting shallowly. Starwanderer was standing over it. The man's horse, lying on its side, had a richly tooled leather saddle over a silk horse blanket. Auragole noticed the insignia on both, but it wasn't one he recognized. The insignia was also on the man's tunic and his cape—two crossed yellow feathers on a horizontal red sword. The beast's left front leg was shattered and its ribs were bleeding heavily from an arrow that was still embedded in its side.

Auragole's heart went out to the creature, which had been a beautiful animal. He returned to the injured man and knelt beside him. The man's eyes were closed and his face was so filled with pain that Auragole wasn't sure the man could hear him.

Nevertheless, Auragole spoke to him. "He can't be saved."

The hazel-flecked eyes opened and sought Auragole's eyes. "Put him out of his. . ." and he passed out.

Auragole raced back into the trees, gathered his belongings from the bushes, and brought them back to where the man lay. The man's breathing was too rapid, too shallow. Auragole needed a fire to brew healing herbs and to clean his knife. It was dangerous, but the would-be killer knew where they were; no need to hide from him. But if there were other soldiers about. . . Still, if Auragole didn't risk a small fire the man would likely die—if not from the wounds, then from infection. And he had lost, and was still losing, too much blood.

Auragole built a small fire, then put herbs and water in a kettle over it to brew. He stood up, swallowed hard, drew his knife, and approached the horse. Its large, rheumy, dark eyes were wild with fear and pain. Auragole touched its great blaze-streaked forehead and said, "You were a good friend to your master. Return now to the great horse soul in the heavens that is your own," and he slit the horse's throat. With a great convulsion, it died.

Starwanderer nibbled gently at Auragole's neck. "It couldn't be helped, old friend." Auragole wasn't able to keep the emotion out of his voice.

He rose, returned to the unconscious man, knelt by his side, and cut away the clothing from his arm. The man was staining the ground with his blood. That wasn't good. Auragole cleaned his knife in the fire, then poured out a large bowl of the herb broth and set it aside. He quickly tore strips of bandages from the supply he carried in his backpack and put them in the kettle with what remained of the broth. He stamped out the fire and carried the kettle the few feet to where the man lay.

Auragole took a deep breath, clenched his teeth, and then cut the arrow from the man's arm. The man cried out, but did not wake up. The wound had pierced the upper arm bone and the fall had exacerbated the break. With great care, Auragole managed to remove all of the arrow.

The blood was flowing freely now. Swiftly, Auragole cleaned and dressed the wound with the herb-soaked bandages, hoping to stanch the blood. He set the arm as best he could. The man groaned with pain as Auragole pressed the bone into place and wound a bandage tight around the arm. But the man didn't open his eyes. It worried Auragole that he seemed so deeply unconscious. Auragole secured the man's arm to his chest so as not to disturb the wound or the broken bone with his movement. Then Auragole cut the man's trousers up the right side and worked the arrow out from his thigh. The man cursed—a good sign—but remained unconscious. The thigh wound bled a great deal, but the arrow, luckily, had pierced no bone. Auragole cleaned and bound that wound, too.

The injury on the man's right side was only a shallow flesh wound and would heal quickly if it was cleaned and bandaged properly. Auragole couldn't tell if a rib or two was cracked, but that was minor and would heal by itself—if the man lived. The head wound too was not deep, but altogether he had lost too much blood. Auragole cleaned both wounds and put herb-soaked bandages on them, then secured them with strips of dry bandages.

Carefully lifting the man up to a half-sitting position, and supporting him from behind, Auragole spooned a small amount of the broth he had set aside into the man's mouth. It dripped back out.

"Take this," Auragole said, his tone soft but urgent. "It's a healing brew."

The man's eyelids fluttered a few times—good—and then he swallowed a few drops. "No more," he murmured.

Well, he's not in a coma, Auragole thought, and felt relieved. He put the man's velvet cloak under him against the hard ground, then gently laid him down on his back. The wounded man was trembling as much from shock and pain as from the cold. Though Auragole had done his best, infection was always a worry with wounds. Warmth was what was needed. But Auragole would not risk another fire. There was no blanket in the man's saddlebag so Auragole used his own, then sat back on his heels and observed the wounded man. He was shaking and breathing noisily.

He couldn't have been traveling alone, a rich person like that—surely not. Where were his friends, the party he had been traveling with? Where were his servants? Perhaps they had all been killed. Auragole wondered if he should go looking. But he didn't dare leave the injured man alone. He needed attending. And what if the cloaked assassin came back? No, it was best to stay put and see the man through the crisis.

If only Auragole could True-sing health into him. But there were two things his teacher, Lorenwile, had warned him not to do once he left the safety of the Woeful Peaks. He must not True-sing, nor even speak of it, and he must not mention the Companions of the Way—those soldiers he had recently stayed with. At least Auragole had bandages and healing herbs. Though the man had lost a lot of blood and was in shock, as far as Auragole could tell, no vital organ of his had been pierced. Surely if Auragole worked with him, tended his wounds, and saw that he drank the eldenmyrr tea he would live—provided that the wounds did not become infected.

Auragole must not let the man dehydrate from lack of fluids and loss of blood. Luckily, there was a creek just at the south end of the clearing. Auragole had herbs, biscuits, dried fish, and meat in his bags and enough dried eldenmyrr for both a poultice and to drink—at least for a few days. Well, it would have to do. If the man made it through the next day, and if the assassin didn't return, then Auragole would consider making another fire.

He picked up his bow and arrow and took his sword from its scabbard. Then he sat down a few feet from the wounded man, his back against the tree trunk and his weapons close at hand. Auragole had better stay alert. It was not yet noon. He had been asleep only a few hours when this business had wrenched him into wakefulness. Auragole had been traveling toward Mattelmead at night in the hope of avoiding soldiers, staying as much as possible within the forests of the Sorren Heights. This small glade was far from any road. He had expected to be safe here until nightfall. From his maps he estimated he was only half a dozen miles from Thorensphere. He was hoping to stay clear of that country—which was still reeling from Ormahn's conquest—and move into the hills between Glovale and Mattelmead, then come down into the southern part of the latter. Once in the country of Mattelmead, the going should be easy. Auragole had a safe-pass to show there, given to him by

Lorenwile and signed by Ormahn himself.

He knew he would be very late meeting Lorenwile in Mattelmead City. Well, that couldn't be helped. Auragole wasn't going to abandon an injured man. If the man regained consciousness, Auragole would ask him what had happened, and where Auragole might find the party with which the man must have been traveling. But for now Auragole had best stay alert. The assassin might try again—but maybe not. Maybe the assassin thought he had already killed his intended victim—or if not, perhaps he expected that the man would die from his many wounds.

Don't fall asleep, Auragole warned himself. He rose, felt the man's head, and was alarmed at how hot it was. Was there infection? Had he not cleaned the wounds well enough? The man was shaking and mumbling incomprehensibly. Auragole carried cold water from the stream in a pot to wipe down the man's forehead. Though some fever was good because it fought infection, this one was too high.

Again and again, as the day wore on, Auragole repeated this routine with at least some success. Periodically he tried to get some eldenmyrr tea into the man. Finally his breathing became less rapid, and his forehead lost some of its heat. In between bathing and feeding the man, Auragole returned to sit against the tree. He kept his sword across his knees and his bow at hand. Through the rest of the day and all through that first night he kept to this routine. But no one came near the clearing. Where were the man's friends, his houschold? Could the man actually have been traveling alone? And had the would-be assassin truly given up?

Just after dawn on the second day, the injured man opened his eyes. Auragole had been attempting to feed him some of the herb broth.

"What happened?" he murmured, his voice low and raspy.

"You've been shot at and wounded," Auragole replied, and

told him what had occurred since he and his horse had stumbled into the clearing.

Memory brightened the man's eyes. "Ambushed. My men and I were ambushed. Gazber will pay for this."

"But surely you knew these hills are overrun with Gazber's men and that he claims this territory. They say he is as skittish as a new lamb because Ormahn of Mattelmead is marching this way."

"You saved my life," the man said, trying to focus on Auragole's face.

"You've been hurt," was Auragole's reply.

"And who are you, if I might ask?"

"Auragole, son of Goloss."

"Ah, Auragole." He said the name as if he were tasting it, then closed his eyes and fell into a normal sleep.

All that second day, Auragole fought the fever—it had gone dangerously up again. He washed the man's feet and hands over and over, as well as his chest and face. He changed the man's bandages and bathed his wounds several times, hoping to clean out any infection. At least the bleeding had lessened. The man opened his eyes occasionally, watched Auragole, but said nothing.

Auragole listened intently to the sounds around him. His hearing was excellent, trained by True-singing. But he heard nothing disturbing, just winter birds, the rustling of branches, and small animals. No sounds of humans at all. Perhaps the company that this man had been traveling with had all been killed by Gazber's men in the ambush, and this one was the only survivor.

When he was not working with the man, Auragole sat against the tree and dozed on and off. "Starwanderer, I've been too long without closing my eyes. You will have to keep guard and waken me if I fall too deeply asleep."

N

chapter two

AURAGOLE SPENT MOST of the second night struggling to bring down the fever. The man had fallen unconscious again, but some time in the night he seemed to pass through the crisis. His breathing became more regular. In the morning, he opened his eyes and they looked alert and intelligent.

"So you are still here, Auragole."

"Where did you expect me to be, sir?"

The man laughed. "What are you doing in these dangerous hills?"

"I'm aware of the danger, and have traveled at night, keeping away from the roads."

"Where are you heading?"

"To Mattelmead. I have a safe-pass, signed by Ormahn himself."

"Do you? That's a rare and valuable commodity. And how did you come by such a pass?"

Auragole hesitated only a moment. "It was given to me by my master. I am to meet him in Mattelmead City."

"And what is it you do, Auragole?"

"I am a singer of songs."

"Ah, now that is welcome news."

"How did you come to be ambushed? And how many were in your party?"

The man closed his eyes, and Auragole thought he had gone back to sleep. But he opened them again and said, "Twenty in all, counting servants. We were on our way to a so-called peace parley with Gazber and his men." There was bitterness in his voice.

"You're from Ormahn's army?" Auragole felt a rush of excitement.

"I am. The army of Mattelmead is not more than a dozen or so miles from here, just across the border in Thorensphere— camped and awaiting word from me. We were hoping to bring Gazber and his territory under Mattelmead's purview without further need for killing."

"And you are called?"

"I am called Solagen."

"Solagen," Auragole repeated, and saw a look of curiosity on the man's haggard face. "Well, Solagen, will not your comrades be out looking for you?"

"Yes, if any of them survived the attempted massacre and reported back to our camp." His eyes looked cold and hard.

Not a man one would want for an enemy, Auragole decided.

"If none survived," Solagen went on, "there will be soldiers from the regular army out looking in a day or two. How long have I been here?"

"Two days, sir."

"And my horse?"

"Dead—too injured to be saved. I removed its finery and dragged the beast into the trees."

"He was a good stallion."

"Yes, I saw that."

30

"It's cold. Perhaps you could make a fire."

"No."

The man raised his eyebrows.

"It's best to be cautious, sir. Gazber's men. . ."

"After that ambush, no doubt they have run as fast and as far from here as they can. Wait around with a great part of Ormahn's army so near? Not likely. But what fools! Who would have thought that Gazber was so bent on suicide? He won't survive this, you know."

"Ormahn's army will go after him?"

"It will indeed. November or not. Even if the snows come today and stay through the winter, Ormahn will go after Gazber." The man's words were harsh.

"You know Ormahn?"

"Yes, quite well."

"Do you like him?"

Solagen laughed. "I confess, I do like him. Yes, you might say I'm extremely fond of him."

"I think it's best if you try to sleep. You're still very weak. We will need to build up your strength if we are to get you back to Ormahn's army before it breaks camp."

"That will be a long walk." The man half smiled.

"But you will ride Starwanderer and I will lead you. I'm sure you will agree that he's as fine a horse as the one you lost."

The man lifted up his head, wincing at the pain, and caught sight of Starwanderer. "Indeed, that is a splendid stallion. How did you come by such a horse?"

"Not the time for stories now, sir. Best rest. And as it is day and there is dry wood, I will risk a small fire to warm you—and to make you some more broth."

"Yes. Thank you."

When he woke later that day, Solagen asked Auragole to describe the man or men who had attempted to assassinate him.

After Auragole's description, Solagen was quiet for some

moments. Then he said, "One man, you say. No doubt belonging to Gazber's ambushers. I didn't see what happened after the first barrage of arrows. I was near the head of our troop and almost out of the short ravine through which we had been traveling. The attacks came from the hills above. I and the guards in front of me were hit in the first assault, but I wasn't unseated so I raced on ahead. Frankly, after two or three arrows struck me, all I could manage was to try to put distance between myself and the ambushers. I didn't know then how many were after me. I tried, obviously unsuccessfully, to elude my followers, and didn't pay close attention to where I was going—but I can't have gone more than a few miles from where we were ambushed. Only one you say?"

Auragole nodded.

"I'm hoping some of the men in the rear were able to retreat. If so, no doubt, they have hastened back to the main army. Well, we will find out in due time."

That third night the fever returned, and Auragole again spent much of it bathing the man with cold compresses. The fever receded with the morning.

"You've not slept much, son. How many nights have we been here?"

"Three, and I am fine. I've catnapped often. No need to be concerned," Auragole hastened to add. "Starwanderer and I are still on guard."

"You said you are a singer."

"I am."

"Then sing for me, Auragole of the Songs."

"No."

"No?"

"Surely you see how unwise that would be? It's enough that I have lit a fire during the daytime."

"And shared your provisions with me."

"Which you barely touched. Now it's best if you sleep, sir.

When you can hold down a whole biscuit, I will consider putting you astride Starwanderer and leading you back to your camp."

"You're sure you can find the way?"

"I have a map. Can you read one? Can you point out the camp's location?"

Solagen chuckled. "I can, indeed. One doesn't get to be a commander in Ormahn's army without learning to read maps."

"Then we shall find our way without obstacle."

Solagen laughed again.

"And hope that the army hasn't moved the camp from where you left it," Auragole added.

"You can be sure that until Gazber is either caught or killed, and until I am found, Ormahn's army will stay put."

"It is best you sleep now."

"Yes, son, I will."

Auragole watched the sleeping man. So he was a commander in service to Ormahn of Mattelmead, one who had been sent to bargain with Gazber, but had been ambushed instead. Once again Auragole felt the old revulsion toward, and confusion about, wars and armies. Because of the foolishness of one man—one petty leader—an invasion of the northern hills of the Sorren Heights would take place. Once again many would die who could have lived if their leader had not been so reckless.

But how would this affect the Woefuls, and Meekelorr's small army, the Companions of the Way? Auragole looked at the sleeping man from where he sat. For all this commander's bragging, how far south into the Sorren Heights could Ormahn expect to conquer? Even an angry leader would not be foolish enough to send soldiers into the snow- and ice-filled Woefuls in November. And in the spring, as soon as the weather allowed, Elarr and Affredda, the children and adults they had brought out of the Ancient Woods, and most of the Companions of the Way would leave for Agavia and the safety of the Gandlese Mountains. Luckily, Gazber was nowhere near the Woefuls.

His territory was in the northwestern part of the Sorren Heights, as Hazahn's was in the northeastern part.

Before Auragole had left the Woefuls, Companions, retreating from their posts in the north, had brought the news to Meekelorr of the fall of Thorensphere. No doubt Meekelorr also knew where Ormahn's army was. Interesting that Meekelorr had anticipated that Gazber's troops would come under attack by Ormahn as early as this fall. If Solagen's words were to be believed, Meekelorr had been right about that.

So long as he felt assured of his friends' safety, Auragole could pursue his own task, one that no longer coincided with the tasks of the Companions of the Way. Auragole was not interested in looking for the evil Nethergod, who, according to the Companions, was incarnate on the earth at present—most likely in the Westernlands. That search had, not so long ago, brought Auragole close to disaster, and had almost cost Elarr his life.

Now that Ormahn and his army had moved into Glovale and Thorensphere, the Companions no longer needed to act as champions to the war-weary peoples of the west. Ormahn of Mattelmead had taken up that task. And with his vast army, he could be of more help to the populace than Meekelorr with his small army of Companions. Now that Ormahn was bringing peace, bit by bit, to the west, Meekelorr could, in good conscience, send most of the Companions of the Way to the Gandlese Mountains, and the hidden Valley of the Agavi. There they could wait for the Last Battle.

How long would Meekelorr and a small band of soldiers remain in the Woefuls? Possibly, Meekelorr would not leave until he knew for sure who the Nethergod was.

Well, Auragole had other concerns now. He had found the life task that he had been searching for, and he wanted to put all his will behind pursuing it. Auragole wanted to be a True-singer, and until he was able to study True-singing again, he wanted to stay close to Lorenwile, and to sing with him in the

Blue Heron Café in the fabled city of Mattelmead.

Auragole wanted to be a singer, certainly not a soldier. Not that he wasn't good with bow and sword. He was very good, he thought, without feigned modesty. And he had been in his share of battles. He was no coward, nor was he unduly fearful. What he disliked, most ardently, was subordinating his will to another's will, as soldiers must do, and submitting to an army's discipline. He had witnessed some of that discipline while he was with the Companions of the Way, and had not approved of it. In this he was the son of his father, who valued freedom above all else. Auragole had left his isolated valley in the Gandlese Mountains when he was eighteen, after the deaths of his parents. Now he was just past twenty. The more he had seen of the world, the more he valued his own freedom. The way of the soldier was a restricted way.

He yawned and tried to stay awake. The area around them was filled with the soughing of the wind through the fallen autumn leaves. No human sounds wafted his way. He and this commander were all alone. Auragole knew that he would be able to hear if people were nearby. Likely Solagen was right. After the ambush, Gazber and his soldiers were probably miles from here and from Ormahn's army. Perhaps Auragole could risk singing. It would help him stay awake, and though he must not attempt to True-sing health into the wounded man, he certainly could sing songs of nature that would aid in some small way. All music was healing, all art was healing. So he had learned in the Valley of the Agavi when he had been nursed back from the brink of death.

Auragole picked up his harp where he had placed it, along with his other belongings, against a tree, and sat down near Solagen. First Auragole played some melodies; then he sang to him. He sang songs of the earth, the mountains and forests, of rivers and lakes, of companionship, and of course, love. It was not True-singing, nor See-singing either. It was plain song—that which most singers do. Still, he knew he sang well.

After half a dozen songs, Auragole stopped and listened. Quiet all around.

"Sing to me again, Auragole."

"So soon awake?" Auragole knelt down and felt the man's head. The fever had returned, but not too high. Best to deal with it, though. "First we must bring your fever down. You must allow me to cool your head with water." Auragole rose, walked to the stream, and filled the pot. He put a cloth in it and once again knelt behind the man's head. He wrung out the cloth and placed it on his forehead.

"Are you from the city of Mattelmead?" Auragole asked, "or from elsewhere?"

"From the city, fortunately, yes." Solagen closed his eyes and was soon asleep.

How long had he been with this man? Four days, Auragole reckoned, though he was losing track of time in his fatigue. And three nights. He had been on the road ten days before that. He was going to be very late arriving in Mattelmead City. Would Lorenwile give up hope of his coming? By the time Auragole had left the Woefuls—more than two weeks after Lorenwile had departed—the northern hills of the Sorren Heights had been extremely difficult to get through. Gazber's men were everywhere. Thank the stars, the good weather had held.

Perhaps he could travel into Mattelmead with Ormahn's army, once he returned this commander to his camp. Auragole did, after all, have a safe-pass. He looked at the sleeping man. He must have been the only survivor of the ambush, or surely Ormahn's men would be out looking for him by now.

Later, that fourth night, as all was quiet about them, Auragole sang again. Then Auragole woke the man. "If you can eat this biscuit, we might in a day or two try to get you to your camp." He propped the man up against his saddle and put a cup of broth in his right hand and a biscuit on his lap.

The man sipped the broth and nibbled without appetite on

the biscuit. "I was sleeping and your songs wove into my dreams. I was waiting on a road and, standing at the end of it, with a face like a beautiful woman, was Death. I began walking toward her. Then I heard your song. It wound itself around me like a garland of roses. I could almost smell them. So I turned back. Swords!" He began to laugh. "I sound like some ethereal poet spouting nonsense in the teahouses of Mattelmead." The laughing turned to a cough.

"Rest again, sir, and I will sing to you."

"Yes, thank you." Solagen closed his eyes. The night seemed unusually quiet and Starwanderer unusually restless. Auragole was exhausted, so to keep awake he sang song after song, mostly of the Deep Earth and her beauty and health in the days before the centuries of war. The songs seemed particularly poignant to Auragole, as if the wounded man and he were about to leave the Deep Earth. In his imagination he could feel Death standing silently in the trees, waiting—but in his mind, Death was definitely not a pretty woman. It was on horseback and wore a long black cloak and a hood that covered not only its head but its face.

Just before dawn he heard a hoarse whisper. "Where did you learn to sing like that?"

Auragole set his harp aside, knelt down next to the wounded man, and put his hands on his head. It was cool. "The fever's gone."

"Good. From whom did you learn to sing like that?"

"From my master," Auragole said, "and compared to him, I sing like a crow."

The man roared with laughter. "Modesty and talent. I like that."

Solagen asked for water and as Auragole held the cup to Solagen's lips, Auragole asked, "Were you with Ormahn when he conquered Thorensphere?"

"I was. Though, truth to tell, there was not much fighting. Everywhere we went, we were welcomed by the people. There were only three. . .no, four it was, real battles. The rest were routs. But the war stories will wait. What I need is a song."

"What we both need is some food," Auragole said, standing and stretching.

Solagen's mouth dropped open and Auragole caught his look of surprise. Auragole sat back down on his heels and said softly, "Sir, I cannot sing well on an empty stomach."

Again Solagen laughed. "Well, let's have those dry biscuits then."

"Sorry I've not been able to hunt. And that little stream has no fish except minnows."

"Nonsense. Nothing is missing here. I call this tea and biscuit a feast fit for a king. After all, I'm alive here to eat it."

After Auragole finished eating, he said, "What shall I sing about? War?"

"Swords, no! Sing about love. A man would far rather hear about love than war—except old men. They love songs of war."

As daylight crept slowly into the trees and bushes around them, Auragole sang about love.

> *What does it matter?*
> *Really, what does it matter?*
> *There are clouds above my head,*
> *and a place to make my bed.*
> *There are horses to ride,*
> *and companions by my side.*
> *Why would anything else matter?*
>
> *What does it matter?*
> *Really, what does it matter?*
> *Oh, yes, autumn brings the rain,*
> *but laughter eases pain.*
> *See, today the skies are blue*
> *and friends are near and true.*
> *Why would anything else matter?*

Let the days go by as they will.
I don't lack for anything
as long as someone waits for me
and I have a song or two to sing.
Why would anything else matter?

What does it matter?
Really, what does it matter?
With good comrades at my back
there is nothing that I lack.
There are stories we can share
To help push away despair.
Why should anything else matter?

Let the days go by as they will.
I don't lack for anything
as long as someone waits for me
and I have a song or two to sing.
Why would anything else matter?

What does it matter?
Really, what does it matter?
I remember fireflies,
moonlight sparkling in her eyes,
as she offered up her charms
while I held her in my arms.
Now why would anything else matter?

Let the days go by as they must.
I don't lack for anything.
Somewhere someone waits for me
and today I have a song to sing.
What does it matter?
Really, what does it matter?
Why would anything else matter?

Solagen's eyes were shiny with pleasure. "You sing like one of the Gods, if I ever believed in such nonsense."

"But you should hear my master."

Suddenly something drew Auragole's attention. There was an unfamiliar sound. It was a long way off. He stood up, sword in hand.

"What do you hear, son? I don't hear anything."

Nor did Auragole, so after a while he sat down, but he couldn't still his uneasiness. "It was probably nothing."

"How would you like to come with me, to serve me, to become part of my household?"

"Where?" Auragole asked.

"In Mattelmead City, of course, where I am heading—now that this campaign is over." Solagen seemed amused. "I promise you, I have one of the better houses in the city."

"What could I do for you, sir?" Auragole said, but his attention was elsewhere. He rose again to his feet. There was something out there, he was sure of it. However, he didn't want to alarm Solagen.

"You're nervous as a cat, son. There's nothing out there except morning birds hunting for their breakfast. Sit down."

Auragole remained standing.

"What would you do?" Solagen went on. "Why, you would sing for me and my friends, of course. There's no singer like you in the city now, and believe me, we've had the best. And I've heard the best of the best."

Auragole gave him his full attention then. The man was serious.

"I'm sorry, sir. I can't."

"No?" came the surprised answer.

"I'm engaged somewhere else."

"Another master? I'll double what he pays you."

"No, no, it's not that. . ."

"Damn it, man. Do you know what I'm offering you? Do

you know who I am?" He stared at Auragole imperiously then, and Auragole stared back.

"I couldn't serve you now if you were Ormahn himself. I gave my promise to someone else. Would you have me go back on my word?"

The man looked first angry and then amused. "Where in all the Grand Continent do you come from? From whom did you learn such independence?" He shook his head. "I admit I see little of it around me. Try running an army with men like you," and he grinned. Then his expression changed. "There *is* something out there."

Auragole nodded.

"Son, you'd better prop me against that tree."

Quickly, Auragole helped Solagen to the tree, then picked up his bow and arrow.

"Listen!" Solagen said.

There was the sound of a single horse moving stealthily in the trees that surrounded them, circling the glade but keeping out of sight.

"Put my sword in my hand," Solagen said. Auragole did.

Auragole hummed for Starwanderer and was on his back in seconds. He sat astride his horse, listening, his sword drawn, his bow and quiver on his back.

"Can you use that sword?" Solagen asked.

"When I have to. Now keep quiet so I can hear," Auragole ordered.

And Solagen was silent.

The man came riding in from the trees to the left of Solagen. Starwanderer and Auragole rode out to meet him. He looked like the same dark-cloaked man who had tried to kill Solagen before. He came charging at Auragole with sword held at the ready. Starwanderer ran at him. The man thrust at Auragole but Auragole veered away from the blow just in time. He turned Starwanderer to the left, hoping to draw the assailant away from

Solagen. But with that incredible hearing developed by True-singing, Auragole knew he had guessed wrong. Twisting on Starwanderer's back, he saw the man galloping straight for Solagen, sword ready for the thrust. What a foolhardy thing for the man to do, to leave his back unguarded.

In one fluid movement Auragole dropped his sword, turned Starwanderer, and pulled his bow from his shoulder and an arrow out of its quiver. He had trained well with Meekelorr. In seconds it was ready for firing. The assassin, heedless of Auragole, had jumped from his horse and was running the few steps that separated him from Solagen.

Steady, Auragole told himself. You have one chance. He loosed the arrow. It hit the cloaked man between his shoulder blades just as he raised his sword for the thrust at Solagen.

No good, Auragole thought. He's going to get Solagen anyway. Auragole kneed Starwanderer into a full gallop, heart pounding. Far off in the woods to the north were the sounds of men on horses, but Auragole's attention was all on the scene in front of him. The assassin had fallen on top of Solagen. Auragole leapt from his horse and ran to them. He pulled the man off Solagen. Too late. Solagen was covered in blood, but Solagen's own sword was in the assailant's chest and the assailant was dead. Auragole dragged the man away from Solagen and knelt down, hands moving quickly over Solagen's body, looking for his wound.

"I'm not injured, son. Your arrow saved me. He must have been dead as he fell on me. If not, my sword finished him. It's his blood on me, not mine."

Auragole sat down hard, drew his knees up, put his head on his arms, and breathed deeply.

"Son, I'm not hurt," Solagen said softly. "That's the second time you saved my life." Then his words became rough edged. "The man was mad to leave his back open to you. He must have thought you were running away."

"Running away?" Auragole raised his head. "Why would I do that?"

"To save your own skin."

"My own. . ." Auragole was indignant.

"An assassin doesn't count on the courage of strangers. And this one was bound and determined to get me."

Who are you? Auragole wondered.

Then he heard and finally paid attention to the sound of horses all around him. He rose quickly to his feet, but his sword was at the other end of the clearing. He held his bow, but had no arrow. How careless he had been in the heat of the kill. He had been so consumed with this second attempt on Solagen's life that he had let his guard down. He ran to stand in front of Solagen, to protect him from the attack, drawing his knife from his boot. In vain, he knew, because pouring into the clearing from all sides were many soldiers. Too many. Before Auragole had a chance to use his weapon, he was yanked aside and held by three soldiers. One put a knife to his throat. Auragole's own weapon was at his feet.

"Drop your knife, soldier," Solagen ordered loudly. The soldier dropped his knife. "And stand back. See that no harm comes to him," Solagen instructed the three who were holding Auragole, as an officer in full battle armor rushed to Solagen. "This young man saved my life."

The soldiers released Auragole.

"Oldwell, let's see who was so bent on killing me that he was heedless of the danger to himself."

The officer called Oldwell rolled the would-be assassin over and drew the hood away from his face.

Auragole could hear the breath go out of Solagen, and the exclamations of the men who stood around the body.

"Bendahl! Bendahl? My sister's son?" and Solagen's words were more bitter than angry. "It seems my heir couldn't wait. Fool. Fool. I would have left him a united Westernlands. Now he inherits only maggots and worms. No," and he spat, "let him be food for the vultures."

The small campsite was quickly dismantled and the fire put out. Solagen was placed in a wagon and Bendahl's body was dragged into the trees.

Auragole, unable to move, watched the activity around him in bewilderment, listening to the orders shouted and the orders obeyed. The officer named Oldwell finally called to Auragole as Oldwell remounted his mare, "On your horse, man. We're off to meet the rest of the army."

Auragole just stared at him.

"Hurry, man. Solagen told me to make sure you are brought to our campsite." He motioned with his head toward the wagon that was now at the edge of the trees.

"Who is he?" Auragole asked.

The commander looked at him as if he had lost his senses. "Solagen, Ormahn of Mattelmead, of course."

In a state of numbness, Auragole gathered up his belongings, climbed onto Starwanderer's back, and followed the procession.

Ormahn of Mattelmead?

chapter three

THEY ARRIVED AT a tent city full of frenetic activity, only a dozen miles from where Solagen had lain wounded. Small campsites sprawled over a wide, short valley and up the sides of the surrounding low hills. As far as Auragole's eye could see, there were soldiers—far more than he had seen at the conclave of the Companions of the Way in the Woefuls. As Ormahn's party rode into the valley in the late-morning sun, Auragole noticed a long ribbon of carts hauling provisions down a winding mountain road from the east. Here as yet there was no snow. Ormahn's party passed several makeshift forges where smiths repaired weapons and armor. On the hills were flocks of sheep, grazing on the late-autumn grass. Hurrying about the new tent city were soldiers, servants, and even some young women.

As their party threaded its way between newly fenced pens where pigs and cattle were kept, soldiers and servants came running from all directions to watch them pass, inquiring after Ormahn's health, cheering as they saw him. A mile before reaching the camp, Ormahn had insisted he ride into it on a horse. The officer in charge, Oldwell, argued with him, but to no avail. So Solagen was propped up on the horse of one of the officers and his cloak was fastened close around him to hide his wounds. His head, however, still carried a large bandage, and his teeth were clamped tight against the pain, despite his attempt at a smile. Looking regal and self-assured, Solagen, Ormahn of Mattelmead, rode into camp.

Chickens ran about, spooking some of the horses. The rescue party passed piles of blankets and, Auragole was told, captured weapons, confiscated grain, and barrels containing supplies. Finally they arrived at several large tents, arranged in a double line. They dismounted before the largest tent, where Ormahn, carefully helped down from the horse and with a soldier on each side of him, entered. He was followed into the tent by a large entourage. Oldwell instructed Auragole to stay near the tent headquarters, and told him that Ormahn would see him soon.

"I'm a doctor," he said to Auragole, "Ormahn's doctor, as well as a commander in his army."

Auragole waited outside Ormahn's tent, watching with interest a steady stream of officers, servants, and messengers enter and leave, but he was also full of his own tumultuous thoughts. By some mysterious twist of fate, he had encountered Ormahn of Mattelmead—the great king and peace bringer of the Westernlands, the hope of the entire Grand Continent. Not only had he met him, but he had saved Ormahn's life. Auragole thought with some embarrassment of his behavior toward the king—his unguarded words, his terse orders, his lack of deference, and overall, his imprudent, perhaps even impudent, manner. Yet Ormahn had responded to him with good grace and humor. And now Auragole was here in Ormahn's camp, and waiting at Ormahn's request.

All fatigue falling away from him in his excitement, Auragole sat down on his pack near the tent where he had been told to await Ormahn's call. Starwanderer grazed on the sparse grass a dozen yards from him. Auragole whiled away the time watching with fascination all the activity. He had been asked to remain and remain he would—at least through the night. If he had not been forgotten by Solagen, Auragole was hoping that he could ask of him permission to travel with his army to the city of Mattelmead.

They had arrived at the camp in the morning. Now the sun was moving down the western sky. Campfires were lit and the aroma of cooking food was making Auragole hungry. He was about to make a meal of dried meat and water when a young page came out of the tent where Ormahn had gone, looked around, spotted Auragole, and went over. He was about fifteen, with freckles and well-groomed short hair. Another young man stood behind him.

"Sir," he asked, "are you Auragole, the singer?"

"I am."

"Then bring your belongings and come with me."

"I shall, but I must see to my horse first."

"Pheel, here," he indicated the other young man, "has been instructed to place your horse with King Ormahn's steeds and to give him grain. Can he be handled by another?"

"Thank you. He can, if I instruct him."

"Then please do so."

Auragole hummed for Starwanderer, who came trotting over to him. He spoke a few words to the stallion and placed the reins in Pheel's hands. He patted the horse and then turned to follow the youth who had spoken to him.

"My name is Breen, and I am page to Ormahn of Mattelmead," the young man said with a smile of pride. He led Auragole to a small tent next to the main one.

There Auragole was given water with which to wash—hot, to his delight—and offered fresh clothes, more elegant than his own. Auragole accepted these gratefully, and put his own soiled clothes in his pack. Breen then led him around to the main entrance and into the large tent. It was filled with soldiers and servants. There was, to his right as he entered what was obviously the headquarters, a long table with several men standing about it. Solagen, dressed now in an officer's uniform, was sitting on a chair near the center. He did not notice Auragole's arrival. Next to Solagen stood Oldwell. Piles of maps were strewn across the table. These seemed to be the focus of the conversation.

To Auragole's left as he entered was a long table filled with food: cooked fowl, bread, cakes, dried fruit, nuts, cheeses, meats, stews, puddings, and a stack of plates and eating utensils. He hadn't seen such a glorious array of food since the Feast of Aa in Agavia. A few people were standing in front of the table, selecting items and conversing with each other. Many of the men at the map table were eating as they deliberated. Men in a hurry, Auragole thought, and wondered if they were conferring about the taking of the northeastern Sorren Heights.

"Help yourself to food, sir," Breen said.

"Thank you." Auragole was about to ask him, then what? But the young man had hurried to Solagen's side. Auragole walked over to the banquet table and helped himself to chicken, puddings, and cheese. He found a vacant stool, sat a little away from the banquet table, and watched everything with unabashed curiosity as he ate. From one opening in the tent, servants moved in and out with a seemingly endless supply of food and drink. Officers came in through another opening in twos and threes, helped themselves to food, and stood about talking in low voices, or joined the others at the map table. Some merely piled their plates with food and left the tent.

Auragole studied them all, but his eyes returned again and again to Solagen, the man he knew now to be the famed Ormahn of Mattelmead. Solagen's face was pale—no sign of fever. The bandage around his head had been replaced with a much narrower one. Solagen's hazel eyes, which looked dark in the candle- and lantern light, followed with alert intelligence the places on the maps that were pointed at by first one and then another of his officers. When Solagen spoke, it was animatedly. Auragole couldn't make out any of the words over the general din in the large tent, but he could hear the tone. Ormahn was in turn thoughtful, questioning, and commanding. Often messengers came with papers, which he read quickly and passed along. Other messengers were given papers and sent off somewhere, as was the young page, Breen. As the officers talked over the maps, servants moved about their table with pitchers of drink.

Auragole finished his first plate of food and went back for a second. It was then that Solagen's doctor, Commander Oldwell, saw him and came over as Auragole stood at the banquet table.

"Ah, Auragole," Oldwell said, taking him by the elbow and moving him to a place where they would not be overheard. "We cannot express to you how very grateful we are. But you must know that. And you did a fine job with his wounds and with the setting of the bones. You would make a splendid physician, and should you wish it, I could see to your training at the academy in Mattelmead. One word from me. . ." He must have caught the surprised look on Auragole's face, for he said then, "But Solagen says you are a singer, and a fine one."

"I am a singer, sir."

"Look at him." Oldwell gestured with his chin toward Solagen. "He should be in bed—I hardly know what's holding him up—but he's as stubborn as a mule and has the constitution of a bear." His words were filled with affection. "We are all in your debt. You were in the right place at the right time. Luck was on our side, good luck," he added.

Auragole nodded.

"Traitorous scum." Oldwell spat out the words. "Arrogant, traitorous scum. His own sister's son. Heir, mind you. Heir! Too much in a hurry, the fool. Well, good riddance. So now, since Solagen has as yet no sons, either Bendahl's twin brother, Veldarr, or Veldarr's cousin, Goredahl, will be his heir, unless. . ." Oldwell's expression turned hard.

"You think them part of the treachery?"

"Was there a treacherous plot? We don't know. May never know. But you can be sure we will not take any chances. Woe to the officers under Bendahl. Guilty or not, they will answer for the sins of their commander." Oldwell looked stern and angry.

Auragole wondered what he meant by that, but did not pursue it. Instead he asked, "How many of your people survived the ambush?"

"Six, thank the stars. The traitor, Bendahl, was part of the troop that was accompanying Solagen to the talks with Gazber. Either Bendahl was in league with Gazber, or he simply escaped the attack, then saw that his uncle was hit and decided to finish him off. It may have just been an opportunity he thought he shouldn't miss."

"How terrible," Auragole said. He wanted to ask more, but felt too much his ignorance. Why would someone who was heir commit such a heinous deed?

"It's a great shock, if I say so myself," Oldwell went on. "I doubt we'll ever know the real truth. Bendahl was a taciturn man, not a man to joke with or drink with—but he was well respected. Handsome, too, and a good commander, well thought of by his men. He leaves a widow and three daughters. Fool. Why couldn't he wait?"

"You said that Ormahn has no sons of his own?"

Oldwell shook his head. "No, he has been married twice, and no children at all. No doubt he will marry again when he returns."

"He has more than one wife?"

Oldwell laughed. "No. The first marriage was declared null and void. His first wife has a nice estate in the south of Mattelmead that he settled on her. The second will do just as well, I'm sure."

"I see," Auragole said, not understanding the ways of wives and sons of kings. "How did you finally locate Solagen?"

"Those six who escaped the ambush saw nothing of the initial attack, for those in front of them had passed round a bend. But when they saw the arrows flying from the hill, they turned about, regrouped, and attempted to climb into the hills to assail the attackers from behind. By the time our men were in the hills, the ambushers had struck and were gone. The six gathered the dead and returned here—but without Solagen and without Bendahl. An hour or so later, Bendahl made it back to the camp just as our troops were about to go in search of Ormahn. Bendahl said only that he had become separated from the rest of the company, and that he thought Solagen had been captured by Gazber's soldiers. That sent our troops off in a wrong direction and lost us much valuable time."

Auragole listened to Oldwell's story of intrigue and deception with a mixture of fascination and revulsion. To be so close to the great Ormahn, and then turn against him. It seemed hardly fathomable.

"Bendahl expected, I guess, that Solagen would die of his wounds. If not, he planned to finish him off before we found him, maybe even lead us to him once he was dead. It must have been a shock to Bendahl to find you still with Solagen, Auragole."

"Why? Would most in Mattelmead desert a wounded man?"

"Most all over the Grand Continent would have run from such a situation. What, stay in a place that had been under attack? How many humans would do that? I think Bendahl expected you to steal Solagen's goods and depart as fast as you could."

"Steal his things! Unconscionable!" Auragole flushed angrily.

"You find that such a strange idea?"

"It was not the way my parents raised me."

"I see." Oldwell cocked his head, then smiled at Auragole.

"When did you suspect Bendahl?"

"There was something in his manner after he returned alone from the ambush. Not all men can act treacherously and hide it. It was a momentous thing he did. If it was unplanned, he might even have surprised and shocked himself, I'll give him that. I've been around the throne all my adult life and I've seen much duplicity and falsehood. There was something a little off in Bendahl's behavior after he returned and told us his story—the one that sent our troops chasing a wild goose. A few of us sensed something was not right, that something had not been told us. Therefore, when a trusted friend of mine saw Bendahl leave his tent and the grounds a few hours before dawn this morning, my friend came for me. I, with twenty of my men behind me, followed Bendahl, keeping our distance. But I nearly lost Bendahl in the dark. Then I heard the unmistakable sounds of fighting, and I called my men to me. We hurried to where the sounds were coming from. We would have been too late to save Ormahn if not for you. Lucky for us that you were alert."

Auragole nodded.

Oldwell swallowed the last drop in his tumbler and set it down on the banquet table. "Young man, you will be well rewarded for your courage, well rewarded."

He walked away, then turned back for a moment. "Solagen has taken quite a liking to you. That's your good fortune." His eyes narrowed thoughtfully, and he gave Auragole a small smile. "Don't disappoint him." And Oldwell hurried back to the map table to stand once more next to the king.

Don't disappoint him? Auragole wondered if Oldwell meant refusing the offer to become part of Solagen's household. Stars, he had been offered a place in Ormahn of Mattelmead's household! And he had blithely turned it down. Had he given offense? Had he made a wrong decision? With those thoughts spinning around in his head, Auragole returned to the table and loaded up a second plate of food.

Just as Auragole placed his empty plate on a cart, a man, dressed in the dark-blue combat uniform of the House of Ormahn, came hurrying into the headquarters, preceded by a breathless page who announced in a loud voice, "Veldarr of Mattelmead." The man moving with decisive steps toward the center of the tent was a tall, handsome, well-built man with curly blond hair.

All conversation stopped, but Auragole could feel the tension in the air.

Solagen rose from his chair, steadied himself, then walked away from the map table and waited. Four officers came to stand slightly behind him, their hands on the hilts of their swords. But Veldarr did not hesitate. He strode up to Solagen, and when he was a yard from him, he halted and with a graceful movement pulled his sword out of its leather scabbard. There were loud gasps. More soldiers rushed to Solagen. The four who stood beside him also drew their swords and moved to block Veldarr's approach, but Solagen motioned them back.

Veldarr, as if he had noticed nothing, stepped forward, dropped to his knees, and placed the sword at the feet of Ormahn. The man, not yet thirty, bore only a slight resemblance to his twin, the dead Bendahl. Veldarr wore no helmet but in all other ways he was dressed like an officer ready for battle. He waited there on his knees with bowed head. He didn't speak. It was utterly still in the tent. Even the servants had stopped moving.

Solagen finally spoke. His words were quiet, intimate, as if only he and Veldarr were in that tent. "Did the messengers not arrive? Were you not told to return to Mattelmead?"

The man said, "Kill me."

Some in the tent gasped, some muttered and then fell silent. "What?"

Veldarr did not look up. "Kill me, Uncle. If you think me the traitor my brother was, then kill me." He moved his hand, and with three fingers pushed the sword closer to Solagen.

"Why should I think you better than your brother?" Solagen's voice was tired now.

His nephew looked up then. "When did I ever follow my brother—except at birth? Not as a child, not as a man. Though we shared the same womb, we have ever been as different as two men can be. Bendahl was born with bitterness and bile, never content. He was as foreign to me as a panther once given to me as a pet."

Auragole watched, mesmerized.

"Bendahl was a good soldier," Solagen said.

"He was a traitor," Veldarr answered.

Solagen was silent.

"If you think duplicity comes with the blood, then kill me, Uncle, for I will not go home dishonored. Kill me or admit me to your council table where I have stood in good faith these six years."

Solagen began to teeter. Fatigue and the wounds were taking their toll. Oldwell rushed to his side.

"Sire, you must lie down. The fever will begin again if you don't take care." Oldwell tried to lead Ormahn toward the entrance of the tent.

"Uncle," Veldarr's voice was hard. "Pronounce my fate now. If I'm to die, let it be now. Or let me resume my place in your council. Is my mother to be bereft twice in one day, or am I still your loyal subject?"

Ormahn was staggering. An officer rushed to take his other arm.

Oldwell spoke harshly. "Can't you see that he is ill? Surely, you can wait, Veldarr, until. . ."

Solagen's voice rose above Oldwell's. "Set up your tent, Veldarr, and join the council. You are not your brother nor must you suffer for his folly."

Solagen didn't wait to see Veldarr rise, but Auragole saw him as he stood up. A triumphant smile played across the man's face.

As Veldarr retrieved his sword, many came up to him to clap him on his shoulders and to welcome him. In a loud voice Veldarr ordered his page to set up his tent, then turned to the table and in moments was deep in conversation with some of the officers.

He's a reckless one, Auragole thought, but brave. Then he turned to watch as the flaps were lifted at the south end of the tent, and Ormahn, Oldwell, and a few others left. Auragole wasn't sure what to do next. He had been asked to wait, but for what? He was hoping that he could stay in the company of Ormahn's army until they reached Mattelmead City. That would certainly ease his journey. Though the army moved slowly, Auragole would at least arrive safely at the gates of the city. He walked about the large tent aimlessly, listening to the lowered voices of the men.

As he passed the map table he heard an officer say to Veldarr, "Your cousin Goredahl has been sent with a large force to engage the bulk of Gazber's army here." And the officer pointed to a spot on the map.

"Does Solagen think that Bendahl was in league with Gazber?"

The officer shrugged.

Another said, "It matters little now. The battle is on."

Veldarr looked no more like his twin than ordinary brothers. But Auragole had heard that it was often this way. The man had the same blue eyes, but his hair was lighter. Auragole had seen Bendahl only in death, but his face had been bony, and his expression in death was one of surprise. The shape of Veldarr's face was softer, and his expression was an amiable one. Veldarr had a way of moving that one might call dashing. From the way he was greeted, Veldarr, Auragole saw, was genuinely popular with the other officers.

Though Auragole would have liked to look at the maps, he knew better than to approach the table, so he returned to his stool and studied the officers. There were two kinds of uniforms, one for the personal house of Ormahn and one for the regular army. They were all dark blue, but the uniforms belonging to the house of Ormahn were distinguished by elaborate gold trim.

After about half an hour, Breen came into the tent and hurried toward Auragole. "Ormahn has requested that the singer come to him," he said.

Auragole rose to his feet, retrieved his harp from where he had left it with his pack, and, heart thumping, followed Breen.

Solagen's tent, a few yards across from the conference tent, was large. It contained a bed, some small tables with candles or lanterns on them, a trunk that bore his clothes, a dining table with seating for six, and a desk and several chairs. There were rugs on the ground and tapestries on the tent walls. Auragole couldn't help but compare this opulent tent with the sparse one Meekelorr, the commander of the Companions of the Way, had occupied. But then, Meekelorr was no king.

Ormahn lay in the bed covered with down blankets and a silk counterpane. Oldwell was bending over Solagen, but straightened up when he heard Auragole approach.

"Ah, Auragole," Oldwell said, "he has strained himself beyond all good sense. He has a slight fever."

"Stop fussing, you old woman, and let the man approach. Go keep that bunch in the conference tent quiet."

Oldwell shrugged, clucked his tongue, and left the tent.

"Draw up a chair, son," Solagen said.

Auragole did as he was asked. He felt shy now, even a little embarrassed, wondering if he had been disrespectful to Ormahn when he lay wounded. Having been raised isolated, with no people around except his parents and their friend Spehn, perhaps had made him too independent. Though Auragole had been taught veneration for elders and good manners by his mother, he had little natural awe for leaders and knew nothing of what was due kings in the way of deference—except from story. Of course, he had felt enormous respect and admiration for the Lady Claregole of Agavia, but that was because something in her manner called forth a kind of reverence. Now, in the presence of a king, *the* king—the one who would put an end to the centuries of war—Auragole was almost speechless. So he sat, quietly waiting.

Finally, Ormahn said, "Will you sing for me, Auragole?"

Auragole swallowed. "Yes, sir. Of what shall I sing?"

"Anything, except of war."

Auragole picked up his harp and began tuning it. He felt more at ease now that he was doing something.

"What did you think of him?"

"Of whom?"

"My nephew. Veldarr."

"Brave, even reckless," Auragole said, uncertain of what was expected of him.

Solagen nodded. "What else?"

Auragole thought for a moment. "He's quite handsome and seems a great favorite with the other officers."

"Oh, he's that all right. And a great favorite with the ladies. He is with the ladies as he is with everything."

"How is that?"

"Excessive. In sport, hunting, dress, he is excessive. Veldarr likes the good life and a fair amount of drama—you saw that display just now. But he's a fair-minded officer, a good soldier, courageous in battle. He's not so hungry as his brother, Bendahl, was."

Auragole looked at him questioningly.

"For power, for fame, to be first, the one at the top." Solagen chuckled. "And he's easier company than is his cousin, Goredahl. You'll meet Goredahl soon, no doubt. He's my dead brother's only son. Bendahl and Veldarr are the sons of my sister." Solagen paused, and in the flickering candlelight Auragole saw something like pain, or perhaps it was anger, cross

Ormahn's face. But in a moment it was gone.

"Goredahl is dour and without humor—though there are few who are as devoted to the army as he is, and few who have his gift at commanding. His cousin, Veldarr, is. . .how shall I say it . . .a lighter personality, though I would hesitate to call him lightweight. He laughs easily and makes others laugh. He is fond of a good joke, and in war, a good joke goes a long way. If I do not have a son soon, one of the two will be king after me." He sighed. "It must be so. They are blood. And that is all-important. We are restoring the meaning of family in our kingdom. Much was lost in the centuries of war when family ties fell apart. Heredity is important. It's our only hold on the future and our only connection to the past. But I shall take my own good time deciding which of the two shall lead after me."

Solagen, Ormahn of Mattelmead, stopped speaking, so Auragole picked up his harp once more and began strumming.

"I don't think Veldarr has it in him to be a traitor. . .no, don't stop playing."

"Why is that?" Auragole asked, his hands plucking at the strings.

"He's too content. He doesn't have ambition like his brother had, nor vision like. . ." His voice trailed off.

". . .like you?"

Solagen laughed. "Vision is not so easily come by, and without it. . . Sing, Auragole of the Songs, and send me into dreams on a river of melody."

So Auragole sang. Often he See-sang, vividly picturing the content of his song so that the listener could see his song also. He sang until Solagen was well into sleep, then stopped. He touched the king's forehead. It was warm, but not dangerously so. Best to leave him now. Auragole rose from his chair and replaced it next to the table. Suddenly he was struck by how silent it had become all about them. The officers and servants in the conference tent must have returned to their own quarters.

I shall have to bed down somewhere, he thought, the fatigue of many hours and nights of sleeplessness suddenly hitting him. Well, perhaps in the conference tent, out of the cold wind.

chapter four

WHEN AURAGOLE STEPPED into the large conference tent, he was surprised to see dozens of men and a few women standing there watching him as he entered.

Auragole felt flustered—why were they looking at him? And then he realized that they must have been listening to him through the thin fabric of the tents. He started to walk past the gathered onlookers, not certain where he was going, when a man blocked his way. It was Veldarr.

"Wait!" His light-blue eyes were bright with interest. "What is your name, singer?"

"I am called Auragole."

It was then that Oldwell hurried over. "This is the young man who saved your uncle's life."

"And therefore also the slayer of my brother."

Auragole flushed.

Veldarr's look was calculating but not unfriendly.

Oldwell said, "Thank the earth for that. Or Solagen would

be dead now."

"Yes, thank the earth and the stars," Veldarr said. Then he smiled. It was a very attractive smile, lighting up his whole face. "I have never heard singing like yours before. It is almost unearthly." He stared at Auragole, his head cocked pensively. "A magical voice, an enchanted voice."

Auragole stared back at the man. Why was he uncertain whether he liked this man or not, or whether he should trust him? He knew only that he had better be cautious with him. Slayer of his brother, indeed! "It's a very earthly voice, sir," he said, measuring out his words. "Nothing of magic in it. I had a very good teacher. There is nothing more to it than that." Then Auragole turned to Oldwell. "May I ask you something?"

"But, of course," Oldwell said. Veldarr inclined his head and moved toward the exit. "How can I help you?"

"Will the army continue its journey to Mattelmead, or will it wait here until Gazber has been bested?"

"The greater part of the army will leave here as soon as Solagen is able to travel, and as soon as we have word from Goredahl about how the battle against Gazber is going. Some troops will be left here either to finish the job or to keep the peace. Then it's off for home for most of us. Why do you ask, son?"

"I, myself, am on my way to Mattelmead City. I wondered. . ." He hesitated. "Do you think it would be too much to ask that I be allowed to travel with the army? I must get to Mattelmead City, and to travel with Ormahn's troops would be by far the surest way to go."

"My dear Auragole, I thought that was understood. Of course you will travel with us. Solagen would insist on it. You are bringing him much pleasure with your singing. Perhaps even health. Of course you must travel with us." Oldwell laughed, then looked at Auragole quizzically. "Man, do you not understand what you have done? You saved the life of the king, protected him, nursed him back to health. You stayed in a dangerous situation when others might have run. Do you think Solagen would take such deeds lightly? If so, you do not know him."

"I did only what was natural, what was right," Auragole stammered. "I didn't know who he was. I. . .I expect nothing, but would be glad of an escort to Mattelmead City."

"Where do you come from, Auragole?" Oldwell eyed him with curiosity. "Yours must be an interesting story, for I must say, you are an oddity. Indeed, a true oddity." And then he laughed again. "But then you are a singer, so that must explain it. I knew a singer once, as odd as you, but maybe not so able with bow and arrow. His name was Lorenwile, the best singer in all of Mattelmead. But alas, he left the city some time ago and has not yet returned."

"But he has returned," Auragole said, excitement in his voice. "Lorenwile should be in Mattelmead City even as we speak. He is my master, the one who taught me to sing, and it is to him I go, to be his apprentice at the Blue Heron."

"Well, well, a small world. But I should have known it. From whom else could you have learned to sing so gloriously?" And he clapped Auragole on the back.

At this moment, Breen came up to them. "I am instructed to show you to your tent," he said to Auragole.

"My tent?" He looked bewildered.

"You didn't expect to sleep on the ground, did you?" Oldwell chuckled. "Solagen is more generous than that. Go with Breen, son, and come back here in the morning for breakfast, and bring your harp. Solagen will certainly want to hear you play again. As a matter of fact, I will insist on it. I will prescribe it for him. Your singing seems to be more beneficial than my remedies."

"Your belongings have been carried to your tent, sir," Breen said. "May I show you the way?"

Auragole followed Breen out of the conference tent and down an alleyway between two rows of large tents, most of them dark now, though a few were still giving off a soft glow.

They had not walked past more than half a dozen tents when Breen stopped in front of one, larger than most. There was a light inside.

"Here it is," Breen said, halting. He lifted the flap and motioned Auragole inside. Auragole stepped through and stood there looking in astonishment at the tent he had been given. There was a large bed, with sheets, down blankets, many pillows. There was a round dining table and four chairs. There was a great trunk, beautifully carved. There were weavings on the walls, rugs on the ground. There were small tables on whose surfaces stood wooden and silver candlesticks holding tall candles.

"Whose. . .whose. . .tent is this?"

"It is yours, sir," Breen said, his tone sober. "It once belonged to Bendahl. As the slayer of Bendahl and the savior of Ormahn, it is yours by rights. Bendahl's personal papers have been removed. But all the rest of his personal things and his clothes are now yours."

"Bendahl's?" Auragole could not move. "This is Bendahl's tent?"

"But no longer. It is yours by rights now." Breen looked at him curiously. "So it always is in war, and when a man has rebelled against. . . Does it not please you?"

"It's not that. . . I'm not a soldier. I understand little of how these things are done," Auragole said.

"Lors, come out of the corner and meet your new master."

A slight boy of about thirteen or fourteen stepped a few feet out of the shadows. He looked uncertain, even frightened.

"Come here," Breen said, almost impatiently. The boy came closer, his face pale in the candlelight. Breen turned to Auragole, who stood staring at the boy, unable to speak. "Lors was page to Bendahl. He is young and small but he is very able. He is now your page. Semp, who has been assigned the care of your horse, will be your groom. Of course, there are other servants who will attend your needs, who will see to your baths and the cleaning and mending of your clothes, the setting up and taking down of your tent when we move. Lors will be your intermediary to all. If you do not find everything to your liking, seek me out and I will take your message to Ormahn himself." A fleeting smile of pride crossed his lips. "Ormahn has left instructions that your every need is to be attended to at once, and that you are to be treated with deference. Those who fail you will be punished." He said the last looking directly at Lors.

Breen bowed and left the tent.

Auragole looked about him in confusion. He stared at the plush bed. He had not slept in such a bed since he had left Agavia a year and a half ago. But Bendahl's bed? The thought of sleeping in the dead man's bed filled him with revulsion. Perhaps he would throw his blanket and cloak onto one of the rugs on the ground and sleep there.

Lors was looking at him uncertainly. "There is warm water for washing," the boy finally said, his voice barely above a whisper. He pointed to a small table on which stood a pitcher and bowl.

"Yes, thank you." Auragole carefully put his harp down on a richly woven rug, and removed his cloak. The boy rushed to help him. At the washstand Auragole found soap alongside the basin. That was a luxury. He stripped off his clothes and washed thoroughly. The boy came up to him and stood there with a towel. While Auragole was drying himself, the boy left him and returned with a sleeping gown. Not since Agavia had he slept in a gown. But this was the dead man's gown.

He saw the boy watching him. Auragole drew a deep breath and asked, "Where do you sleep, Lors?"

"I sleep here, sir. I roll out my rug and sleep here." The boy looked wary. "Is that all right? Unless I am instructed to sleep outside. Do you have a woman tonight?"

Auragole shook his head. It was cold outside. November cold. He was not going to drive the boy out into the wind so that he himself could sleep on a rug instead of in a dead man's bed. "Set up your bed rug then, Lors. It is late."

The boy nodded.

Auragole put on the gown. "Shall I put out the candles," Auragole asked, "or will you?"

"That is my job, sir." Lors hurried to the bed and pulled back the covers. Auragole walked toward it, brushed the back of his hand across his forehead, and climbed in. The sheets felt crisp and cool. As Lors pulled the blankets over him, Auragole remembered Bendahl, dressed in black from head to foot, looking like the very personification of death.

The boy unrolled his own rug, then put out the candles. Auragole heard him crawl into his bedding. Soon all was silence. I shall not close my eyes for a minute tonight, Auragole thought, then rolled over and fell into a deep sleep.

THE ARMY STAYED at the camp for another week. Twice each day Auragole sang for the king, once after lunch when Oldwell insisted that Solagen nap so as to regain his strength for the upcoming journey, and once at night, sending Solagen into sleep with his melodies.

During the day, Auragole often sat in the conference tent and watched the comings and goings of officers. Lors, if he was requested to, stood near him and told him their names. Solagen spent much of his day at the map table conferring with all who came and went. Auragole ate in the tent with the officers, and knew that was also a special privilege. He never moved close enough to the conference table to hear what the officers were planning. That would have been beyond what was welcome, he felt sure. Oldwell, who spoke to him often, said they were conferring over the conquest of the northern Sorren Heights and then its governance. The battles were going well, apparently.

On the fourth day in camp, Auragole was witness to the

coming of Goredahl, Solagen's nephew and cousin to Veldarr. He was a tall man, thin, dark haired, with a gaunt face, in his mid-thirties. He looked like a man given to scowling frequently, like a fussy and fastidious man, one not easy to please. How different from his cousin Veldarr. Oldwell later told Auragole that Goredahl had brought the news that Gazber was dead, and that Mattelmead's troops were in possession of the northwest part of the Sorren Heights. Solagen then put Goredahl and his soldiers in charge of the territory they had won. In the spring Solagen would send relief troops and another commander to take Goredahl's place.

Auragole walked often through the camp, curious to learn how a successful army travels, and was intrigued by what he saw. Lors, who had finally lost his fear of Auragole, accompanied him, and told him much about the conquest of Thorensphere. Auragole found this enlightening, and his admiration for Solagen grew. Every day Auragole took Starwanderer out for exercise, riding into the hills where autumn was belatedly giving way to winter. Semp was a good groom, and Auragole soon grew used to the help. Sometimes he marveled at his own good luck. Here he was in the middle of Ormahn's army, treated with great courtesy, and singing for the king himself. What a tale that would be to tell Lorenwile.

Auragole eventually lost his squeamishness about living in Bendahl's tent. He became accustomed to using Bendahl's things and wearing his clothes. It was accepted as his due by those around him. That is the way of war, he told himself. This is what Ormahn himself has bestowed on me. Learn, adapt, and do not give offense.

He was sometimes called into Solagen's tent just to talk, rather than to sing, which seemed odd to Auragole. Solagen was, after all, Ormahn of Mattelmead. He could speak with anyone. Yet again and again during that week, Auragole was asked into Solagen's quarters merely for conversation.

Solagen asked about Auragole's life. Little by little he told the king his story—or most of it. Auragole was not given to dissembling, but some inner reticence he hardly understood kept him from speaking of all that he had experienced since he left his home in the Gandlese. Was it for the safety of old friends he was concerned, or was it to keep himself in a good light, a safe light? After all, he didn't know who were the king's enemies and who were his friends. And he had seen at first hand how harshly the king's enemies were dealt with. So Auragole didn't ask people in Ormahn's camp whether they knew the whereabouts of his old friends as he had asked the Companions of the Way at that first conclave in the Woefuls, more than a year ago.

Auragole gave a full description of his childhood to Ormahn, but skimmed over the months he had traveled with "some people I met on their way to Mattelmead," purposely not naming them. Nor were the names of the Lady Claregole, Pohl, or Meekelorr ever mentioned, since he left out any description of his sojourn in Agavia. He merely blended in the trip after Agavia with the trip before. To make up for his lack of candidness he described in detail portions of the Westernlands that he thought Solagen would be interested in—and indeed he was: the foothills of the Gandlese and the roving bands there, the walled country of Isofed and its army outside the East Gate, the Deep Forest south of Isofed with its strange ailments, and Wildenfarr-low-desert and the two tribes there.

Auragole told the king that he had become separated from his first travel companions in a river accident. Then he told him how he had set off for Mattelmead alone, and had met Lorenwile on the way. Lorenwile was, of course, well known to Solagen. Hearing Auragole sing, Lorenwile had taken him on as an apprentice. Auragole skipped over his time with Meekelorr and the Companions of the Way, his adventures with Elarr and Affredda through the Ancient Woods and the town of Little

Thoren. If he made it seem as if he had been on the road a shorter time than he had, and that he had sojourned with Lorenwile for a great many months instead of only a few, well, so be it. As instructed, Auragole did not mention True-singing, or even See-singing, saying only that he and Lorenwile had roamed the Sorren Heights together while Lorenwile instructed him in the fine art of singing. Auragole never mentioned the Woeful Peaks. To his profound relief, Solagen seemed satisfied with what Auragole told him, and questioned him only about that which might some day be tactically useful.

Occasionally, when Auragole and the king were alone, Solagen spoke about his dreams for the west, for a united Westernlands filled with peace and order. He spoke about a renewal of the Golden Century in science, in commerce, and in all the arts. When Auragole asked Solagen about religion, he tossed his head deprecatingly.

"It is provided for those who need it. All the remembered religions are represented on the Street of Temples. People are free to attend, if they choose, and the priests free to practice, as long as they speak about the other world and don't sow seeds of dissatisfaction in this one. However, when science has rediscovered what was lost after the Golden Century during all these years of war, when science even surpasses the Golden Century, there will be no more need for religion."

"So my father also believed," Auragole said. And he brushed quickly from his mind the thought that his father had once been a priest of the King God who had lost his faith.

"I'm a great believer in science—and scientific institutions receive much money for their research from my government. The earth, this marvelous earth, will provide answers to all our questions. And I, Solagen, Ormahn of Mattelmead, will do everything I can to make it happen." Solagen's eyes sparkled, and his tone was one of boyish enthusiasm when he spoke of all that he had done in Mattelmead City to establish hospitals, academies, and centers of research.

Auragole listened fervently, drawn into Solagen's great vision. The dynamic Ormahn would bring peace, would help humanity in a way that Meekelorr could not. Ormahn would create a new world, far grander, Auragole was sure, than the Companions of the Way could create, noble as their intent was. The Companions were too few, and Ormahn's army grew larger each day. Yes, Ormahn was the answer to peace and hope in the west. Then perhaps, in time, he would carry his noble vision to the east, to the whole of the Grand Continent. How lucky to have met this great leader. Sometimes the marvel of it kept Auragole awake long into the night pondering his good fortune.

Solagen seemed particularly interested in Auragole's experience with Isofed and Wildenfarr-low-desert. One day Solagen invited Auragole to the conference table, pointed to a large map of the west, and asked him to show the officers where Auragole and his friends had traveled. Auragole was able to correct their maps of Wildenfarr and to draw in for them the Deep Forest that lay south of Isofed, and to amend their drawings of both the Isofed River and the Roaring River. "You're very good with maps, son," Solagen said to him.

"My father taught me," Auragole answered. "I like it very much."

"And when you choose to be," Solagen said, "you are very observant and very detailed in your descriptions."

Auragole blushed. Did Solagen know that he had glossed over much in the telling of his journeys? Nevertheless, he decided to keep his secrets—he wasn't sure why. Some intuition, no doubt, not to bring misfortune down on the heads of his former companions—and a desire to protect from the world the lovely people of the Valley of the Agavi. Why cause them trouble? Or himself? Until he knew whom Ormahn considered his enemies, Auragole would keep his own counsel.

About the Deep Forest, Solagen said, "That sounds a bit like the Ancient Woods in Thorensphere—some lingering illness there from the time of the Golden Century or the earlier wars. Something like the Northern and Southern Desolations. We shall have to do something about those forests when the whole west is ours."

Auragole only nodded, but he felt great relief that Affredda and the children had been brought out of the Ancient Woods to the Woefuls by Elarr and his troop, and would be on their way to Agavia come spring.

Solagen's health was improving daily. It would take time for the bones to heal and the wounds to mend, but the fever was gone. It was decided, though not to his liking, that Solagen would ride home in a covered carriage. Still, he was a sensible man.

One cold, rainy day at the end of November, a week after Auragole had arrived with Solagen in the camp, they began their slow, cumbersome journey north.

chapter five

GLENELLE HAD BEEN waiting for three days. The mansion had been scrubbed from top to bottom. She herself had supervised the cleaning, had been quite severe with her servants, making them do over and over the floors and windows until the house shone and the servants were exhausted. Finally, the note arrived. He would come tonight. The meal had been planned in every detail, the cooks scolded and threatened, Glenelle's clothes carefully laid out. They would dine in her bedchamber. It was a large room, but more intimate than the great dining hall, or even the breakfast room, and intimacy was what she wanted. A table in front of the fireplace had been set with her best china. The bed had silk sheets underneath the down coverlets. All that was needed now was for her to bathe, dress, fix her hair, and wait.

Veldarr came at nine. She met him downstairs, offering him her hand. After the formal greeting, after the servant had taken his cloak and hat, Glenelle led him upstairs. She dismissed her maid, saying she would call when they were ready for the meal.

As the door closed behind the maid, Glenelle moved quickly into his embrace. He said little, enveloping her in his arms, lifting her off her feet, and carrying her to the bed.

After the supper dishes had been cleared away, and with them the talk of the Thorensphere campaign, but while they were still sipping tea, Veldarr asked her, "Do you remember telling me about a young man named Auragole?"

The question was unexpected. "Auragole? Of course. It was when I told you how he became separated from us while we were crossing the Noonbarr River in two boats. Why do you ask?"

"I think I've met him."

Glenelle nearly dropped the cup she was holding. "My Auragole?" She carefully set her cup down. "Is that possible? But Auragole's a fairly common name. What does this Auragole look like?"

And so Veldarr described him, and told her the story of how Auragole came to be part of Ormahn's victorious march home.

"It must be he! The description. The singing. But I was sure Auragole was dead," she shook her head in wonder, "drowned in the Noonbarr River when my brother and I and our friends were captured. This is incredible, really quite amazing. You say he saved Solagen's life?"

"And murdered my brother in the process."

Glenelle was suddenly quiet, unsure of what she should say next. Veldarr had never been fond of his brother. Still. . .

But Veldarr continued. "However, the important thing is he saved the king, is that not so?" he said, with a show of even, white teeth.

Glenelle nodded, still trying to read his expression.

"Auragole has been given my brother's house, all that is in it, and all his servants. No doubt he will be given his country estate, too."

"What has happened to Bendahl's wife and children?"

"Sent away to her parents in the south—with little more than the clothes on their backs. And now all of Bendahl's top officers have been put in prison and their families exiled. . ." He stood up and walked to the fire and began poking it. "Well, that is the way of wars and worlds," he said. "My brother was stupid. He was heir, chosen above Goredahl, who is older. And me." Veldarr shrugged. "If it had been Goredahl who. . .but it wasn't." He turned to her and smiled. "Fool. What was Bendahl's hurry?"

Glenelle waited, for she knew the question was rhetorical.

"I always thought of my twin brother as rather plodding and unimaginative. I could never figure out why Solagen chose him as his heir."

Again Glenelle waited. Veldarr came over to her and kissed the top of her head, then sprawled in the chair opposite her. "Who would have thought that Bendahl had that much deceit, or even courage, in him? Perhaps it was simply opportunity. No doubt, he was wary of this new marriage that will take place as soon as Solagen has set aside his present wife—worried that Solagen might father a son who would usurp Bendahl's claim to the throne. I doubt Solagen will ever father a son. Two wives and no children, not even girls. And all those women in the camp. . ."

Glenelle listened and watched.

"Enough of my brother. I want to speak to you of Auragole."

"Do you really think it's the Auragole of my acquaintance?"

"Don't you?"

She nodded.

"Then I'm sure you will want to see him."

"But of course. Does he know I'm here?"

"Not from me. I never heard him mention the names of any of his earlier companions. If he heard your name from others, well, after all Glenelle is also not so unusual a name." He grinned at her. "And you are not the same waif who was traveling with him—hardly that."

Glenelle laughed and knew how attractive her musical laugh was by the softness she saw in Veldarr's eyes. "I think if someone had described to Auragole a Glenelle that this someone knew in Mattelmead," she said, "Auragole would not think it was the Glenelle he had traveled with. And my brother and Don and Sylvie are not in society much. It's possible, really quite possible, that he has no idea that any of us arrived in Mattelmead safely. The last he knew of us was that we had been captured at the southern border of Glovale. I must get in touch with him."

"Not yet, my love. Wait a month, or perhaps two. Then you might invite him to one of your soirées."

"Why wait?"

"Indulge me in this." He leaned toward her and smiled brightly. "Let's give him some time to settle in. Mattelmead City is quite a wonder for people coming out of the east, as you well know. He's soon to sing at the Blue Heron with the famous Lorenwile, whom you have not yet heard, have you?"

She shook her head, still uncertain why she should wait—but if that's what Veldarr wanted. . . "There must be an interesting story behind this. Sing with the famous Lorenwile? How did all of that come about?"

"I'm sure it's a very interesting story. But he's shared his tale with no one other than the king. However, thanks to you, I know some of his past. I do wonder how much he has told the king. I suspect not much at all. If he has prevaricated as well as skipped over many details, that would trouble me. After all, I am ever concerned with the king's welfare."

"But, of course," she said, keeping her eyes unwaveringly on his face. "Well, Auragole was always a quiet, private sort of person, with a rather simple nature. He seldom let people know what was going on inside his head—if anything." And then she smiled. She knew she had a charming smile.

"Indeed? Then if he withheld things from the king, you would not find that out of character?"

Glenelle hesitated a moment, then said, "It was the way he was raised, you see—so isolated. No doubt he held back nothing of importance. He was never, when I knew him, a skilled liar."

"Yes, you told me about his childhood. Well," he laughed, "perhaps he is, as you say, a quiet, private sort of a person, and the things he has not spoken about are innocence itself." Veldarr set down his teacup. "In a month or two, you might send him a letter—or better yet, visit him at the Blue Heron. Tell him you had only just heard he was in Mattelmead. Befriend him again. In the meantime, let's give him some time to adjust to the wonders of Mattelmead. Visit the Blue Heron, say, sometime in February."

"But that's more than six weeks—it's a long time to wait. He's an old friend and I owe him much."

"Do you? But it wasn't he who saved you after you were captured—you, your brother, and your friends."

"No, you did that, Veldarr," she said.

"Let's give him a little time to adjust to our wondrous city before he encounters yet another surprise." He rose from his chair, came over to hers, and lifted her to her feet. "My darling, I cannot stay the night. My wife is. . .well, let us say I'm home too short a time and I do have my duties. She'll get used to things again in a few weeks." He kissed her and walked to the door. Glenelle followed him. "Ormahn has taken quite a fancy to your Auragole. Let's see how that turns out. What I can't understand is why he would want to sing for his living, when he has showed up in Mattelmead with enough jewels—no doubt also from your fabled land of Agavia—to buy a dozen mansions. . ." He opened the door. "Bring him into your circle, my dear, in due time. I'm sure he'll be very happy to see you again."

"But, of course," she said, escorting him down the stairs to the front door. "After all, he's an old friend. Should I not want to see him again—in time?"

"Good girl."

AURAGOLE SEEMED TO have one overriding emotion, Lorenwile observed as they walked down street after street in

Mattelmead City. It was amazement. He was perpetually startled by what his eyes were taking in and what his ears were hearing. He often looked like a deer flushed out of hiding. Lorenwile had taken Auragole on several tours of the city since he had arrived in the midst of Ormahn's army. Now Auragole's fascination with the grandeur of the city both delighted Lorenwile and caused him some concern. After all, Mattelmead City could be very seductive. This must look like Adelmorr come to life, he thought, recalling Auragole's emotional reaction to the ruins of the grand city that Meekelorr had taken him to see in the Woeful Peaks.

That his young apprentice should have been befriended by Ormahn had at first caught Lorenwile by surprise. But he quickly accepted the machinations of destiny. Now it seemed right that Auragole should have so quickly come into the circle surrounding Ormahn. How much time it saved. Lorenwile would have introduced Auragole to members of the ruling class, person by person. But that task had been taken out of his hands. Beyond any part Lorenwile seemed to have in it, destiny continued to work its will on young Auragole. It had brought him to all the important meetings in his young life—Meekelorr, Pohl, the Lady Claregole, himself. And now Auragole had befriended Solagen, Ormahn of Mattelmead, and consequently all the significant members of his court.

If Auragole had a part to play in the Last Battle, for good or for ill—and Lorenwile was sure that he did—it was not merely luck that had brought him to the aid of the wounded king. Though destiny often surprised and even amazed, there was always wisdom in it. Someone high up in the leadership of Mattelmead must be the Nethergod. And because Auragole had been drawn into that circle, Lorenwile felt even more certain of it. The Adversary Being had incarnated—and only a small group of people on the earth was aware of it. If you knew how to look, all the signs pointed to his being on the earth at this time. Lorenwile had long suspected that the Nethergod was close to Ormahn. He had told this to Meekelorr, to the Lady Claregole, to her brother Galavi, and to Pohl. It was because of this—call it intuition—that Lorenwile had chosen Mattelmead as his home and place of work. It was because of this that he returned again and again to this great city after trips away to "visit my aged and ailing mother."

But who at the court was it? Goredahl, Veldarr, Oldwell? Or one who was less well known, but had the king's ear? Perhaps he was even Ormahn himself. And now Lorenwile's apprentice was a favorite at the court. And watched, no doubt, by the Adversary God himself.

Lorenwile looked at his young friend, who was gazing intently at a building that housed a theater. What would Auragole do when the Last Battle came? After all, destiny only brought about the meetings in these world days; it did not bring about their outcome. Would Auragole serve the Creative Gods and tip the scale in their favor, or would he become an ally of the Nethergod and help pull the Deep Earth and all humanity away from its rightful goal? Lorenwile sighed out loud.

Auragole looked at him. Lorenwile merely smiled.

Well, at least while Auragole is here and singing with me, I can keep an eye on him. And, should things work out for the good, Auragole does have the makings of a great True-singer.

"Come, would you like to see the inside of this theater?" Lorenwile asked. "I know the man who manages it. I'm sure he'll let us roam around both the stage area and the auditorium."

"Yes, I would like to see a theater very much."

Soon they were standing at the back of the empty theater, staring down the dark aisle to the raised stage, which was lit by a few lanterns scattered across its bare floor.

"Can you imagine seeing a play such as the Agavians perform at their festival times in a space like this?" Auragole said, excitement in his voice.

"No."

"Why not?" Auragole turned to Lorenwile.

"Because the plays that the Agavians perform are done only on their holy days, not for entertainment. Besides, the Agavian plays are too religious for the people of Mattelmead."

"Too religious? There is a whole street of temples in this city. You took me yourself to see them."

"Officially sanctioned religions."

"And what's wrong with that?"

"Someone to tell you what you should believe and what you should not, someone getting between you and the Beings of the Creative World? Would you like that?"

Auragole was silent.

"There was a time in history when leaders and priests needed to tell humans what they should believe—in humankind's infancy and childhood—but no longer. In our day—indeed, it has been true now for many centuries—a human being must forge his own individual relationship to that higher world. He must do it out of the 'I' one uses to True-sing."

"But not everyone can True-sing," Auragole said.

"No, not everyone can True-sing, but everyone in these times has access to his higher 'I.' Only he must want to cultivate it and to work out of it, not just out of his everyday 'I.' A human being is free—free to do that or not. After all, the higher ego is not just for those who can True-sing. That might have been true in ages past. Not now."

Auragole did not speak, so Lorenwile went on. "Have you ever wondered why the Nethergod has come just at this time to the earth? Surely you have. Surely you know that he has come to prevent humanity from working out of the 'I.' After all, from where do you think genuine, unfettered love emanates? And where do you think true freedom originates? The Adversary God loathes freedom and love, would prevent people from experiencing either."

In the months he and Auragole had been together in the Woefuls, Lorenwile had purposely refrained from speaking of humankind's evolving history, or of the Creative World. Everything he had spoken of then, he had related to the performing of True-singing. Auragole was a man of will. In the act of doing was his way to the truth.

Lorenwile started down the aisle to the stage. Enough of this preaching, he decided. "You have heard all of this before—from Meekelorr, from Elarr, from Pohl. You don't need a lecture from me. Still, I must warn you, particularly as you have been befriended by Ormahn himself, that freedom and individuality are not to be openly championed in Mattelmead City."

They were now standing at the foot of the stage. In the dim lantern light Lorenwile observed a thoughtful expression on Auragole's face.

"Since you believe as Meekelorr does, that such a Being as the Nethergod exists, whom do you think this Nethergod is?"

"Now that is the great, and as yet unanswered, question. If I knew for a certainty, we wouldn't still be in Mattelmead." And without waiting for Auragole to respond, he moved past him and ran up the stairs to the stage. "Come, Auragole, hear what singing sounds like from up here."

Auragole followed him, his eyes drawn upward to the great fly space of the stage. "This is a marvel," he said.

They sang then, without accompaniment, two voices blending together in harmony. Lorenwile could see the wonder and joy on Auragole's face. A sense of hope, like warm wine, spread through Lorenwile's body.

As they were about to leave, Lorenwile, his words barely audible, said impulsively, "Perhaps we can get off somewhere this summer and True-sing—at least for a few weeks." And he was gratified to see the pleasure in Auragole's eyes. I haven't lost him yet, he thought.

GLENELLE SAT DOWN at her writing table to compose a letter to Sylvane and Donnadorr. Writing letters was what she did every morning after a light breakfast in her bedchamber. There were dozens of people with whom she wanted to keep in contact. Most were still in town—it was early March—but some had already left for their country estates. Glenelle didn't much like the country, and seldom went to the estate she and Glen owned as was the custom among the rich. She loved the city and all that it offered in the way of culture, society, and excitement. Often she wrote invitations for one of her many parties that would be hand-delivered to friends and acquaintances. Her parties were now famous in Mattelmead, and she prided herself on knowing the cream of Mattelmead society. Only Solagen had not attended one of her parties. But she hoped one day to entice him. That would certainly be a feather in her cap. She loved giving parties, had a gift for it. More important, Veldarr loved it. And right now, Veldarr was the brightest jewel in her well-jeweled crown. Now that she was healthy, there was nothing she enjoyed more than her evenings—her galas, Veldarr called them. Well, perhaps shopping in the stores for clothes. For jewelry, she did not need to shop. There were many presents, and not all from Veldarr.

"Dear Sylvie and Don,
"I've been meaning to write this letter to you now for weeks, but there is so much to do in Mattelmead City that time just gets away from me. I hope that this letter finds you both in good health. It is months since the three of us met, many months, and I miss you. I had hoped that you would come to town for the winter, and now it is March and you haven't arrived. The caretaker of your house here in the city said that you didn't plan to come until late spring, and then only for a few weeks. I think my news might induce the two of you to come sooner, if the weather permits.

"First, let me tell you that Glenorr and I are quite well. The medicines that I have been given by my doctor continue to be effective and I have had no recurring incidents of that old malady. Glen still lives most of the time at the academy, and visits our house no more than once a week, unless he chooses to look in on our country estate. Well, someone must. He continues to make excellent progress in his scientific studies, and is, I must confess, very happy at the academy. That assurance over with, let me come finally to my news.

"Auragole has come to Mattelmead! Yes, that's right, our Auragole! He is alive, is well, and has grown quite handsome. After we were separated (is it now almost two years?) he spent months looking for us, but could not pick up our trail. While looking for us, he met Lorenwile. Did you ever hear of him? He's that famous singer who used to perform at the Blue Heron, but was away from the city when we first arrived. Well, Lorenwile met Auragole on the road, and took him on as his apprentice. Auragole was always a good singer, but now he's extraordinary. You should hear him. You should come to town and hear him. You would be quite proud. He's most eager to see you and has asked me to contact you. His work keeps him much engaged and he cannot get away to come to you.

"Oh my, there is so much to tell. I barely know where to begin. But the telling of most of this wondrous tale must be left until you come. Two things I will, however, tell you. The first is that Auragole is a great favorite of Ormahn's! It seems that Auragole saved the king's life when there was an attempted assassination against him on Ormahn's way home from the war against Thorensphere. No doubt, you will have heard that news, even in your self-imposed isolation—but did you know that it was our Auragole who was the hero of that story? Ormahn was badly wounded—though that news is not widely known. It was days until Oldwell and members of the army found the king, and Auragole stayed with him, caring for him and guarding him. He even saved him from a second murderous attempt. You can imagine how grateful the king is to him. Auragole's popularity with Ormahn makes him sought after by all those close to the throne. He is being entertained by all the important people in the city. Is this not a marvel?

"The other thing I want to write you about is our first meeting, for it was quite dramatic. Glenorr and I went to the Blue Heron one night, but sat way in the back of the room so as not to startle Auragole. Then after the performance, we went backstage. It was filled with people wanting to say hello to him and to Lorenwile, to issue invitations to them. Some I think just wanted to be noticed by them. I'm told that Ormahn himself has gone on more than one occasion to the Blue Heron—you can imagine what excitement that causes—and Auragole has been invited to the palace frequently. He's been here less than three months and he's already a regular at the palace! Well, good luck always seemed to cling to Auragole. But back to my story.

"Glen and I stood at the edge of the crowd, waiting to get through to his dressing room, and finally we did. I think at first Auragole didn't recognize me. Well, I have changed—thank the stars for that—and am no longer that skinny, gaunt, pale thing that I was on our long journey here, traveling in rags, and ill. Auragole recognized Glen first, and then Glen introduced me and I think Auragole almost fainted. He turned white and could barely speak for several moments. He thought I was dead, you see! Remember the blue cloak that the Agavians gave me? Well, Don was carrying it when we disembarked from the boat, and when Don took that wound to his leg, the arrow went through the cloak first. I remember that I screamed and screamed, fearing Don had been killed. There was blood all over the cloak. Don must have dropped it on the dock where Auragole found it. Auragole thought I had been killed. So I was suddenly this ghost reappearing. Isn't that astonishing? We went out to dinner that night, the three of us, and we told him all that has happened since we were rescued by Veldarr's soldiers from that band of thieves that could have been our death. Auragole did try to find us, but had no idea in which direction we had been taken. But I'm sure he'll tell you when you get here about what happened to him after we were separated.

"Auragole was especially happy to hear of your marriage. I must say, it took him by surprise. But I think it gave him great pleasure. He and I see each other quite often. I include him in my little galas, which he comes to after singing at the Blue Heron. Though why he has to work is beyond my understanding. He has a great house here in the city—grander than yours or mine, and also a country estate, which he has not yet visited. And all those jewels from Agavia. But I think he stays on at the Blue Heron because he truly loves the singing—and feels a certain loyalty to Lorenwile.

"Lorenwile is quite the character. He doesn't have a serious thought in his head, for all the glory of his singing talents. But that's the way it often is with artists, don't you think? All talent and few brains. Lorenwile's been to my evenings also and is the perfect person to have at one's social gatherings. He's very funny, even a little irreverent, but apparently the palace and those around Ormahn find him witty and amusing. So though he's not really society, and though he possesses no great wealth, it's all right to include him. Besides, he's the most outrageous gossip. And gossip is fun.

"Auragole has urged me to write you and beg you to come as soon as you are able. When the weather clears up a bit, do hasten to the city. I shall make a little party, just for the five of us. It will be like old times, only better. I adore you both. We don't see enough of each other.

"Love, Ellie"

N

chapter six

IT WAS EARLY March and Auragole was struggling to write a song about the first night he and Ellie had made love. He was sitting on the edge of his bed. He had just breakfasted, though it was nearing noon. But then he hardly ever made it to his own bed until the early hours of the new day. More than three months in the city, and still he couldn't get used to the largeness of Bendahl's house that was now his. He could not imagine sitting all alone in the great drawing room to play on his harp or to create songs. The magnificence of Mattelmead still overwhelmed him. Lorenwile, and occasionally Ellie, had taken him about the city—and by now he thought he knew every square foot of it. He still wasn't used to the attention of so many strangers all wanting his friendship. He wasn't used to so much happiness, so much unalloyed joy. He was in glorious, fabled Mattelmead City, and the reality was even better than the fantasy. Ellie was alive, and his beloved. He was singing with Lorenwile, and that was going amazingly well. He was friend to

Solagen, Ormahn of Mattelmead. That was still like a dream from which he kept expecting to awaken. And perhaps this summer he would continue his study of True-singing. It was all too much, and some days he needed to be by himself, away from the nightly parties, away from the sightseeing, away from the conversations about the latest scientific discovery, the newest stage play, the current dance performances or concerts, or the most recent art exhibit. Some days he needed to saddle up Starwanderer and ride up into the hills around the city where there was a view of the Western Sea. He needed to be alone, to be with his own thoughts. And some days, and this was one of them, he needed to be in his bedchamber, the room that seemed most his own, and create songs.

How many songs of love had he written about Glenelle after they had been separated and while he thought she was dead? How many songs had he written about love in general? But what had he really known about love before? Now he knew about love, now he understood it from inside its depths, inside its glory. Auragole wanted this song to be perfect, the most beautiful love song ever written in the whole history of the Grand Continent. Many singers from past ages who had loved well had written about their first encounter with that consummate joy, and some of these songs had been passed down—and he and Lorenwile now sang them. But his song would surpass all of them. After all, wasn't he now both a See-singer and a True-singer, capable of living intensely into things?

Auragole flung himself on his back across the foot of his bed and thought about that first night. If he had been too quick or too awkward in his lovemaking, Glenelle had not seemed to mind because he had come to her with such ineffable bliss. How many nights had he been with her now in the month or so since she had found him? Many—perhaps most. And his skill as a lover had increased. Of course it had, but still, that first time. . .

Some nights he would just sit in her room and stare at her.

Her eyes were liquid blue universes. He created stars in them. Her hair to his touch was softer than any of the silks in Agavia. She lay on her bed as languidly as when he first saw her lying by that stream in the Gandlese Mountains, sleeping and ill. She was not so pale now, not so thin. She had told him, in her musical, almost caressing speech, that the doctors in Mattelmead City had cured her of her terrible spells. "I no longer dream my fears or speak them," she said one night, lying in his arms. "I need only take two pills a day," and she had reached across him to the little table next to the bed, opened a drawer, and removed a bottle. She dropped it on his chest.

"Ouch," he had said, and removed the bottle and put it back on the table. Then he drew her close and said, just before his lips covered hers, "I have medicine for you, also."

Some nights they would linger in front of her fireplace sipping wine, and Glenelle would ask him questions about what had happened in the nearly two years since they had separated. He was telling it to her, a little at a time, detail by detail, everything— except True-singing. He held back from mentioning True-singing, and it made him feel at times ashamed of what might seem like a lack of trust in the beloved. But Lorenwile had warned him to keep silent. And he owed that to Lorenwile. Lorenwile had told him not to speak about the Companions of the Way, or Meekelorr, or Agavia, while he was in Mattelmead. But Ellie also knew Meekelorr, knew that Meekelorr was in the west. She knew about the Companions of the Way, knew Agavia, so what reason was there to hide any of his encounters with them from her?

Therefore, he told her about Elarr and Affredda, and their adventures together, about the Ancient Woods and Little Thoren. She seemed enthralled by his stories and he rejoiced in the telling of them, sharing his life with her, and his past. About his time with Lorenwile, he said only that they had traveled together while he learned to sing better. And there was no question that he was singing better now than when he had sung with Donnadorr. She could hear that. So if he held back the mention of True-singing, was that so terrible an omission?

Auragole often sang to Glenelle in the privacy of her rooms, songs that he had created for her when he had thought her dead, songs about her beauty, her goodness, her courage, and songs of his undying love. An unbidden image came just then, and Auragole sat up. It was the memory of a time when they were together and he was singing to her—a prelude to lovemaking. Glenelle was lying on her bed, a silk sheet draped lightly over her long, exquisitely curved body, and he was sitting in a chair at the foot of the bed. He looked at her face, and for a moment her expression startled him. She seemed so remote, so removed, as if her thoughts were miles away and not where his song was. At that moment he wanted desperately to crawl into her thoughts, to penetrate her feelings, to True-sing her being, to go into her soul as he would in a few moments go into her body.

At that moment he stopped singing, appalled at himself. Why did he want to go where no human was allowed to go? Hadn't he learned the folly of that from his experience with Kaynadahhn, the horse-man he had sung to his death? Hadn't Ellie given Auragole enough—her body, her love? Must he also desire to violate her soul like a rapist? He must have gasped.

If Glenelle's thoughts had been somewhere else while he was singing, she noticed when he stopped his playing. She yawned and stretched like a cat. "Come, my beautiful pet," and she held out her white arms. He rose and went to her. All other thoughts fell away as he let her arms enfold him.

But enough. He wanted now to recall only that first night. To celebrate it in song, to create a hymn to that first time when he had experienced such ecstasy, such total giving. It was a night locked in his memory, not to be equaled, but to be brought now into melody and words. He sat up, rose quickly from his bed, picked up his harp again, and moved to his favorite chair before the fireplace. And he began.

IT WAS THE beginning of April, and Donnadorr had just returned home from his club in Mattelmead City. He had taken Auragole to lunch there, to show him where he spent much of his time when he was in town, and where some of the members of Ormahn's court, and many of the officers in Ormahn's army, also passed their time in the winter. There was a fine dining room in the club, and gaming rooms, a room for cards, billiards, one for fencing, and a library. He thought perhaps Auragole would like to become a member, and Auragole said he would think about it. Donnadorr returned home worried, and he spoke his worries to Sylvane.

"Auragole is besotted," he said to her after dinner, when they were sitting in front of the fire in the little drawing room that they favored over the larger, more formal one.

"Besotted? By what?"

"By whom, you mean. By Glenelle, of course."

"Oh, that's an old tale, Don. He fell in love with her the first time he set eyes on her."

"But he doesn't know her, not really. . .what she's become."

"Don. . ."

"No, you know what I'm speaking about, Sylvie. Let's not have pretenses between us. In truth, I don't believe Ellie is in love with Aurie."

"No?"

"Do you?"

Sylvane lifted the cup of tea to her lips. "Well, yes, perhaps. In her fashion."

"In her fashion. You will ever think well of her, Sylvane."

"She is my sister, Don."

"Foster sister."

"We were raised together and have come through much together."

"We have all come through much together," Don said, stroking his red beard. "How often do you see her? How often does she invite you, us, to her parties?"

"It's not because she doesn't care for us, Don. It's we who do not care for the social life that Glenelle craves, and she knows it. Even Glen attends very few of her evenings."

"Lass, you know what everyone else knows, that she is mistress to Veldarr."

"I've heard the rumors, too," Sylvane said. "People in this city love to gossip, as you well know. And much we hear is false."

"If she is mistress to Veldarr," Don pursued it, "what is she doing with Aurie?"

"If she *is* mistress. . ."

"Come, Sylvie, you know it's true."

"Then why is she so taken with Auragole?" she asked him, her face thoughtful.

"That's the question I just asked you, my love. But you might have phrased it differently. Perhaps it is Auragole who is taken with Glenelle."

"Don, this makes no sense. If she is mistress to someone as powerful as Veldarr, she wouldn't allow Auragole to court her."

"Unless. . ."

"Unless what?"

Donnadorr rose and took her by the hand. He picked up the candelabra and they walked through the halls and up the stairs to their bedroom. "Unless Veldarr knows and is even encouraging it," he finally said.

"Preposterous. If she is his, he wouldn't. . . To what purpose, Don?" She looked at him, troubled.

"Sylvie lass, you will ever see only the good in people. You know how much intrigue and how many machinations go on at the court of Ormahn—everyone wanting to get closer to the king, to be in his favor. Why, that crowd there would climb over whomever it takes, and tell whatever secret or lie it takes, to ingratiate themselves. It's enough to make one's head spin. I far prefer the officers at the club who are not so high up at the court. Their genuine patriotism is admirable."

"But Veldarr is as close to the court as one can get. He doesn't need Auragole to help him make that climb."

"I know. I know. I don't understand it. But there is something here that has a foul odor to it. Frankly, Sylvie, if it weren't for Auragole, who might need a friend or two soon, I would pack us both up and return to the country. It's a far easier and a far safer place to be."

TWO DAYS LATER, Sylvane was waiting for Donnadorr when he returned from his club. She stood in the hallway with a sad expression on her face.

"You're in early today, Sylvie," Don said, dropping his cloak on the chair near the door. A servant rushed to retrieve it.

"They've closed down the orphanage—all the orphanages in the city." Helping out at an orphanage was where Sylvane spent much of her time. There was one near them in the country as well as one at which she worked while in the city. Until she was able to have children of her own, she wanted to be near them.

"Closed them down?" Donnadorr took her by the hand and led her into the small drawing room and up to the hearth, where there was a warm fire.

Sylvane held onto his hand and stared into the fire. "Refugees will no longer be allowed into the city," she said, "unless, of course, they have gold or jewels to buy or build themselves houses or have positions waiting for them. The orphanages and other refugee-clearing institutions will be set up far from the city. Since the war with Thorensphere, there are so many people pouring into the country. . ."

"Come, come, my love, is that such a tragedy?—other than that it takes away an institution in Mattelmead City where you feel useful?" He lifted her small hand to his lips. "The countryside is a far better place for children to be nurtured. As for the adults, single or in families, many are taken in by the city. There is still a need here. That is the talk at the club. And because they are needed they are welcome. There is much work in the city, not only for the skilled, but for the unskilled as well. The city is growing at a phenomenal rate—houses and buildings mushrooming up everywhere. You worry unnecessarily. What you need is a nice cup of senta tea." He led her to a chair, then rang the bell for the servant and sat down on the sofa. "Don't trouble yourself so, lass. Everyone is cared for here in Mattelmead—if not in the city, then away from the city. No one goes hungry. And those young men who have no usable skills, and who pour into this country every day, are taken immediately into the army. It's a good life for most, even a noble life," his voice turned a little wistful, "in the service of Solagen, Ormahn of Mattelmead, peace bringer and hope restorer. No one is starving under Ormahn's rule."

"Yes, yes, I know you're right. Even those who can't work, or are too old, are looked after, sent off to special camps in the country— no doubt where they are well provided for and given all that they need to sustain them," Sylvane said, but she still felt uneasy.

"Then what troubles you, girl? Everyone is accounted for, cared for, through the generosity of our king."

She sighed and stood up. "I know you're right, Don. But now I don't have anything to do in the city to occupy my time. I can't bear to be idle, planning parties or attending them, shopping endlessly for clothes and gossiping with the ladies, or dining at fancy restaurants." She came and sat down next to him. "When shall we return to the country, Don? At least there I can garden, and walk or ride in the woods. It's April and time for planting. I don't want to leave it all to the gardeners. And besides, there is an orphanage there. . ."

They stopped talking as the tea tray came in and the table near the fireplace was quickly set. Sylvane dismissed the servant, telling her that Sylvane would serve the tea herself. They sat at the table and she poured. They drank for a time in silence.

Then Don leaned toward her across the small table and reached for her hand. "Wait just a little, Sylvie. Let's see what happens to Aurie. I worry about him."

"I know. . .I know. You think he might need his old friends?"

"I do. By early summer, I'm sure, we will return to the country. By then. . . Well. . . Are you willing to wait?"

"For Auragole, you know I am." She smiled at him.

"That's my girl." He came around the table and lifted her to her feet, took her in his arms, and kissed her.

"What a good man you are, Don," she finally whispered in his ear.

"You mean, what a lucky man I am."

GLENELLE WAS IN her own bed, lying in Veldarr's arms. The scent of April flowers drifted in through the open window, filling the room with a voluptuous aroma. Auragole had received a request to go to the palace that night and would not call on her. She was certain that Veldarr had arranged it.

"Do you think he knows the way to Agavia, Ellie?" Veldarr said, covering her neck with kisses.

"I haven't asked him. Do you want me to? Is it important?"

"Important? Not yet—but someday it might be a useful piece of information to have. So, yes, I want you to ask him. If I bring that information to Solagen. . . But first, it would be helpful to know the whereabouts of the main camp of the Companions of the Way in the Sorren Heights."

"I told you. In the Woeful Peaks."

"That, my darling, is partially useful. But the Woefuls comprise a large and mostly unpopulated area. The mountains there are very high. One wouldn't want to go roaming around with an army looking behind every peak."

She rolled over him and kissed his mouth. "If this information will help you become heir to the throne, then I'll get it for you, my pet."

"Now who says I want to be heir to the throne?" He slapped her rump playfully. And there the conversation stopped.

chapter seven

AURAGOLE AND GLENELLE were dining in one of the finest restaurants in the city. Lorenwile had recommended it. "Much too rich for my blood, boy, unless someone from Ormahn's court takes me, hoping for gossip. I'm purported to know more secrets than anyone else in the city, and it's probably true. With a little wine, and a delicious meal, I tell all."

Except that you are a True-singer, and in search of someone known as the Nethergod, Auragole had thought then.

But because of Lorenwile's recommendation, Auragole had arranged to take Glenelle to the Lavender Goose. From the expression on her face, Ellie seemed quite taken with the place. She had never been there before and that pleased Auragole. The food was superb and the wine excellent. Wine from Glovale, the best one could get, available only at the top restaurants and at the palace. Glenelle was very gay and talkative that night. She was busy telling Auragole who most of the diners were, how close they were to the court, or how wealthy they were. She pointed out who was society, and therefore very rich, and who were merely well-to-do merchants out with their wives or comrades for a special celebration. Many people had risen to greet Glenelle as she and Auragole had entered the restaurant. Most were quite effusive when introduced to Auragole. Everyone, it seemed, had heard him sing, and they showered him with compliments. Auragole still blushed at the attention. It had taken some getting used to—all the adulation he had received since coming to this great city. Some, he knew, was for his singing, but most he suspected was because of his friendship with the king.

Auragole sighed inwardly as they put down their forks and stood for the fifth time that evening, to greet friends of Glenelle's. He had hoped for a more intimate evening, but he should have known better. The Lavender Goose was a place where people came to see and be seen—that was obvious. And it suited Glenelle. She was having a grand time. Her face glowed with the attention she was receiving. She was happy, and that should make him happy. The truth was, he couldn't get enough of her. For more than two months he had been seeing her, and he still couldn't believe his good fortune. How beautiful she was, how healthy she seemed. Glenelle was now his love, the way he had so often dreamt it. No, better than his dreams, because not only was Ellie his, he was also singing with the great Lorenwile. And Auragole was a favorite of the king's, and living in Mattelmead City. What more could Auragole ask? He could barely eat, he was so full of the abundance life had bestowed on him.

"So why do you do it?" Glenelle was asking him.

"What?" He realized that he had stopped listening to her words, and had been simply looking at the wonder of her.

"I asked why you continue to sing at the Blue Heron."

He was surprised at her question. "Why shouldn't I sing at the Blue Heron? I love singing."

"Because, my pet, you are very rich and extremely well

connected. Because you don't need to work for your living. Because you are accepted at the court and are closer to the king than some of his relatives." She hesitated a moment, and then plunged on. "Because to be a performer is not. . .is not. . ."

"Is not what, Ellie?" He looked at her lovely face, at her golden hair piled high on her head and sparkling with jeweled combs. But her forehead was wrinkled ever so slightly now in perturbation.

"Well, performers are not in the same society as you are—what with your wealth and your contacts."

"I'm not sure I understand you," and his head tilted slightly, his eyes questioning.

"I think you do, Auragole. You just don't want to admit it."

"Admit what, Ellie?"

"That you could aspire to something higher."

"What is lacking in my life that I should aspire to anything else?" He took her hands and looked deep into her eyes, willing her to see how much he loved her. Then he released her hands and sat back. "Besides, I adore singing. Why shouldn't I sing? It seems to give people pleasure."

"At present you belong to the very top echelon of society. But you must know that if it weren't for your connections at court and for Solagen's indebtedness to you, that as a singer you would be only in Lorenwile's class—despite your wealth. Surely you know that, Auragole. You've been in Mattelmead long enough to know that. To know what is important and what is. . . well, of less importance. Singers are. . .well, artists."

He straightened his back, but his eyes never left her face. What was this all about? Surely there was no stigma attached to being a singer. The king called on him frequently to come to the palace, sometimes to sing for him alone as well as for Solagen's guests. "I don't understand what you are getting at," Auragole said.

"Auragole, you will ever be that independent innocent who was born in the Gandlese Mountains and raised away from people." She shook her lovely head and her blond curls shimmered golden in the candlelight. "Surely you see how society is formed here in Mattelmead."

"It bothers you that I sing and earn money doing it? If I sang only for pleasure, that would be more acceptable?"

She was quiet for a moment. Then she smiled brightly and said, "Forget what I said, Aurie. Do as you please. Let's order dessert. They say the desserts here are marvelous." She motioned for the waiter.

Auragole was quiet while they drank their tea and ate their plum-and-whipped-cream concoction. He was bothered by what Ellie had said. What was wrong with being a singer of songs? It was true he didn't have to earn his keep by singing. But he loved singing—and it apparently gave people pleasure. Could there be anything more glorious than singing with Lorenwile? Should he spend his days gaming or hunting? Was that more acceptable? Should he become an officer in the army? Was that what she was hinting at?

His thoughts were interrupted by a party of four that was following the headwaiter to a table. He saw Glenelle flush, and then he looked up. It was Veldarr with some friends. Veldarr stopped when he saw Auragole.

"It's good to see you again, Auragole. I understand Mattelmead City has taken quite a fancy to you." He offered Auragole his hand. "I'll have to come soon and hear you sing. I'm sure my wife would enjoy that."

Auragole stood up and took the proffered hand.

"Let me introduce my friends." And Veldarr named the three men who were with him.

Auragole shook the hand of each. "Let me introduce my. . . my friend," Auragole said. "This is Glenelle."

Glenelle blushed and offered her hand to each of the men.

Veldarr smiled as he took Glenelle's hand. "Yes, I know Glenelle. She's quite famous, considered the best party giver in all of

Mattelmead. Nice to see you again," he said, and gave her a little nod.

"Nice seeing you," she said.

Veldarr turned once again to Auragole and gave him a brilliant smile. "Auragole, you amaze me. Here so short a time and you know the best restaurant in the city. And you've made the acquaintance of one of the most beautiful ladies in all of Mattelmead. Luck does seem to follow you."

Glenelle's face glowed. Veldarr bowed slightly and led his friends away, following the headwaiter to a table in the center of the large room.

Auragole looked at Glenelle thoughtfully. "I didn't know you knew Veldarr. How did you two meet?"

"It was he and his soldiers who rescued us from those awful thieves when we got separated from you." She smiled brightly at Auragole. "I thought I told you about that."

He tried to remember. "Yes. . .I suppose you did." Trouble was, he was so often caught up in just looking at her that he didn't always hear what she was saying.

"He's come to some of my parties. Not often, but he has come."

"With his wife?"

Glenelle hesitated. "Seldom with his wife."

"Do you know his wife?"

Glenelle was looking away from him. "Yes, I've met her. She's not very social, so the gossip goes. She comes out into society only when it is necessary. She is one of those happy homebodies. A woman busy with her family. Not my type, really." And Glenelle laughed and turned back to Auragole. "Now, my pet, how would you like to go to a quaint little club I know and have some wine and listen to some exquisite music?" She reached over and stroked his face.

What beautiful eyes she had. Her features were small and delicate, and, he thought, perfect. Veldarr was right—Ellie was, no doubt, one of the most beautiful women in Mattelmead.

In Mattelmead? In all the Westernlands. On the whole Grand Continent.

"Anything you want to do, my love, is fine with me," and Auragole took her hand from his cheek and kissed her palm.

THAT NIGHT, LYING in her bed after they had made love, Auragole was falling asleep when Glenelle sat up. "But I can't imagine it," she said, "where Meekelorr and the Companions are camping in the Woefuls. The tallest mountains are in the Woefuls. How do the Companions who report to him find him?"

Auragole rolled over and yawned. They had been talking about this as they were riding to her home in his carriage. Glenelle seemed very much to admire Meekelorr. "No doubt they have maps," he said.

"And you, do you have a map?"

"I don't need a map. I could find my way back there without a map. Have found my way back there."

"And Lorenwile, does he have a map?"

"Lorenwile has an uncanny sense for where things are. I don't think he needs a map."

"But if you had to tell someone how to get there, could you draw him a map?"

"But I don't have to tell anyone how to get there."

"I know. I know. But could you?"

He was sitting up by then. "Of course I could. I could do it in five minutes—if I had some paper."

He fell back on the pillows and yawned again. She rolled on top of him and began kissing his face and tickling his ribs. "Braggart, you could not."

"I could," Auragole said, laughing. He swung Glenelle over onto her side of the bed. He was becoming aroused again.

"No," she said, pushing him away. "Show me first. Show me that you're not just a braggart."

He fell back on his pillow again. "You are a little vixen. You know I'm good with maps."

Glenelle sat up and opened the drawer in her bedside table. She drew out a pad of paper and a pencil. "Prove it," she said, with a roguish twinkle in her eye.

He sat up. "Give them to me. See, here are the Sorren Heights." He was drawing rapidly. "And the Woefuls are here. These are old roads and these roads lead to a valley called the Doldarr. That's where Meekelorr is. Now, have I proved it to you? Was that less than five minutes?"

She took the paper from him and stared at it. "Auragole, you are amazing. I apologize for calling you a braggart." She slipped the pad of paper into her drawer and leaned over to kiss him. "For proving me wrong you get a little reward." And soon she was on top of him, and her hands and mouth moved over his body so deliciously that Auragole forgot maps, forgot sleep, and simply gave himself up to the wonders of loving Glenelle, body and heart.

THE MESSAGE CAME just as Auragole was about to leave his house. The note said he was not to come to the palace that night. Some pressing business had come up; therefore that night's dinner party had been canceled and there would be no need for his services. Auragole stood and looked at the message for a few moments.

"Is there an answer, sir?" the messenger asked him.

Auragole shook his head, "No, only to say I have received it."

The messenger bowed and walked to the door, where a servant let him out.

Well, Auragole thought, I'm free tonight.

"Shall I have the coach returned to the stables?" his servant asked him.

"Yes," Auragole said, "but I would like my horse saddled. Tell Semp I'll be ready in fifteen minutes." He bounded up the stairs two at a time to change into clothes more suitable for riding. In fifteen minutes he was guiding Starwanderer out of the courtyard and into the streets. It was a lovely May night, the stars were bright, the moon just past new. He thought for a moment of riding over to Glenelle's, but she was having one of her galas that night. He wasn't in the mood for dozens of people, for light banter. He had been saved from a long night of polite conversation at the king's palace, and frankly he was relieved. An evening to himself was a rare event. When he wasn't performing at the Blue Heron, or attending Ormahn, then he was with Glenelle. He savored the idea of a solitary ride into the western hills above the city that protected it from the winds off the Western Sea.

So Auragole rode up into the beautiful park. It was filled with green balsam firs, mountain ash, white spruce, black spruce, maple, and oak, and his favorite, the trembling aspen that would turn golden in the fall. If it were day there would have been seagulls, bald eagles, terns, cormorants, yellow and purple finches, red-tailed hawks, chickadees. He knew that beside the path there were all kinds of growing things—wood wort, black napweed, fireweed, and a rainbow of wildflowers. It was dark, but in his mind's eye he could picture it all. Auragole loved the view toward the sea, and rode along a ridge with the sea appearing now and again below and to his left. Sleeping or hiding were deer, squirrels, foxes, even black bears. A great peace came over him as he turned his thoughts to all that had happened to him since he had come to this city. There was much to think about, much to be grateful for.

He must have been riding the better part of three hours when he decided that he would head down to Glenelle's. If the party was still on, he would go home. If not. . .

He turned his horse in the direction of Glenelle's house and in less than an hour he was there. The lights in the house were out. Good. The party was over. He would take his horse into the stable, give it to the groom there, then walk around to the garden, which was at the back of the house. Glenelle's room was on the second floor, overlooking an array of May flowers and elegantly shaped bushes. There was a small door opening into the garden from the house that was used mostly by the servants. Auragole had a key to it that he wore around his neck on the same long chain with the token given him by Pohl, one that had belonged to his mother's uncle, now dead.

Auragole dismounted and walked his horse into the barn. The lights were still on, and a groom he didn't know was brushing a large stallion. The horse was familiar but he could not for the moment place it. Glenelle's groom, Bode, had been talking with the new groom, but he jumped to his feet when he saw Auragole enter leading Starwanderer. Bode looked rather startled and glanced quickly at the new groom, whose face was turned away from Auragole and who was suddenly brushing the horse in his care with great diligence. Auragole took a coin from his vest pocket and tossed it to Ellie's groom. "Will you give Starwanderer some oats and water, and keep an eye on him till I return?"

The groom caught the coin and merely nodded. His eyes had widened, but the usually loquacious young man said nothing. It was later that Auragole would remember this. But at that moment he merely walked out of the stable and gave the horse and the two grooms barely a fleeting thought. He was so intent and happy at the prospect of seeing his beloved that it didn't occur to him then that she might have a guest. Later, he would wonder again and again at his stupidity in not recognizing the horse.

Auragole walked past the outbuildings of the mansion and entered the garden, as he so often had, by a gate at its far end. He turned to walk toward the house down a path flanked by flowers, then glanced up at Ellie's room. Good. The lights were on. She was still awake. There was not a doubt in his mind that Ellie would be glad to see him. Wasn't she always? The curtains were not drawn, the windows were open, letting in the fragrant

May air. He looked up at the window in happy anticipation as he moved down the path toward the house. And there coming to the window was Ellie herself, in a flimsy negligee, her long hair billowing down past her shoulders. He stopped to look at her. Could she see him? Probably not. With only a sliver of a moon, the garden was encased in shadow. How beautiful Ellie was. He almost called out to her, but thought better of it. He didn't need to wake the whole household. He was about to move again toward the door when he saw someone come up behind Ellie. The figure was tall, male. The man's arms moved around Ellie and clasped her about the shoulders. She smiled. He brushed her hair from her shoulders, then kissed her neck. Auragole moved quickly off the path to stand half hidden and dumbstruck behind a topiary. The man turned Glenelle slowly in his arms, kissing her neck, her throat, her chin, then her mouth. She flung her arms about him. Without removing his lips from hers, the man lifted her off the floor and carried her away from the window.

Auragole was so shocked he almost forgot to breathe. Then he began to shake. He stood there for some time, unable to stop the shaking. He saw the lights go out in Glenelle's room. Suddenly his chest was heaving with anger. His head began to spin. He sat down hard on the ground, taking in great gulps of air. Afterward he didn't remember going to the stable to retrieve his horse. He knew he had not gone directly home. But where he had ridden, he couldn't say. All he knew was that it was past dawn when he returned his horse to Semp. He let himself into the house, climbed the stairs to his room, and threw himself on his bed, fully clothed. He fell quickly into a deep but troubled sleep, and dreamt of his father, of standing at his father's deathbed, of hearing once again his father's last words to him.

"I must warn you," he whispered, and Auragole put his ear close to his father's mouth, "as I warned you about the Gods."

"About what, father?"

"About love." He looked at Auragole and Auragole could see yellow flames burning deep in his father's sunken eyes. "If you seek it, you will find illusion. Forget what you have heard in song and story."

"But. . ." Auragole started to interrupt.

"Let me speak, Auragole, for I cannot fight the blackness much longer. Everyone will speak to you of love and sing its praises. The thief will tell you he loves you as he takes your goods. The king will tell you he loves you as he takes your freedom. The priest will tell you he loves you as he takes your will. And the woman will tell you she loves you as she takes your manhood. They will all lie. They will all entrap you in the name of love. Don't be fooled. Don't succumb to their illusions. There is no such thing as love. Accept what rises in the blood but don't call it love. Admit what lives in the instincts but don't call it love. The people of the Easternlands killed or were killed with slogans of love on their lips." He gasped. "Don't succumb and you will be free, free." Then the flaming eyes saw no more.

Auragole didn't get up until late afternoon.

"WHAT WAS WRONG with you tonight, boy? You sang as if your mind was as far away as Agavia. What was going on inside you? I felt I was all alone out there." Lorenwile stood in the doorway of Auragole's dressing room and stared at him quizzically.

Auragole, sitting at his dressing table, lifted a face, pale now without his makeup, and turned to Lorenwile.

That look is ice. It could freeze the blood, Lorenwile thought. What ails the boy?

"What do you know about Veldarr?"

"What do you mean?" Lorenwile came in and sat on the sofa in Auragole's dressing room. But he guessed now where this conversation was going.

"Tell me about Veldarr. Not the things that I already know,

but the things I don't know."

"He aspires to the throne, no matter how indifferent he pretends to be. As it stands now, unless Solagen's new wife produces an heir, the succession is between him and his cousin, Goredahl."

"I know that."

"He will do a lot to ingratiate himself with his uncle. Murder, no. That I doubt. But whatever else it might take."

"Tell me about his marriage."

Ah, we are coming to it. "It's like all the marriages among the rich and important families in Mattelmead. A marriage is only an alliance between families, between fortunes and land. And his is no different. Veldarr has made a good alliance with a large and influential family, and he will have need of that family should he in time make a bid for the throne. I would venture to say his is a better alliance than his cousin's, Goredahl's."

"You're saying that love doesn't enter into marriage here in Mattelmead."

"I'm saying that it doesn't *necessarily* enter in."

"And then. . .?"

"And then, what?"

"Does a man in such a marriage look for love elsewhere?"

"Listen, boy." Lorenwile stood up. "You've been here, what, five months? Surely you know that it's quite common and even accepted for a man to find his pleasure elsewhere, outside the marriage bed."

"And Veldarr, does he find his pleasure elsewhere?"

"So it is rumored."

"Where?"

"Auragole, why ask me?"

Auragole stood up. He moved toward Lorenwile and thrust his face, white and threatening, into Lorenwile's. "Because you know everything, all the gossip, all the secrets. People confide in you. You have boasted of that yourself. So where is it that

Veldarr sleeps when he doesn't sleep in his own bed, Lorenwile?"

Lorenwile moved away from him and strode toward the door. "Ask her yourself, Auragole. Why ask me?"

"Wait."

Lorenwile slowly turned around.

Auragole was standing where Lorenwile had left him, looking young and bereft, no longer threatening or angry.

"Does everybody know this except me?"

Lorenwile nodded, and left Auragole to work it through. Well, Lorenwile thought as he left the club and looked for a horse and carriage to take him home, everyone gets disappointed in love at some time.

SYLVANE WAS NOT at home that afternoon when Auragole arrived. Donnadorr led Auragole into his small sitting room on the second floor near his bedroom. Beyond the large eastern windows the sky was gray and cloudy and a light spring rain was falling.

"Why didn't you tell me, Don?" Auragole's voice was hollow.

Donnadorr sighed. "It's hard to tell someone who is. . .was as much in love as you were, that the beloved is not the woman he thinks she is. You probably would have punched me in the nose," he added lightly.

But Auragole was in no mood for humor. He sat stiffly in a chair opposite Donnadorr, his eyes never leaving Donnadorr's face.

It was hard to take, that intense look. Donnadorr went on, however, knowing that Auragole needed to hear what he had to say. After all, wasn't it for this that he and Sylvie had stayed in the city? "It wasn't long after we arrived in Mattelmead that I realized what it was that Glenelle desired. I say that not to judge her harshly, Aurie. But, as we've already told you, our wealth rapidly opened many doors for us. We were taken up by society, because it is money that makes one eligible to become part of society. Perhaps in the years to come it won't be money, it will be family and one's ancestors that count. We are heading in that direction. Well, that's not what we were talking about, is it?"

Auragole didn't respond. He merely watched Donnadorr with anxious eyes.

"As I said, money is what counts here in society, and because of the jewels bestowed upon us by the Agavians, and the jewels the other three had brought with them from their home, we came here wealthy. And being wealthy, we purchased mansions and country estates, as was the custom, and were taken up by society. Glenelle loved it. Sylvane and I, well, we loved some of it. I cannot say I don't relish the easy life and all the comforts after so many hard years. I do. But I soon saw what it was that Ellie wanted. And then I saw what Sylvie wanted. I had never appreciated Sylvane's quiet strengths, her moral character, her goodness, her wisdom, her loyalty, or how pretty a woman she genuinely is. I was too besotted by Glenelle, her lovely gestures, her ephemeral beauty, her seductive charm, her wit—even her neediness. But you know this, Aurie."

Auragole nodded imperceptibly.

"Glen quickly found his place at the Academy for Nature and Categorizing. And Glenelle found her place in society. Men have always admired Glenelle, you know that. You and I, Auragole, were only two in a long line of admirers. Ellie has always had men around her who adore her. She has come to expect it. Here in this great city she knew she would shine, would be admired as she always had been since she was a child. Glenelle loves that admiration—even needs it. It's like medicine for her. Perhaps it does more for her than the remedies she takes."

Still Auragole did not take his dark, searching eyes from his, so Donnadorr continued, "Does she love Veldarr? Perhaps, if Ellie can love in the way you and I and Sylvie think of love. But

Veldarr is not the only one. There are others, not so consistent as Veldarr, not so important to her as he is, I would venture to guess—but others. And why should she give up everything for Veldarr, lad? Oh, I'm sure she is useful to him, and he to her. But Veldarr has a wife whom he will never set aside for Ellie. Frankly, I don't think Ellie would want that. This way she is free, free to be admired by many, free to take pleasure where she chooses. She has her own money, after all, and need never rely on anyone to take care of her. If you ask my opinion, I don't think Ellie will ever marry. She will have men around her as long as she is beautiful, and she will be beautiful, even as she grows into old age. No, there will always be those to admire her."

Finally Auragole lowered his eyes, rubbed his forehead, and stared at his hands. He sat wrapped in that silence Donnadorr remembered so well from their travels together. Donnadorr rose, poured Auragole a glass of wine, and brought it back to him. Then Don sat in the chair opposite, watching him.

Auragole sipped the wine absentmindedly, his face white with inner struggle. Finally Auragole said, with a quick shake of his head, "I don't understand it, Don. Frankly, I don't understand it. What is love? Can she not love?"

"I can't answer that. But think about yourself, Aurie. What did you love in her? What did I love? Was it not some ideal woman that we had turned Ellie into? Did we not impose our idea of who she was on her? Did we not fall in love with our own idea of love, making her its ideal?"

Auragole shook his head. "My father warned me."

"About what?"

"He said there was no such thing as love. That love was merely an illusion, a bodily need. That it would entrap you, take away your freedom."

"Do you believe that, friend?"

The look that crossed Auragole's face was a bitter one. "Why should I believe differently? I feel like a fool. And right now I think I hate her as much as I've ever hated anyone. What else does she deserve from me? She used me for some purpose of her own, that's all. Probably for her own amusement. Another man to conquer. And everyone around her knew it and was laughing at me, and waiting to watch me fall. Then waiting to see if I would pick myself up again. Was she laughing, too? Was she waiting for me to fall? She knew from the beginning that it wouldn't last, that eventually I would find out about. . .about her. She had to know that. I don't see anything at all admirable in her. You only excuse her."

"I have Sylvane, I can afford to be kind," and the thought filled Donnadorr with great peace. "Auragole, why don't you take some time off, go out to your estate? You've never been there. The house is quite marvelous, I am told, and the land around it superb, overlooking the sea. The weather is becoming warmer, the rains are slackening, so why not go? Or if you don't want to be alone, come to our country estate with us."

"Yes, yes," Auragole's face brightened, "that makes sense. I've never seen Bendahl's. . .my country estate and it would be beneficial to get away." He stood up. "Thank you for your offer, Don. Don't think me ungrateful—express my thanks to Sylvie, but I'd like to be alone for a while. I'd not be good company now."

"I understand."

Auragole rose and began pacing about the room. "This city is overwhelming, too often overwhelming. I sometimes feel I can't breathe, and then I have to ride up into the hills. Society and its ways are too much to take in. And now everyone knows about this, about me and what a fool I've been, how like a lapdog I've been. I'm gossip on everyone's lips, and it's hard to bear. I'm not used to having my affairs so scrutinized. There is much about being a public person that I don't like, I tell you true." He stood before the fireplace and stared at Donnadorr. "I'm not used to so many buildings, not used to the lack of privacy—especially in that cavernous house I've been given, what with all the servants one nearly falls over every time one takes a step. . . I'll take Starwanderer, Lors, and Semp, and go to my country estate. Maybe in the morning. Yes, I must get away." And he moved toward the door, as if he could not wait another minute.

Donnadorr followed him. "Have you spoken to Glenelle?"

"Why should I speak to Glenelle?" Auragole stopped, but did not turn around. "What can she say that will not add to my humiliation? No. Let her wonder what happened. I have no wish to see her again."

"Aurie, if there is anything Sylvie or I can do, let us know. Anything."

Auragole turned to face Don then and thrust out his hand. Looking distracted, as if he were already on Starwanderer riding out of the city, Auragole muttered, "Yes, yes, thank you. Thank you."

And he left, running down the stairs, not waiting for his host to escort him to the outer door.

Poor lad, Donnadorr thought, slowly descending the stairs. He takes everything so hard, takes everything in too deeply. Well, life will teach him. His position in this world is not so bad, after all. He's a friend to Ormahn, which puts him in the topmost tier of society. He's a much-admired singer, singing with the great and popular Lorenwile, and he's very wealthy. Surely, a month in the country and he will be over it. Life will open up for him in new ways. There are, after all, many pretty women in the city. And Auragole has grown into a very handsome man, and has become a remarkable singer. Well, lucky man to have had Lorenwile as a teacher. And Donnadorr felt a slight twinge—of what? Jealousy? He hoped not. Perhaps remorse that he himself had not found another one to guide and teach him—like Aiku. He did love to sing and had sung hardly at all these past two years.

Oh, well, there was nothing to stop him from singing. He still had his Agavian harp, thanks to Veldarr, who had insisted that it come with them after he had rescued Don and the others from their captors. Maybe when he and Sylvane returned to the country, Don would begin to play again. And now that Auragole was leaving for his own country estate, there was nothing to keep Sylvie and him in the city. Time to think about returning to the home he really loved.

WHILE HE WAS in the country, Auragole thought often about what his father had said, on his deathbed, about love. He decided his father was right. Love is for fools.

chapter eight

WHEN AURAGOLE RETURNED from the country a month later, he went immediately to Lorenwile's house to see him. He had written Lorenwile, of course, but still Auragole wanted to see Lorenwile face-to-face.

"You've grown thinner, Auragole. Your cook there not so good as the one here?" was all Lorenwile said by way of greeting, as soon as Auragole was shown into Lorenwile's drawing room.

Auragole ignored the comment. "You received my letter?"

Lorenwile nodded.

"Do you think I've made a wise decision?"

Lorenwile shrugged. "You made a decision. That's your right. So off with the army and Ormahn in a few weeks."

"But not to fight. I go as a singer, not as a soldier. Frankly, I'd rather not to be in this city at present."

"An invitation from the king is a hard one to turn down. He wrote you?"

"Sent a messenger—who would not leave until he had my

answer. But I am sorry about the True-singing we planned for the summer."

"It was no doubt an imprudent plan. I should not be leaving Mattelmead again only months after I've returned. Might cause some unnecessary gossip." Lorenwile's tourmaline-colored eyes, with their tiny red specks, reflected the June light spilling in from the windows, making them seem odd and unreadable. "So it's Noonbarr that's next on Ormahn's list."

"You heard that? I thought it was a secret."

"A huge army keep such a secret? Not from me, boy. The main part of the army has gone already. And you will follow with Ormahn in a few weeks?"

"Yes. Until we leave I'm to train with his Elite Corps. Though I don't intend to fight, I do need to be ready to protect myself. I look forward to the training. I need to do. . ." he stood up, ". . .something more physical than play the harp and sing songs. I'm restless. Frankly, it was good to spend some time in the country. Bendahl's estate. . .my estate is very large, I had no idea. . .near the Western Sea. I rode and hunted and didn't sing a note until the last week. It felt good."

"The hunting or the singing?"

"Both. I'll return to Mattelmead at the end of the summer, or by the fall at the latest. Then I'll come back to the Blue Heron," he hesitated, ". . .if you'll have me back."

"And why would I not have you back? We sing well together. We're very popular. We draw great crowds." Lorenwile slumped back in his chair. "It'll be quiet in the city while you're gone. Most of the men will be with you."

"Well, those in the army."

"And every important man is in the army."

"There are some who will remain here. I understand Veldarr is to stay and act as his uncle's regent while he is gone."

Lorenwile nodded.

Auragole stood up. "I'd best report to the palace. It's good to see you again, Lorenwile. I've. . .I've missed you." Auragole colored. "Someday, before too long, I hope the two of us can go off and. . ."

"Yes, well, that will come in time."

"I do miss it, you know."

"It's hard not to miss True-singing, once you've tasted it."

Auragole looked almost pleadingly at Lorenwile, willing him to understand. "Ormahn is doing something important, Lorenwile. If there is a genuine hope for peace in our world, I think it is Ormahn who will bring it."

"Well, you might be right."

"Perhaps Meekelorr and he will join forces. They both want the same thing."

"Perhaps they will."

"Well, good-bye for now. I'll stop in again before I leave."

"I would expect nothing less." Auragole offered his hand and Lorenwile took it. "And Auragole, send word, if you can when you're gone. I should very much like to know how you are faring."

At that Auragole's eyes lit up. Those might have been the warmest words Lorenwile had ever said to him.

IT WAS A cool November evening and Donnadorr was writing a letter to his wife. He had come to the city earlier than Sylvane, who would arrive in another month. He had been impatient in the country and Sylvane had urged him to go to the city the previous month, there to await the return of the army. She understood that his inability to be part of Ormahn's fighting force, because of his leg injury, was galling to Donnadorr. He had been restless and short-tempered, not at all himself. If only he could find some way to cure his injury, to rid himself of his marked limp and the intermittent bouts of pain.

"The bulk of the army," Donnadorr wrote, "has returned from the east, with much fanfare, many formal ceremonies, and a spate of parties. I'm sorry you're not here to attend them with me.

"The campaign was a huge success. Everyone at my club is talking about it. All of Noonbarr is now Ormahn's. There were several battles. Some say Noonbarr was harder to conquer than Thorensphere. That's probably because life was not so terrible there as it was in Thorensphere, so Ormahn of Mattelmead was not greeted with so much enthusiasm in Noonbarr as he was in Thorensphere. But he won each battle. What a fantastic army our army is! Now only the rest of the Sorren Heights, Isofed, and Wildenfarr-low-desert remain to be conquered. Can there be any doubt of the outcome?

"The most important part of this letter is that I have news of our Auragole. He's quite the hero, and the whole town is talking about him. It seems he saved Solagen's life once again. Apparently, he ended up fighting as well as singing. And when I see him—if I see him—I'll ask the lad how that came to be. He has more than once told me that he doesn't like soldiering. So there has to be an interesting tale there.

"Auragole must finally be over Glenelle for the city is rife with rumors about his women. He is seen everywhere in town, at all the best parties and at all the finest restaurants and entertainment clubs with a different woman on his arm each night. Well, I'm happy he's gotten Ellie out of his system. Speaking of Ellie, I've not tried to get in touch with her. I'll wait until you come and let you do that.

"More news—gossip, really. Auragole has not gone back to sing at the Blue Heron. Some say he won't ever return there. Interesting, don't you think? Well, he doesn't have to earn his keep by singing. It seems Auragole has begun to enjoy, and revel in, what this city has to offer a rich, handsome young man. Our old friend is apparently no longer overwhelmed by this city.

"And speaking of Auragole. . . Just after I wrote those last words, I received an invitation by messenger from him. He's giving a party in a week's time at his house, and you and I are invited. Well, you won't be here, but I'll certainly go. And then write you all about it.

"I miss you. Can't wait until you come. I'm on my way to attend one of the services on the Street of Temples. I feel a need to hear something about the Creative World. But no doubt I'll get a sermon on our brave soldiers and how to be a good citizen of Mattelmead. Oh, well, it still does me good.

"Love,

"Don

"P.S. I've gone to the doctors again about my leg. I still hope they can find something to help with the stiffness. I would so love to be part of Ormahn's conquering army when it next goes out. It's dreadful to feel able-bodied and walk like an old man. I can still ride. I shoot well with a bow and arrow—you know I practice at the club. Sorry, my lovely lass—I didn't mean to complain. The Gods have been so good to us. And we have each other."

AURAGOLE WAS DREADING this meeting. He had received a note from Lorenwile asking him to come to his house that evening for dinner. Auragole had been back two weeks from the war and had not returned to the Blue Heron, nor had he seen Lorenwile. After his arrival in the city, he had sent him a note saying he needed a few weeks of rest. Of course, he hadn't rested. After the harshness and the intensity of battle, he had been ready for the fun and lightheartedness of Mattelmead City society. And so he had gone from party to party, and was, in fact, about to give one of his own in a few days. Lorenwile was invited to that. Auragole knew he had to talk to Lorenwile, but he had put it off. It would be an uncomfortable meeting and he wasn't quite ready for discomfort. However, it seemed Lorenwile was no longer willing to wait. Auragole had sent him a note declining dinner, claiming a previous engagement, but wrote that he would come at five so that they could talk. There was no point in delaying this encounter.

He stood in front of Lorenwile's small but attractive house in the artists' and performers' part of the city, but hesitated before he knocked on the door. Down the street his carriage and driver would wait for him. He had about an hour and was glad that he didn't have longer. He had thought about but put off this inevitable meeting. Not that his mind wasn't made up. It had been made up during his months away.

A manservant came to the door. Auragole entered and gave him his cloak, hat, and gloves. "Master Lorenwile is waiting for you in the drawing room, sir." The servant motioned to the stairs. "I'll show you the way."

"No need, Arforr. I can find my own way. I haven't forgotten where the drawing room is," and Auragole bounded up the stairs, taking the steps two at a time. As he reached the top he heard the strumming of a harp. He took a deep breath, and then turned to his right to walk a short distance down the hall.

Lorenwile's drawing room was not large, but comfortably furnished with sofas and chairs. The hearth, with a fire burning brightly in it, had a chair on either side. Lorenwile was sitting in one, playing. He smiled as Auragole came in, but he didn't stop playing. After a moment's hesitation, Auragole came and took the other chair. And waited. "What do you think?" Lorenwile finally asked.

"It's lovely," Auragole answered, knowing Lorenwile referred to the new tune he was playing.

"There are words. Would you like to hear them?"

"Yes, please." This was not going to be easy.

Lorenwile sang a song of war, a sad, poignant song of the loss in war. When he finished he said, "I'll teach you the harmony, if you like." Lorenwile didn't look up but kept strumming the harp.

Auragole rose and began to pace around the room. "Lorenwile, I have to tell you something."

"Yes, I gathered you had something to tell me—from so many days of silence." He looked at Auragole finally, his tourmaline eyes sparking red in the firelight, and grinned impishly. "You look remarkably well, Auragole, for one who has recently come from battle. You seem a little taller, a little broader of shoulder. How old are you now? Twenty-one?" Lorenwile didn't wait for Auragole's answer. "I must confess, that is a very striking outfit you are wearing. Sit down, Auragole. It is hard to have a serious conversation while you are moving about, and I see that this is going to be a serious one." He set his harp down and once again Auragole slid into the chair opposite him.

"Lorenwile, I. . . I. . ." And once again he was on his feet.

"I gather you no longer want to sing with me at the Blue Heron."

Auragole sat down. "How did you know that?"

"For a man who was too tired from battle to meet with an old friend after such a long absence, you have certainly not taken to your bed to rest. You've been seen all over the city at festivity after festivity with a host of different ladies."

"You've heard about that." It was a statement, not a question.

"Everyone gossips with me, Auragole." He shrugged. "I'm the confidant of many men whom you know. That's not news to you." Lorenwile stood up and went to a table, brought back a decanter of wine and two glasses, and returned to his seat. "Do you want to tell me why you no longer care to sing with me?"

Auragole looked down at his hands, then brushed his forehead, and began, "It's not that I don't care to sing with you. I love singing with you. It's. . .it's. . ."

Lorenwile watched him with those remarkable eyes of his, and waited.

Nothing to do but plunge ahead. "Ormahn is doing something great, Lorenwile. It won't be long before he unites the entire Westernlands under his banner. He is bringing peace, the peace people have been dreaming of for so many centuries, my. . .my. . .parents included. It's so grand, what he is doing."

"Yes, it is very grand. Peace is a glorious thing."

"I want to be part of it." Again Auragole rose. Excitement propelled him now. He moved about the room, and when he spoke his voice was passionate. "It's not what you think. I don't want to join the army. You know my feelings on that subject." He was standing at the windows, looking across the room at Lorenwile. "Though I confess, I did do my share of fighting in Noonbarr. Well, I couldn't sit among the baggage with the women, the pages, and the animals. I couldn't just wait while others fought to protect us. So I fought. And I fought well."

"So I've heard." Lorenwile's voice was soft. "You say you don't want to join the army. What is it you want to do, boy?"

The word *boy* pricked at Auragole's nerves. How long had it been since he had been called boy by Lorenwile, or by anyone? He didn't like it. He was no boy. No one who had been through as many battles, or had made love to as many women, as he had, was a boy. He was now twenty-one, and a man by anyone's reckoning. Auragole turned to stare out the window. The streets were filled with people hurrying home from their activities. Did any of them have such heavy decisions to make? He allowed his irritation to slide away. He wanted Lorenwile to understand. Needed Lorenwile to understand.

Auragole turned around to look at the man he was talking to. "It seems Solagen has taken a liking to me." He shrugged deprecatingly. "And I want to serve him in every way I can." Auragole walked back to stand behind the chair he had vacated. "He's going to save this world, Lorenwile. If he can achieve his dreams, perhaps there won't have to be a Last Battle, and the Agavians can go on living in peace as they have for thousands and thousands of years."

Auragole felt Lorenwile's eyes searching his face. He tried to allow it, tried to keep his own eyes on Lorenwile's. Why was it so hard to know what Lorenwile was thinking? "Let me try to explain what I mean," Auragole said. "If Ormahn succeeds in doing what he intends, perhaps the Nethergod, whom you say is incarnate, will not be given the opportunity to wreak havoc on humanity." Was he being too patronizing—speaking to Lorenwile from inside Lorenwile's beliefs as if they were his own?

"You think the Nethergod so weak?" Lorenwile's words were matter-of-fact, and his expression unreadable.

Auragole tried again. "Lorenwile, I don't know if there is a Nethergod or not. I've never seen him. For all I know it may be mere superstition; forgive me if that sounds condescending. What I do know is there's an Ormahn, and he is doing wonders here in the west. That's what I can see with my own eyes and know with my own heart. The other. . ." He walked around the chair and sat down.

Lorenwile's eyes followed him. "So what is it you want to do, Auragole?"

"I want to serve the king in any way he wants me to. I want to do what I can for him."

"And do you know what that is?"

Auragole picked up the decanter and poured wine into the two glasses. He took his own and drank down half of it. "Right now that means being available for him. Sing for him when he wants me to. It means going to the palace when he calls for me. I know that doesn't sound like much, Lorenwile, but sometimes . . .sometimes he likes to talk strategy with me. Maybe it's because I know maps, because I've been to parts of the Grand Continent that none of his officers has been to. Whatever. . . He has invited me to his war council table time and again."

"And if you sing at the Blue Heron?"

Auragole took a deep breath and let it out. He looked down at the wineglass in his hands. "If I sing at the Blue Heron, I'm not available when the king wants me." Then he drank the rest of its contents.

"Has he asked you to give up your work?"

Auragole shook his head. "No, he wouldn't, not after. . ." He put his glass down on the table next to Lorenwile. "Solagen knows I love the singing and that I have given you my promise, and he honors that."

"It is said you once again saved Solagen's life."

Auragole made a deprecating gesture, then nodded.

"So you want me to release you from what you consider your promise?"

Again Auragole nodded.

"You've made no promise to me, Auragole. You're free to do as you please, to leave the Blue Heron or not."

Auragole knew that relief showed in his face. He could feel his cheeks grow hot with satisfaction and embarrassment. "Can you understand why I want to, Lorenwile? I'm not giving up singing. It's only for a time, don't you see? Do you think I make any sense at all?" To his mortification, he heard the appeal in his own voice. Why was this so hard? He hadn't meant to ask Lorenwile anything, only to tell him, only to explain.

Lorenwile stood up then. "Auragole, follow your heart." He squinted at him and then gave him a crooked grin. "If you know your heart, then follow it."

"Lorenwile, I'd hate to lose your friendship. Will I?"

"You know where I work, and you know where I live."

It was an answer, but not quite the answer Auragole wanted. Lorenwile hadn't mentioned True-singing. Nor had Auragole. Should he?

But Lorenwile was walking out of the drawing room and Auragole realized that the meeting was over, so he followed Lorenwile down the stairs and to the door. The servant appeared immediately with Auragole's cloak, hat, and gloves.

Lorenwile extended his hand. "Follow your heart, Auragole. Listen deeply to it, and follow it."

Those words seemed odd and sentimental coming from Lorenwile. However, Auragole took the extended hand and said, "I think I am, Lorenwile. I think I am." And he walked out the door, relieved, yet feeling somehow unsatisfied and sad. He was following his heart. Of that he was sure. Goloss would have approved. Yes, his father would have approved.

Well, he thought as he climbed into his coach, what I need is a little more wine and definitely some diversion.

"MY DEAR DON,

"Yes, I do know that the army is back. By the time your letter arrived, most of the men from our neighborhood had returned. I may come just a little later to the city if you can bear it. I know I said early December, but would it be all right if I came toward the end of December? The orphanage closest to our estate has had an influx of children these last weeks and it needs all the help it can get. I don't think too many have wended their way here from Noonbarr yet; however we do have many still coming from Thorensphere. They are such dear little things, Don, and there is such a shortage of help. It's good, as we have often said to each other, to be of use. And right now I feel especially useful. If only they hadn't removed all the orphanages from the city, there would be a reason for me to hurry back there. Sometimes I think they don't want anything to mar the beauty of the city or the sense of well-being of its inhabitants. It's as if those who live there do not want to see how much people are hurting elsewhere. But who am I to quarrel with Ormahn's policy? We have been given so much. And Ormahn will bring peace. In that goal, I believe implicitly.

"I miss you. And you know how bad I feel about your leg. But don't give up hope. They are making new discoveries in medicine all the time. And no one will ever convince me that you are not a whole man.

"Love,

"Sylvie"

"MY DEAREST SYLVIE,

"It is late in the afternoon. I confess I slept past noon today.

I went to Auragole's party last night. It was quite a fête. I'm so sorry you weren't here with me because—can you believe it?—Ormahn came—which I understand is a rarity—and stayed at the party an hour. Auragole introduced me to him! Charming, charming man. He exudes vitality and amiability. I must say, I was quite thrilled. I haven't felt such awe since we met the Lady Claregole in Agavia.

"Auragole looks remarkably well. I think he's still growing! How old is he? Twenty-one or twenty-two? I think it's twenty-one. Anyway he's even taller than when he left on the campaign, and definitely broader in the shoulders. He has cut his hair to just below the ears, and wears it much like Ormahn wears his. I didn't find a moment really to speak to him privately, because he was surrounded by so many people, all wanting to be near him and to speak with him—but then he did introduce me to the king.

"Now I want to make you jealous, and perhaps hurry your coming. There were so many beautiful and finely dressed women, I could scarce do anything all evening but look. I did speak to one or two. But I think not one of them had eyes for anyone except Auragole. Even the married women. Glenelle and Glenorr were not there—well, that's not a surprise. Nor did Lorenwile come after his performance at the Blue Heron, and that was a surprise. But Veldarr was there—interesting, and his cousin, Goredahl. What a taciturn man Goredahl is, tall, straight backed, and very sure of his importance. He came with his wife, as did Veldarr. Veldarr's wife is not so beautiful as Ellie but she was handsomely attired and bejeweled. She was rather quiet and stayed near her husband for most of the evening.

"The party was perfectly organized. Auragole has certainly become the cosmopolitan. The food was exceptional, the service at dinner superb, and he entertained us with a play hired from one of the theaters in the city. He must have engaged dozens of extra servants for the evening, all elegantly attired in uniforms that had his crest on them. Have you seen his crest? It's an A and an M, with a feather across both letters. Auragole of Mattelmead, he now refers to himself. Remember how quiet, even shy, he was when we were traveling together? Well, he's not shy now. He was the center of much conversation and laughter and joke-telling all evening. How strange a thing destiny is. I could not have predicted this remarkable turn of events for Auragole— could you? But I must say I am happy for him, if he's happy. Now why did I write that? What would make me think Auragole unhappy? Everyone who is anybody in this city dotes on him, including Ormahn himself. He must be happy!

"Oh, surely you have heard the news that Ormahn's new wife is pregnant. That gossip has been filling the clubs for a few weeks now. Did I write you that before? Everyone says she's a pretty thing, quite young, not much more than twenty. I think this has given both Goredahl and Veldarr something to worry about, or so the gossip goes. But why worry in advance, I always say. It could be a girl.

"I've gone frequently these last weeks to hear Lorenwile at the Blue Heron—did I write you that it is a certainty now that Auragole is no longer singing at the Blue Heron? It was Auragole's own wish, I understand. What a marvelous singer Lorenwile is. Auragole is good, very good, even superbly good, but Lorenwile, well, Lorenwile is a master. And his singing reminds me of my beloved Aiku. Since Auragole introduced us to Lorenwile last spring, I have felt it all right to stop backstage after his performance and say hello. Because I've gone so often, we've taken to talking together and even to having a drink or some supper after the performance. Tomorrow, he will come to my club for lunch.

"What can I do to hurry your arrival? I'm beginning to feel like an orphan myself. Did we not plan to spend the fall and winter in the city? If you really would rather stay in the country over the winter, I'll return there before the weather makes traveling impossible. Let me know immediately. I'm sure I'll find something in the country to keep me occupied.

"Love,

"Your husband, Don"

"THIS WINE THEY say is from Glovale. Surely there are no vineyards in Mattelmead to equal the vineyards in Glovale, particularly the ones in the south," Lorenwile told Donnadorr. "What do you think of it?"

They were eating a late supper at a very small, very elegant restaurant, not far from the Blue Heron.

"Very fine," Donnadorr said, and sipped the drink appreciatively.

"And how do you find the duck?"

"Excellent, excellent. You do know the best places to eat in the city, Lorenwile."

"I pride myself that I do," he agreed.

"You sang especially well tonight," Donnadorr said.

"That's kind of you."

"You know, some of the songs you sing are songs that I wrote with Auragole. Delightful to hear them sung so well."

"I understand you are a fine singer yourself."

Donnadorr reddened. "No, no, it's a small talent. I learned from a man who traveled with me for some years when I was a child. Aiku, he was called."

Lorenwile's eyes narrowed slightly. "So Meekelorr told me."

"Meekelorr told you? To what purpose?"

"Because I knew Aiku."

Donnadorr sloshed wine on the tablecloth and immediately began mopping it up with his napkin. "Sorry. But I had no idea. It's so rare to meet someone who knew Aiku." Don could feel, to his embarrassment, tears welling up in his eyes.

"What happened to him?" Lorenwile asked.

"I don't know. He found me when I was a child. We roamed the east together for several years, but he went away one day—

this was when I was still in the Easternlands and quite young—and he never came back. He told me to wait, but he never came back. I looked for him everywhere I could, singing so he could hear me. But I never found him. How is it that you know him?"

"He was my teacher," Lorenwile said.

Donnadorr almost knocked over the glass again, but he caught it in time. As he steadied it, he asked, "Where? When?"

"Oh, many years ago. In the Easternlands, in Stahlowill, in its high northern hills. He liked to take his pupil, if time permitted him, into nature, away from people, and spend some months with him, just roaming the woods and hills, looking at the beautiful and the magnificent in nature, and singing."

"How long ago was that, Lorenwile?"

"Probably before you were born, Don, or soon after. Before the wars came finally to the once safe hills of Stahlowill."

"Auragole's family came from Stahlowill."

"Yes, so I've heard."

"Sometimes this vast world seems small indeed." Don shook his head. "When did you last see Aiku?"

"It's been many years now. Earlier than your encounter, if I understand you rightly. Rumor has it that he is dead."

Donnadorr exhaled—a sad sound. "Yes, so it must be. He was heart-father to me."

"As the Agavians would say."

"Yes," Don looked curiously at Lorenwile, "as the Agavians would say."

"When we finish our dinner, come home with me—if you can spare the time," Lorenwile said. "I should like to hear you sing. And perhaps learn other songs of yours."

"You jest."

"Yes, very often. But not now. Not this time."

"I should be honored."

chapter nine

AURAGOLE WAS RIDING through the hills west of the city of Mattelmead on Starwanderer. It was January and the city below him lay covered by a fresh winter blanket. He hadn't been in the park since the previous May—the night that he discovered Glenelle's duplicity. He wondered why he had stayed away so long. This mountain park that protected the city from the sea winds had nothing to do with Glenelle. As he rode along the trails, he was glad it was scarcely used at this time of the year. But Auragole, mountain born and bred, was used to winter, and it now provided him with the solitude and quiet that he still craved from time to time. Ormahn had given the park to the city and it was a favorite place for its residents in more-clement weather.

Auragole rode up to the higher hills and stared out at the great Western Sea. He wondered what lay on the other side of what was said to be a vast ocean. The people of the Grand Continent were uneasy at best on the water, fearful at worst.

There was little sailing on the rivers of the Grand Continent or on the oceans that surrounded it. Staring out at the ocean gave Auragole a sense of space he had experienced only in the desert, certainly not in the mountains of his first home. There, every vista was interrupted by a mountain. There, only the sky seemed vast and remote.

It was early in the morning. Auragole had barely slept the previous night after the party he had attended. Like many Mattelmead parties it had lasted almost until sunup. But he was restless and had something on his mind, so, after no more than an hour or two of sleep, he had risen from his bed, dressed, and left the house. In the stable, he had roused Semp, who slept in a room there, and soon Starwanderer was saddled. In the gray air under gray skies, Auragole set forth. He had a decision to make, one that might set him on yet another new road, unlooked for and unplanned. Uncertainty sat in his soul like a hot coal.

Solagen had sent for him the previous day, and Auragole had arrived at the palace carrying his harp.

"I haven't called you to play for me, Auragole," Solagen said when Auragole was ushered into Solagen's war room.

There were half a dozen commanders, several pages, and servants in the large room. Auragole knew all the commanders, most from the campaign in Noonbarr. He greeted them with either a wave or a nod.

"I want to talk to you about something. Leave your harp, keep your cloak on, and come walk with me in my garden." A page rushed to hand Solagen his cloak.

As soon as they were outside, Solagen moved briskly along the swept path, and without preamble said, "You say you don't like soldiering, Auragole, yet you are one of the best fighters I know. You're as good as any in my Elite Corps. You can shoot from a saddle more accurately and faster than any one of them. You're good with a sword. And you're smart. When we were in Noonbarr last summer, you gave me better advice than some who now stand around the war table with me. You, Auragole, have a natural talent for soldiering."

"I have a natural talent for singing, which you know I love."

"We can't always do what we love most."

Auragole turned his head to look at Solagen.

Solagen was gazing at the snow-covered garden, but his jaw was tight. "If each man were allowed that, there would still be chaos reigning in the west."

Auragole had no answer to that but his heart began to beat faster. The garden was cold, its manicured lawn obliterated by the snow. Only the paths were free of it. Still, their boots made a snapping sound as they walked.

"Listen to me, Auragole of Mattelmead. I have an offer to make you." Solagen stopped walking, forcing Auragole to halt also, and to look at the king. "And this truly is an offer. You can refuse if you want, and if you do, we will go on as we are—or nearly. I give you this chance of deciding, out of friendship. With any other man, I simply would have given him an order, and he would have obeyed. But I've not forgotten what I owe you."

Auragole waited. In the upstairs window of the palace Auragole saw someone watching them, but as he caught sight of the figure, it withdrew.

Solagen resumed walking along the path, and Auragole walked alongside him, staring at his own boots as they moved. As he listened to Solagen's words, he could feel Solagen's eyes on him.

"I'd like to offer you a commandership in my army. Come spring we go south. Where is not yet decided. Even now emissaries have gone to Wildenfarr-low-desert. On your advice we are speaking first with Tul-farr in the north. If he will ally himself with us, accept me as overlord and king, then he can rule over all Wildenfarr in my name. We will offer him our help in dealing with And-ul-farr. Or. . .we might set Wildenfarr aside for the time being and move first into the Sorren Heights."

Auragole felt uncomfortable under Solagen's gaze. Solagen

was waiting for his response.

He cleared his throat and swallowed. "What would you have of me, should I accept, that you do not have now, Solagen?"

"I have invited you many times to the council table, Auragole. You have been in Wildenfarr. You have been at the gates of Isofed, in the Deep Forest, and throughout the Sorren Heights. None of my officers has." Solagen slowed his brisk pace and spoke each word carefully, emphatically. "No one who is not one of my commanders, or one of my soldiers, has ever sat at war council. You, Auragole, have been the exception. You have been given special privileges. I would like you by my side through the deliberations this winter. I would like you by my side when we go to war this summer. But I tell you this, Auragole, I can no longer take advantage of what you know and of your skills, other than singing, if you do not accept my offer. It sows too much dissension within the ranks of my officers."

Auragole stopped moving to look at Solagen. Solagen's words shocked him. Dissension?

But Solagen continued walking, and Auragole hurried to keep pace with him. "And it is there that I need harmony most of all. I don't want my commanders to resent anyone I trust because I have bestowed on that someone unusual privileges— but not the discipline. Can you understand that?" And now he stopped and faced Auragole.

Auragole saw in Solagen's eyes the complexity of his life, the many decisions, the many considerations.

"Never before has someone not in the army had such access to me and to my plans for the future."

Auragole didn't know what to say. "I. . . I. . ."

"Wait, son, before you accept or refuse too hastily. Let me say this to you," and he strode forward again.

Up above at another window, Auragole caught a glimpse once again of someone, with dark hair or hooded, watching them.

"Think carefully on what we are doing here—we privileged

few. We are uniting all the west. We are bringing all the battling, unruly countries under one flag, ridding the world of petty tyrants and dictators. We are restoring hope to people who have lived without it so long that they don't even know what hope is. We are bringing a halt to the centuries of wars. We are bringing peace and prosperity to everyone, and giving work to all. Have we not accomplished much?"

There was a quality of boyish enthusiasm to his words and Auragole couldn't help but feel thrilled.

"Is this not a noble task, worth giving one's efforts to, even one's life? And the army—my army—is the instrument that is bringing it about. Because of this army, there will be schools and hospitals, scientific academies and theaters, concert halls and art galleries all over the west, not just in Mattelmead City. There will be cities like our city in every country in the Westernlands. Just imagine it, Auragole! And all because of the army and what it's accomplishing.

"Is that not a fair mission for any man to participate in?" But Solagen didn't wait for Auragole's response. "And when the entire west is united under the flag of Mattelmead, then you and Lorenwile can travel to city after city, in peace, and bring your music and song to all who have not yet had the privilege of hearing the two of you. You sing exquisitely, Auragole, and give pleasure to all who hear you. I respect and value your talent. Believe that I do. But lift your eyes a little higher, son. Be part of this inexorable movement that is bringing peace and order to the Grand Continent, that is making it possible for singers like you to fulfill your private dreams. But for now, give something greater to the world than a song."

"Sir, truly I am honored by your offer." Auragole finally found his voice. "But must you have my answer at this moment? I had not anticipated this. May I have a day or two to think it over?"

Solagen was quiet and Auragole was wondering if he had offended him.

"I understand this in you, Auragole, that you are a thoughtful man. I admire this in you. I will wait for your answer."

"Thank you."

"But no more than two days."

Starwanderer stepped confidently on the park paths, his hooves making crunching sounds.

What should he do? Auragole wondered. Become a commander in Ormahn's army? For years he had shunned the idea of becoming a soldier, had felt it as a giving up of his freedom, no matter how skilled he had become in the soldierly arts. And he had become skilled. There was no denying that. He had fought alongside Ormahn of Mattelmead, the great hero of the Westernlands, in the war against Noonbarr. Auragole had not been able to sit out the fierce battles along with the servants and pages, with the sheep and chickens, with the supply carts and the women. So he had mounted Starwanderer and had fought and killed and had saved lives. If he hadn't entered the fray, would Solagen be dead now? But he had entered the fray. And he had sat at council tables during the campaign and had offered his advice freely and thoughtfully.

Whom among the commanders was he offending? But that was not the question he needed to think about now. He needed to give Solagen an answer the next day. What was it that was holding him back from making this step, from accepting the uniform, from accepting. . .accepting both the discipline and the command of others? Would he be giving up the freedom that he so cherished? He wondered what his father would have recommended, or Meekelorr, or his friend Elarr. Elarr had said that freedom for the soldier community called the Companions of the Way came in choosing to join the Companions or not to join. If one joined the Companions, then one accepted the hierarchy of command and discipline. Well, that was true of the Companions of the Way, but it was not true of the soldiers of Mattelmead. The foot soldiers in the Mattelmead army were conscripted. There was no freedom or choosing there. The officers, however, all from the wealthy families in Mattelmead and the conquered lands, purchased their commissions and then were trained, and trained hard. That was a choosing of sorts. After all, to be an officer conferred on one great status. To be an officer in Meekelorr's small army of Companions conferred nothing except responsibility. But there was a different need here in Mattelmead. There was a great, achievable goal here. All because of Solagen, Ormahn of Mattelmead, and his great army.

And wasn't Solagen right? The goals of Solagen were great and mighty goals—to bring peace to the west, even to the whole Grand Continent. That, too, was what Auragole's own father had wanted. Goloss had wanted his son to be free of the rules imposed by men and Gods, but he had also longed for peace. Surely the lack of peace was what caused his father to lose his faith, to give up the priesthood in service to the King God, to abandon his belief in the Gods. It was the terrible wars that had driven his father off his farm in Stahlowill and sent him deep into the Gandlese Mountains looking for peace—at least for his small community.

From what Auragole knew, Meekelorr was after the same thing: the cessation of the centuries of war. Of course, Meekelorr saw the achievement of that peace through other means, through the finding of the Nethergod and the fighting of the Last Battle. But surely a war in the faraway Gandlese—even a great war—would not bring an end to the wars in either the Easternlands or the Westernlands. So who was doing more for humanity, Meekelorr or Ormahn? Auragole was sure what the answer was. Let Meekelorr wait for his Last Battle. In the meantime, Solagen, Ormahn of Mattelmead, was achieving what Meekelorr could not—peace in country after country.

But there was something else that troubled him should he accept Solagen's offer—and this was, he realized, the crux of the problem. If he was admitted as an officer to the council table, would he not have to speak about what he really knew of the Sorren Heights, of the Woeful Peaks, of the Companions of the Way? The thought made him uncomfortable. He had withheld much from Solagen, not wanting to betray the whereabouts of Meekelorr and his Companions. Auragole was riding now through a grove of stately maple and oak trees, their large trunks rooted and secure in the ground that held them, their branches asleep until spring woke them. But Auragole's mind was elsewhere.

If he accepted Solagen's offer, it would not be right to hold back information. If he became Ormahn's man, then he would have to speak of what he knew. The best thing would be to say "No" to Solagen. That, also, filled him with great discomfort. After all, Solagen had been good to him, and was now offering him a role that could make a difference in the lives of so many, a difference even to the whole world. Solagen had admired and praised his talents on the battlefield. He, Auragole, could be one of those who helped make the dream of peace come true, his father's dream of peace, the dream of peace of all good men. Should he withdraw from such a challenge, keep his secrets, and serve only his own wants and pleasures? Should he continue to live as richly as he had been living, and sing only for his own pleasure and for the few who heard him? Should he stay free and unfettered while others fought for his freedom? Should he disappoint the king? Or should he ally himself with Ormahn of Mattelmead, give up his cherished independence and accept the discipline and the command, and help in the great goal of peace?

But what about the things he had not told Solagen?

It was a dilemma he could not resolve. As he was riding and thinking he decided to go speak to Lorenwile. He turned his horse and headed back to the city.

He stopped at Lorenwile's home, but to Auragole's disappointment Lorenwile's servant told him that his master had risen early that morning and had gone out. He wasn't sure where. "Perhaps he's off to the Blue Heron, sir," the servant suggested. "He mentioned something about needing a new costume the other day."

"Then I'll look for him there," Auragole said. He wrote Lorenwile a note and asked the servant to give it to Lorenwile the moment he returned.

Auragole rode through the neighborhood that housed many of the artists and performers in the city. Auragole liked this part of the city, and often came here to sit in its cafés and talk with its denizens. If artists and performers were approved of by Ormahn's government, they were given houses, a staff to manage them, and a generous stipend.

"We will be a cultured people," Solagen had said, "and the arts bring culture as well as pleasure."

Auragole looked at the houses. They were not so big as the ones in his neighborhood, but then his neighborhood was the richest in the city, and its homes the largest. He rode past house after house in the quiet morning and thought that once he would have been content with one of these. But he knew it was no longer true. Could he have given the parties that he had given? Would as many of society's elites have come? Of course, they went to Lorenwile's parties. But not even someone as much admired as Lorenwile could afford to give parties like the ones Auragole had given and would continue to give. Once he had entertained his guests with an entire play. The actors had been brought in from one of the theaters in the city, much to his guests' delight, and to the pleasure of the actors allowed to mix in such society. Auragole's house and how he had won it were symbols of his status, and he liked his status. He liked being a friend to the king. He was envied and admired, and what was wrong with that? After all his years living in isolation in the Gandlese, society was a tonic. Would he lose all he had gained if he should turn Solagen down?

He rode the several blocks to the Blue Heron. It had been

many, many months since he had sung there, and to his surprise he felt a pang of loss. As Auragole dismounted from his horse, and a groom came to take Starwanderer from him, he thought that perhaps he missed the performing, missed singing with Lorenwile. Auragole still sang, but it was now only for Solagen and his friends and guests—the cream of Mattelmead society. Still. . . Maybe he should say "No" to Solagen, maybe he should return to the Blue Heron and to Lorenwile and simplify his life, keep his secrets, and do what he loved most, sing.

Auragole entered the Blue Heron. All he found there was the cleaning crew. No one had seen Lorenwile that morning. Auragole wrote a note and slipped it under Lorenwile's dressing room door, requesting, as he had in the note he had left at Lorenwile's house, that Lorenwile please come to Auragole's house. There was something urgent he had to discuss. He would stay home all afternoon waiting for Lorenwile.

After Auragole returned home, he tried to nap but was too restless, so he walked from room to room and waited. Where on earth was Lorenwile? Surely he would respond with haste after receiving Auragole's urgent note. Lorenwile always returned to his own home in the afternoon for a rest and a light, quiet dinner before the night's performance. He must have received the note by now.

When evening came and he still had not heard from Lorenwile, Auragole dressed, ordered his coach, and went to the Blue Heron. He entered late to avoid attention and to avoid meeting and talking to people he knew. He was given a table in the rear when he asked for it, and a bottle of the best wine. Auragole was drinking his third glass and wondering why the performance was so late in starting when he caught sight of the proprietor of the club. Auragole rose from the table and went to him. "What's happened? Why is Lorenwile so late in starting?"

"He's not here," the man said, obviously agitated. "He hasn't come in yet. This is not like him. And my customers are getting restless. I sent a man to look for him at his home, but he's not there and hasn't been there all day. He left early this morning with his harp and pony but he's not returned, and he left no word with his servants. I sent another man for Suwell, a good-enough singer, to come and take his place, at least until Lorenwile shows up. But what could have befallen the man? I hope no accident." And he hurried off.

Auragole listened and something in him froze. He couldn't have had an accident, not Lorenwile. He was too wily, too alert to what was around him. But to go off somewhere and not tell his servants, that was not like Lorenwile. And it wasn't like him to miss a performance. Auragole thought, with a spasm of anxiety, of the Security Forces. And Goredahl. But surely not. His servants had said that Lorenwile had gone off alone on Surefoot.

Auragole threw some coins down on the table and left the club, just as Suwell arrived on stage.

That night, lying in bed with Duneeze, a woman he knew, asleep in his arms, he tried to overcome his worries, but he could not. He was concerned about the disappearance of Lorenwile, for disappearance was the way he thought of it. But impinging on that worry was what he was going to say to Solagen the following evening. Well, he would get up early and see if Lorenwile had returned home, or if they had heard from him at the Blue Heron. He needed to speak to someone, someone who knew Meekelorr and the Companions of the Way, knew about Agavia and the Lady Claregole. If not Lorenwile. . .

Donnadorr. Sylvane.

Auragole felt a twinge of embarrassment. It was weeks since he had seen either Sylvie or Don. He had deliberately avoided them—because they knew Ellie, because seeing them would remind him of his foolish infatuation. Well, be that as it may, Don and Sylvie would understand Auragole's dilemma in accepting Solagen's offer. By now Auragole knew that it was this worry about revealing the whereabouts of Meekelorr that stood in the way of his acceptance.

The following morning Auragole went first to Lorenwile's house and then to the Blue Heron, but Lorenwile had not returned home, nor had they heard from him at the café.

Auragole found Don at his club. They sat in two large, overstuffed chairs in front of a roaring fire in one of the club's private rooms.

"That's quite an offer," Donnadorr said, after Auragole had laid out his problem. "What will you do?"

Auragole brushed his hair away from his forehead. "I don't know what to do. There's this dilemma, you see. What would you do?"

Donnadorr picked up his glass of wine. "If I didn't have this game leg, lad, I would have purchased an officership long ago."

"How is your leg?" Auragole asked, remembering.

"It's stiff, hates the wet weather. And there's often pain. But I'm alive, and living well, thanks to Ormahn's policies, so I can't complain."

"Then you think I should accept his offer? But what about Meekelorr? What about the Companions of the Way? When I am asked in council about the Woeful Peaks, can I pretend I know nothing about them? Can I out-and-out lie? I've withheld information, Don, but I've never actually lied to Solagen."

"Perhaps they already know about Meekelorr and the Companions."

Auragole looked at him quizzically.

"Glenelle. She's close to Veldarr."

Auragole's face paled and he turned away for a moment. How very much he had told her. How trusting he had been. How much had she passed on to Veldarr? Auragole was about to voice his anger when he saw something shut down in Donnadorr's usually open face. His own bitter words dissolved inside his mouth as he looked at his friend.

Donnadorr's words came out haltingly, almost cautiously. "Perhaps you. . .worry for nothing. Perhaps Meekelorr and his troops have already left the Woefuls. . . If not, perhaps they will leave very soon."

"What do you mean? How can you know that?" Lorenwile! "Do you know where Lorenwile's gone, Don?" Auragole had heard that Lorenwile had befriended Donnadorr.

"I didn't say I knew that. And if I did know, I. . .I couldn't tell you. I can only say that if you are worried about betraying Meekelorr's whereabouts to Ormahn, and that's what's holding you back, then I say to you, forget your concern. If you want to be a commander, take the offer."

"What are you not telling me, Don?"

Donnadorr placed his glass on the table next to his chair and leaned forward. "What I can't tell you, Auragole. Let it go at that. I've already said too much. But feel free to give your service to Ormahn with a full heart, as I would now if I were asked. Isn't that what you came to ask me?"

Auragole looked penetratingly at his old friend. Don knew something. It was obvious that Auragole was no longer trusted by Donnadorr, whose life he had saved more than once. Auragole stood up, bewildered and hurt. "Well, thank you, Don, for your advice—and. . .and for your information." He offered his hand.

Donnadorr rose and took it. "Sylvie and I miss you, Aurie. You should come to dinner one day."

"Yes, I'd like that," he said, trying his best to hide the unhappiness he was feeling in his heart, an ache he did not know how to describe. It was as if vast distances, fields, mountains, and rivers, had opened up between himself and Donnadorr, and Auragole didn't know how it had happened, when it had happened, or how to leap over the chasm.

"I'm sure Sylvie will be in touch soon."

"Yes, thank you. Good-bye, Don."

"Good-bye, Auragole."

LORENWILE WAS STANDING inside the mouth of a hidden cave in the hills of southwest Mattelmead. Above him he could hear the sound of hoofbeats, of armed men on horseback. There were perhaps thirty of them, the highly skilled mounted soldiers, belonging to Mattelmead's internal Security Forces that were under Goredahl's command. Lorenwile had been aware of them for more than a day now, and he had kept out of their sight, thanks to the keen hearing developed by True-singing.

Lorenwile had left Mattelmead City quickly, going off one morning without a word to anyone. He had been prepared for such an event for some months, keeping food, a change of clothes, and other necessities in a safe place in the stable. Only to Donnadorr had he mentioned that if he should disappear one day, Don was not to worry, neither about him nor about Meekelorr nor the Companions of the Way. Good that Lorenwile had friends in high places. He had been casually warned, warned that Goredahl's men had been making discreet inquiries about him. Lorenwile had been expecting trouble ever since Auragole had taken up with Glenelle. He was certain Auragole had talked too freely to Glenelle, and she in turn to Veldarr. And obviously Veldarr had spoken to his cousin for his own purposes. Had either of the two rivals for the throne passed the information to Ormahn?

Well, Lorenwile had stayed on in Mattelmead far longer than he had thought possible at first. Now he must get to Meekelorr. It was time for all the Companions of the Way to retreat to Agavia, as early in the spring as possible. Better not to stay in the Westernlands any longer—it was far too dangerous, what with Ormahn's army growing daily and his slow but steady consolidation of the countries of the west. The Companions were too few. And however few they were, they would be needed in Agavia at the Last Battle.

It was with feelings of deep regret, even with some sense of personal failure, that Lorenwile turned his thoughts to Auragole. What could he tell Meekelorr about him? That Auragole was now a close companion of Ormahn of Mattelmead? That destiny had placed this young wanderer in the highest ranks of Ormahn's court? Well, that was a tale worth a night's conversation. That Auragole would be a player in the Last Battle, Lorenwile was as certain as Meekelorr. But for or against the Agavians? Frankly, he didn't know. And it was because he didn't know that Lorenwile felt his own failings. Then he shook off the feelings. He had left Auragole free, as the Gods had done. He could do no more than the Gods had chosen to do. Auragole's choice was Auragole's choice. As it had always been.

When the sounds of the mounted soldiers had disappeared into the night, Lorenwile left the cave. Leading his pony, Surefoot, he moved stealthily south.

chapter ten

AURAGOLE HELD STARWANDERER in check as he overlooked the Doldarr Valley. This was the very place he had stood with Elarr two and a half years before—both of them anxious, both wondering how Meekelorr would receive them after they had betrayed his trust. Then it had been midwinter. Now it was July and the familiar valley was covered with summer grass, and the trees were full-leafed. On the mountain road with Auragole were some twenty members of his Elite Corps. Auragole and his men had been sent to confer with the Companions of the Way, if they were still in residence there. Accompanying him were Veldarr and twenty of the regular army. Ormahn and the rest of their brigade were waiting in the hills ten miles north of the Doldarr.

After Auragole had accepted Solagen's offer, and had become the commander in charge of the Elite Corps, he had not felt it necessary to speak of the Companions of the Way—that is, not until Goredahl broached the subject. It was at a war conference, and suddenly Goredahl had said, "Haven't you had some dealings with that strange little people's army who call themselves the Companions of the Way?"

Auragole had looked up to see Goredahl watching him with unreadable eyes.

"What little army is that, Goredahl?" Ormahn had demanded.

"Why not let Auragole tell it?" Goredahl smiled that obsequious smile that Auragole so disliked. "He knows all about them, or so I've heard."

Solagen looked at Auragole curiously.

Auragole had been prepared for such a challenge. He hadn't been sure when it would come, and from whom, but he had been prepared for it. "The soldiers that Goredahl speaks of, called the Companions of the Way, are not in opposition to you, Sire." He turned to look directly at Solagen. "They have been called a group of 'do-gooders,' a small army of men who are willing to help others in need, help those who are oppressed by cruel leaders. They worked in the Easternlands for decades. And they've worked here in the west for several years. They fought hard against the rebel Boreen in Thorensphere, but also against its king, Nolen, because of those leaders' excessive cruelty. The Companions are not looking to conquer any country. Only to make life a little more tolerable for the common folks."

There was a small laugh from Goredahl.

Auragole looked over at him and then back at Solagen. He held Solagen's eyes. "I'm surprised, since Goredahl apparently knows of them and seems more concerned about them than I, that he hadn't informed you of their presence in the west."

Solagen turned once again to Goredahl, and the smile slipped momentarily from Goredahl's face. But he recovered and said, his voice edgy and high, "They were a small group, doing no harm—and as best we could tell, harrowing our enemies. I didn't think them very important."

You'd better watch your back, Auragole told himself. If Goredahl had not been his enemy before, he was certainly his enemy now.

Goredahl paused, and then turned a cold eye on Auragole. "And since you too seem to have known about them, how come you haven't reported them to Ormahn yourself?"

As Auragole turned to meet Goredahl's challenge, his eyes brushed past the face of Veldarr, who was watching the goings-on with polite interest. "I've met many people and groups of people in my travels in the west, and as you say, Goredahl, the Companions seemed to be doing only good, preparing the ground, one could say, for Solagen, Ormahn of Mattelmead. Like you, I saw no need to trouble Solagen with something inconsequential." He gave Goredahl a cold, crooked smile.

"Do you know where their headquarters are in the Sorren Heights?" This time it was Veldarr who spoke.

"I did pass through it, and stayed for a time, hoping to find word of the friends I had lost on our journey to Mattelmead. At that time, I didn't know that you had found my friends and had brought them here." He gave Veldarr what he hoped was a friendly smile, then turned back to Solagen. "I think I told you, Sire, when we first met, of my search for my friends."

Solagen looked thoughtful, as if he were trying to remember.

It was Veldarr who once again spoke. "Do you think you can find the Companions' headquarters?"

"If Solagen wishes, and the maps are good, I think I can."

"Well, if there's an army in the Sorren Heights, no matter how small, or how friendly, I think we had better take a look at it," Solagen said.

At those words, Goredahl's expression was one of triumph.

Auragole returned his look with one of defiance and, he hoped, indifference.

Despite the terrain, the army of Mattelmead had an easy time moving through the Sorren Heights. The band of troublemakers that had constituted the army of the self-styled Duke Gazber in the northwest had dispersed after Gazber's death. Ormahn's army, now divided into three brigades, was moving steadily south and southeast. None had encountered much opposition, so messengers had informed them. Goredahl and three other commanders headed the brigade in the west. Ormahn, Veldarr, and Auragole were heading down the center of the Sorren Heights, where they expected to traverse the Woeful Peaks and continue through them south to within a few miles of the Noonbarr River and the northern walls of Isofed—if the weather held all the way. Oldwell and two other commanders were moving along the border with Thorensphere, seeking Hazahn, the self-appointed leader in the eastern Sorren Heights, and would eventually turn south as they neared the country of Noonbarr. The Sorren Heights was a mountainous land, and sparsely populated. The few shepherds and homesteaders that Ormahn's army passed were ready to accept the new rule, ready for the sake of peace to provide some of the livestock and fresh produce that the army needed. When Ormahn's division arrived at the Woefuls, the only enemies encountered were the mountainous land itself and the changeable weather.

As they traveled through the Woefuls, much of it seemed poignantly familiar to Auragole. He had, after all, spent some months here with Lorenwile. Auragole couldn't help but think of True-singing, and the one who had taught him, with a sense of loss. As the days passed Auragole became more and more taciturn. If his comrades noticed, they said nothing. He tried to keep them to the lower narrow valleys. He did not take them directly to the Doldarr Valley but recommended that they camp about ten miles away in some hills. There they conferred. It was Auragole who had suggested that first he and a small troop of men go to the headquarters of the Companions of the Way in the Doldarr and ask for a conference with the leaders there. Ormahn agreed. The message he sent with Auragole was that the Companions were to put themselves under his leadership or risk a battle within days. If they were willing to cooperate, the leader or leaders were to accompany Auragole back to Ormahn's camp, where they would talk terms. Auragole was to go with twenty of the Elite Corps. Solagen also decided that Veldarr should accompany Auragole with twenty of the regular army. So, Auragole thought after the meeting, I'm being tested. He prayed that Don had been right and that Meekelorr had long deserted the camp and had returned to the Gandlese with all the Companions of the Way.

The night before they left for the Doldarr Valley, Auragole spent an hour with Veldarr, bent over the maps in Veldarr's tent, pointing out everything that was known to him about the valley and its surroundings. How much Glenelle had told him, Auragole wasn't sure. He assumed it was everything that Auragole had revealed to her. Therefore he was not going to risk holding back what he knew about the layout of the Woefuls. He even pointed out the Adelmorr Valley on the map. "That is a place worth seeing, if time and our needs permit."

"What is worth seeing?" Solagen came striding into Veldarr's tent. He walked over to the table and stared at the map. Auragole once again pointed out Adelmorr. "The ruins of an ancient city that once existed in a rather large valley. The ruins are quite impressive. The city might once have been as big as Mattelmead City itself. It is said it was the largest and most beautiful city in the Sorren Heights. It's been deserted for centuries."

"Directly west, I see. Well, we shall have to take a look at these ruins," Solagen announced, "if we don't get into a big battle with those comrades of yours."

"Yes, Sire," Auragole said, keeping his eyes on the map.

Auragole, sitting on Starwanderer, looked down into the Doldarr Valley. The buildings that Meekelorr had erected one spring and summer were still standing, looking fairly sturdy even after the winter's ravages. But there was no life around them, no tents on the campground, no signs that inhabitants had been there recently, certainly not since the snows had melted. Auragole and his men, with Veldarr behind him, descended into the valley, their white parley flags held high. They looked into the buildings. They were empty. Tables and chairs remained, but all personal items were gone, and all weaponry. Auragole led the group of soldiers across the valley to the hills in which there were caves. These had been home to the Companions before they had erected the buildings in the valley. Auragole looked into each cave, including the one where he and Elarr had spent a winter. He was not prepared for the upsurge of emotions that enveloped him, nor for the relief he felt at finding the Doldarr Valley empty, even though he had anticipated that it would be so, nor for the joy he felt knowing his friends were likely safe, nor for the sweeping sadness and sense of loss he felt.

Those long-ago days, before he had found his way to Mattelmead, but after he had lost his first companions, had been hard days but also good days, filled with a kind of camaraderie, he realized, he had not found in Mattelmead. In those days he had made two exceptional friends, and exceptional friends were rare. But Elarr and Affredda were more than just friends, they were brother and sister to him. He prayed they were safe in Agavia waiting in peace for a war that would never come.

"Are you satisfied that they are no longer in this valley or the hills around it, Veldarr?" Auragole asked him, keeping his voice as neutral as possible.

"Yes, satisfied that they have left this place. But should we assume that because they are no longer in this valley they aren't somewhere in the hills?"

"Hard to keep an army together in these high mountains unless there is a valley where they can camp. And you can see that this camp has not been used for a while."

"True."

"There is no other valley large enough for an army, Veldarr," Auragole said, "except Adelmorr, and that's a few days from here."

"Another good reason for visiting your interesting valley, is it not?"

Auragole, his eyes still on the Doldarr, finally said, "Yes."

"Where do you think they've gone, Auragole?"

"Into the Gandlese, would be my guess," he said, keeping his voice flat. "Perhaps on their way back to the Easternlands, where there is still need. They must have decided they are no longer needed here. Not with Ormahn subduing the west and bringing peace to the land." He was not going to speak about Agavia. Even if Veldarr knew about Agavia, Auragole was not going to speak about it.

But if Solagen should ask about it? Well, Auragole would face that one when and if it happened.

Veldarr gave Auragole a crooked smile and then turned his horse. "Let's get back to Solagen with our news," he said, and led the way across the Doldarr, up into the hills, and north toward where the king waited. At the top of the hill, Auragole turned back to look once again at the empty land below. Just beyond one of its farther hills, he could see part of the ruins of the amphitheater where he and Lorenwile had sung for the Companions. Something stuck in his throat and something stung his eyes.

Solagen moved his army into Meekelorr's deserted camp. They spent a week there, while patrols were sent out daily to check the hills nearby. Not a soul was found, not even a shepherd.

Once they were certain there was no army, small or large, waiting in the hills above them, Solagen said, "Auragole, take us to this other valley of yours and show us this great ruined city."

So Auragole led the way to Adelmorr, retracing the route he had once taken with Meekelorr. It, too, was empty of people or armies. They camped once they reached level land. The next day

Auragole took Solagen, Veldarr, and a few officers to see the ruins of the city.

They spent ten days in the Adelmorr Valley, giving the soldiers a rest before proceeding south. Day after day, at the king's request, Auragole, Solagen, and, occasionally, some of the officers rode through the ruined city. Auragole told them the story of the city even as it had been told to him. "I was here with Lorenwile while he taught me to sing," he told Solagen. What he said was true. However, he didn't mention that he had been taken here first by Meekelorr. He wasn't sure why he obfuscated. It just seemed too late to tell Solagen how much time he had actually spent with the Companions of the Way. It was no longer important, he told himself.

As they rode through the ruined town the king's demeanor was serious and thoughtful. He listened and looked and took in everything. "Someday, Auragole," he told him on their last visit before they left the valley, "I will rebuild this place. I will restore it to its full glory. I will make it even a grander place to live in than it was at its height. I swear it."

And Auragole believed him.

Auragole had not taken the king through the temple. He had pointed it out, but had not walked through it. Solagen was not interested in religion. One day, however, Auragole visited the temple alone. Leaving Starwanderer to graze on the summer grass before it, he walked through the ruin. This was where he had first heard Lorenwile True-sing. Lorenwile had True-sung the temple back some of its health, had True-sung its history to it, had sung the story of the countryside around it, singing of when nature had been healthy. While Lorenwile sang, Auragole had seen it all in clear and sometimes dreadful images. They had shown themselves to him as if Auragole himself was back in those times and had been a witness. He saw the despoiling by men of the temple and of the city. And then he saw it whole—such was the power of True-singing.

Auragole walked out behind the temple, where a stream flowed. It was here that Auragole had first attempted to True-sing, here where he had first felt that longing rise up in him as an ache never to be forgotten. The sight of the stream caused a sharp pain in his heart. Someday, he told himself.

As he thought about Lorenwile, he felt another ache. It was half a year since Lorenwile had left Mattelmead without so much as a good-bye. Stop being concerned with Lorenwile, he told himself. Lorenwile was gone and that was that. And Auragole's present life was far greater than anything he had ever dared dream of for himself. He was a commander in Ormahn of Mattelmead's army, friend to the savior of the Westernlands. And he was acquitting himself admirably.

Frankly, to his own surprise, Auragole had discovered that he liked what he was doing, liked the campaigns, the physicality of them, the sheer energy that poured through him when he was in battle—the opposite of what he felt singing, especially True-singing. Singing he had been open, had been a breeze flowing through everything. True-singing needed peace within, attention without. And it was extraordinary, nothing like it in the world. But battle, and its preparation, brought feelings of exhilaration, of power, of confidence. That too was good, that too filled some inner need.

Auragole walked out of the temple and looked at the grassy slope before it. He and Meekelorr had camped there, and eventually Lorenwile had joined him. And it was here, deep in the night, that he had first met Elarr, who would become so important in his life. Auragole mounted Starwanderer and turned him toward the camp where Ormahn's army waited. When the west was conquered, there would be time to seek out Elarr, Affredda, and Lorenwile again. He promised himself that he would do so.

There was only one time during their rout of the Sorren Heights that Auragole felt any trepidation. It was when he and his soldiers had come unexpectedly upon the little valley and flat-topped hill of Wihl, the Starmaster. It, too, had been abandoned—the garden overrun with weeds, the cabin swept clean. The furniture was still there. But all the maps were gone. Lorenwile must have come for Wihl as well. Likely the Starmaster was now in Agavia with all the Companions, with Meekelorr, and with Mondrief, another master of the stars. Auragole sincerely hoped it was true. Perhaps someday he could once again look at the incredible maps of the heavens that Wihl had charted. Heartily he wished it to be so. Let that lovely people, the Agavians, live in peace. Ormahn was the world's champion now, and there would be no need for their sacrifice. Ormahn and his commanders and soldiers were all the sacrifice the world needed.

N

chapter eleven

DONNADORR WAS SITTING on the banks of the lake on his country estate in late October, fishing. It was growing cold and he was wrapped in his winter cloak. The last of the autumn leaves still clung to the trees. All the crops on his estate were in, and the previous night the first frost had come. He and Sylvie would stay in the country that winter. Nothing in the city now drew them. Last winter, Auragole had accepted a commandership in Ormahn's army, and, Don had heard, was quite content with his new life. No need to worry about his old friend now.

Donnadorr would hunt for a few more weeks. He hunted rarely in the cold months. The larder was well stocked: vegetables and fruits canned, meat and fish smoked. The winter would be a good time for reading—a skill he had learned from Aiku—and Donnadorr had acquired a small but fine library. He would practice his singing again; Lorenwile had been so encouraging. And he would try this winter to reacquire his skill as a harp player. It had been much too long since he had sung and played in earnest. Singing those late nights with Lorenwile last year had stirred that hunger in him. And he would write songs, too. Perhaps songs of Mattelmead and its splendors. And songs of Ormahn and his feats. There was so much to put into words and melody, so much that he had encountered since going to Mattelmead City. But he had not done so, had sung little. He wasn't sure why. In the early days it might have been the separation from his singing partner, Auragole. Or maybe it had been the adjustment to Mattelmead. Because of the precious stones he and his traveling companions had been given as gifts from the Agavians, he and Sylvie were wealthy. He lived well. He moved freely in Mattelmead society. Others were artists—performers and singers—not he. But those several times when he had sung privately with Lorenwile, a fire had rekindled in his heart. He would sing again—if only for himself, if only for Sylvane.

Sylvie had her work at the orphanage. He knew it pained her that they did not yet have any children of their own. It seemed a cruel blow of fate not to give children to this woman who so adored them and would, in all ways, be a splendid mother. However, there were new children coming every month to the orphanage, and that was where Sylvie spent most of her time.

Their days should be quite filled with activity this winter. Sylvie and he scrupulously abided by the laws of their new country. After all, they enjoyed privileges they had scarcely dreamed of when they had each set off for Mattelmead. And for them, since arriving—other than being childless—life had been good. They had met several families from the neighboring estates whose company they enjoyed. Many of the men were officers in the army, of course, but the army was expected back any day now from the campaign in the Sorren Heights, and the men would be returning to their homes as soon as Ormahn released them. The winter would be bright with social festivities, and stories of the latest victory for Ormahn and Mattelmead. It seemed that defeat was simply not a possibility. Ormahn was invincible.

"Don."

He turned slightly at the sound of his name. Sylvie was hurrying down the path from the house toward him, carrying something in her hand.

"What is it, lass? And don't shout, you'll scare away the fish."

"You have a large enough basket of fish already," she said as she drew near. "You're going to have to give away most of it to our tenants. How much can we two, and our servants, eat?" She sat herself down on a rock near him.

"You know fishing gives me a chance to think. Not that there's much to think about these days. And soon it will be too cold to sit out here."

"Then let me give you something to think about. I've had a letter from Glenelle."

"Glenelle? Truly? It's been months, hasn't it?"

"Yes, months."

"What does she say?"

Sylvane brushed the wrinkles from her skirt with her free hand. "She says that Glenorr has been offered a position in research at the hospital at the academy, and he has accepted it. He continues to live at the academy most of the time, and she still sees him only about once a week."

"It's what Glen always wanted. I'm glad for him."

"It's perfect for him," Sylvane said. "I think Veldarr put in a good word with the powers that be at the academy. Don't look for that in the letter. It's my guess."

"A good guess, lassie." With his free hand he brushed a stray lock of red hair from his forehead.

"But the big news is that the army and Ormahn are back. The men in our own neighborhood should be returning within days. The Sorren Heights is entirely in the hands of our king."

"As expected. Oh what a glorious time we live in, Sylvie. To think we should be subjects of that king who is bringing peace to the world, after all we went through in our youth."

"Yes, thank the stars."

"Any news about Auragole? Is he safe and well? Or does Glenelle hold back from writing about him?"

"She does write about him. Put down your pole and read it for yourself." She offered him the letter.

"In a few minutes—one more fish, I think. Just tell me first and I will read the details later."

"Auragole is safe and well. The brigade under Veldarr, which Auragole and his Elite Corps were attached to, and with whom Ormahn was also marching, met little in the way of conflict until they arrived in the south, not far from the Noonbarr River. There they had a few fierce battles. It seems that the Elite Corps under Auragole's command performed beyond expectation. And Goredahl, at the head of another division that marched south along the Glovale border, won battle after battle. All the Sorren Heights is in Ormahn's hands. In the east, Oldwell did well, also, conquering as he went. The loss of life was low—only one commander was killed."

"Ormahn's army is becoming more and more remarkable with every country it conquers," Donnadorr said. "An indomitable army, I would call it. Oh, how I would like to be part of it." He sighed, then grinned. "Enough of that," he scolded himself. "Does Ellie say anything about Veldarr?"

"She does, and it's only in passing. He's been put in charge of the Sorren Heights and will be there at least until the spring."

"Her heart must be breaking," Donnadorr said.

"Don't be unkind. I'm sure she feels it. But Glenelle has so many acquaintances. She won't be friendless this winter."

He raised his eyebrows.

"None of that, Don," Sylvane scolded.

"I wonder if Auragole has yet made peace with her. It's been more than a year, hasn't it?"

"More like a year and a half. And the answer is 'No.' That's the purpose of Ellie's letter. She writes to urge us to return to the city for the winter, and to act as her emissary to Auragole, whom she says she truly cares for and cannot understand why he shuns her."

"Can she not?"

"I think she's sincere, Don."

"Do you? She will always be the sweet, ailing sister whom you took care of for so many years. Are you ready to drop everything and go to the city?"

Sylvane slowly shook her head. "I have my work here. I'm needed here."

"Good girl. I think Ellie wants to make it up with Auragole because he is close to the throne and she is apparently being shut out of events because of the so-called rift between them. He's interfering with her social advancement, and that's what's motivating her."

"Oh, Don, you've become such a cynic."

"Have I?"

"I think it's because you cannot forgive her yourself for not being the woman you idolized."

"Sylvie, you're such a dunce. You think I still harbor resentment toward Ellie, that I'm bitter because she turned away from my attentions, that I'm like Auragole?"

"Perhaps, a little."

Donnadorr pulled his pole out of the water and put it on the bank. He stood up and walked over to her and pulled her to her feet. "You refuse to believe that I woke up one day and saw who was really the superior woman, the one who loves and expects nothing back, the one who has courage, the one who truly understands people, who is kind, generous, and moral." He wrapped his large arms around her and drew her to his burly chest. "When I saw that, all thoughts of Ellie disappeared from my head. And they have not, not even for an instant, come back."

"THANK YOU FOR seeing me, Sire," Auragole said, as he strode into the room that was the private office of Solagen.

"You sent word that it was urgent," Solagen said, and motioned Auragole to a sofa, rose, and joined him there. "Now what is urgent?" He pointed to his desk piled high with papers. "As you see, I have much work to attend to."

Auragole took a deep breath. This had better be important, he told himself. Solagen does not take kindly to being petitioned needlessly. "I've done some thinking since our campaign."

"Yes."

"I have an idea for some new weapons that would make our campaigns easier. . .I think."

"Yes." Solagen watched Auragole without blinking.

"I wonder if the metalworkers who make the weapons for our army could make us some swords that are both lighter and shorter. Swords that could be wielded in one hand, once our bows are of no use."

Solagen's eyes narrowed.

"Only for the Elite Corps, Sire. Or, if they prove successful, for all the horse-soldiers."

"And why do you see this as a worthy idea?"

"If our horse-soldiers learn to fight holding a sword in one hand and a knife in the other, I think it would give us great advantage over our foes, whether on horseback or if we become unseated." Auragole couldn't keep the enthusiasm from his voice. "Let the foot soldiers carry the longer, heavier two-handed swords."

Now Solagen looked thoughtful. Auragole waited. It seemed as if many minutes crept by—but perhaps it was only seconds.

Finally, Solagen spoke. "I shall set up a meeting between you and my master armorer. Tell him your plan. If he says it can be done, then let it be done—but at present only enough for the Elite Corps." He stood up. "I'll send you a message when the meeting has been arranged." He moved toward his desk.

"Thank you, Sire," Auragole said, relieved, and headed toward the door.

"Auragole."

Auragole stopped and turned to face Solagen.

"It's a good idea. Now let's see if we can make it work."

"Yes, thank you." And Auragole bolted from the room. Please, he thought, let it work.

IT WAS EARLY December. The snows had blanketed the city for three days. The once naked trees, now dressed in white, looked burdened under their heavy, moist load. Auragole had risen early and was walking down the Street of Temples. His head ached from too much wine the previous night. He had left a woman sleeping in his bed whose name he couldn't remember. Well, she would be gone by the time he returned. His servants would see to that.

The gray ash and cinders, spread out on the walkway in front of the temples, made a satisfying crunch beneath his boots. He hardly knew what had caused him to pick this street to walk on. No, that wasn't true. Since his return from the wars, he had begun to dream about his father. They didn't speak to each other in the dreams. But his father seemed to be watching him. Whatever crazy turn the dream took, however ridiculous the activities in the dream, there was his father hovering in the background, watching, just watching. Perhaps it was because Auragole had started to think about the Gods again. It had started in the Woefuls during the campaign the previous summer. His father, and questions about the Gods, had been at the edge of his thoughts ever since he and his men had found the camp of the Companions of the Way in the Woeful Peaks. And even more so since he had camped in the Adelmorr Valley.

There he had had that conversation with Meekelorr. The two of them had been sitting on the grass in the park. Meekelorr was looking out at the ruins of what had once been a fine city.

Auragole stared at the sad wreck of a city, which seemed more eerie in the approaching twilight. No human walked there now save him and the commander of the Companions of the Way. He shook his head. "I can't imagine it, can't think so many people in one place, so many buildings. Hardest of all is to think its destruction." His voice cracked and to his embarrassment he struggled to keep the tears at bay. And then he was angry. "Where were their Gods when the enemy came?"

Meekelorr looked at him through half-closed eyes. "You think that because there is war, there can be no Gods?"

"I can't understand how you come to your beliefs, frankly, Meekelorr. You have one set of beliefs, the Agavians another, the people of Wildenfarr-low-desert another—no, each tribe there has a different set of beliefs and they fight each other over them. Why is your belief better than others? Or more true? How do any of you know that there are Gods at all?"

"Do you believe only what you can touch with your hands and see with your eyes?"

Auragole sighed and looked out at the dead city. "No, I can easily believe that there are hidden things, hidden forces, things we can't see. I believe that because I've experienced such things. Strange ailments in the Deep Forest, for instance, and strange Beings behind the wind, for so I experienced it in the Deep. Not only myself, but Don and Ellie and Sylvie and. . .well, I'm not sure about Glen. But that only gives me a. . .a. . ." Auragole paused and couldn't go on.

"A sense of something behind the visible?"

"Yes, a sense. But that is not the same as knowing. There may well be Gods, Meekelorr. But you say that there are good Gods, whom you call the Creative Gods. And you say that there are evil Gods called Adversary Gods, led by someone called the Nethergod. You say he is on earth right now, that it is your task and the Companions' and the Agavians' to find him and do battle with him. And to that you devote your life. But what I

don't understand is how you know all of this. Pohl told me that there is a path to the Gods, but I don't understand how that can be." His voice cracked with intensity. "I don't understand how you can claim to know something in its reality, its true reality, if it is hidden."

"Well, young Auragole, how do you know anything?"

Auragole answered without hesitation. "I know something if I have experienced it."

"Good," Meekelorr said. "That's a beginning. And someday you will have to tell me what you mean by experience.*" And he rose in a fluid, graceful gesture and whistled for Sunflight.*

Meekelorr could have told him then that his father had once been a priest of the King God, but he hadn't done so. How angry Auragole had been when he found out that Meekelorr knew and had withheld that information from him as he had withheld the fact that Auragole was cousin to the Lady Claregole and her brother Galavi. But Auragole's father had withheld that fact from Auragole as well. All those years, as he was growing up in the Gandlese, Auragole had been told that his father had been a farmer back east.

Another early riser came toward him, gave Auragole a small nod, and moved past him.

His father. . .his taciturn father. Would he have been proud of Auragole now that he was a commander in the army of Ormahn of Mattelmead? Surely he would have been proud. Perhaps that was why his father had come to his dreams.

But it wasn't just his father who was the cause of Auragole's edginess. Perhaps it was only post-battle restlessness. Nearly two months had passed since the army had returned from the Sorren Heights. But after such active, enlivening, and purposeful months, to be back in the social, almost silly whirl of Mattelmead City seemed a bit of a letdown. He was still war-weary, Auragole told himself, with a little shake of his head; that's all this agitation was about. But he knew it wasn't true.

Visiting the temple in the Adelmorr Valley where he had first heard True-singing, and seeing the little stream where he had first True-sung. . .

He sighed audibly. Well, that's the way it would have to be. He had made a decision. True-singing was a personal striving, and Solagen, his sovereign, had convinced him to raise his eyes higher, to do something to help humanity. He, Auragole, had answered that call. And was doing fine. Just fine.

Auragole stopped in front of a beautiful building with the symbol of the King God, a crown whose points were candles, on the lintel over its magnificently carved front doors. Had his father's temple looked something like this? He would go in and just sit there and think about his father.

"AURAGOLE." SOLAGEN CALLED him away from the council table one day in February and said, "It's come to my attention that you have been frequenting many of our temples."

"I've made no secret of that, Sire." But he felt uncomfortable.

Solagen waved his hand in a dismissive gesture. "I'm not criticizing you, Auragole. How you choose to spend your free time is your own affair."

"In truth, none of it is very inspiring, but it puts me in mind of my father."

"Yes, yes, you've told me about your father. . . But I have a request to make of you."

Auragole waited, a small spot of tension in his stomach. A request.

Solagen's tone was brisk, businesslike. "There's a little temple on a side street—I'll show you on the map. It's not an official temple, but it's not exactly outlawed either. I need to know what goes on there. It's dedicated, if my information is correct, to the Prince God. I wonder why they are not satisfied with the official temple to the Prince? As you know, we're interested now in this Prince God because we expect to ally ourselves with

Tul-Farr of Wildenfarr-low-desert in a campaign against And-ul-farr."

Auragole nodded and waited.

"Both of these desert leaders and their people worship the Prince God, though they have different beliefs, and fight over those beliefs. Didn't you tell us that?"

"Yes."

"I need to know more about this God. I've already spoken to the priests at the official temple. Not very satisfying. What makes this Prince God so important? What makes him stand out from all the other Gods, in the opinion of those who worship him? Tul-farr speaks of a God who walked on earth as a man millennia ago. But his nemesis, And-ul-farr, believes that is a heresy, that the Prince never descended to the Deep Earth. Frankly, it's all childish nonsense, this running after the Gods—but until our science makes more progress it's to be expected, I suppose."

Auragole could feel the color rising in his cheeks.

However, Solagen didn't seem to notice. "I never underestimate my enemies, nor my allies. Therefore, I need to know more about this Prince. Go to that little temple. Attend its service. See what you can find out about their beliefs— perhaps something that will help us understand the desert people a bit better. Also it will let us know whether what they are preaching there is seditious."

Auragole said nothing.

Solagen looked at him, a slight frown on his face. "Surely this is an easy thing to do, Auragole. Why are you so quiet?"

"You have others who do this kind of work, Solagen, why ask me?"

Solagen laughed. "Sometimes you are too fastidious, Auragole. I ask you because you are the only one of my commanders who goes into any of these temples. That you should find your way to theirs might not be looked at as out of the ordinary. Those *others* you mentioned would be noticed immediately because that little temple has a very small congregation, and its members will notice strangers. Therefore, the priest there, or whatever he is, might alter what he teaches, and preach accordingly."

"I'm also a stranger."

"But a stranger who is interested in the Gods."

"And I am also well known in this city."

"Auragole, I expect you will be able to talk your way into that place in some plausible way. Go for several weeks. Befriend some of the congregation. And report back to me."

Auragole could hear the impatience and irritation in Solagen's voice and made no more argument. "As you wish, Solagen."

Solagen looked at him coolly.

"If it's important to you, Sire, I'll do it."

"Good. There's nothing to this, Auragole. You're doing me a service and it will be easy for you." Solagen clapped Auragole on the shoulder and returned to the council table.

Auragole stood a few moments, rubbing his forehead, an unhappy feeling spreading throughout his body. Do this for Solagen, he told himself, and returned to the table. When he had taken his place he looked up and saw Goredahl watching him with a triumphant look in his eyes. So that's where the idea came from, Auragole thought with distaste. He didn't like the man, though he respected his abilities on the battlefield. But his other job Auragole found odious. Goredahl was commander of the Security Forces, an extension of the army whose task it was to ferret out possible acts of sedition, or even the thought of sedition. Yes, that's something this dour man would like.

And now he's got me involved. Well, what else was there to do? Solagen had requested it.

ON THE FIRST day of the week, the day when the temples offered their services, the day when people rested from their labors, Auragole knocked on the door of a small house in one of the poorer residential sections of town. All the streets in Mattelmead were clean, and all its houses well maintained. That was the law. There was nothing to distinguish this house from its neighbors except, as Auragole had stood down the block and watched it, a dozen or so people had come up to its door and knocked on it, and were admitted. The hour was early. Auragole guessed that the inhabitants of most of the neighboring houses were still sleeping, taking advantage of this day of rest to stay in bed a little longer. All shops were closed on this day by order of the king. The normally bustling city was uncharacteristically quiet.

For a long time, Auragole, too, had slept late on the first day of the week, until he had started going, in the late morning, to services at the various temples. In the beginning, he had gone only to the temple of the King God, hoping to connect there with something that would help him understand the part of his father that he had kept secret from Auragole. That his father had been a priest of the King God who had lost his faith was a large, indigestible stone in Auragole's gut. Like the memory stones of Agavia, this one cast a long shadow over his recollections of his childhood.

The temple of the King God had been disappointing. The allusions to this supreme ruler among the hierarchy of Gods, who looked down beneficently on Ormahn of Mattelmead, his chosen instrument on earth, usually turned into a harangue about good citizenship and the importance of obeying the will of Ormahn and his government. So Auragole had gone elsewhere. He had tried one temple after another, looking for something that he could not put a name to. But it was the same wherever he went. There was a temple to the Prince God. There was a temple to a God of Battle, who Auragole thought must be Elarr's Defender God. There was not one temple to a Lady God such as the one Auragole had experienced in the Ancient Woods in Thorensphere, or the one Elarr had called the Goddess of Wisdom, or the two female Goddesses of the Agavians called

Oahla and Demeda. However, there were temples to the Gods of Crafts, of the Fine Arts, of the Performing Arts, of the Animals. And many more. He had visited most of them.

For weeks, he had continued to rise early on the first day of the week—he wasn't sure why—and had attended some temple or other. After a while it ceased being about his father. He was looking for something that none of the places of worship in Mattelmead, with their abstract allusions and their exhortations to good citizenship, provided. Something holy, some sense of reverence for the Gods, something he had experienced in Agavia, something similar to what he had heard from Pohl and Meekelorr, and from his good friend Elarr. But why now, when long ago he had decided that knowing about the Gods of the Creative World was less important than understanding the Deep Earth and its needs? That was why he had turned to True-singing—True-singing was about knowing the earth. And that was why he had joined Ormahn's army, which was the means for bringing peace to the earth. He decided he was just restless after all the months of war, of excitement, decided he just missed the sense of purpose battle gave him.

And yet he had persisted, week after week, that winter—though there was little satisfaction. From those who also came to the temples all he experienced was what Auragole termed "an intolerable passivity"—people sitting, listening, nodding, smiling at their neighbors, and then, no doubt, going home to good dinners. Most were from the merchant class and the laboring class. Few artists were there, and none that he could recognize from his own class. He had decided to stop going when Ormahn had made this "request" of him.

Auragole stood at the door to the little, unofficial temple to the Prince and hesitated. He didn't want to do this. He didn't want to be here. He was no spy. He sighed. A request. From Solagen, Ormahn of Mattelmead, the king—his king, the high commander of the army. His commander. Auragole took a deep breath. And knocked on the door.

A woman answered. She was perhaps in her late twenties, with a small face and rather plain features. The exceptions were her large, hazel eyes, which were quite beautiful, and her long, thick brown hair, which she wore down and tied back. Her dress was worn, cut simply, but clean and well pressed. The smile on her face faded momentarily when she saw Auragole at the entrance.

"Can I help you?"

"I've been told I can find a temple to the Prince God here," Auragole said.

The woman hesitated for a moment. "There is a temple to the Prince God on the Street of Temples no more than half a mile from here," she said, and gestured down the road.

"I've been to that temple, to all those temples, actually, and I cannot find what I'm seeking there," Auragole told her truthfully. "Is this not also a place where one can worship the Prince?"

The woman searched his face and he allowed it, wondering if she could see more deeply than he wanted. He willed himself not to blush.

"Come in, sir. You are welcome. My name is Meraleese. I am the priest's wife."

She led him down a hall into a small room. There were some twenty chairs there facing a wooden altar, on which stood a white cloth and a twelve-branched candelabra with unlit candles. The room was painted a soft pink and was lit only by some candles on a table in the back of the room. There were about a dozen people sitting there. No one turned as he came in. Auragole sat down in the last row, feeling uncomfortable. But after a few moments, as no one looked his way, he began to study his surroundings.

This was nothing like any of the temples he had been in. This was no grand room filled with statues and paintings. This room was tiny and simply decorated. The official temples could seat from three to five hundred; this one, no more than thirty. When one entered those other temples, before the service began it was noisy, with children running down the aisle and people standing about talking to each other, dressed in their best clothes and admiring one another's finery. Here there were no children, though he could hear the occasional raised voice of a child coming from above them. No one in the chapel was talking. Here there was utter quiet. He wondered if the people were praying. But he couldn't see their faces. Their clothes, from what he could make out in the soft, dim light, were plain and unadorned, much like those of the woman who had answered the door. There was no one there, as far as he could tell, from the upper class—his class.

Auragole forgot his discomfort as he waited. He could feel around him a rising sense of anticipation. After about seven or eight minutes, a man, apparently the priest, entered from a door to the left of the altar. He was dressed in a long white linen robe and carried a candle. From just behind his chair, Auragole heard a harp playing lovely chords, hardly a tune, yet rather moving. The priest walked to the altar and lit the twelve candles. He put the candle he was carrying into a holder on a small table not far from the altar. Then he returned to the altar and picked up a book. Turning toward the congregation, the priest opened the book and began to read.

"From the life of the Prince God when he lived on earth."

Auragole straightened up, tense with excitement.

For several minutes the priest read about the activities of the Prince God on earth, how he had healed the sick, how he had taught those who were his followers about the Creative World, and about the task of the Deep Earth. Auragole listened with astonishment. Where had the priest found such a book? It was thought that all the books about the Prince, about all the Gods, had been destroyed in the terrible centuries of war, and that all

166

that was known now about the Gods were only stories—vastly differing, vastly conflicting verbal accounts. Auragole had only to think of the two versions of the Prince God's life that created enmity between the two tribes of Wildenfarr-low-desert. How had this book survived, the one that the priest was reading from?

Then the priest put down his book and turned to the congregation again. The harp music stopped. "Now let me offer you some thoughts of mine. You know that in the centuries of war all written records of the Prince were systematically destroyed. Destroyed, not by those who believed in nothing, but by those who professed belief. One religious sect destroying the works of another."

Auragole could feel the eyes of the priest on him, and wondered uncomfortably if the priest was aware of his thoughts.

"I have told you, time and again, that the stories that have survived and come down to us orally are distorted and many essential facts have been either lost or altered. Some facts have even become the opposite of what they once were. That need not concern us here. This book, of the life of the Prince, I myself have written down—as most of you know. Written from my own research, for all the events of all the epochs of human history are etched into the spiritual substance of the stars, which is the Creative World itself, and access to them can be found by all true seekers. I want to say to you, as I have said to you for the years we have been coming together, that I have done nothing that you cannot do at least in some measure yourselves. I read from the record in the stars about the Prince's life, as he led it on earth many, many centuries ago. And I write it down. Then I bring it to you as a reminder of what the Prince brought as his manifold gifts to humanity."

Auragole leaned forward. Wihl, the Starmaster, had said something similar when he said he needed no books to tell him the history of humankind—that he could read that history from the stars. Was this priest a master of the stars? He stopped his thoughts to listen to the priest's words.

"The Prince God brought not just his teachings, not just the healings, but most important of all, his being. That is the main point. His being. And his descending to earth, inhabiting the soul, the life, and the body of a man, has changed forever what we human beings have consequently achieved as our own earthly and spiritual faculties, and what we will achieve in the centuries and millennia to come. Even if not one of us remembers or acknowledges him, it has happened. One could call the most important deed of the Prince his self-bestowal. And this self-bestowal enabled humanity to step forward into its future. It enables us now to move, if we only will it, past the centuries of violence and decadence into a time of more and more freedom and more and more love. This we have spoken about many times. This is our certainty and this is our hope.

"Today I wish to remind you that the God died but did not die. And that when we die, we, too, die but do not die. Death is the great lie whispered to us by the Destroyer God. When we die, we only set our earthly bodies aside, and our individualities go on for a time in spiritual realms, and then we return to the earth.

"However, to look only at what the Prince did centuries ago can become meaningless, can become pretty story, comforting story. But to find the Prince again where he is in our times, that is what is significant for us now. I say to you that he has left the heavens once again and dwells in his life body—not in a physical body that one can see with one's eyes and touch with one's hands; he dwells in his life body in the spiritual life element that surrounds our earth like the clouds. One could even say that he is once again on the earth, that he has returned to us as was promised so many centuries ago. And each of you can find him and can experience him and garner strength for your life. He is very close to each of you.

"Do not be afraid. You carry within you great capacities, but you must will to use them. If you use them, you will find the Prince. If not, then these latent capacities in you will become the possession of the Destroyer God. But if you use them, they will develop and become stronger, and then you too will be able to find the long history of humankind where it is recorded in the stars. And then no destruction of records or books will ever again throw the earth into darkness and forgetfulness. Now let us pray."

The priest proceeded to recite prayer after prayer—all, Auragole deduced, of the priest's own making. Most prayers were to the Prince, but others were to the King and to a goddess he called "the Wise One." Hearing the prayers, Auragole forgot why he was there and just listened into the words, and was both excited and moved. When the prayers were done, the priest picked up a candle snuffer from the little side table and slowly put out the candles. And then he left.

The congregation sat quietly for a while, then one by one rose and exited the sanctuary. Auragole did the same. In the reception room, people were standing around talking quietly. When Auragole entered, the wife of the priest left the group she was talking to and came over to Auragole. It suddenly became quiet as people noticed the stranger in their midst.

Before the woman could say anything, Auragole bent his head in greeting and said, "Thank you for letting me attend your service. May I come again?"

"Yes, if you find here what you are seeking."

"Thank you," he said, nodded again, and left the house. He dismissed his carriage, which was waiting down the street, and walked the many long blocks home, thinking about what he had seen and heard, thinking again of Wihl, of Meekelorr, of his dear friend Elarr.

chapter twelve

THAT NIGHT AURAGOLE had a disturbing dream—one he had dreamt before.

Again he was walking aimlessly through a light snow somewhere high in the Gandlese Mountains. He turned around a bend in the road and there, spread out before him, was the beautiful, hidden Valley of the Agavi. He stopped to look. Something was happening down there. Auragole sat, ate his lunch, and watched the scene below. He saw clearly that there was a war going on. The Agavians and the Companions of the Way were fighting against several armies dressed in a rainbow of uniforms. The Companions and the Agavians were hopelessly outnumbered. The people of the valley had no weapons to speak of and were battling with sticks, rocks, and farm tools. Auragole saw faces distorted in pain, heard shouts of anger and screams of agony, the familiar sound of metal on metal, and the roaring, rushing sounds of war. He gnawed on a chicken leg and watched. No one was spared in the battle—neither men, women, nor children. Artists and poets, singers and dancers, actors and reciters, all were struggling with the invaders. Most were dying. As each child fell, Auragole noted it, and brushed another crumb away from his mouth.

He saw Galavi struggling with a soldier in black in the Lady Claregole's garden. On the steps of the Lady's mansion, outnumbered by a host of the enemy, was his old friend Pohl. He was wielding his sword well; really, Pohl was an excellent swordsman. But of course Auragole knew that Pohl couldn't survive, and he bit into his dried apple.

In the fields behind the Great Mansion, Meekelorr on gray Sunflight was encircled by dozens of red-clad soldiers. Near him was a handful of Companions of the Way. They couldn't hope to come out of this alive.

Look, there were Glenorr and Glenelle, Sylvane and Donnadorr, all battling from horseback. But weren't they in Mattelmead, safe from wars? Ellie had been healed by the doctors there; she shouldn't go risking her life again. Someone should tell her that, he thought, and took out his flask of water and drank deeply.

Suddenly all was in flames. The Lady Claregole's mansion, which had stood from the beginning of time, was enveloped by fire. So too were the golden meadows, the dark Agavi trees on the hills surrounding the valley. There was a roar as if all the marble and precious stones in the mountains had imploded.

Time to leave, Auragole thought, standing up. He watched the hills begin to tumble into the valley like children's blocks, then got up to walk away, when he heard the sound of people on horseback coming from behind him. Auragole shouted to one as he passed by, "Who has come to destroy Agavia?"

The man who leaned down toward Auragole was very young. "The Dark Breather," he called as he passed, "the Dark Breather has come."

Auragole was suddenly stricken. The Dark Breather? The

Nethergod? The Destroyer?

Sylvane came riding by. "It's all because of you, Aurie. You could have saved us," and she shook her head and rode off.

"Sylvane, wait!"

Auragole turned to stare down at the burning valley. Was everything really gone? The stately Agavi trees, the colored marble that supported the mountains like bones, and all the precious jewels? All gone. He could see that they were all gone. The mansions, the manor houses and cottages, the exquisite sculptures and tapestries in the Lady's beautiful home. The Lady herself and all the wonderful people who had nursed him back to health when the beast from the cave had nearly killed him. Gone. Gone. Why was he doing nothing? Shouldn't he do something? He tried to find the road but it had disappeared. He must find the road down to the valley. But it was too dark.

And then he woke up, drenched in sweat. He rose from his bed and began pacing about the room in his bare feet, indifferent to the cold. His half-awake mind went over and over the dream. Why had he dreamt of the destruction of Agavia again? And why had he, once more, dreamt of his indifference to that destruction? Surely that would never be. As he came more into wakefulness, he was able to put the dream in its proper context. Hearing the words of the priest at the little temple that day had made him think of Agavia and those he knew there—particularly his two cousins, the Lady Claregole and her brother, Galavi. The more he had thought about them, the more determined he was not to allow the so-called Last Battle ever to reach the Valley of the Agavi. Ormahn would put an end to the plans of the Nethergod, whoever he was, when Ormahn conquered all of the west. Then there would be peace. Then there would be no need for a Last Battle.

When Auragole was finally convinced the dream was only a reminder of his worry concerning the lovely Agavian people, he returned to his bed, more determined than ever to help Solagen bring peace to the entire west—and then, who knows, eventually to the war-torn Easternlands.

AURAGOLE WENT BACK to the little temple the following week. Again there was a reading from the life of the Prince. Again there was a talk. And then there were the prayers.

In his talk, the priest said, among other things, "You don't know what you carry within you. The fact that you can say 'I' and mean only yourself, mean the 'I' that is carried in your body, mean exclusively your single self, and not your whole community, that 'I' is a sacred gift of the Prince. To give this gift, the Prince came to earth; this was his self-bestowal, for it is part of himself that he gave and still gives. In the past, the further back we go, humans were not so separate, not so isolated within their own skins. They felt themselves also in those around them, and also in their ancestors, those who had come before them. In an ancient time, even their memories reached back to their ancestors' memories."

Yes, yes, Auragole thought, that's like the Agavians! Just like the Agavians even in the present time.

"We have lost that, lost the ability to feel into and be a part of another, to feel into and be a part of the nature around us. We are cut off from each other. We live as if locked within our own skins. It makes us lonely. It makes us hostile to others. But yet I have called it a gift of the Prince—even a sacred gift. Why is it a gift? It is a gift because humanity has a great goal here on earth. To become Gods ourselves one day, Gods of freedom and love."

Auragole sat up. He had heard the same from Pohl in Agavia, then also from Meekelorr and Elarr. Did this priest know them? He leaned forward as if to listen harder.

"Only human beings can become free—not the animals, not the plants, not the stones. And only a free human being can truly love—love another human and love the Gods. Without the Prince, living on earth as a man, this individualization would not have taken place. For what one being can do while dwelling in a human body, in time all others can do. Without this gift, perhaps we would feel more a sense of community, perhaps there would be less war. But without this gift of the Prince, we would have been more like the animals—living out of our instincts and in tribes, but not free, not thinking beings, not individuals, not capable of change. We would have been perpetual children, incapable of growth, cared for by the Gods as infants are cared for by their parents, but never reaching maturity and individuality. Cherish that gift, the gift of the 'I,' with all its dangers, and out of that most precious gift work hard to know and then love another."

Auragole felt a stirring of memory in him, of a dream, but he could not draw it up into consciousness. And then he thought of the Seusadahhn, the horse-men of the Woeful Peaks. They too had been bereft because they could not change, were willing to lose much of the magnificence of who they were so that they could change, could grow, could become human.

After his second visit to the temple, Auragole again thanked Meraleese, and left quickly. He had not yet reported his visits to Solagen, and Solagen had not yet asked. What would he say when Solagen did? Auragole hadn't decided. But here was nothing seditious, that he knew. Only worship and reverence.

IT WAS A few days after Auragole's second visit to the small temple that he was invited by Solagen to a state banquet. It was in honor of In-tul-farr, son of Tul-farr, who was now allied to Ormahn of Mattelmead. In-tul-farr had come to confer with Ormahn about the planned campaign in the fall. Auragole was looking forward to the festive occasion. He had very much liked In-tul-farr when he had met him in the desert of Wildenfarr. Because of him, Auragole and Ellie, Don, Sylvie, and Glen had been saved from dying in the desert.

The night of the banquet Auragole, dressed in his finest attire, arrived at the palace in his coach. The reception hall in Solagen's palace was grand. It was a tribute to the fine craftsmanship that had been developing in Mattelmead in the past twenty years. There were marble fireplaces and floors; there were both wooden and granite columns holding up a beautifully painted ceiling. The walls too were painted with scenes of Ormahn's conquests.

Everyone who was important to the life of the army and of the city had been invited—at least two hundred persons. There was a reception line, and all the guests passed through it. When Auragole finally stood in front of In-tul-farr, who was dressed in his own fine desert robes, Auragole was not recognized.

"In-tul-farr," Auragole said, with a small bow of greeting, "don't you recognize the young man whom you rescued, along with his friends, from Wildenfarr a few years ago?"

In-tul-farr raised his eyebrows and recognition dawned slowly in his eyes. "Tell me not that you are one of those with whom we sang and played for a few precious and welcome days in the sands of our home?"

"The same."

"So it is that the days fall back upon themselves. We meet again, Auragole of the Gandlese. The Prince is good."

"Indeed he is, In-tul-farr. Indeed he is."

In-tul-farr clasped Auragole's shoulder and looked at him with a half smile, dropping for a moment that carefully composed countenance the people of Wildenfarr cultivated. "But look at you. You have become a man in these short, world-changing years, so tall and broad of shoulder. Recognized you would not have been, had we met without introduction. But we are well met here, are we not, young friend?"

"Well met indeed, In-tul-farr."

"And now both of us are allied to Ormahn of Mattelmead, I see. For Ormahn has acknowledged the Prince Who Walked. And for my father, that is enough."

As Auragole was standing in the reception line talking to In-tul-farr a familiar voice from behind him said, "Auragole, aren't you going to introduce us to our old friend?" He turned, and there she was, Glenelle, and with her, Glenorr. But of course she would be here. She too had known In-tul-farr. He felt the color rise in his cheeks and was glad for the soft candlelight that he hoped hid his blush. "In-tul-farr, do you remember Glenorr and his sister, Glenelle? They were with me in the desert."

In-tul-farr's eyes lit up at the sight of Glenelle. "Happy am I to greet you in this great city, for I see you are well. I hope that soon we will meet, we four, and our acquaintance renew. And where are the other two that were with you on your journeys?"

"Alas, they live most of the year in the country, and so were not able to come to this banquet in honor of you," Glenelle said, looking into In-tul-farr's eyes.

"Sylvane and Donnadorr are married now," Glenorr added.

"Ah, a happy thought. And children?"

"No, no children yet," Glenelle said. "But I shall tell you all about them at the dinner table, for I understand that Glen and I are sitting on one side of you, and Auragole on the other." She gave Auragole a dazzling smile and took her brother's arm and walked away from the reception line.

Auragole watched her as she moved off to stop at a cluster of people she knew. When he turned back to In-tul-farr, he saw In-tul-farr watching him through carefully veiled eyes. "We don't see so much of each other any longer," Auragole said, with a small shrug.

He was about to move on when Solagen, who had been standing next to In-tul-farr greeting guests, turned to him. "Auragole, you and I must meet tomorrow early while our guest, and those who accompany him, are taken on a tour of our army training grounds."

Auragole nodded and knew that Solagen would now want

that report. What would he say? Well, at least he could repeat the bare bones of the story about the "Prince Who Walked"— though much of that knowledge Solagen had heard before in his briefings about In-tul-farr.

"I hope," Solagen was saying, "that you have social time for our guest in the next few weeks, Auragole. Now that you have become reacquainted, you two no doubt have much to say to each other."

Another request from Solagen. Only this was one he would very much enjoy.

As Glenelle had said, Auragole was seated next to In-tul-farr at dinner, in the great banquet hall, and she on his other side. Well, the noise in the hall would make it impossible to carry on a three- or four-way conversation. And he couldn't avoid Glenelle forever. What did he feel at the sight of her? Other than a twinge of embarrassment, nothing, he was surprised to note. Nothing, neither pain nor anger. He breathed out a long breath. It was over. He was over her. Thank the Prince, it was done.

The well-designed banquet hall was beautifully decorated, and easily held the two hundred guests. The pillars here were all of marble, as was the floor. On the wood-paneled walls hung many, many paintings, all done by Mattelmead artists. They were of the great buildings of Mattelmead, or of the land around the city. However, on one wall was a large painting of Solagen, his current wife, and the two baby daughters she had given him.

"Beyond my grandest dreams is this city," In-tul-farr told Auragole in a low voice, his face carefully composed. "I wish my father were well enough to travel, for remember long he would this sight. But ill he is, not unto death, I think. So come I as his emissary to the great king here. But recover we must, you and I, the days that have turned since we last met. Shall we two meet in the weeks I am here?"

He was glad that In-tul-farr had not said "we four" again.

"We shall, indeed—at the request of Ormahn and to my own

joy. Tomorrow when you return from looking at our training ground I shall be here to greet you. Then we will talk, you and I."

"Ah, the Prince is good," In-tul-farr said.

"I understand that you will train Ormahn's Elite Corps in some special techniques of desert warfare."

"Asked, I have been. Therefore, willingly I shall accede."

"Then it is I whom you will train, I and my men. For I am commander of Ormahn's Elite Corps."

"Wonders increase," In-tul-far said, "in a wonder-filled world." And again the carefully schooled countenance permitted a smile to appear. He then turned to Glenelle, and Auragole turned to the woman who sat to his right.

THE NEXT MORNING Auragole met with Solagen in Solagen's private study. He told the king some of what he had seen at the little temple and what he had heard—some of the narrative that he had heard from the priest. But he withheld the fact that the priest had claimed to have researched his story directly from the spiritual world. And he withheld the parts about love and freedom and the importance of the individual. Why bring trouble down on them? They were such a small and genuinely peaceful group. He knew that Solagen believed that an individual must sublimate his individuality to the needs of the community, to the needs of the state. It made Auragole uncomfortable to withhold, but he did it anyway. He spoke at length of the Prince God as a great teacher and healer. Had he told Solagen enough to satisfy him?

"It sounds like a lot of fantastic stuff, hardly makes any sense," Solagen said.

Auragole answered carefully, "That may be so, but it certainly has nothing of the seditious in it."

"Perhaps not, but why can't they content themselves with the official temple to the Prince? That's what I would like to know. That's what that temple is there for. Swords, I've built a whole street of temples for people like them. Why can't they be satisfied? Why must they do it their own way?"

"Maybe they like it all a little simpler." Auragole almost added, "deeper," but held his tongue.

"I doubt if simplicity enters into it. That fantasy they've created about the Prince's life is certainly not simple. Can you imagine if every one of the temples had its little offshoots? It would create confusion among the people, perhaps even dissension. They would begin to feel that something was wrong with the official temples. I don't like it."

Auragole was quiet, and somewhat ill at ease.

"Have you talked to people in the congregation?"

"Not yet."

"Well, man, how long must you wait?" Solagen said, with slight irritation.

"I've only been there twice. I didn't want people to think I had some other. . .other agenda. I wanted them to think that I came merely for the satisfaction of the service."

"Stay after and talk to someone the next time."

Auragole took a deep breath. "Yes, Sire."

Solagen watched him with calculating eyes. "Too much independence is not good for the country, for its stability and for its peace, Auragole. Remember that."

Auragole nodded, and wasn't sure if Solagen meant the little temple or him.

Suddenly Solagen smiled, and it was a welcome relief. "I want to talk about In-tul-farr. Tell me again everything you know about him, his country, and his beliefs, and what you know about And-ul-farr. I know we've been over it before. But one can't be too well prepared."

chapter thirteen

FOR SEVERAL WEEKS the Elite Corps trained almost every morning with In-tul-farr and the half-dozen men he had brought with him.

Roradahl, a captain, second in command to Auragole, was fascinated with the techniques they were learning from In-tul-farr. He and his small group of men were certainly giving the Elite Corps, despite their new swords, a bit of a shaking up. Their second day at the training grounds outside the city, In-tul-farr said he wanted to show them something, and asked the others to watch while he and Auragole demonstrated.

"With bows and arrows, you will begin the battle," In-tul-farr said, so all could hear, "and most skilled you are—as are my men. But show you I must what will happen when the battle is close and of no use are bows."

"You mean when we take up our swords?" Auragole asked, but In-tul-farr did not answer him.

The two men then mounted their horses. Auragole was holding

the short, light sword that had been created for the Elite Corps. Roradahl felt sure Auragole would be able to best In-tul-farr with his new weapon, and the knife he carried inside his boot.

In-tul-farr called to Auragole to charge him.

"Where is your sword?" Auragole called back.

And indeed, Roradahl saw that In-tul-farr had no sword.

"Wait and see," In-tul-farr responded from the opposite end of the field.

What is going on? Roradahl wondered. Doesn't the man know that few on horseback can best Auragole with a sword? In-tul-farr's sword must be under the large cape he wore. Roradahl watched eagerly from the sidelines to see just what the desert prince had in mind.

The two men charged at each other. Auragole held his sword in readiness. But still no sword appeared in In-tul-farr's hand.

"Where is your sword, man?" Auragole yelled as he drew closer.

"I don't need it."

"This is foolishness," Auragole shouted as he drew nearer, waving his sword in one hand. "I could kill you easily."

As Auragole came close to In-tul-farr, ready to swat him across the chest with the flat of his sword, In-tul-farr suddenly knocked Auragole's sword out of his hand with a flick of his voluminous desert cloak. Auragole was overcome with surprise and before he recovered he was spun off his horse with another lightning maneuver of In-tul-farr's cloak.

Roradahl could hear the laughter around him. In-tul-farr leapt from his horse and reached down to help Auragole rise.

"I can stand on my own, thank you," Auragole said, ignoring In-tul-farr's hand. Roradahl heard the irritation in Auragole's voice.

"Feel no shame, Auragole of the Mountains. I have seen you in the practice field and no one can best you with bow and arrow, nor with a sword, even I who am the most skilled of my clan."

"That was remarkable," Auragole said, and Roradahl saw the irritation pass as quickly as it had come, and a smile appear on Auragole's face. Auragole got to his feet and dusted off the seat of his trousers. In-tul-farr's men gathered round, looking proud. Auragole gestured for his own men to come and join them.

"This is what you will have to contend with, if you fight in the desert, when the fighting is close and bows are of no use," In-tul-farr said, holding out his cloak. "And I will show you, all of you, how to use such a one as this."

"So, Roradahl," Auragole said, clasping him on the shoulder, "it seems we have much to learn from these guests of ours." And then, with a wide grin, he offered his hand to In-tul-farr, who took it with a rare smile of his own.

AFTER AURAGOLE'S THIRD visit to the little temple, he entered the reception room when the service was over and stood there for a moment, wondering to whom he should speak. But the priest's wife, seeing his uncertainty, came up to him. "Won't you stay and have a little breakfast with us?" she asked, gesturing at the others in the congregation who were waiting there. "And won't you meet my husband?"

"Thank you, I will."

She motioned Auragole through a door to a second room, where the breakfast was served. It was simple fare. Tea and dried fruit, bread and cheese. Auragole stood alone, tea mug in hand, ill at ease, watching the men and women clustered together in small groups. The talk in the room was subdued. Often people looked at Auragole, furtive glances, but no one approached him. He was considering leaving, despite Solagen's request, when the priest entered the room. He was tall and slender, and had a full head of light-brown hair. He was dressed now in simple, well-worn trousers and a shirt with a knitted vest over it. Auragole watched him, fascinated, as the crowd surged toward him, greeting him, asking him questions. The man looked warmly at each one who approached him, grasped his or her hand, and smiled. He listened to the questions posed him and answered briefly, often suggesting a time for a meeting. After five or six minutes of this, he lifted his eyes beyond those who hovered around him, and met Auragole's.

"But we have a guest," he said, and he walked through the group of worshippers to where Auragole was standing. All eyes were now on Auragole, and he blushed slightly. The priest walked up and offered his hand. "Welcome, welcome, sir. You have come back yet a third time, I see." He put his arm around Auragole's shoulder and led him off to a quiet corner.

"It's not every day," the priest said, his eyes kind, "that we have a commander in the king's army attending our service."

Again Auragole reddened. How did the man know that about him? Was there someone in the congregation who knew him? Someone who, perhaps, worked at the palace? How else?

"I've been to the other temples," Auragole said. "And I haven't found what I was seeking." That at least was true.

"And what is it you are seeking, sir?"

Auragole hesitated. "Knowledge," he finally answered.

"Knowledge of the Prince?" the priest asked. There was a smile on his lips, but his eyes now were probing.

Auragole looked away and didn't answer him directly. Instead he said, "I had done much traveling before arriving in Mattelmead. Among my traveling companions at various times have been those who looked into the deeper mysteries of the Prince, far deeper than what is presented at the official temple here. I am thinking now of one companion who learned about the Prince in a school in the Easternlands at Stahlowill."

"Ah, yes, the last school to teach about the Gods in the east before it finally fell."

"Yes, that's right." The man knew about that school! "Are you from the east, yourself?"

"No, I was born and raised here in Mattelmead, and I have not ventured very far from this city. I earn my keep as a shoemaker."

"Then how did you know. . .?"

The man laughed. "Many travelers come from the east to our city, is that not so?" Auragole nodded. "Shall you come again to our service, sir?"

"If you will permit me."

"We withhold nothing from a genuine seeker."

Again Auragole felt himself redden. He brushed his hair from his forehead.

"And will you offer us your name?"

"Forgive me, I am called Auragole. Auragole, son of Goloss."

"And also, Auragole of Mattelmead?"

"Yes."

"Then you are that hero of Mattelmead whom we have heard so much about?"

Auragole shrugged his shoulders. The word *hero*, in this place, made him embarrassed.

"And you are a fine singer, I understand. One who has sung with the great Lorenwile."

"Do you. . .did you know him?"

The man shook his head. "But I have heard him sing. My name is Timorr. And I welcome you, Auragole of Mattelmead. Perhaps some day you will sing for our small congregation?"

"Yes, yes, I would be happy to do that. Thank you for asking me."

Auragole left, feeling relieved. But also uneasy.

DURING THE LATE days of winter and throughout the spring, Auragole trained with In-tul-farr, and went weekly to the little temple. By the end of spring, In-tul-farr was gone, and Auragole had continued to attend the services at the temple. He had given two concerts for the congregation, and had dined at the home of Timorr, Meraleese, and their young son, Glorr. He reported his meetings to Solagen when requested, and tried to assure the king that there was nothing seditious going on there, certainly no disloyalty to the kingdom. Only a deep interest in the nature of the Gods, and in particular the Prince God.

"What harm can come to Mattelmead by such seeking?" he asked Solagen.

"That remains to be seen, Auragole. You are attracted by independence, but I tell you, too much independence can disturb the peace that we have fought so hard to bring to Mattelmead and to the west."

For that Auragole had no answer. But he found himself telling less and less of what he heard in Timorr's home and in his services, glossing over the deeper claims to knowledge the priest had said was his and was available to any who sought it.

The training for the campaign in Wildenfarr continued into late spring. The army would leave from all parts of Mattelmead and Glovale in early August for the slow march through Glovale, and assemble in the hills south of the Noonbarr River. There it would meet In-tul-farr and his army, and together march into Wildenfarr when the heat of the summer had subsided.

During the early days of summer, Auragole continued to attend the little church of Timorr and to visit with the priest's family. He was growing fond of that family and was happy to be in their company, to be away for a time from Mattelmead's society and its intrigues and pettiness. To be with this family, who lived simply, reminded him of home, of his own family. It gave him a place to breathe and it satisfied a deeper longing of his soul. Auragole brought them food, and toys for Glorr. They accepted all with thanks. Often when he left them, he would spend hours walking and thinking about the months of True-singing he had experienced with Lorenwile. How deeply he had lived into things then; how shallow, albeit interesting and of service, was his life now.

In early July, Solagen said to him, "Your independence, no doubt, has made you a good leader, Auragole. But too much independence can bring you troubles. To be plagued by war and the anarchy it brings is the world's greatest evil. Don't you agree?"

Slowly, Auragole nodded. But he caught the hard look Solagen gave him.

"You need no longer go to that little temple. We have found out what we need. I think we know quite enough about the Prince for our campaign in Wildenfarr this fall. Yes, it would be best if you did not return to that little temple."

It was with an aching heart that Auragole said, "As you wish, Sire."

"Good," Solagen said. "I am giving the officers and their men a few weeks off just before we begin our march toward Wildenfarr. I suggest you go up to your country estate then and get some rest."

So Auragole sent a message to Timorr and Meraleese saying that he was now deep in training for the next campaign, and then would spend a few weeks at his country estate. Unfortunately, he would no longer be free to come to their temple or to visit them. Along with the note, he sent a large basket of food and wine, and some clothes and toys for Glorr.

IN THE FIRST week of August, the army of Mattelmead began its long trek to the northern border of Wildenfarr. Ormahn led the army. At his side, along with a dozen commanders, were Veldarr, nephew of Ormahn, and Auragole, commander of Ormahn's Elite Corps. Goredahl, Ormahn's other nephew, remained in Mattelmead to oversee the running of the country in the king's absence.

Sometime in September, just before the battle began, Auragole passed his twenty-third birthday without marking it.

giving
and getting

PART EIGHT OF AURAGOLE'S JOURNEY
AURAGOLE OF MATTELMEAD

N

preface

IT WAS WHILE he and his party of soldiers and servants were still in the desert of Wildenfarr, but on their way home to Mattelmead, that Auragole had a dream about his father.

In the dream he was also in the desert and also asleep. In the dream he awoke and sat up. His father was calling him. He saw his father standing at the edge of the oasis where Auragole and his men were sleeping. Goloss was wearing the clothes Auragole had so often seen him wear back home in the Gandlese—well-worn clothes, often-mended clothes, the ones he had put on in the evenings after he came in from the fields.

Goloss beckoned to him.

As Auragole stood up and started toward him, his father turned and moved away from the oasis with its dim firelight. He was heading toward one of the outcroppings of rock that were everywhere in this part of the desert. Near the rocks, Goloss stopped and waited for Auragole. It seemed quite natural that he and his father should be together—as if there were no barrier between death and life. His father wanted to speak with him, so Auragole approached Goloss and waited for his father's words.

Goloss sat down on a rock and motioned Auragole to one opposite him. Above the two men the overarching sky was ablaze with stars, and a great full moon gazed down on them with an "oh" of surprise on its face. It always amazed Auragole how close to the earth the stars seemed to hang in the desert. How beautiful their designs were, the intricate script of the Gods. Up there in the starry sphere, the Creative Beings live and speak and the stars are their words, he thought, as he waited for his father to tell him why he had come.

"You are looking well, son."

"Thank you, sir. And you? Are you well?"

At first Auragole thought his father hadn't heard him. He seemed to be looking out at the moonlit desert with concentrated interest. Finally, Goloss turned to Auragole, his eyes intense, and said, "So you are part of the army that is bringing peace to the west."

"I am. Do you approve?"

Again his father did not answer, but asked a question of his own, his eyes never leaving his son's face. "Is this peace enough?"

Auragole was puzzled by the question, puzzled at the troubled expression on Goloss's face. "What do you mean, father? I don't understand your question."

At these words Goloss again looked away from his son, and again stared out at the vast desert. Long moments elapsed before Goloss spoke. And then he repeated the question. "Is this peace enough?"

"Enough for whom? The west is almost totally under the control of Ormahn of Mattelmead. He intends to bring peace to every inch of the west, and then if he is successful, and I believe he will be—for most of the people greet him gladly—he will march to the east and bring peace there. Is that not enough?

More than enough?" His tone, he realized, was defensive.

His father's look was long and unwavering. Auragole felt naked beneath that scorching gaze. What did his father want from him? Was he not proud of him? Did he not see how he was making a difference in this war-torn world that had driven his father and mother away from their home in the Easternlands into the isolation of the Gandlese Mountains?

"You will have much success in the coming years, son. But also much sadness and much trouble. You will need all your courage for those dark days—and all your wisdom." His father rose. "I am sorry I was not able to give you the understanding you will need for the momentous times to come. I was too angry in life, and that anger made me selfish. I never said this to you when I was alive, Auragole—I love you. I know it is not adequate for the hard days ahead. But it is all I have to give you. All I have to give. . ." And he looked sorrowfully at Auragole, rose, and walked away into the desert.

"Wait," Auragole called out. He started to follow him. "Wait!"

And he woke up. Someone was shaking him by the shoulder.

"What's the matter, Auragole? You called out 'Wait.' Wait for what? To whom were you speaking?" It was Roradahl.

Auragole sat up. "Sorry. It was just a dream, that's all. Nothing important." It was still dark. There was no moon—not like in his dream, just the stars hanging like lanterns close to the earth. He was glad that he lay far from the banked fire so that Roradahl could not see his face. There were tears streaming down it. "Go back to sleep," he told his friend.

And Roradahl did. But it was hours before Auragole could let go of the dream and fall asleep himself.

chapter fourteen

IT WAS THE end of March, just past the spring equinox. The snow still lay thin on the ground in Mattelmead, but there were crocuses and daffodils pushing up through the white dusting. After more than eight months away, Auragole rode up to his mansion on Starwanderer, accompanied by his servants, Lors and Semp. It was night and late. He and Roradahl and many of his Elite Corps had been riding for some weeks now, through all of Glovale, and more than half the length of Mattelmead, and finally through the city. They were back at last from Wildenfarr-low-desert.

At Ormahn's request, Auragole had remained in Wildenfarr for a time after the war had ended to help administer the newly won territory. Now he was finally home. After a long, hard, and hurried ride back, Auragole was bone weary. He felt he could sleep for a week. But his obligation was to report to the king first thing in the morning. Solagen would want to know how the government fared under the vassal kingship of Tul-farr.

First, Auragole would have to tell him that Tul-farr, ailing for years, had died, and his son In-tul-farr was now undisputed king. That would be, he thought, to Solagen's liking. Solagen knew and approved of In-tul-farr, and would be happy for his youthful and vigorous leadership.

Leaving Semp to attend to his horse, and Lors to take care of the baggage, Auragole climbed the steps to his front door and knocked loudly. After a few moments a servant opened the door. Soon the entire household was up, dozens of excited servants, preparing him dinner, readying his bedchamber, lighting candles, and kindling a fire in the hearth.

In less than half an hour Auragole lay in a hot tub, soaking away weeks of road dust and thinking about his time in the desert. The war had lasted three months and had been hotly contested. And-ul-farr had been a formidable opponent, but finally, after And-ul-farr had been killed, the opposition had collapsed. Now after nearly a century's enmity, Wildenfarr was reunited. In-tul-farr was vassal king. Auragole's own short term as overseer was over. Another officer, one who had not been in the battle, had come to take his place. After eight months' absence Auragole, along with most of the soldiers assigned to him, and all of his staff, had finally returned to Mattelmead City. He was home.

Home, he thought, looking around at the small room devoted entirely to his baths. He had never counted the rooms in his mansion. More than two dozen, he was sure, and that was not counting the servants' quarters or all the outbuildings. It was his by right of battle. He had won it by slaying Solagen's nephew Bendahl, after Bendahl had attempted to assassinate the king.

Later in his bedchamber, sitting at a table in front of the hearth with a bowl of soup, bread, and cheese in front of him, he thought once again of home. Where was his true home, the place to which he most belonged? Was it in that small, isolated valley in the Gandlese where he had been born and had lived nearly eighteen years? Now he was past twenty-three. Auragole of the Mountains, he had thought of himself back then. Or Auragole, son of Goloss. After his parents had died, Auragole had become a wanderer, encountering on his journey good friends but also foes. During that time he had thought of himself as Auragole of the Way.

And now he was. . .Auragole of Mattelmead.

He had earned that title for he was not only a citizen of that great country, he was friend to its indomitable king. And Auragole was the commander of Mattelmead's crack Elite Corps.

But Mattelmead, home? Truth was, sometimes he felt homeless. Rootless.

Living those months in Wildenfarr, in the desert amidst its stark beauty, its unadorned simplicity, its elemental way of life, he had felt almost cleansed of encumbrances. And for a while he had liked that. But in the end it hadn't been enough, so he was glad when his replacement had come and he was freed from that responsibility. For a few crazy hours, after taking leave of In-tul-farr, he had thought of not returning to Mattelmead, of sending his men on ahead and making his way to the Gandlese Mountains and to the Valley of the Agavi, of seeking out his cousins, the Lady Claregole and Galavi, of finding Lorenwile again. Of becoming Auragole of the Songs. No, not Auragole of the Songs, Auragole, True-singer. He had thought of True-singing often while living in the desert. To roam the desert with Lorenwile, to True-sing that remarkable wilderness. . .wouldn't that have been something?

There had been times when he had been tempted to ride off by himself and try it. But he hadn't. No, he hadn't. Not only because Lorenwile had warned him not to True-sing anywhere, but because he no longer felt he had the right. He had given that up to become Ormahn's man. And how could he show up in Agavia, even if the fantasy had stayed with him for more than those few hours? Would he be welcome in Agavia now that Lorenwile had come to distrust him? That thought still cut into his heart like a dagger.

So he had honored his commitment to Ormahn, and had returned like a good soldier to Mattelmead City to continue the work for peace and order in the Westernlands. He had to face the truth squarely, had to let go of this obsessive longing. He would never become a True-singer. He had lost that chance—no, had given it up. And now Lorenwile was gone. Off to the Valley of the Agavi with Meekelorr and the Companions of the Way to await there the Last Battle, which, Auragole was sure, would never take place because of Ormahn of Mattelmead.

Surely that was something to be proud of. He, Auragole, had helped save the future for that remarkable people, the Agavians. The Last Battle was no longer needed because Solagen had brought peace to the entire Westernlands. . .well, almost the entire Westernlands. There was still Isofed, but the Isofedians bothered no one. They were an insular people, fighting only to keep others from their borders, fighting only to keep their ancient religion—one devoted to the King God—from becoming contaminated by those who were not of their blood. Perhaps Ormahn could negotiate a treaty with that people.

Auragole ate a little of his supper and climbed into bed. Auragole of Mattelmead, that's who he was now, and why not? He had been asked by Solagen to lift his eyes a little higher than his own personal life fulfillment. And Auragole had accepted Solagen's challenge. Auragole was now a leader of men and a warrior. He had, in fact and to his surprise, liked it—liked leading, liked the battles with their heightened energy, even their sense of terror. He liked the victories and the winning, liked the enhanced feeling of power battle gave him, liked driving himself to the edge yet keeping his balance, liked also the accolades. But most of all, he loved the great ideals of peace and order—Ormahn's ideals. He loved the sense of having made a difference, of having in fact changed the world. Surely this was the task he had been longing for since childhood.

So why these silly, almost childish worries about who he was and to what place he belonged? He was Auragole of Mattelmead, friend and servant to Solagen, the king of Mattelmead, who was now overking of Glovale, Thorensphere, Noonbarr, the Sorren Heights, and Wildenfarr-low-desert. And Auragole had helped bring that about. Auragole was a commander in Ormahn's great army. That's who he was—and it was enough, had to be enough. "Yes," he should have said to his father in that dream, "peace is enough. Better than enough. It's the best the Westernlands has ever known."

He would stop spiraling around in this soul muck. It was time to sleep. Tomorrow he must report to the king.

"BUT WHY NOT attempt a treaty?" Auragole asked at the council meeting a couple of weeks later. "Isofed is not out to conquer anyone's territory. Its people have never challenged us, never obstructed Mattelmead's progress toward unifying the west."

"Because they have an enormous army," Goredahl spun out his words slowly as if to impress Auragole with the idiocy of Auragole's stance, "the largest standing army of any of the countries we have conquered, and they are the best trained of any army we have met in battle. Just because they've made no attempt to fight us doesn't mean that they won't try it if we get too complacent."

"Then what do you suggest, Goredahl?" asked Solagen, sitting at the head of the table.

"We fight, that's what I suggest. This summer."

"Why rush headlong into a fight, cousin?" Veldarr, with half-hooded eyes and slouching in his chair, asked. "Why not first try to negotiate a treaty, as Auragole here suggests?"

"You are ever wanting to take the easy way, Veldarr,"

Goredahl said. "Does your stomach fail you at the prospect of another battle, this final one before all the west is ours?"

Veldarr merely chuckled.

Auragole spoke up then. "Veldarr makes sense. Our army has marched out year after year to do battle. Our soldiers are brave, but also exhausted. If there is a better way, why not take it? Must we always take the most arduous approach? Give the valiant men of our army some rest, a time to be with their families. Should men's lives be wasted needlessly, in a war that may not be necessary?"

"What exactly are you suggesting, Auragole?" Solagen asked him.

"I'm suggesting that we send an envoy to the leaders in Isofed. Tell them that we will leave their land in peace, if they acknowledge the overkingship of Ormahn of Mattelmead, acknowledge they are now a vassal nation and owe tribute to the king yearly. Some proposal like that."

"And that they retire their army, keeping only, say, ten percent of their men on duty," Veldarr added.

"They won't agree to that," Goredahl scoffed.

"How do we know if we don't try?" another commander said.

"Goredahl is right. They won't disperse their army. They'll tell us they will, but how can we trust them?" someone else said.

"We'll have to keep an administrator there and an occupying army to make sure they do," a third said.

"They'll never agree to that," Auragole said. "They won't let foreigners touch the soil of their land for fear that outsiders would contaminate the land consecrated to the King God. They're more fanatical about their God than And-ul-farr was about his. If we tried to enter their land, it would be all-out war. They won't stop fighting until every one of them is dead—man, woman, and child."

"There, you see," Goredahl said. "How can we negotiate with a people who will not allow any oversight of their land? To trust them would be foolhardy."

The argument went on for another hour. When the conference was called to a close, nothing had been decided. The argument, Auragole thought with fatigue, would go on for a few more weeks until it was resolved by Solagen's decision.

AFTER HIS RETURN from Wildenfarr, Auragole moved slowly back into the social life of the city. Once again he was much sought after by society. He attended parties, listened to music at the concert hall, and went to look at art in the galleries around the artists' quarters. He went to poetry readings in the teahouses. Often Auragole met with the officers of the army at their clubs and talked about the war that had just passed. He rode and hunted with them in the king's forest some miles east of the city. He gave parties and amused himself with the ladies. He spent a few mornings a week training with his Elite Corps. He refurbished his wardrobe, much of which was now too small.

He sang for Solagen less and less. Ormahn was busy and seldom called on him for what he referred to as "entertainment." Auragole sang occasionally all alone in his room, but it was not satisfying without an audience to hear him, even an audience of one. He never sang for the women who came and went in his life. He wasn't sure why.

One evening, about a month after he had returned from the desert, Auragole was dressing to go out to a party. As Lors was buttoning Auragole's vest there was a tentative knock on his bedchamber door.

"Come in," he called.

A man who worked in the kitchen stood there, twisting his apron in his hands.

"What is it?" Auragole asked, turning his head to look at him.

"Begging your pardon, sir, but there's a woman come to the back door and she begs you come to the kitchen and speak with her."

"A woman? What woman of my acquaintance would come looking for me at the kitchen door?" Auragole asked, somewhat amused. "Give her some food and send her away."

The servant had turned to go when Auragole called out, "Wait. Did she say what she wanted to talk to me about?"

"No, sir, but she says she knows you and begs that you come and speak to her."

"Well, did she at least give a name?"

"Yes, sir. She said she is called Meraleese."

"Meraleese," Auragole repeated, startled. He moved away from Lors, who was still working on his buttons. Auragole felt a twinge of guilt. He had hardly thought about the woman, or her husband, Timorr, since he had gone off to war. The little temple to the Prince God. . .how easily he had set aside those times he had spent with the priest and his family. How easily he had forgotten the remarkable, the comforting hours spent in their little temple. But Solagen had told him to stop going there, and he had stopped, had driven the desire right out of his mind. That was an uncomfortable thought.

"Show the lady into the small drawing room. I'll be down as soon as I've finished dressing. And do send us some tea and cakes or sandwiches."

Fifteen minutes later, Auragole, dressed elegantly for a dinner party, entered the small drawing room. Meraleese was standing near the hearth staring into the flames, and apparently hadn't heard him enter. He stood just inside the doorway looking at her. How plain she was, Auragole thought, how drawn and thin. How different from the ladies he had grown used to—those society women with their elegant gowns that enhanced their figures, with their elaborate hairdos and their painstaking makeup. This was someone simply attired—with no makeup, no jewels except for her wedding ring. Her thick, long brown hair was piled haphazardly upon her head, as if she had thrust it up there with little thought, and with only a few hairpins. Something stirred in him. She seemed acutely vulnerable, unpretentious—and somehow real.

"Meraleese?"

She turned a pale face to him then; her hands flew to her mouth. Her large, hazel eyes were wide with anxiety, and she looked as if she were about to faint. Alarmed, he rushed to her side and helped her into a chair, then bent over her. Her hair slipped out of its precarious bondage and fell down her back and the sides of her face. Before he could ask her what ailed her, a maid from the kitchen entered and placed a tray with tea and cakes on a table. Auragole straightened up. The maid gave the two of them a peculiar look that Auragole did not fail to catch. Damn the servants, he thought, and damn their snobbery and their judgments. He dismissed the maid, who had remained, ready to pour the tea and serve the cakes, then watched until she had closed the door behind her. He turned back to Meraleese.

"Are you all right?" Auragole asked.

"I. . .I. . .yes," she whispered.

He sat across from her, poured her a cup of tea, and pushed the cup toward her. Meraleese picked it up with shaky hands and drank from it, a few long draughts, as if she had an unquenchable thirst. Or perhaps to put off the moment of speaking. Finally she placed the cup back in the saucer. Auragole offered her the plate of cakes but she refused them.

Her voice was barely audible when she spoke. "Forgive me for coming, Auragole. But I have no one else to whom I can turn." She breathed in as if to stifle a sob.

"What is it, Meraleese? Tell me."

"You've heard what has happened to the temple. . ."

"The temple?"

She looked up, pushing strands of hair out of her face, and peered at him. "But surely you have heard what happened?"

He shook his head.

"I know you were away, but I thought that by now you knew. . ." There were two small lines between her brows.

"Knew what, Meraleese? I've been gone a long time and haven't caught up on all the news."

"They closed it down."

"Who closed it down?"

She swallowed hard, picked up the teacup, took a sip, and said, "The Security Forces. While you were away at war. While Solagen was away at war. They came, tore down the altar, took away the candelabra and candlesticks and the wine cup, my husband's books. . ." Her hands were trembling, so she carefully put the fine china cup down on the table.

Auragole felt a tremor of shock.

"You didn't know?"

He shook his head again. Goredahl. He had been in charge of the country while Solagen was gone. This was obviously the work of Goredahl. Ever-vigilant, ever-worried Goredahl. What harm did he think these people could have done to the state?

"But that's not the worst of it," and now she began to sob. With a sense of foreboding, he pulled out his handkerchief, leaned forward, and handed it to her. She took it. "Forgive me, but I'm so bereft, and have been unable to do anything all these long months, not anything."

He waited while she wiped her eyes. He could feel apprehension growing inside himself, and anger.

"They've imprisoned my husband."

"Imprisoned him? When?"

"About a month after the army left."

"But that's eight months ago!"

"Yes."

"On what charges?"

"Sedition," she said.

"Sedition? That's insane."

She nodded and the tears flowed from her eyes as she tried to stifle the sobs.

"Have you heard from him?"

Meraleese shook her head.

"Do you know where he is?"

"No. Possibly in the main prison here in the city, but by now he could be. . .maybe in one of the work camps. I'm not sure. That's what I was hoping you might find out. That and. . ." And now she buried her head in her hands, and her shoulders shook uncontrollably.

Auragole came quickly to his feet, moved around the table that had divided them, and knelt by her chair. He pulled her hands away, brushed the hair gently from her face, and lifted her chin up so he could see her eyes. They were large in that tiny countenance and overflowing with tears. "Tell me the worst of it, Meraleese, and I promise I'll do what I can to help."

"They've taken my son."

"What? What do you mean, they've taken your son?" He leapt up, her words shocking him into movement. He began to pace.

"They said I was an unfit mother, and so they took my son and placed him in some orphanage. I don't know where." She sobbed and sobbed, hands once again covering her face.

"Unconscionable. Goredahl. If Solagen had been here, none of this would have happened. Well, we'll see about this. Taking away your son." He could feel the fury inside him rising as he strode about the room.

The woman broke off her sobbing to watch him. "Please, please, Auragole, do nothing that will bring trouble down upon yourself. You must be careful. I had only hoped for a discreet inquiry. I wouldn't want to see you end up in that awful prison."

"Nothing will happen to me, Meraleese. I'm a friend to our king. And he's a good man. He just wasn't here." Auragole crouched down beside her again.

"Many have ended up in that prison. Others who have been close to the king."

"Well, it won't happen to me, if that's what you're worried about."

She shook her head. "Listen to me, Auragole. You must be careful. Please. I haven't come here to cause you trouble. I. . .I just didn't know to whom. . . Timorr and I knew you were ordered first to come and then not to come to our temple."

Auragole's face colored. "You think I had something to do with this dreadful business?" The thought that she might horrified him, and it must have shown on his face.

"No, no. That never occurred to. . . Therefore, you must take care."

"Please don't worry about me, Meraleese. It's not necessary. I've been at the court long enough to be aware of the intrigues there. I've stayed out of them. No one there has any fear of me."

She looked at him dubiously. "I wouldn't want to endanger you in any way, Auragole. It's just that I was hoping you might find out which prison, or work camp, my husband is in, and if he is faring all right. And. . .and where my son is."

Auragole nodded and drew her from her chair. "Tell me where you are staying."

"I still have my house. I. . .I don't know for how long."

"But what do you live on?"

"Friends bring me food."

"Come with me to the kitchen. You shall have half my pantry. Then I'll send you home in my carriage."

"No, no. That would be very unwise." She pulled back from him in alarm. "No one must know I came here. I've been very careful."

"Nonsense. . ."

But she shook her head.

"Look." He took her by the arm again, and led her gently to the door. "If I can't persuade you to take some food, let me give you some money. You can't live without money."

She hesitated.

"Good, that's all decided. Come with me."

THE PARTY THAT night was tedious. Auragole sat in a corner most of the evening drinking wine and thinking about what Meraleese had told him. The rage kept rising up into his throat, unabated by the wine. He could barely wait until the next day when he would confront Goredahl in the palace.

Later, when he returned home, he knew he had been rude to more than one lady. Tonight he would sleep alone. And with that he was content.

N

chapter fifteen

"BY WHAT RIGHT do you question me, Auragole, and in such a tone?"

"By my right as a commander in the army of Ormahn of Mattelmead, by my right as a citizen of Mattelmead."

"A citizen of Mattelmead?" Goredahl stood up behind his desk, put his hands on his hips, and gave Auragole a sour smile. "As a citizen you have no rights other than what Ormahn says you have or, in his place, I say you have."

"That was a harmless little temple, with a congregation of only a handful of peace-loving individuals, who only longed to understand the Prince God better."

"There is an official temple to the Prince provided for the people by Ormahn. Those who go their own way, Auragole, Song Singer," and he spat out those words as if they were distasteful, "are a danger to the state. If they want to worship some God or other, fine and good, but not in a way that makes God more important than the king."

"This is nonsense, Goredahl. . ."

"Oh, is it?" Goredahl's words were high-pitched and filled with irritation. "And who are you to say so?"

"I say so because I know that family, those people. I spent time with them, as you recall—no doubt at your request. And I tell you, as I told the king, they are a harmless lot. Why did you ask me to go there, if you paid no heed to what I found out?"

"You think your judgment infallible, Auragole? Well, internal security is my affair. And I say they were not harmless. Why, that congregation looked up to that priest as if he were a God himself, or even a king. They would have followed him anywhere. . ."

"A handful of people? What could they do against the army of Mattelmead?"

"There is only one king here, and that is Solagen."

"That's right," Auragole said. "And I shall take this matter to Solagen."

"It won't do you any good."

Auragole stopped at the door and turned to look at him.

Goredahl sat down again. "He already knows. And besides, the priest is dead."

"What?" Auragole moved toward Goredahl.

Goredahl pulled a drawer open and lifted a knife out and held it loosely in his hands. "You'd better leave now, Auragole. There are things I know about you that could cause you trouble if the king were told."

Auragole stopped in his tracks. "What are you talking about?"

"All the things you withheld from the king, such as your true relationship to that rebel band called the Companions of the Way and to its leader. How much time you spent with them. Many things."

Auragole advanced again, his fists clenched. He could feel the blood throb in his temples, his face redden.

"And what about Lorenwile? Both you and I know he was a

spy and a traitor. If the king knew that, how safe would your own position be? You might end up in prison yourself. Others have for less."

"You bastard," was all Auragole said. He wheeled about and stormed out of the room before he completely lost his temper and did something rash. He would speak to Solagen himself.

"PERHAPS GOREDAHL IS a little overzealous, I agree, Auragole," Solagen said, when Auragole had told his story. Auragole had waited outside Solagen's office for almost two hours before the king could spare him a few minutes. "Granted, he might not have acted so hastily if I had been here. But what's done is done. That temple is not needed. Best that it's closed down."

"But why take the child away from his mother? That seems inexcusably cruel." Auragole was standing in front of Solagen's desk, leaning toward him.

"Sit down, Auragole. Don't hover over me like a bird of prey."

Auragole sat down, and the king eyed him soberly.

"Do you see these papers piled up on my desk? From all over the United West. Decisions have to be made that concern the running of Glovale, Noonbarr—every conquered country. And as you know, Auragole, there are great and weighty matters to consider now—foremost the problem of Isofed. And each matter waits on my will and my resolution. Can I worry about every child and mother in the empire?" Solagen didn't wait for Auragole's answer. "Obviously not. That's why I've delegated the responsibility for many duties to others. Yours is to keep the Elite Corps battle ready and able to respond at a moment's notice. Veldarr's is to oversee the regular army. The list of delegations goes on and on. Oldwell, a good commander and a good doctor, trains and oversees the assignments of men who can care for the injured in battle. It is Goredahl's duty to handle internal security. And he does a good job with it, for all that he is as fastidious as an old aunt. My advice to you is to leave this matter alone. I told you to stay away from that family and that temple months ago. Why are you mixing in now?"

"The woman came to me. . ."

"Auragole, I will not have dissension or open quarrels among my commanders. Let each do the job I've given him, and let each respect and not interfere with the job another is doing. Now, I've given you all the time I can." He rose, walked around his desk, clasped Auragole on the shoulder, and led him to the door. "But I'll see you tonight at the dinner party I'm giving for the trade delegation from Noonbarr. We haven't heard you play in a long time, and we're looking forward to that. This other matter, Auragole, leave alone." He looked sternly at Auragole.

And Auragole knew that this was more than a request.

"Yes, Sire," he said, and turned and walked out of the office.

LATER, AURAGOLE STOOD before the fireplace in his room, staring at the flames, trying to think. Solagen liked him. But Solagen was not a man to cross. However, Timorr the priest was dead—and though Auragole had been forbidden by Solagen to involve himself with the priest's family, he would have to inform Meraleese. How could he not? But it couldn't be tonight. Tonight he must sing for the king. And he must sing well. There were members of Solagen's own family whom the king had imprisoned or exiled, for who knew what offense. Auragole would have to tread carefully.

And that was a new idea. Meraleese had known and had warned him.

Was he afraid? The thought disgusted him. He had known for a long time that Goredahl disliked him. It had never troubled him before. Goredahl disliked many people. And what did his threats mean? It must have been Veldarr who had told Goredahl stories about him. Facts he had gotten from Glenelle. How much had Veldarr repeated to Goredahl? But why would he say anything to Goredahl? It was common knowledge that there was no love lost between the two cousins, that both were rivals for the throne. Or had the information come to Goredahl directly from Glenelle? Well, that would be like Glenelle, making certain she was friend to any man who in the future might be king. He wondered if Veldarr or Glenelle had told Goredahl also about Agavia. Why had Goredahl, who apparently knew things about Auragole, withheld what he knew from Solagen? For some devious plan of his own, no doubt. Knowledge he would use when it suited him.

Well, Auragole had certainly increased the enmity between them. He pounded his fist into his hand, then began pacing about his bedchamber. How he loathed all these machinations. Goredahl was probably the most powerful man in Mattelmead, next to the king. He was more ambitious than his cousin, Veldarr, which was probably lucky for Veldarr. Solagen would not interfere with Goredahl in matters he thought were minor. To Solagen one man and his wife and child were minor when looked at in the context of his great vision.

Auragole would have to see Meraleese, and the thought filled him with dread, even with shame. He was bringing her terrible news about her husband and had found out nothing about her son. What could he do now, when the king had refused him help? How could he find out anything about Glorr? And do it discreetly? He didn't know where to begin. The only one of his acquaintances who knew anything about orphanages was Sylvane.

Sylvane!

It had been a long, long time since he had seen her or Don, and he had written to them only once while he was away in Wildenfarr. He would sit down that very minute and write a letter to her.

No. He had better not put any of his questions in writing.

Auragole paced around his bedchamber, from hearth to wall to window to wall. A visit. Yes, that would be good. He would go visit the two of them at their country estate as soon as the council had decided what to do about Isofed. He would write them today, but the letter would contain only a request for a visit when Auragole's work here was done. Nothing suspicious about wanting to see old friends. No hasty departure. A leisurely decision for a time in the near future. Nothing to connect that visit with this matter of the priest and his family. Auragole would have to be careful now. Meraleese had been more astute than he. He must keep up his old life as if he hadn't a care in the world. He must do nothing to arouse suspicion. Was it possible that Goredahl could destroy the king's trust in him? Not now, he thought. Not yet. After all, hadn't he saved Ormahn's life? Goredahl would not act against him without the king's permission. Against those who held no position in society or at the court, yes, but not against him. An unwanted stone came and lodged itself in Auragole's stomach. For the first time since coming to Mattelmead, he felt uneasy, even vulnerable. But this is foolishness, he thought.

IT TOOK AN effort of will, but with the concentration born of True-singing, Auragole sang well for Ormahn and his guests that night. Auragole then flirted with the ladies, and even took one home with him. If Goredahl watched him, it was no doubt with satisfaction. He must certainly have thought that he had Auragole cowed.

THE NEXT NIGHT, after attending a party, Auragole returned home without a woman in tow. When the servants were in bed, and all the lights in the house and stable were out, he dressed in dark clothes, slipped out the kitchen door, and on foot made his way to Meraleese's house. It was a long walk. But he didn't want to arouse any suspicions by taking his horse out of the stable. He stayed out of streets that might be filled with night revelers. He trod lightly, something he had learned from his father when they were tracking game. And he kept his eyes and ears open. There was no one following him. Goredahl had not put a watch on him. Not yet. Not, he hoped, while he was still a favorite of the king.

It was nearly two o'clock when he arrived at Meraleese's house. There was no light coming from the shuttered windows. He tried the front door, but it was locked. So he tapped softly. There was no answer. He didn't dare knock louder and alert the neighbors. He walked around to the back door. It too was locked, so he knocked again. And waited. No answer. He would have to get in somehow. Through a window, perhaps. He moved stealthily around the house, trying one after the other of the windows on the ground floor. All were locked. However, in the back there was a tree with branches that overhung a small porch, and on that porch was a door leading to the second story of the house. If he could climb onto that. . . He circled the tree and found that with a running jump he could reach its lowest branch. He climbed into the tree, moving as quietly as he had done as a child looking for birds' eggs. With great care he made his way up and around the tree until he came to the branch hanging above the upstairs porch. He slid out on it and dropped as silently as he could onto the porch. There, to his relief, he found the door unlatched. He opened it and let himself into the upstairs hall. He knew where he was now. The nearly full moon cast its light like a beacon into the hallway where he stood. This level held the rooms where the family had lived. The first level had been converted into a chapel and meeting rooms. He walked past the door that led to the dining/sitting room, past the one to the kitchen. At the end of the hall were two rooms, one that led to Glorr's room and one that led to Timorr's and Meraleese's bedchamber. He knocked loudly on her door. From inside the room, he heard an intake of breath, but no answering call.

"Meraleese, it's Auragole. Please don't be frightened."

In a few moments, the door opened and Meraleese stood before him, a shawl over her nightgown, her feet bare, her thick, brown, sleep-tousled hair hanging below her shoulders. Her eyes, in the moonlight, were huge and filled with anxiety and uncertainty. She didn't say anything but waited, her hand on the doorknob.

"Forgive me for coming to you in the middle of the night, but I thought it was best to be discreet."

She said nothing, but searched his face.

"Meraleese, may I come in, or will you come out to the sitting room?"

She walked past him then, down the hall, into the sitting room. She was about to light a candle when he said, "Don't do that. Don't do anything you wouldn't ordinarily do."

The sitting room was dark. Heavy drapes covered the windows. He walked to the window and pulled the drapes open a few inches, to let some moonlight in.

"Let's sit on the sofa, Meraleese. I've come with news."

They groped their way to the sofa and sat. Soon his eyes adapted to the dark. He could just make out the features of her face several inches from his own, but not its expression. He sat there unable to speak, struggling to find words that would temper the dreadful news he had brought.

It was Meraleese who broke the silence. "Timorr is dead, isn't that so, Auragole?"

He didn't answer immediately.

"Auragole?"

"How did you know?"

"Timorr was so much a part of me that when he was gone, truly gone, I felt it. And then, he has come so often to me in my dreams. . ." Her voice broke and she began to sob. For a moment he sat there frozen, shut out of her pain. And then he took her in his arms. She buried her face in his shoulder and cried and cried. He stroked her hair and said soothing, meaningless things. "It's all right, Merry," he said, calling her by the pet name her husband had used when he spoke to her. "It's all right. I'll help you. It will be all right."

Finally, the tears subsided and she sat up. "When," she asked, "when did my husband die?"

"I'm not sure, but not long after he was taken, I suspect."

"So now I know truly what my heart has known and wanted to deny for so long. I shall begin the prayers for the dead for him. . ." she hesitated, "as soon as I'm alone. But tell me. . . Glorr, have you found out anything about him?"

"Not yet. But I'm working on that. Don't give up hope. I have a plan for finding out. Meraleese, I'll need to come to you again. But I must come in secret."

"Ah." And he could almost see her nod.

"Are you afraid to leave a window unlatched downstairs?" He rose.

"No. There's nothing to fear from my neighbors—only from the Security Forces. And if they come, they will kick down the door. No lock will stop them."

Auragole rose then, feeling ashamed. He must be careful not to bring more trouble down on this woman. "Meraleese, I hope you know that I had nothing to do with this."

"I know," she said.

"Do you have enough money? Enough food?"

"I have enough."

"I'll leave you a little money anyway. I don't know how soon I can get back. But as soon as I have news, I'll come to you. I ask you to be patient."

"Yes. Thank you." She offered him her hand. The slender smallness of it filled him with an unexpected poignancy. "Auragole?"

"Yes?" He tried to see her face, her eyes.

"Be careful."

"I will," he said, and hurried out of the room, down the stairs, and out the front door.

As he walked home through the dark streets, the feeling of shame never left him. Had his reports to Solagen contributed to the closing of the temple and the imprisonment of its priest? He had told Solagen there was nothing to fear from the little congregation. He had gone there merely to help Solagen obtain more information about the Prince God, so Solagen would better understand his ally, Tul-farr, and his enemy, And-ul-farr.

He had told Meraleese that he was not culpable in the death of Timorr. But perhaps Meraleese, in her heart, blamed him. Perhaps she had turned to him only in desperation.

Auragole despised Goredahl for the work he did. But was he, Auragole, any better? Had he overlooked too much in an attempt to please Solagen? Had he given up too much in his desire to see peace and order come to the Grand Continent, to stop once and for all the wars that for centuries had destroyed countries, cultures, destroyed so much knowledge, and worst of all, had turned humans into little more than animals? Had he given up too much?

Peace and order.

Surely those were admirable goals, great goals even. Why couldn't he be satisfied with that, as others were in Mattelmead? He had no answer. When he finally crawled into his bed, he took the shame of Meraleese's plight with him, and couldn't sleep.

TWO NIGHTS LATER, he returned to Meraleese's home, bringing with him a basket of food. As had been planned, a ground-floor window was unlatched. Again he knocked on her bedchamber door and she followed him into the sitting room.

"I haven't any news to offer you yet, Meraleese, but I do have a plan. However, it will take a little time. I. . .I just wanted to see how you were faring." He pointed to the basket. "I brought you some food and money."

"That's very kind of you. I'm doing as well as can be expected. I have many friends. . . They are all now saying the prayer for the dead for my husband. That's quite helpful, you know, for the dead on their journey—these prayers of love. It's like, well, it's like this." And she lifted up the cover on the basket that sat on the sofa between them. "It's like food."

"Is it possible. . . I mean, could you teach me that prayer?"

She was silent.

"Or is that inappropriate? I mean a prayer from me. Would it be offensive to him. . .to you?"

"No, no. Not at all. Well, yes, I can teach it to you, if you'd like."

"I would."

And so she recited the prayer. After a few times through, he knew it. He had always been quick to memorize, even as a child.

"How often should I say this?" he asked her.

"Well, perhaps once in the morning and then once again at night."

"Good. I'll do that."

THE ARGUMENTS ABOUT Isofed were becoming more heated. The council itself was divided almost equally in its opinions. Most of the time, Solagen listened. In the end, the choice would be his. Auragole longed for the decision to be reached. He wanted to leave for his visit to Sylvane and Donnadorr. He wanted somehow to help Meraleese find news of her son. He didn't allow himself to think what he would do about it after that. First he had to obtain the news. That's what he would concentrate on. One step at a time.

He found himself going often to visit the woman. He didn't know how she felt about the visits, but he went anyway.

They would sit in the parlor and talk, often about her husband's beliefs, for that seemed to bring her comfort. In return, Auragole spoke to her of what he had learned about the

Gods from Pohl in Agavia, from Meekelorr, and from Elarr. He had told most of it before, sitting around their kitchen table when Timorr was alive and Auragole still permitted to visit the little temple. But he had to offer her something. In her bereavement he wasn't going to talk about the campaign that had ended only months before, or his part in it. And he certainly wasn't going to talk about those inconsequential things he bantered about with the other ladies he knew.

Meraleese listened to all he had to say—politely, he thought, because he couldn't see her face. Often her comment would be, "Yes, so my husband saw, and so also I think." One night Meraleese asked, "You've been to the official temples?"

"Yes," Auragole said.

"What troubled my husband and caused him to begin our little congregation was that the official temples speak only vaguely about the Gods, only vaguely about a higher world. Mostly the priests tell people to obey the law, and to follow and be grateful to Ormahn. They know little of the true reality. They don't speak about a world that works into our own. A Creative World."

"No."

Auragole had first come partly out of guilt, bringing food and money, and partly to help console Timorr's widow. But more and more it became about their conversations. Auragole was reluctant to admit it, but it had been a long time since he had really talked earnestly with a woman. Not since his travels with Affredda and Elarr. Not since—yes, he had to say it—not since his affair with Glenelle. But then it was he who had done most of the talking. The women he knew in the city, the society women, loved to gossip, to speak about fashion, about the latest theater piece, the latest dance concert, the newest entertainment club, who was sleeping with whom amongst their acquaintances. He found the women amusing, many of them beautiful, many satisfactory sexual partners.

But this woman, this plain woman, with her lovely, gentle voice, sat with him in the dark and talked about things that seemed so vast and so deep in their implications that all other conversations he had had with women paled. He hadn't intended to, but soon he was speaking about his childhood, his travels, even his sojourn in Agavia. She listened intently and asked many questions.

"They believe that in their valley and its surrounding hills," Auragole told her, "a Last Battle will take place."

"A Last Battle? And who will fight in this Last Battle?" she asked.

"The Agavians, for that is the destiny that has been awaiting them for thousands of years. The Companions of the Way—I told you about them. Some others."

"And against whom will they fight?"

"Against an incarnated evil God that the Agavi call the Dark Breather, and the Companions call the Nethergod or the Adversary God."

"Ah, yes, that would be the Destroyer God that my husband spoke of. One of the two evil beings who have set themselves up against the evolution of humanity."

"Yes, yes, that is what is taught in the Last School, and also by Pohl and Meekelorr. That is what is believed by all the Companions."

"The Destroyer God and the Deceiver God," Meraleese commented.

"The Deceiver God. . . That would be probably the Light Eater of the Agavians."

"And when is this Last Battle supposed to take place?"

"Soon. For years they've been searching for the one who is the Nethergod. They are convinced he is incarnate now. Yet he will seem only a man, like all others, living somewhere near a seat of power—so Meekelorr and Pohl both believed, and so did my dear friend Elarr."

"Yes, my husband saw that, too, felt that his incarnation would be in our times. Thought even. . ." she hesitated.

"Thought what, Meraleese?"

"Thought that he might be someone here in Mattelmead, at the court of Ormahn."

The idea pained Auragole. It had been a long time since he had entertained the possibility that Ormahn or someone at the court might be the Nethergod, for he truly didn't want to believe in the Nethergod's existence. And yet he knew that Lorenwile had thought it possible. That was why Lorenwile had been in Mattelmead. And Meekelorr too had thought it a good possibility. "Who? Did Timorr say?"

She shook her head.

"But surely not Ormahn. Look at what he's done in a few short years. Look at the peace he's bringing to the people of the west. Why would your Destroyer God incarnate here? Better somewhere else where there is still war and still chaos."

"And where is that now, Auragole?"

He was silent for a moment. The entire west, save Isofed, was under the control of Ormahn of Mattelmead. "Perhaps, now that there is almost complete peace in the west, the Nethergod will incarnate in the Easternlands where there are still terrible troubles and anarchy."

She didn't answer him.

"You don't think so, do you?" he said.

"I don't know. But if the Destroyer God is to wield great influence, if he is to corrupt humanity, would it not make sense that he be near a seat of power, even the seat of power?"

"A seat of power, yes, I give you that. But not this seat of power, no, I can't believe that."

There was silence for a moment, and then Auragole went on. "If Ormahn can complete his conquest of the Westernlands, then perhaps he will turn to the Easternlands and also begin to bring his peace there. If he does that, the plans of the Nethergod could be foiled, and there will be no need for a Last Battle. Ormahn's determination and opposition could simply undo the Destroyer God's original plans."

"Is that what you believe, Auragole?"

"Yes." But did he?

"I know nothing of a Last Battle, but this is what I believe, Auragole; that despite the terrible times we live in, we have the ability to be a single self, to be free from the wholeness of the community, all because of the Prince God. Only a free human being can love, truly love, another human being, or God—even love his or her own self."

"I have heard this—more than once. But that love is so lofty, it hardly seems achievable."

"But it is achievable. It must be achieved." Her words were almost a cry. "Why else has your Adversary God come if not to counter this freedom, this love? But sadly, most human beings are unaware of what is possible—and this was my husband's great sorrow. Therefore the Destroyer God could succeed."

"Then you also believe that, to turn humans away from their rightful path, the Nethergod must corrupt humans, must bend them to his will," Auragole said.

"I do. Do you think that human beings are not corruptible?"

He didn't answer her.

"So why not here in Mattelmead, Auragole? I know that there is much to admire in this land. But is there freedom in Mattelmead?"

He made himself think about freedom as she spoke of it, and thought then how his father had valued it—perhaps above all other things. Then he thought how he had felt himself to be free—until he had joined Ormahn's army. Had his so-called freedom been more than mere dream? And where was his freedom now, when he had to sneak around to visit a woman because he had been forbidden to do so?

"Is this peace enough?" his father had asked him in a dream.

His father had longed for peace. But his father had also longed for something else, a gift he wanted to give his son, a virtue he had tried his best to instill in him as he grew up. The desire for freedom. What about freedom? Where did freedom fit into these great ideals of Solagen's? Auragole feared it didn't fit in, at least not now. But first things first. Surely someday, after the wars were over and peace reigned. . .

"What about peace and order, Meraleese? Where do these belong in your God's plan?"

"You tell me about peace and order. Tell me about their cost," she said.

And he was once more silent.

Is this peace enough?

IT WAS AT the end of May that Solagen finally called a halt to the conferences on Isofed.

"Done," he said. "I have listened and listened and have found merit on both sides. This, however, is my decision. We will not go to war this summer or this year. I agree that our men have had enough of war. And as Isofed has made no aggressive moves against us or its neighbors, let all our soldiers rest. Let them train minimally. Let our commanders visit their country estates and one another's. At summer's end, I will send an emissary to Isofed asking for a meeting to be held halfway between us—say, somewhere in Glovale—before the winter snows. I will go there myself, with a party of officers and soldiers. Who of you will be in that party, that I will decide later. I, too, will take my wife and my daughters and go to our country home for the summer. I must confess, I am bone weary of war and talk of war. I want to hunt and fish, and look upon faces other than the ones I see here."

Auragole was relieved. He would give his Elite Corps a summer vacation, spend a little time in the city, for appearance's sake, then go visit Don and Sylvie, who had answered his letter with a wholehearted invitation. Sylvie would surely know something about the orphanages in the country. Then back to Mattelmead City to tell Meraleese what he had found out, and then off to his own country place away from the city, the army, the women, and all those nagging questions that he couldn't rid himself of. Five or six weeks of fishing, hunting, and riding. Rest and recuperation. That's what he needed.

And Meraleese? What would become of her while he was gone? Well, he would see that she had enough money to take care of her needs over the summer. What else could he do? He certainly couldn't take her with him to the country. Not after Solagen's reprimand. Not after Goredahl's snooping.

Still. . .

It was an intriguing thought.

chapter sixteen

IN THE LATE afternoon, ten days into June, Auragole left for Donnadorr and Sylvane's estate. It was a beautiful ride north on Starwanderer. Auragole traveled leisurely on the off chance that someone was watching him. It didn't seem likely; still, it was best to act as if he had nothing but pleasure on his mind. He spent the night at an inn, and rode up to his friends' estate midmorning the next day.

Sylvane and Donnadorr rushed out to meet him as he alighted from his horse. After the warm greetings were over, Auragole felt awkward, almost tongue-tied. Here were two people he had once cared about, who had once cared about him. He and they had gone through much together, shared so many memories. But since Auragole's arrival in Mattelmead, more than three years before, they had seen less and less of each other. Of course, Don and Sylvie preferred the country to the city, but Auragole knew that wasn't the reason for this estrangement. Had he been too busy with Mattelmead society and his acceptance at the court to bother with his less-ambitious friends? Had he turned too proud? Had he, without admitting it, felt he had outgrown them? That was an ugly thought.

After Auragole had washed and changed from his travel clothes, he met his two old friends on the terrace overlooking their garden. It was a perfect June day, comfortably warm and sunny. Sylvane poured tea and Donnadorr told him about their estate. Auragole listened with half an ear. He was thinking about trust, about where the trust had gone between Don and him, and for that matter, between Lorenwile and him.

"Would you like to take a ride out to see the property after lunch?" Donnadorr broke into Auragole's musings.

"Oh, yes, I'd like that very much."

There was an awkward silence between them now. The three stared out into the garden. Finally, Auragole spoke. "Sylvie, tell me about your work in the orphanage near here."

"Oh, the little ones." Her eyes glistened with tears, which she quickly wiped away. "They're so dear, Aurie, and so sad and frightened. You should see them. They come from all over the Westernlands, brought by relatives, refugees themselves, who can't care for them, or by our soldiers who have found them wandering about—lost, or parents dead—or brought by kind strangers. War creates orphans, and children are those who can least care for themselves. That, I think, is the worst of what war does. And Solagen has seen to it that there are no children roaming about the countryside or in the city uncared for and uncared about. Not like it was in the east." She glanced over at her husband. "Not like what happened to Don." And she took his hand and smiled at him with a fondness that Auragole envied. She then turned back to Auragole. "Every month there seems to be a new group of children arriving. Some of the lucky ones have been adopted by families in the area."

"Do you know how many orphanages there are in the country?"

"I hear about ten, possibly as many as twelve," she answered. "And they're building more. Some, I understand, are now being built in the conquered countries—there are just too many war orphans."

At that moment the steward who oversaw the estate farm came up to them. "Master, may I speak with you for a few moments?"

"Will you excuse me, Auragole?"

"Yes, of course."

"I'll take Auragole for a walk through our gardens," Sylvane said, "and meet you in an hour for lunch."

"Good," Donnadorr said, and left, following his steward.

As they walked down the paths of her formal garden, Sylvane talked, naming the flowers and telling Auragole what new plants they intended to set in that month. But when they moved into a more rustic part of the garden, far away from the house and from the gardeners, Sylvane halted. Auragole turned back to her.

"Aurie, something's troubling you." Her expression was one of concern. "You've come for some purpose—not just to be social. Isn't that true?"

"Yes," he said, with a big intake of breath. He let it out slowly. "You always could see through me, Sylvie," he said, with an upsurge of affection. He walked back to her.

"What troubles you, my dear friend?" She put her hand on his arm.

And so he told her the story, as they slowly walked through the rustic garden, then out onto the woodland paths. He told her all of it, from the beginning—about his initial contact with Timorr and his family. He even told her about his surreptitious meetings with Meraleese since he had returned from Wildenfarr.

"Yes, the Security Forces," Sylvane sighed. "They're like a blight on the promise of Mattelmead. Last month the husband of one of our acquaintances was taken off in the night, and no one knows where or even why. And that's the second time that's happened here in the country to someone we know. And in the city, three people we know, three with whom we had dined, disappeared. In one case, the whole family was taken off, the Gods know where." She shook her head. "I don't understand it. I don't understand the need."

Auragole was silent, thinking about this. If there was a Nethergod here in Mattelmead, a Destroyer God—Auragole thought about his conversations with Meraleese—who was it most likely to be? *If* there was a Nethergod, it would likely be Goredahl. No one else around Ormahn possessed that much cruelty.

"Auragole?"

"Yes."

She hesitated, then asked, "What do you know about any of this?"

He had to admire her forthrightness. Sylvane had always had courage, had always been direct. You knew where you stood with her.

"Nothing." He brushed a lock of hair from his forehead. "Truly nothing. It's Solagen's nephew, Goredahl, who is in charge of inner security. I have nothing to do with it, and am never consulted about inner security matters. I have my own work, the Elite Corps." He looked at her, willing her to believe him. She smiled up at him.

"I admit Goredahl is an odious man," he went on. "Yet, he is likely heir to the throne, since Solagen has only daughters, and establishing a pattern of family inheritance seems very important to Ormahn." Auragole inhaled deeply. "May Solagen live forever. The thought of. . . I tell you, I despise Goredahl— I think because he loves his job as head of the Security Forces so much. But Solagen says it's necessary, even if Goredahl makes mistakes on occasion."

"Why is his job necessary?"

"For the sake of peace and order, so Solagen told me himself."

"But what about the fear that it instills in the population? I must say we feel it here. You only have to be accused of the thought of sedition by someone, even if it's not true, and. . ."

"I don't know how to answer you, Sylvie. Ormahn of Mattelmead has done great things, really great things. It's impossible not to admire him. And he says the Security Forces are necessary. We don't know about the plots to overthrow him. We think everyone in Mattelmead is as happy as we are with Ormahn's rule." He glanced over at her, but she was staring at the ground, her brows furrowed.

They were walking now through a small copse of birches, with their burgeoning green leaves.

"You came here for something, Aurie." It was a statement and he didn't dispute it. "How do you think Don or I can help you?"

"I guess I was hoping you would know where the orphanages were located, those other ten or eleven."

"Oh, Aurie, I'm sorry. I don't."

She looked so crestfallen that he put his arm around her shoulders and gave her a little hug. "Is there some way you can find out?"

"I'll try. What's the name of the child you're searching for?"

"Glorr, the boy's name is Glorr. I know it's a common enough name. . ."

"Glorr? When was he taken from his mother?"

"About ten months ago."

Sylvane stopped moving and covered her mouth with her hands.

"What is it, Sylvie?"

"There was a boy who was brought to our orphanage around that time. His name is Glorr. About six years old?"

"Yes, yes! That's right!"

"Describe him."

Auragole did.

Sylvane was silent for a moment, staring down at her toes.

"What is it?" Auragole could feel the excitement building in him. "Does your Glorr fit that description?"

"I think so. Our Glorr came about that time. It must be he. When he came to us," she said, starting to walk again, "he wouldn't speak, though we were told that he could. He hasn't spoken for all these months. I. . .I've taken a liking to him and have spent extra time with him. I tell him stories. He listens and I know he understands, but he doesn't speak. I take him for walks. I think he likes me because he holds so tightly to my hand. The other children make fun of him sometimes. But not cruelly. He is well cared for."

They walked back to the house without speaking. Auragole could hardly believe what had happened. He had found out where Glorr was! He was sure of it. He had anticipated making discreet inquiries at orphanage after orphanage. This Glorr that Sylvie was talking about must be his Glorr, Meraleese's Glorr. He wished he could visit him. But he knew that would be unwise.

Now what? The boy was obviously suffering—that would break Meraleese's heart when he told her. What was to be done now? How could mother and child be reconciled? He had no plan for that. And he couldn't go to Solagen. So what could be done?

At lunch Sylvie told Donnadorr the content of their conversation.

"Is this the child you've been speaking to me about, Sylvie?" She nodded.

Donnadorr fingered his red beard absentmindedly. Auragole watched him with interest.

"Auragole, is there no way you can bring child and mother together? No one at court who could help you? What about Solagen?"

Auragole slowly shook his head. "No. I've been told to let this matter rest. And to stay away from Meraleese."

"Stay away. . .? If you're caught, Aurie. . ." Donnadorr looked concerned.

"I won't be caught. I'm careful. I feel I owe this woman. . . I have to help her somehow."

"Lassie," Don turned to his wife, "we've been talking about this, lo, for many weeks now. I say let's do it."

Sylvie's face lit up.

"Do what?" Auragole asked.

"Adopt the boy," Donnadorr answered. "Sylvie and I haven't. . .yet been able to have children of our own, you see. And this little boy. . . Well, Sylvie has taken quite a fancy to him. This is no perfect solution for your Meraleese, Aurie. But if there's no way to bring them together. . .at least she will know that he has found a good home."

"You'd do that?"

"For our sake as well as for the boy's and his mother's," Donnadorr said, his face reddening.

"Oh, Aurie, you should see him." Sylvane clasped her hands together and held them to her breast. "He's so small and so afraid and so lost. My heart just goes out to him. I think I fell in love with him that first day. And now. . . Now that I know. . . that we know who he is, and what the circumstances are, it makes me want him even more. I'm sure we can in time, with love, get him to speak."

"Of course we can," Donnadorr said heartily. "And I'll teach him to ride and to hunt and fish. Maybe even to sing. Yes, yes, I like the idea, I really do. We both want children—so very much."

And Auragole felt enormous relief. How good these people are, he thought, and once again guilt filled him.

THAT AFTERNOON WHEN Donnadorr and Auragole were riding through his property, Don asked him about Glenelle.

"I've seen her a few times at parties. We don't seek each other out. She doesn't invite me to her parties and I don't invite her to mine. Frankly, I cannot bring myself to trust her. I think she has spoken too freely about. . . Well, of course, I, in my infatuation, shared too much knowledge with her. But then, she already knew a lot. As does Glenorr."

"As do Sylvane and I."

Auragole looked over at his friend.

"Don't worry. There was no need to speak of that dear people to any of our acquaintances. Sylvane and I decided long ago to protect Agavia."

"As do I," Auragole said, and continued where he had left off. "Occasionally Glenelle and I are at the same social event. Can't avoid that since we are both in society. But if what you really want to know. . . ," and he grinned, ". . .is have I gotten past my childish infatuation, the answer is yes—just as you did."

"Two fools, we," Donnadorr said, then absently stroked his red beard. "Remember how cavalier we were, trying to decide between us who should get the prize—as if a woman were something to give or take, like a prize cow." And Donnadorr laughed.

"Appalling." Auragole smiled and shook his head.

"But I understand you don't lack for women."

"No," Auragole said. "No, women there are aplenty, but. . ."

"Lucky you. I've seen some of them." And Don grinned and rolled his eyes.

"No, my friend," Auragole said, "you're the lucky one. It would be nice to have. . ."

"To have what?"

"What you and Sylvane have."

"Yes, that I can wholeheartedly wish for you. I am a contented man, Auragole. A very contented man."

MERALEESE WEPT AND wept when she heard the news. Auragole held her until the tears subsided. How fragile her warm body felt against his own. He wasn't sure which of them was trembling the most—but only one of them from. . . Thank the stars, she was too caught up in the emotions of the moment to understand.

She finally pulled herself gently away. "Thank you," she said, "this is more than I could have hoped for."

It was then that he asked her. He had thought about it off and on, but had not made up his mind until that moment. "Meraleese, how would you like to come to the country with me for a few weeks?"

"What?" She brushed the tears from her eyes and brought her face closer to his so she could read his expression in the pale light.

"Come to the country with me. Be my guest at my estate," he said, pulling back slowly. He didn't want those eyes, that mouth, so close to his own.

"That's insane, Auragole." He could hear the genuine surprise in her voice. No, it was shock.

"Why?" He stood up then. She was only a shadowed form on the sofa. "Who will know? None of the other officers lives within a dozen miles of my place. My estate is on a small northern peninsula surrounded on three sides by the Western Sea. It's extraordinarily beautiful there. We'll give you a different name." He was becoming more animated as he spoke. He wanted this. "I don't think anyone will be surprised if I bring a lady guest with me. After all, I have. . ."

"Auragole, be sensible. Light a candle and look at me. I'm a poor woman. I have few clothes. Fewer perhaps than your servants have. If I were a society lady, I imagine there would be nothing but a little idle talk on the part of your servants. But if you come escorting a poor field mouse to your estate there will be plenty of gossip."

He sat down on the chair opposite her. "That can be remedied," he said quietly.

"Auragole, no, it's too dangerous. You could get into terrible trouble going against the wishes of the king. Think what you're suggesting. You don't owe me this."

"This is not the repaying of a debt, Meraleese." His tone was almost harsh.

The more she fought the idea, the more he wanted her to go, to get her into the clean, fresh country air, to see her cheeks become rosy in the sun, to see the sparkle return to her large, sad eyes.

To just be in her company.

"In the country we'll be far from the court, and it is well known that I socialize very little when I'm at my estate. We'll get you some new clothes, give you a different name. . . And perhaps later on, at the end of your visit, we can go to Sylvane and Donnadorr's home to. . .it's a little less than a day's journey east."

With that last enticement, it was decided.

chapter seventeen

MORE THAN ONCE, Auragole had purchased items of clothing for women as gifts. It was accepted practice in Mattelmead for men to buy gifts of clothing for the women they admired. But he bought only a few things in the city for Meraleese, not wanting to arouse suspicion, just enough so that Meraleese could arrive in the country looking like a society lady. There would be dressmakers in the village on his estate to make whatever else she needed.

So one night at the end of June, Auragole left his mansion, riding Starwanderer, with Semp driving the coach. They stopped at the gate leading to a large house where a woman with a small case was waiting. Tied to the back of the coach was his trunk and a smaller one. Meraleese, wearing clothes that Auragole had delivered to her home a few nights before, stepped into the coach. Starwanderer walked alongside. They rode the rest of the night, and arrived at Auragole's country estate the following morning.

Later that same day, after they had rested, Auragole summoned the dressmaker from the village.

"This friend of mine has only clothes that are suitable for the city. Can you make up some clothes better suited for country life—for riding and hiking and swimming, as well as for more-formal occasions? And can you make them up quickly?"

The woman readily agreed. "There are three other women in the village who would be happy for the work and the extra money," she said. "The lady. . .you, sir, I mean, need only tell me what she needs and I will come back before evening with samples of fabric for you and the lady to look at, and to take her measurements."

Meraleese protested at what she said was an unnecessary extravagance, but Auragole only smiled, and when the seamstress returned, he picked the fabric and ordered many, many items.

The woman was as good as her word, and in days the clothes began arriving.

"It's foolish, you know," Meraleese said. "I'll be here for hardly more than three weeks, Auragole."

"You could stay the whole summer, you know," he countered.

"No, that would be too risky."

He started to answer her, but she put her fingers on his lips. "For me as well."

Auragole tried to give her a friendly grin. "Then these clothes will be waiting for you when next you come."

She shook her head, but he saw that her eyes were glowing.

There were several invitations waiting for him when he arrived, invitations to dine at other estates in the area, but Auragole declined them as he had done time and again in the past. It was well known that the social Auragole of the city was somewhat reclusive when he came to the country. The pattern had been established long ago, so nothing much was made of it.

He knew people were thinking that the man had a right to some rest, if the tales about him and his exploits with women were true. And no doubt, many had heard that he had brought a lady with him this time.

The reaction of Meraleese (now called Anneese) to the large, richly furnished house was astonishment. Auragole saw, as they moved through room after room, that Meraleese loved beautiful things and had, he thought, a wonderful discernment. When she admired something it gave him a little lift of pleasure, and he shared with her in particular those things he himself had purchased for their craftsmanship and beauty—not just what had belonged to Bendahl before him.

He showed her the grounds with their many gardens and their own small lake. He walked with her through the farm fields, the kitchen garden, the orchard, the woods with their numerous paths for hiking or riding. But what Meraleese loved above all else was looking out at the vast sea that surrounded his estate on three sides.

In her new clothes Meraleese looked rather pretty. She was not very tall, coming up just past his shoulder. Now that she was away from the sadness of her life, she looked less frail, slender still, but also sturdy. She could sit a horse well, and they rode through the woods and fields on Auragole's vast estate almost daily. Sometimes he put her on Starwanderer for the sheer joy he saw in her eyes at riding so extraordinary a horse. Often they stopped to stare out at the Western Sea from one vantage point or another.

As the days passed, Meraleese seemed to bloom. Like a flower she took to the fresh air and to the sun. When the weather was good they swam in the lake on his property. He noticed she had a fine figure—nothing plain about that. Her figure was one many of the corseted woman he had known in the city would have killed for. Meraleese took to wearing her long, dark-brown hair loose and down, letting the wind blow through it. "To let the sun shine on it again," she told him. It was thick, and with the help of the lady's maid he had brought in to attend to her needs, it was looking healthier and shinier. How sensual a woman's hair is, just loose and flowing, Auragole thought one day, riding behind her through an old maple grove. He was watching it billow in the breeze. In the city the women wore their hair twisted tightly or wrapped in silk or tortured into curls.

"I come from a farm family in the south," she told him, as they were picnicking on a bluff overlooking the sea not long after they had arrived. He was lying on his side, his elbow bent, his head in his hand, watching her. "Not a small farm, but of course not an estate either. Nothing like this." She flung out her hand in a wide arc. "My father worked on his land, as did my brothers, but he also had many workers under him. I was one of six children—two girls, four boys. My sister and I helped my mother. We were taught our manners, taught to read, and taught our numbers, and a great deal more. To play the flute. . ."

"You play the flute?"

She nodded.

"Then this evening after dinner shall we make music together?"

"If you like." She plucked at the grass around her. "I was also taught the care of the house, how to tend the vegetable and herb gardens, taught to cook—even to sing."

"Ah, now that is even more delightful. Tonight we shall play together and sing."

"I'm only an amateur, you know. But if it will please you. . ." she said.

"Not if it will please me." He sat up and frowned. "Don't do things to please me. I. . .I didn't bring you out here so that you would please me."

"Auragole, what have I said?" She sat up straight and began wringing her hands in her lap. "I meant only that doing something for you would please me as well—perhaps more. Why are you scowling so?" And she suddenly laughed. It was a musical laugh.

His heart lightened. "I'm scowling because what I want is to please you. And you must admit that no one would believe that the infamous ladies' man, Auragole of Mattelmead, would invite a lady out to his estate, place her in a room at the other end of the house, and keep his hands to himself, even though she is in every way desirable."

The laughter left Meraleese's hazel eyes, turning them into gray clouds. She looked away.

"Meraleese, I'm sorry I said that." He reached out and tentatively touched her arm. "I didn't mean anything by that."

"Auragole, I loved my husband very dearly. . ."

He wanted to kick himself. "Meraleese, I was merely joking." How could he be such a fool? And why had he said that? Had his feelings of fondness, of tenderness, of protectiveness become too sexual? Heavenly stars, was that need so great that he couldn't behave appropriately, couldn't act like a gentleman instead of a lustful animal?

"He's a distant cousin, you know. . .was. . ." She pulled up some wildflowers that were on the grass near her and sniffed them. The thin wedding band she still wore on her right hand sparkled in the sunlight. "His father used to bring Timorr to our farm from the city a few times a year when I was still a child and he a teenager. He always let me show him the ways of farm life. I think he pretended ignorance of where milk came from, or that wheat came from the earth, just to make me feel special. He was like that. I think our families knew that someday we would marry. . ." Her eyes filled up.

"Meraleese, I behaved like an ass. Don't take my jesting seriously."

She turned and gave him a long, solemn look.

"Come," he said, standing up and offering her his hand.

"Let's walk in the woods out of the sun for a while. We can pick some herbs for the cook, and a bouquet of wildflowers for our table this evening." He looked at her and smiled a smile he hoped was not provocative.

She took his proffered hand, and he helped her to her feet. Then he gently withdrew his hand. As they walked she told him more of her childhood, and he told her about his. The conversation became livelier, and the earlier awkwardness disappeared.

That night, after dinner, they sat in the large sitting room. He handed her a small flute, which she fingered appreciatively.

"Bought from the best flute maker in Mattelmead," he told her. He picked up his harp and sat down. "All right, you begin."

She played a haunting melody, one that he had never heard. "Beautiful," he said. "Play it again, and I'll try to follow you on my harp."

And for hours they played, melodies they both knew, or new ones that she taught to him, or he to her. It was a most satisfactory evening.

As he lay in bed that night, sleep eluded him. He was beginning to have feelings for Meraleese that he knew he shouldn't have. In some ways they surprised and troubled him. Meraleese was a widow, still in mourning, a woman he had been explicitly told not to see. And she was not in the least interested in him. Why should she be? She had been married to an exceptional man, even a great man—kind, caring, and unique. Who was he, Auragole, under all his finery and possessions? A soldier, a singer, a doer of someone else's deeds. Her husband had carved out his own road, and if that road had deviated from what was acceptable in Mattelmead, he had walked on it fearlessly. And died for it.

That Auragole could be brave in battle, he had already proven. Fight for Solagen's beliefs? Yes, that he could do. But what about his own beliefs? What about his own road? What thoughts were his? What thoughts were Ormahn of Mattelmead's? All his life, before arriving in Mattelmead, Auragole had gone his own way—with Pohl, with Meekelorr, with Elarr, even with Lorenwile. Had he given up his own sense of self for another's vision for and of him?

He was drifting toward the border of sleep when suddenly the words *"Find me with what is most yourself, then you will never lose me again. . ."* floated past him. He sat bolt upright, remembering a dream, one he had dreamt years ago after he had fought the beast from the cave and had saved Meekelorr's life. But he himself had nearly been killed. He had hovered between death and life then, had dreamed of a golden being, one he wanted to stay with forever.

"Too soon, my child," the Beautiful One said. His voice was all around Auragole, gentle as mist.

Auragole shook his head and tried to speak. *"You are not on the Deep Earth,"* he cried. *"Why should I return there?"*

"I am on the Deep Earth."

"But how, when you are here?"

"Only a memory of me lingers here."

Auragole did not understand. He wanted desperately to stay with the Sweet One. *"No one remembers you on the earth, not even I. Let me stay here, for here I can see you. Here I can know you as I have in ages past."*

The Sweet One, the Beautiful One shook his head. *"You knew me before, child, with powers that were not as yet your own. We met as my gift to you. But in these terrible and crucial world days you can know me through your own efforts. And it will be your gift to me. You are now able, in your inner isolation, in your deepest solitude, to find me, though all deny me. Step by step, you can find me with your most human quality. Find me with what is most yourself, then you will never lose me again."*

"I don't understand. What is most myself?"

He touched Auragole's face, and light and quiet rest drifted through him. If Auragole had tears, then he was crying, for he understood him—but only for a moment, and then forgot again.

Auragole lay back down again. That dream. . .that dream had been at the edge of his consciousness so many times, but he had never been able to pull it into clear thought. And now suddenly here it was. The first time it had come was when he had been wounded severely. He had wanted to die then so he could stay close to the Beautiful One. But he'd been sent back into life, told to find the Beautiful One who was now on the Deep Earth. Told to find him with what was most truly himself. But he had not found him. He had not even searched for him.

What had the Being said to him? *"Find me with what is most yourself, then you will never lose me again."* What was most truly himself?

He spent hours going over the dream so he would never forget it again. In the morning he would tell it to Meraleese.

He fell asleep just as the dawn was breaking, so he was late rising. When Auragole went down for breakfast, Meraleese had eaten and was in the garden picking flowers for the house.

"Anneese," he called to Meraleese, striding purposefully toward her. "I need to talk to you." He took her by the hand and, without looking at her, led her away from the house toward the lake and then into the woods.

When they had reached the woods, out of earshot of anyone, he said, "I want you to tell me what you think of this dream I had."

"Last night?" she asked, removing her hand from his.

"No, more than five years ago, in Agavia, before I woke up feverish and injured to find myself in the Healing Tower at the Last School. I'm sure there have been other times that I dreamt it, but always upon awaking I would lose it. Last night I remembered it. I'm not sure why it came to me so clearly just at this time." And he recounted the dream.

She listened carefully, though he was so intent on the telling that he hardly looked at her. When he finished, he stopped and turned to her. "Well, what do you think?"

She stared at her boots, drawing little circles in the dirt. "I'd say that you had a dream about the Prince God—if dream you could call it."

"The Prince? And what do you mean if I could call it a dream?" The back of his hand brushed across his forehead.

"Well, when you first had that dream, you were hovering between life and death, you see. You were at that threshold, and you had an encounter."

"An encounter? Me? With the Prince? A genuine encounter with the Prince?" He knew his voice sounded incredulous.

She smiled at him. "Why not? He loves humanity."

"But why? Why me? I was never a follower, never a believer." He remembered the strange encounter Elarr had had with the Prince when Elarr had been filled with despair and remorse, but wasn't that different? After all, Elarr had once studied to be a priest of the Prince.

"You think now only of this one life. Tell me again what he charged you with."

"To find him on earth with what is most truly myself. What does that mean? What is most truly myself?"

Meraleese laughed and started down the path once again. "Well, I don't think he meant your beautiful clothes, or your handsome face, or your well-made body." And then she blushed, and hurried a little ahead of him.

"What did he mean, then?" Auragole insisted, striding to catch up with her.

"Oh, Aurie, that's an easy one. Surely, with all you have learned about the Prince God in your travels, this is an easy one."

He slowed down and stared at the ground as they were walking. "You mean the higher ego, the part of the human being the Prince came to quicken, the 'I' whose name only I can call myself, the part of me that comes back again and again to earth, the ego that can separate itself from the group, follow its own dreams. . ." The words tumbled out of him until he suddenly realized what he was saying, and stopped.

So she continued, ". . .while loving the community it comes from, while wanting to give of the self in a loving, helpful way to the group."

Auragole thought about True-singing then. The "I" that could enter into nature, into animals, into the rocks, earth, mountains, and hear the song that was their essence, that was the "I" that was most truly himself. Not his earthly, everyday "I" but the one he had awakened with True-singing. The one he had allowed to fall into sleep again. Suddenly, Auragole was filled with an overwhelming sense of loss and melancholy.

"I understand now," he said, when he saw she was watching him.

After that they walked in silence. Auragole was so caught up in his own distress that he didn't notice with what intensity Meraleese was looking at him.

THAT EVENING, AS they played their instruments and sang, Auragole suddenly stopped in the middle of a melody he had been playing for her.

"What is it?" she asked.

"I want to sing a song for you. It's very old, I think. I heard it first from my mother when I was still in my crib. And then when I, too, was able to sing, she taught it to me. When I asked her about it, where it came from, whom it was about, she said she didn't know. Will you listen carefully to the words, and tell me whom you think it's about?"

She nodded.

And so he sang:

There is a riddle
here in my song.
The tale is short
but the melody long.

I sing of a prince
not born of a king.
He wears neither crown
nor does he wear ring.

He has no silk cape.
He has no silk shirt.
Will this prince heal
or will this prince hurt?

Who is his father?
Who is his mother?
Some say he has
neither one nor the other.

Is he one cursed
or is he one blessed?
Will he bring strife
or will he bring rest?

Will he bring peace
or will he bring war?
Seek you the answer?
Then search for the door.

Some call him wise.
Some call him fool.
Where is his kingdom?
Whom does he rule?

Where is the door?
Where is the gate?
Where is the young prince?
Why does he wait?

So here is my riddle.
One you can ponder
whether at home
or whether you wander.

Will he bring love
or will he bring hate?
Would you an answer?
Look for the gate.

Yet where is the door?
And where is the gate?
And where is the young prince
for whom we all wait?

So here is my riddle
and here is my song.
The tale has been short
but the melody's long.

I sing of a prince
not born of a king
who wears neither crown
nor does he wear ring.

Auragole watched her eagerly as he sang. When he finished, he said, "Well?"

"Hmmm. It's what is called a riddle song, isn't it?"

"Yes." Now he was excited.

"I'm not sure I have an answer for you, Auragole."

"But couldn't it refer to your Prince God? I mean, 'not born of a king/he wears neither crown/nor does he wear ring.'"

"Yes," she answered slowly. "That part fits."

"Or 'Who is his father?/Who is his mother?/Some say he has/neither one nor the other'?"

"Yes, that would also fit. But the part about his bringing either peace or war, or strife or rest, or love or hate. . ."

"But don't you see, the wars came to the Grand Continent at first because of the fighting between various religious groups with different beliefs. So that could also fit." He was sure he had solved it. But the look on Meraleese's face made him wonder.

"Well," she finally said. "It could be about the Prince God. What you say is true about the wars—how they began. The various factions finally annihilated one another and one another's beliefs—for the most part. And then the wars just went on. Everyone fighting everyone else. It is hard to imagine the Prince inaugurating such events."

"But that's because he didn't reckon with the Adversary Being, with the Destroyer, preparing to come to the earth. What about this part? 'I sing of a prince/not born of a king/who wears neither crown/nor does he wear ring'?"

"Yes, that too could fit. But might it not be some human being, just as easily?"

"What human being? Kings have been done away with in the west and in the east. Perhaps there are kings somewhere else in this world, but not on the Grand Continent. Even Ormahn, whom one can call king, has no son. And if he did, that would be a legitimate prince, and therefore not the one in the song who is not born of a king."

"I don't know, Auragole. I simply can't say for a certainty that the prince in your riddle song is the Prince God. It could be. . ."

"But you don't think so."

"Let's just leave it at 'I don't know.' Sorry."

"That's all right," he said. He saw that she was troubled and knew that she hated to displease him. He wished it weren't so, but it was. "It was just a thought. Not important. A boyhood curiosity, that's all."

He picked up his instrument once again. "Now you sing me a new song, and I will try to follow you on my harp."

And she did.

N

chapter eighteen

A FEW DAYS into their third week in the country, after they had finished playing songs together, Meraleese asked Auragole when they could go to his friends' estate, so that she could see Glorr. She asked him hesitantly, as if she were afraid he would tell her that it was not a good idea.

But he answered, "Yes, it's time to do that. Our days here together are drawing to a close." He felt a stab of sadness at the thought. He had postponed their visit to Glorr, selfishly loving the days and nights he was spending with her. But she had a different purpose in visiting him. So he said in a voice he attempted to make cheerful, "We can leave early tomorrow morning. The roads there are not very good, but if we stop to rest the horses two or three times, we should arrive there before evening."

"Oh, Aurie, thank you." She rushed over to him and gave him a warm hug, then hurried out of the room.

TWO EVENINGS LATER, Meraleese and Auragole returned to

his estate. They sat on the same side of the carriage, each huddled in a corner. Auragole couldn't bear sitting across from her, watching the tears flow down her face. His heart ached for her.

The meeting between Meraleese and Sylvane had gone well. Good, kind, understanding Sylvie. She had greeted Meraleese like a long-lost sister, and then had brought the boy to her. The boy, upon seeing Meraleese, had cried, "Mommy, Mommy, why have you been away so long?" They were the first words he had uttered since he had first been brought to the orphanage so many months before, and all the adults had cried as Meraleese gathered Glorr up into her arms. And then Sylvane had taken Donnadorr and Auragole off and had left the mother and son alone.

What a generous heart Sylvie has, Auragole thought, and Don, too. How could he have ignored them for so long? What better friends did he have in Mattelmead, now that Lorenwile was gone?

Auragole hadn't asked Meraleese how she had answered her son's wrenching question, or how she had explained to the boy that he must remain with Sylvane and Donnadorr, or what she had told him about his father, the priest Timorr.

When they had stood at the carriage ready to depart the following evening, Meraleese had knelt beside Glorr. "You must now speak with words to Sylvie and Don. They love you and will take care of you, just as your father and I would if we were able. This is a lovely place in which to live and you will be happy here if you try." The boy nodded solemnly. "You know I love you, will always love you. You know that I pray for you, that your father looks down on you from the land of the Gods and keeps watch over you. After all, didn't he bring you to these good people who will care for you and act as parents? We've talked about why we can't be together now. It is not out of lack of wanting, you understand that, Glorr. But we cannot in this world always do as we would wish to do. You be good, listen to your new guardians, return their love. I will come again if I can.

And I will send you messages when I can." She had looked at Auragole then, and he had nodded, understanding that he would have to be the conduit for letters between herself and her son.

Auragole looked over at his companion. She was sitting in the corner of the coach, her hands folded in her lap, holding tightly to a handkerchief, staring out at the dark night. They had decided to stay only one day—better for the boy not to get too attached again to his mother. He would be unwilling to let her go then. And, too, they needed to protect Don and Sylvie. Auragole didn't want them to have to explain to the many visitors who dropped in on them what all these strange relationships were. So he and Meraleese had spent the night and the next day, and had departed that evening.

Auragole was feeling a mix of things, as he tried not to watch the woman at the other end of the coach—and many of his feelings were at war with each other. He was glad to have been able to arrange this meeting between mother and son, glad he had been able to locate the child in the first place. Still he couldn't help but feel guilty for having been a party to the destruction of her family and their little temple. The question of whether he was culpable had haunted him since the day she had come to him begging for information. Yet had he never set foot in the temple, someone else would have been sent in his place. The results would have been the same—the temple would have been closed down and the priest arrested and slain. And if it had been someone else who had been sent, Meraleese would never have found her son. So there was no need for all this guilt, this sense of personal responsibility.

But he couldn't drive them away.

And what did he feel for this woman? He was younger than she by perhaps five years—but did that matter? Not to him. To her? Timorr must have been at least ten years older than she and possessed of great maturity. Perhaps she saw Auragole as young and callow.

Auragole glanced sideways at Meraleese again, but her face was turned away. He remembered how she had looked one day coming up out of the lake on his property, her hair streaming like a river down her back and shoulders, and her swim garment clinging to all the curves of her well-shaped body, laughing, unconscious of the effect she was having on him. She could be called pretty, but not beautiful. To be beautiful in society meant to employ a lot of artifice, and Meraleese did not bother with artifice. She displayed, with no attempt at concealment, a weariness that most women he knew would have hidden with hours of careful grooming. And Meraleese certainly was not fashionable, nor consciously seductive, as were so many of the ladies he knew.

But there was something unique about her—her depth of heart, her ability to accept and hold up under terrible suffering, her wonderful wisdom and kindness, the endearing mobility of her face when she spoke, and those large, changeable, and knowing eyes. These made her more desirable than she could possibly realize. And, frankly, it shook him up. He wasn't sure what to do about it, wasn't sure what he wanted from her. He didn't think she felt anything for him other than gratitude. She had been married to an extraordinary man; why should she even look Auragole's way? He sighed, and Meraleese turned a tear-streaked face toward him. He just smiled and shook his head, then peered out his window. But the longing to hold her, to comfort her, was almost overwhelming.

He took off his gloves and dug his fingernails into the palms of his hands. One pain to distract him from another. Get hold of yourself, he scolded himself silently. What is it you want? To live as Don and Sylvie live, mostly in the country, with some good, warm, and wise woman like Meraleese? To be in love and to be loved—if there is such a thing?

Sometimes. But only sometimes. He had to confess he liked his life—most of the time. Only a fool would turn his back on such a life. And he hoped he wasn't a fool. He liked being admired by both men and women, liked being close to the throne, liked being a commander in Ormahn's army.

Yet there were times when he felt that he was only half a man, and maybe not even the best half. For wouldn't that other half seek something he had begun to find in True-singing? *"Find me with what is most yourself, then you will never lose me again."* Wouldn't the self that he had pushed away want to find what Meraleese and Timorr, what Pohl and Meekelorr and Elarr, what Lady Claregole and the Agavians wanted to find, what even his father in his youth had wanted to find—his connection to the greater universe? They longed to know about the Creative Beings, called Gods, that they claimed worked into all the events on the Deep Earth, as did also the Adversary Gods. These friends of his didn't want to remain bound only to the earth, caring only for bodily needs and little for the soul and nothing for the spirit—because, as Meraleese had explained, the earth and the body were only a small part of reality.

But Ormahn, also, claimed to be interested in satisfying the soul. Wasn't that why he had built a city that loved and supported all the arts? Wasn't that why he had allowed the temples to the various Gods to be built and attended? What more did one need? Why should Auragole not be satisfied? After all, he was helping Ormahn bring peace and order to a chaotic world. Without it people would have no time or inclination to search for the Gods, only for food. Surely bringing peace to the Deep Earth should satisfy the Creative Beings—if they indeed existed.

Stop torturing yourself, he told himself, and looked at the blood that trickled down his hands almost in surprise. He put his gloves back on. Right now, your task lies with Ormahn and with the saving of the earth from anarchy and destruction. And as things go in this world, that is not a minor task. Let the Gods note this effort and be content.

He looked over at Meraleese, whose eyes were closed, and whose head lay back against a pillow crushed into the corner of the carriage. Something stirred in his heart. But what about this woman? What was he to do about this woman?

AURAGOLE SPENT ANOTHER week at his estate with Meraleese, a few days longer than he had intended. She had not argued with him when he had suggested it. She was more subdued now, less talkative. But if he asked her to walk or ride with him, she did. Often they sat on a bluff overlooking the Western Sea, without speaking. If he asked her to sing and play the flute in the evenings, she did. It was gratitude, duty, Auragole felt, and it left an ache in his heart and an ache in his body. But he couldn't leave the woman, or thoughts about the woman, alone.

Finally they had to return to the city.

Auragole spent a few days at his mansion, seeing Meraleese only once, for she warned him away. "Go back to the country, stay there for the rest of the summer, that's what all the commanders are doing. That's what Ormahn suggested you do. Best if you keep to your original plan, Auragole."

"I'd rather be in the city now," he told her, his voice thick with a caring he couldn't fight.

"No," she said, and then her voice softened. "Don't be unwise, Auragole. Don't cause speculation. Return to the country. Perhaps when you get back, you will come. . ."

So he returned to his estate, which now felt large and empty. And he couldn't wait to return to the city.

While he was in the country, he visited Donnadorr and Sylvane once again. The boy, Glorr, was doing well. He was talking and had begun to take an interest in games and in learning. He listened solemnly when Auragole brought him regards from his mother. As Auragole was about to enter his carriage to return to his own country estate, the boy flung his arms around Auragole's neck and whispered in his ear, "Tell my Mommy that she is still my best Mommy, and that I will always love her."

AT LAST, IN early September, Auragole returned to the city. Within a week of Auragole's arrival, the war council convened. It was decided that the conference with Isofed would take place on a grand estate in Glovale. The delegation accompanying Ormahn would include Auragole, Goredahl, Veldarr, and a large contingent of the army. Oldwell would remain behind, taking charge of what was now called the United West. Auragole was glad of that. Oldwell was a strong leader, but all in all, a kind man. And Auragole wanted Goredahl where he could keep an eye on him.

Auragole had been to see Meraleese three times in the three weeks he was in the city before leaving for Glovale. He had tried while he was back at his country estate to get her out of his thoughts, but he had been unable. Every room in that house, every inch of his property reminded him of Meraleese. When had he felt this way before—so obsessed by a woman? While he had been on the road searching for his friends, he had yearned for Glenelle, his lost Ellie. Yes, he had to admit that was true. And finally he had found Ellie, alive and well. And they had had an affair. What he had felt then had been intense, euphoric, a kind of madness. But had that been love? He long ago had decided that it had not. The woman he had thought Glenelle to be had not been real, only an ideal he had created in his mind.

And all those other women, who had come and gone in and out of his life since then, what were his feelings for them? Only lust? Lust surely—but more than that. It was simply good to be around the femaleness of most women—their charms, their flirtations, their desires and attentions focused so obviously on him. But he had known that none of it was love. In some ways he had stopped believing in love. How often since his involvement with Glenelle and its painful, embarrassing ending had he remembered his father's admonition about love? Goloss had spoken to him about it moments before his death. His last words had been a warning against love. He had said love didn't exist, that it was only instinct, that it could entrap you. *"The people of the Easternlands killed or were killed with slogans of love on their lips,"* he had said. *"Don't succumb and you will be free, free."*

But something existed between Donnadorr and Sylvane. And something had existed between Meraleese and Timorr. Was that not love? And something had existed between his father and his mother, between his parents and himself. Surely that had been love. His father could not have been right. Auragole had witnessed love. There were Elarr and Affredda, Meekelorr and the Lady Claregole. And didn't all those who said they loved, love out of freedom? Perhaps he was the only one who couldn't experience the reality of love. Perhaps he was incapable. Perhaps because he had been raised in isolation, with no others near his own age, he was unable to love.

Then what was it he felt for Meraleese? Admiration? Pity? Sympathy? Some sort of moral debt? Yes, all those things. But there was something else, something more. These feelings were so much quieter than anything he had felt for Glenelle. But was it love—that which Don knew and Elarr knew? Well, whatever these feelings were, they went deep. Sometimes they felt so deep they cut him like a knife, causing a wound whose blood he could not stanch for days. Sometimes they felt as warm and embracing as the water in the lake he and Meraleese had swum in earlier that summer. Meraleese was real, substantial, without artifice, without coyness, and without pretense. So three times he had gone to visit her in the middle of the night. She received him gladly, handed him notes to send to Sylvane for her son, spoke with him for as long as he chose to stay, but Auragole never felt that she returned any of his feelings. He was glad that he was going to be away for several weeks. Maybe this impossible infatuation, this obsession—for that was what it must be—would finally disappear.

In the last week of September, the delegation left for Glovale. And Auragole's twenty-fourth birthday passed uncelebrated.

AURAGOLE HAD A curious conversation with Veldarr one night on their way to meet the negotiating party from Isofed. The envoy had camped for the night. Auragole was about to prepare for sleep when Veldarr's servant came to him.

"My master asks you to his tent. Will you come?"

Auragole, curious, agreed. When he arrived at Veldarr's tent, Veldarr took his hand and shook it vigorously. Though intrigued, Auragole was also on his guard. Veldarr knew too much about him, about those things he had kept hidden—even from Solagen. What had Veldarr told Goredahl? Auragole had better be cautious with this man. Veldarr could be a formidable enemy if he chose. Veldarr led Auragole to a small table laden with wine and sweets, dismissed the servants, and invited Auragole to sit down.

For a while the two men, sitting opposite each other, spoke about the upcoming conference with Isofed. Then, as each was drinking his second glass of wine, Veldarr said, "I want to speak to you about Glenelle." Auragole could feel his face grow cold. But Veldarr went on, "It galls me that because of Glenelle, you and I have not become friends. Oh, yes, you and I attend the same parties, attend each others'. But we have stayed shy of each other—even wary. And I think that is not good for either of us." He eyed Auragole over the rim of his wineglass.

Auragole, having quickly regained his composure, held Veldarr's eyes. He had long ago learned to school his expression. In that, he was far from the boy whose every thought had been written on his countenance.

Veldarr went on, "Glenelle is a lovely woman, fun to be with, excellent in bed. . ."

Auragole, to his own surprise, flushed. And Veldarr saw it.

". . .but not serious about any man. Not capable really. She adores many, and even loves some. But he who would be close to her knows that she is not a bird to be caged by the love of one person. She's a free spirit who will never be tethered to one man. We must take her the way she is."

"It is long since I've thought about Glenelle, so why this conversation now, after so much time has passed?" Auragole's words were soft and measured.

"But is the anger gone?"

Auragole smiled, then laughed. "Probably not." Why he should confess this to Veldarr, he wasn't sure. But then why, after all these years, should Veldarr speak to him about Glenelle?

"Did you know that she counts Goredahl among her close associates?"

Auragole raised his eyebrows. "No," he said. "But I have wondered."

Veldarr grinned. "Yes, to be expected, of course. Since Goredahl may be Ormahn someday, it is natural that Glenelle would seek him out."

So, Auragole thought, that's how Goredahl knew about Meekelorr and the Companions of the Way. Odious man. But Veldarr was talking. Auragole stopped speculating to listen.

"It's not Glenelle I particularly wanted to speak to you about, Auragole. It's about the two of us. I fear that my own involvement with Glenelle, superficial as it is, has been the cause of this chasm between us. If not for her, we two might have become friends long ago. It is this that troubles me."

"I feel no enmity toward you, Veldarr. As you just said, I've been to your house and you to mine. . ."

"No, but you feel no friendship either."

Auragole was silent.

"And I think we two should be friends."

"Why?" Auragole was blunt.

For a moment Auragole thought Veldarr was going to laugh. But he didn't. He said, quite seriously, "Because we see eye to eye on so many things. Look how often we agree in council. If it had been left up to Goredahl, we would be going to war, instead of a conference, with the Isofedians. You and I have a less harsh approach to the uses both of war and of governance, is that not so?"

Auragole nodded.

"It is not known yet upon whom the mantle of Ormahn will fall when my uncle dies. He has not yet divulged his preference, but knowing Solagen's interest in family and inheritance, it will fall either on Goredahl or on me."

"I know that. Unless Queen Deena has a son. And she is pregnant again."

"Yes." Veldarr nodded. "If Solagen produces a son, then all of this conjecturing is only that. But should something happen to Solagen before the boy is of age, one of us would have to act as regent. I ask you to think which of the two of us, Goredahl or me, would make the better king or regent for our country, for the entire west?"

Auragole said nothing. But he thought, so Veldarr is more interested in the throne than most people think.

"I'm not asking for your loyalty, Auragole." Veldarr's eyes glowed with the seriousness of his words. "It's far too early to ask for such a thing. After all, Solagen is a healthy, vigorous man. I only want you to think of the Westernlands governed by my cousin—a sour, fearful, cruel, tyrannical man. The prisons would be filled to overflowing. We would have to build more." There was no heat in Veldarr's words. "And the man has no vision. I doubt he could remain in power very long without an uprising. Under his repressive rule, the Westernlands could once more break up into petty warring states. Good governance takes a lighter touch, takes a more human approach, takes someone who knows people, who likes people, who can work with people."

"If it's not loyalty, what is it you are asking of me, Veldarr?"

Veldarr laughed, then quickly finished the wine in his glass. "Nothing—except to suggest that you think on these things. And that you at least accept my offer of friendship. Don't forget, Auragole, you too have a great following. You are popular with the people. And most important of all, you are commander of the Elite Corps, who, I am told, would follow you anywhere. Now that is something that might worry Goredahl should he come into power. He is at present in command only of the Security Forces, a small but admittedly lethal group. He has his way of finding things out, as I'm sure you know." He looked straight into Auragole's eyes and held them.

What does that mean? Auragole wondered while he, unwaveringly, returned Veldarr's gaze. What was he hinting at? Finally Auragole reached for the decanter and poured himself another glass of wine. He could ask Veldarr. But if indeed, by some chance, Veldarr did not know about Agavia and Meekelorr's involvement there, he wasn't going to reveal it. Most likely Glenelle, wishing to ingratiate herself with both cousins, had revealed things to each of them. Auragole sipped his wine and raised his eyes once again to Veldarr's.

"Yes," Veldarr went on, reaching for a small sugar-coated cake. "Goredahl commands the Security Forces. However, I am in command of the regular army. You and I together control a formidable force."

"You are thinking of opposing Goredahl should he ascend to the throne?"

"Did I say that?" Veldarr raised his eyebrows, then placed the cake he was holding carefully down on his plate and wiped his fingers with his napkin. "I said no such thing. I said only think about these things. You know how hard-hearted a man

Goredahl is. As commander of the Security Forces, he has used his power in extreme and harsh ways. I needn't tell you that. Those close to you have felt his heavy hand."

Auragole looked sharply at Veldarr then. But Veldarr's expression was unreadable. He rose and offered Auragole his hand. "It's late and we will be off early in the morning, so we'd best call it a night. All I'm asking of you," he said as he walked Auragole to the tent opening, his arm about Auragole's shoulders, "is that you allow our own friendship to blossom. We have much in common, I think, so why should we be estranged over a woman? That makes little sense."

"I'll think about what you've said."

"That's all I ask," Veldarr said, and slapped him gently on the back.

Auragole walked the several yards back to his own tent. He had been around the court and its intrigues long enough to understand what inference to draw from Veldarr's seemingly casual comments. If something should happen to shorten Solagen's life, there would be a battle between Goredahl and Veldarr for the throne—no matter which of them was named heir. Whose side would Auragole be on? It didn't take much thought to answer that one. And Veldarr knew it.

THE CONFERENCE WITH the Isofedians went smoothly. Solagen called upon Auragole to take a leading part in the negotiations, and he did. Apparently he acquitted himself well. The Isofedians accepted Ormahn's offer. All they asked in return was that no outsider come inside the walls of Isofed. Twice a year an emissary party from Isofed would bring the tribute into Glovale at an agreed-upon meeting place. The Isofedians would also withdraw their army to within their gates and reduce its size, and they agreed to contingents of the army of Mattelmead setting up camp outside their gates. They would send an ambassador to Mattelmead City in the spring.

Ormahn was in high spirits on the way back—the largest country in the west was under his authority. He was now overking of all the Westernlands. He was especially complimentary to Auragole for his delicate handling of the negotiations and for his good advice at council. One night when they had been drinking and Solagen was particularly effusive, Auragole looked up to see a cold, hard look on the face of Goredahl. A shudder ran up his spine. That man did not just dislike Auragole, he was an enemy who would attempt to destroy him if Auragole didn't stay alert.

Five weeks after they had left Mattelmead City, they returned. It was early November. By that time Queen Deena had given birth to her third daughter.

chapter nineteen

ONE WEEK AFTER the negotiating team had returned from Glovale, in mid-November, Ormahn called Auragole in for a talk. When Auragole arrived at his office, Solagen was signing papers. Two aides were standing next to him. Solagen motioned Auragole to the seat in front of his desk. Auragole sat and waited for him to speak. Finally, Solagen looked up. "This paperwork is endless. With every new conquest, more work," and he motioned with his hand at the tall stack of documents on his desk.

Then he dismissed his aides, and when the door was closed, Solagen said, "Thank you for coming in."

These words of gratitude caught Auragole by surprise. He was, after all, obeying a command.

Solagen fiddled with his pen and glanced down at the stack of papers. Then he set the pen aside, folded his hands on the desk, and looked at Auragole. "I need to send a large troop of soldiers to take up posts outside the gates of Isofed in accordance with our agreement. Well, not at the South Gate. That, you have told us, opens up into the Deep Forest and, as they have never kept soldiers there, why should we?"

"Yes, you mentioned that at the last council meeting."

"And I need a commander, maybe two, to see to the deployment and then to take charge. This commander could be away from four to six months."

Auragole had known some commander would have to go. He had hoped it wouldn't be him. He waited for Ormahn to go on. But Solagen sat watching him without speaking for a long time. The scrutiny made Auragole uncomfortable. Was he supposed to say something? He finally did.

"Have you decided which commander it should be?"

"Not quite. But I have narrowed the list down."

Auragole nodded and waited to hear Solagen's disclosure.

Solagen rose suddenly and said, "Come, Auragole, I need to get away from that confounded pile of papers. And since the snows are late this year, let's take a stroll around the garden." Solagen picked up his cloak, which lay carelessly tossed on a chest, moved to the glass doors, opened them, and walked out into one of the many courts of the large palace. Auragole put on his own cloak and followed, convinced now that it was he who was to be sent to Isofed.

Solagen waited for him near the marble fountain that stood at the center of this inner courtyard. During the warm weather many streams of water shot up from it, crisscrossing each other in a pretty pattern. It was dry now. Nothing looks so cold as marble in winter, Auragole thought as he approached Solagen. The king, without a word, walked toward the arch set into the palace's right wall, and then through it. It led to one of the palace's many walled gardens.

Auragole followed Solagen, then strode alongside him, wondering if this was about something else. Surely, if he wanted Auragole to take command in Isofed, Solagen could have announced it, set up an appointment to go over the details with him, and then dismissed him. Auragole began to be a little worried. Was Solagen angry with him? Had he found out about Auragole's visits to Meraleese? Was he about to get a tongue-lashing—or something worse?

But Solagen didn't look angry. He looked pensive. Finally, without slowing his step, the king began to speak. "Auragole, you know how often I have chided you, even chastised you, for being too independent, too unwilling to conform. . ."

Auragole swallowed hard and his heart began to beat wildly. It must have to do with Meraleese.

"I have told you time and again that a good soldier, a good citizen must conform, must subordinate his own personal will to the good of the state, must let those in charge do the thinking and the deciding." Solagen stopped then and looked solemnly at Auragole.

"Yes, Sire," Auragole answered him, his voice soft and low. He tried to hold the man's gaze. It was a penetrating one. Auragole hoped his face did not reveal how uneasy he felt.

But after a moment, Solagen once again strode forward. "Well, what I said was true. But there is an exception. Let me explain. So that there can be a state, an empire that is peaceful and orderly, people, and especially soldiers, must comply with the rules of that state, that empire."

"So you have told me, Sire." Auragole's heart was racing, but he hoped nothing but passivity showed on his countenance, because Solagen was watching him as they walked.

"But that has a drawback." Solagen waited for Auragole's response.

"A drawback? And what is that, Sire?"

"It doesn't foster the development of—what shall I call it?—vision, creative vision. Individuals who can do more than fight wars, plot, connive, or gossip. It doesn't foster the development of individuals who can see beyond the present, see into a glorious and new future."

Auragole tried to formulate an answer, but Solagen held up his hand. "Let me finish. Would it surprise you to know that that inability troubles me? Oh, not as a rule, you understand. As a rule we don't want people of vision, people who have ideas that differ from the state's. We want compliant, cooperative people. This you understand."

"I think so, Sire."

"But in its supreme leader the country needs a man of vision, of far-reaching sight, even of independence."

"And they have it, Sire, in you. You are admired greatly for that."

"Don't flatter me, Auragole. I don't want that. . .not from you."

Auragole flushed. Had he been flattering? Had he been fawning?

But Solagen was not looking at him. "Now take my two nephews. They are good commanders, good soldiers. But does either have vision? Can they imagine what might happen in the future, and deduce from that insight what action is needed now? I'm not saying they aren't clever. They can scheme, can plan with great deviousness something in their own self-interest. But can they envision a larger plan for the future of the Grand Continent?" He shook his head. "Let me give them their due. Both are good soldiers. But could either lead in peace as well as war, hold together seven countries, each with its own obstreperous leader or leaders?"

Did Solagen expect an answer from him?

However, Solagen went on. "I fear for the Westernlands, Auragole. Now that we have brought peace and order, I fear for the future. How long do I have left? No one knows that answer. But I think it unlikely that I will ever have a son of my own, at least not one I can train carefully from infancy to adulthood to be a leader with creative vision. And if I were to have a son, and I didn't live to see him grown and capable of taking on the rulership of so vast an empire, someone would have to act as regent."

Solagen was looking down the length of the path they were walking on through the large arch that led into the wilderness garden, as if in the far trees the future was beckoning. "Neither Goredahl with his heavy-handedness and his shortsightedness, nor Veldarr with his easygoing manner, will make a good king—a commander of soldiers, yes, but king? No. Of a small country, perhaps, but of an empire? No." Solagen turned to look directly into Auragole's eyes. "Auragole, these words I am speaking must remain confidential, only between the two of us. I have never spoken of this to anyone, not even to Oldwell, whose friendship and advice I highly value."

Auragole was bewildered, but he said, "You have my word, Sire."

"I have another idea." He stopped walking and Auragole followed suit. Solagen crossed his arms and the look he gave Auragole was unwavering, almost piercing. "You."

Auragole stared at Solagen. The confusion that he felt was written all over his face. He made no attempt to hide it. "Me, what? What do you mean?"

"You have vision and independence and can think boldly and creatively—if I don't manage to hammer out those unique kinks in your thinking in a few years."

Auragole reddened. Was Ormahn complimenting him or reproaching him?

"Now we come to the heart of it, Auragole." Solagen sat down on a bench at the far side of the garden and motioned Auragole to sit down next to him.

Auragole sat down and waited. Before them was a formal garden, much of it still green, and beyond it the large and imposing palace that was home to Solagen and the seat of the government. Only the Lady Claregole's mansion in Agavia was more beautiful, Auragole thought. But he was brought out of his reverie by Solagen's words.

"I'd like to adopt you, Auragole. That would make

everything legal, make you legally my son, and therefore heir to the throne. I'd like to bring you into the palace to live, begin tutoring you in all the things you would need to know in order to govern well. You have all the qualities required. All you lack is experience and knowledge."

He looked sideways at Auragole, whose body had gone rigid with the shock of the words he had just heard. Auragole was too stunned to notice the look of satisfaction on Solagen's face as Solagen turned from him to stare up at the palace.

"You're intelligent, a person who can listen, a leader of men. You're quick-witted, an able soldier, you're still quite an independent thinker, a creative and original thinker—look at your ideas about new weaponry. Look at what you were able to accomplish at the conference with the Isofedians. It was your ideas that resolved everything. You, Auragole, have those rare qualities—insight and vision, and the ability to synthesize various and often opposing arguments into something new and workable. It was you who understood the Isofedians' need to keep their land from being trod upon by outsiders, no matter how superstitious the rest of us thought them. You were the one who came up with the plan they finally accepted—their soldiers withdrawing within their walls, ours encamped outside. If we had listened to Goredahl or some of the others we would have been drawn into never-ending battles. And that group of zealots would have fought us without letup if we had pushed our way into their country. There would have been a constant harrowing of our soldiers, constant bloodshed and endless war because of their fanaticism—battles worse than anything we've seen in Thorensphere. Religion. It makes people crazy."

Auragole didn't see Solagen turn to look at him. Auragole was staring out at the autumn garden, too astonished to answer, too amazed to keep his face from exposing his feelings.

Solagen went on. "No other in my circle has your foresight. Afraid to think, that lot. I don't know why I go to them for advice. I can see their minds busy working, trying to figure out what it is I want to hear. That, you must admit, is not much help." He stopped speaking and turned his head to look at Auragole, who now was staring at him, pale and dazed.

"Don't tell me you have never thought of being Ormahn, of ruling all of the Westernlands?"

"No. . .I never. . ." He couldn't go on.

Solagen put his arm around Auragole's shoulders. "Let's move. You're holding your breath. Just breathe deeply." They rose and resumed their walk.

And Auragole breathed deeply.

"Listen to me, son. I am coming to you with a request, not a command, for there is much you must give up and much that you must take upon yourself—even powerful enmity—should you acquiesce. If you accept my offer, you will move into the palace. You will leave your house and your society life behind, or most of it. You will give up visiting that woman—the wife of the priest—yes, yes, I know all about it. You will have to follow me about all day and halfway into the night, studying and learning the ways of governments and governing. I warn you there is nothing glamorous in most of this work."

When Auragole's words finally came out, they were barely above a whisper. "I hardly know what to say."

"That's why I'm not asking for your answer just now. Take three days. But confide in no one. This is something you must want, Auragole, not something I can command you to do. You must take your own counsel. If you decide yes, I will send both my nephews as commanders to Isofed. While they are away, I will arrange for the adoption, and prepare the papers for the right of succession. It will all be completed before either of my nephews gets wind of this, before one or the other takes some unwise and desperate action against you—or me. However, if you say no, then I will send you as commander to Isofed for six months, for in truth you are the better man for Isofed. If you agree to my offer, then half a year away will give the two hopefuls time to adjust to my decision and to cool off. They won't even hear of the adoption ceremony until weeks after it is over."

"What. . .what can I say, Sire? I never. . .I always assumed. . ." Auragole's head was spinning and for a moment he thought he was going to pass out. He breathed deeply, and then focused hard on a maple tree with some of its leaves still clinging to it.

Finally, Solagen said, "Auragole?"

Auragole turned to him, his face drained of color, a feeling of vertigo wobbling his knees and making him light-headed. He did observe Solagen's look of deep gratification.

"Go home now, son, and think hard. Take three days to come to terms with what is being offered you. But look at this offer from all sides. There is much you will have to sacrifice for this. You will have to put aside all personal dreams, perhaps even your singing and song-making, for there will be little time for that. You realize you will become a powerful man, next only to me in authority, and many will fawn on you or dote on you because of who you are. And some will plot against you, and you will have to be wary at all times about whom you can trust and with whom you should be circumspect. But despite that power, despite the popularity, the adulation, in the end your life will be one of sacrifice to the public. And of loneliness." He paused for a moment, then went on in a more hearty voice. "However, what you will gain, son, when you take over the throne, is the satisfaction of a united Westernlands, and perhaps by then, a united Grand Continent. Come, I'll walk with you to the stables."

FOR AN HOUR after returning from the palace, Auragole strode distractedly through his large house. But he couldn't think. If his servants gave him strange looks, he didn't notice it. He couldn't get past the shock of Solagen's unexpected offer.

Finally, he had Starwanderer saddled and he rode out of the city into the park to its west and above the sea. The sound of the horse's hooves kept time with the words in his head. "Solagen has offered to adopt you, to make you his heir. Solagen has offered to adopt you, to make you his heir. His heir, his heir. . ." For a while his heart expanded till he thought it would burst. He, Auragole, son of Goloss, could one day become Ormahn of Mattelmead. It was unbelievable.

But he couldn't do it.

He didn't have the abilities. He was merely the son of a hardworking farmer. He had been raised in solitude in the great Gandlese until nearly eighteen years of age. He didn't know anything about governing. He didn't know anything about being a king. Or about life. Or about people. Granted, he had learned much in the years he had been in Mattelmead, and much in war, and even much from his earlier travels, from their hardships, before coming to Mattelmead. He was far from the child he had been when his parents were alive. Far from the youth who had started out on his journey six years earlier. He was twenty-four now, an able soldier, capable of planning a campaign and of leading it, of moving an army over vast territories, with all its equipment and food. He knew something of administration. He had learned that while he was Ormahn's emissary in Wildenfarr. But become Ormahn of Mattelmead some day? King? More than king, overking of the United West?

What would his father think of him now?

Auragole rode through the crunchy autumn leaves for an hour, feeling enormous pride. To be second in command in the entire Westernlands, second only to Solagen. To be adopted and to become the legitimate son and heir of Solagen. It was too much, too much. He laughed at the wonder and the absurdity of it; then he was weeping uncontrollably. Finally, he took hold of himself. Think, he said, think for a moment of what you will give up for the honor of being Solagen's son and heir, and measure the shadow side before you become weighed down by pride and haven't a rational thought left.

And so he began to think.

First, it would mean leaving his own house, which, despite dozens of servants, afforded him some measure of privacy and a great measure of freedom. If he moved into the palace, he would be under scrutiny night and day, probably never allowed to go out without a retinue of guards to accompany him. He could not move in society as he had before, at his own choosing and disposition. Could not have guests or parties. How did he feel about giving up the ladies, or at least the ladies of his own choice? That bothered him less, since his heart had turned again and again to Meraleese.

Meraleese. He would not be able to see her. How sneak out of the palace at night? He had thought about her often while he was away in Glovale, had dreamt of her night after night. If he had hoped that being away would cool off his infatuation with her, it had not.

Give her up, Ormahn had told him.

But if he stopped seeing her, how would his heart manage? Fool, some part of his being answered him. She cares not a whit for you. All she feels for you is gratitude. Would you give up a kingdom just to be in the presence of someone who cannot love you? But someday, when he became Ormahn of Mattelmead. . . But how would Meraleese manage without his help? Who would see to it that Meraleese's letters to her son were sent to Don and Sylvie?

Auragole moved through the park, which was almost empty of visitors on this autumn day, unable for a time to turn from the concern he felt for Meraleese, for her ability to survive and be kept from the work camps—until he realized that there was something else, something deeply a part of him and his identity that he would have to sacrifice to become heir.

Singing.

What about singing? Solagen saw it merely as a pleasurable pastime. He enjoyed listening to Auragole sing, but he didn't truly value it. Not when he compared it to soldiering, to governing, to bringing peace and order to a war-torn world. But was Auragole ready to give it up, to sing only for his own pleasure all alone in his rooms—if he were ever really alone?

And then there was something else. Auragole, True-singer.

"Find me with what is most truly yourself."

Wasn't that True-singing? Wasn't it while True-singing that he was most himself, his best self?

Auragole pulled Starwanderer to a halt. Had he really hoped that one day, in the not-too-distant future, when the west was united and peace reigned, he would be free to seek out Lorenwile and once again study True-singing? Auragole had made an excellent beginning. But perhaps he had forgotten it all. Perhaps he could no longer do it.

The thought of never again True-singing brought him as low as he had been high at the thought of being a king.

But the west *was* at peace now that Isofed had been brought under Ormahn's governance. He could go now in search of Lorenwile. He could leave soldiering behind and resume his tutelage under Lorenwile. Yes, he could do that. However, if someday he would be Ormahn, then he could do anything he wanted to do!

Think! Solagen was in his forties, in good health. He would probably live well into his sixties. It would be twenty-five years before Auragole could bring Lorenwile back to Mattelmead. But if Lorenwile was still alive, he, too, would be in his sixties.

No good. Ormahn or True-singing. Not both.

"Find me with what is most truly yourself."

Perhaps this was it—this unexpected offer. To become the next Ormahn of Mattelmead, to be a peace bringer—not only to the Westernlands but possibly to the whole Grand Continent. As a True-singer he could offer something restorative to those who could hear him, could even bring healing to the earth, as Lorenwile had when he sang health back to the war-damaged temple in Adelmorr and the land about it. But was that a task to equal what Ormahn could do for the known world? Was True-singing more a selfish longing? Still, the thought of giving it up, and the thought of giving up all contact with Meraleese, weighed heavily on his heart.

No gain without sacrifice, he thought. Sometimes incredible sacrifice. And that's what Solagen was demanding of him.

No, that wasn't right. Solagen was not demanding, he was asking.

Auragole turned his horse around and rode back through the streets of Mattelmead to his home. That night he tossed and turned and could not come to a decision.

The following day he walked—sometimes aimlessly, sometimes purposefully—through the streets of the city, looking at all that Solagen had wrought there. It was a marvelous city, a beautiful city, full of grace and charm, filled with all the trappings that made a city vibrant—great architecture, all the fine arts, the performing arts, science, commerce, fashion, society. Solagen had plans to bring to all the countries he now occupied something of what he had caused to happen in Mattelmead City—along with peace, order, and compliance. Replicas of Mattelmead City all over the west.

Compliance. He sighed.

What was wrong with compliance? It had rid the west of war. Compliance was a good thing.

But you, Auragole, are not always compliant. You have found opportunities to go your own way. You have disobeyed orders when they seemed unjust. Still, isn't that what Solagen admires about you?

But another voice said, Nonsense. Your transgressions are minor ones, hardly worth noting. Like any good soldier or any good citizen, you serve and you obey. You take orders and do as you are told. You are not the independent man you once were, or thought you were.

Yes, but I have given up that personal freedom for the greater good. For the peace and stability of Mattelmead, of all the west.

Yes, so you have, but don't give yourself airs. You are not the free man your father had wished you to be.

But he would be proud of me all the same.

Are you so sure?

Maybe he had given up too much. Maybe the independence Solagen saw in him was just a little bit of high spirits. Were his ideas really so creative, so full of vision? Or when offering his ideas was he just intuiting what Solagen wanted to hear and speaking for Solagen's approval? Was Auragole so different from Veldarr or Goredahl?

He wished he had someone to talk to. He needed to converse with someone about this. But he had been forbidden. He walked past the closed-up house of Sylvane and Donnadorr, who now stayed year-round at their country estate because of Glorr. He walked past Meraleese's house, hoping for a glimpse of her, but he had none, and he could not call, not in the daytime. And maybe never again. Even if he saw her, he wouldn't be able to speak of this. He had been told to speak to no one of this.

Auragole walked and walked, past Lorenwile's old house, now occupied by a sculptor and his family, past the Blue Heron where he had sung with Lorenwile in those first happy months after his arrival in Mattelmead. He felt again the old sorrow of Lorenwile's leaving Mattelmead without informing him, felt the hurt of Lorenwile's lack of trust. If only Auragole could talk to him. What would Lorenwile tell him to do? Auragole wondered. What would Don tell him to do, or Sylvie? He suddenly thought of Agavia, of his cousins Galavi and the Lady Claregole. What advice would Claregole give him? Or Pohl? Or Meekelorr? Surely his old friend Elarr, if Auragole were able to talk to him, would give him clear advice. And Affredda; she had a way of seeing right to the heart of things. But none of these old friends was near. And even if they were, he wouldn't have been able to ask them.

He tried for a fruitless hour to imagine what each might say if he or she were there and Auragole allowed to ask. But his imagination was his own and he heard no new arguments. He had made them all himself.

That night, exhausted from his long walk, he once again had that terrible recurring dream about the destruction of Agavia. He woke up in a cold sweat and sat upright. Horrible, he thought. Horrible. It's only that old worry, he told himself, breathing hard. But as Ormahn's heir, I could see that it doesn't happen. If we keep peace in the west, that will keep Agavia at peace. There need not be a Last Battle. I could be instrumental in seeing that the west stays peaceful.

After a few moments, he lay back down and fell into a dreamless sleep. When he woke later, the earlier dream had faded from his memory.

Today was his last day. Tomorrow morning he would have to tell Solagen his decision. He ordered a hot bath, sent the servant away, and lay in the tub until the water was cold and uncomfortable. Afterward, he sat in his robe in his chair before the fire, going over and over the arguments. Finally, he said to himself, "Stop this. Think of something else. Do something else. You will decide tonight. Leave it be."

So Auragole picked up his harp and played and sang for hours, songs he had sung with Donnadorr, songs he had sung with Lorenwile, with Meraleese. Songs he had written while he was in Mattelmead. He refused lunch and did not stop singing until late in the afternoon. Then he napped. When he woke up he had made his decision. He had one more thing that he must do late that night.

chapter twenty

WHEN ALL THE servants were in bed, Auragole rose, put on dark clothes, and walked through the crisp November city streets until he came to Meraleese's house. He had seen her once, two days after returning from the conference with Isofed in Glovale. The moment he laid eyes on her, all the old feelings had come rushing back. What is this, he had asked himself that night on his way back home, if this is not love? Feelings that cannot be driven away with other distractions, what are they if not love? But his father had warned him. . . And this was definitely not the spiritual kind of love that Meraleese had spoken to him about.

There had been a woman in Auragole's bed every night after that visit—until Solagen's offer. But too often, inappropriately, Auragole's thoughts had strayed to Meraleese. He had even imagined once that he was making love to Meraleese, and had been especially ardent that night. Afterward, he lay awake, elbow on his pillow, leaning on his hand, looking at the woman he had pretended was another. She was exceptionally beautiful, even in sleep, with her long blond hair lying about her, framing her head with a hundred silver curls. The expression on her flawless face was one of deep contentment. He felt a little guilty. What male acquaintance of his would not have been overjoyed to have such a beauty in his bed? But he had thought of another while making love to this one—thought of a plain woman with thick brown hair and large, hazel eyes, a woman not like this one, but one who would walk unnoticed and undesired in a crowd.

The window Meraleese left unlocked for him was still unlocked. He climbed in, walked to the second floor, and knocked on her bedchamber door. In a few minutes, a large shawl covering her nightgown, she opened the door. Auragole moved toward the sitting room without a word, and she followed him. He sat on the sofa and she took the chair opposite him.

When he didn't speak, she finally said, "Auragole, what troubles you? How can I help?"

"Meraleese, I wish I could tell you. I wish I could share my concerns with you, but I can't. I've been sworn to silence about this. . .this problem. Sorry to sound so mysterious. In a few weeks you will know and understand everything." He stared at her, not needing to hide his sorrow in the dark room.

Her voice held a note of anxiety when she spoke. "You're not in trouble, are you?" And she leaned forward as if to see him better.

"No, no, nothing like that. But after tonight, I can no longer come to visit you. Not just because I've been forbidden—that you already know, and it hasn't stopped me. But I can't come to you because I'll be unable."

"You're going away?"

He shook his head. "No."

"Nothing bad is going to happen to you?" she asked, and he could hear the alarm in her words, and it gratified him.

"No, no, nothing bad at all. In fact, it might be something wonderful. . . I can't say more than that. But there's no need for you to worry on my account. I've come to say farewell—at least for a time. And to tell you that somehow I will see to it that you are provided for. However, I'm not sure that I can send your messages to Glorr."

"Oh," she said in a small voice.

"I'll try to arrange something. But you must have patience and give me time."

"I'm not sure I understand, Auragole. This is all so mysterious."

"I know. I know. Meraleese, this is all very painful for me, this parting. Surely you know the way I feel about you." And his throat ached as the words passed his lips.

She didn't answer. But in the shadowed light he could see her downcast face.

"And I know that my feelings are unreciprocated. I understand. Who could compare to the man you already had?"

"Auragole. . ."

"No, it's not necessary for you to say anything. I understand it and am resigned. Please don't be concerned on my account. I've come to say good-bye, and to tell you not to worry. You won't be left without help. I'll see to that, no matter what." He rose to his feet. "I. . .I don't want to prolong this. It's best if I leave now."

She stood up and came to him. He took her hands and then gave her a hug. He walked quickly to the door of the parlor.

"Auragole?"

He stopped mid-flight and waited without turning toward her.

"Auragole, when you think of me, think this. There are many ways to love. Not just one. Each relationship creates its own unique bond of love. It need not be like another, nor compared to another. Go, with the guidance of the Prince. I will miss you greatly."

278

And Auragole flew down the stairs, for if he had stayed for one more word, he might have reversed his decision.

HE WAS AT the palace, waiting outside Solagen's office, at the appointed time the following morning. When he walked through the door toward Solagen's desk, the king stood up, his face registering first curiosity and then something that Auragole could only call dismay. Ormahn was afraid of being rejected! He wanted him as son, as heir. Auragole's heart lifted a bit, and he gave Solagen a smile.

Solagen sat down and motioned Auragole to the chair opposite him. "Well?" he said, when both of them were seated.

"I have thought hard these few days, Sire. If I said the decision was easy, I would be lying."

Solagen cocked his head and looked curiously at him. "So difficult a choice, Auragole?"

"So overwhelming an offer, Solagen. It needed weighing. You place a lot of faith in me. I feel, frankly, inadequate to the task."

Solagen dismissed Auragole's concern with a wave of his hand. "We will quickly remedy that. You have years to learn. I do not intend to leave this earth so soon, not until the entire Grand Continent is under my banner."

"May the Gods grant you that wish."

"Well, we won't rely too much on the Gods, but on our own good health and abilities. So, other than the fear that you are not able enough for the job of Ormahn, do you have other qualms?"

Auragole stared at his folded hands, then looked up at Solagen. "You yourself have named the things that I must give up, and I have thought long on them."

"And?"

Auragole could hear the impatience in Solagen's voice. He wanted an answer. "I've come to say yes—but with one stipulation."

Auragole watched Solagen's face register first relief and then amusement. "And what is this stipulation?"

"It has to do with the wife of the priest, the woman called Meraleese."

Solagen's eyes narrowed.

"I want you to understand just what the relationship is between the two of us. We are not lovers. I'm very fond of her, but we are not lovers. I am willing, since you requested it, not to see her again. But I cannot desert her entirely, cannot leave her without a means of support, left only to the charity of friends because of the overzealousness of Goredahl. I cannot leave her to the work camps. I feel culpable for her plight, and I cannot back away from my sense of responsibility toward her. I have a proposition for you. If you can accept it or something like it, then I will give you my word to quit visiting her."

"And if I don't agree to your proposition or something like it?"

"Then you will have to send me to Isofed. I will not accept your generous offer."

Solagen stared at him coolly. For a moment Auragole thought, all is lost, I have been impudent and there will be no adoption and no Isofed, maybe something far worse. But suddenly Solagen was laughing, and it was a delighted laugh.

"All right, Auragole. Tell me your proposition."

"I want some arrangement for money and food to be sent to the lady monthly."

"That seems like an easy thing to arrange. And for this arrangement you will promise to stop seeing her in the night or taking her to your country estate for clandestine visits."

Auragole's face reddened. So, Solagen knew that, too. How foolish Auragole felt. But he nodded.

"Then, Auragole of Mattelmead, let me make you a counteroffer. I will agree to a monthly stipend for the lady—on the condition that she be removed from Mattelmead City and sent to live somewhere else. Then there will be no concern on my part, and no temptation on your part to break your word and visit her."

"But where would she be sent? You propose to send her to live as a stranger somewhere?"

"Does she not have family?"

"Those outside the city no longer are in touch with her."

"Friends outside the city?"

Auragole shook his head. And then an idea, like lightning, struck him. "I know of one couple whom she knows, who might be glad to have her as governess to their child."

"And what are their names?"

"Donnadorr and Sylvane. They live many hours from the city."

The laughter rolled out of Solagen. "Auragole, you are something. I might call you devious, but perhaps I shall simply say you think quickly. So you would have the priest's wife become governess to her own child?"

Auragole's face registered the shock he was feeling.

"I like it. I like the irony of it. I think that quite a crafty proposition."

"You do?" Auragole could not keep the surprise from his words.

"And I'll tell you why. If your friend is reunited with her child, if she is given a stipend, and if she is far from you and your concerns, then I think I have the better part of the bargain. Because then, Auragole, soon to be heir to the throne of Mattelmead and of the United West, you will put her out of your mind and no longer feel any sense of obligation toward her, and put all your thoughts and concerns on learning what it means to be prince of Mattelmead." Solagen's words had become cool and challenging. "Now have I understood your stipulation?"

Auragole gulped and nodded.

"And have you understood and accepted my counteroffer?"

"Yes, Sire."

"And have you understood clearly your end of the bargain?"

"I have."

"And do you now agree to the adoption and to become heir to the throne with an untroubled heart?"

"Yes."

"So quiet a yes?"

"I must in honesty say that I will regret only that I must set aside my singing. But I am willing."

"Then, son," Solagen said, rising, "come in to lunch with me." His tone was light, and a note of pleasure sounded in it. "And after lunch we will discuss how soon we can arrange these matters. This must remain secret for a while—just between the two of us. Before nightfall I will summon both Veldarr and Goredahl to the palace. They will be told to ready themselves to leave for Isofed within the week." And he came round the desk, took Auragole by the arm, and walked with him out of the office.

THE FOLLOWING WEEK Auragole's mood went from the heights of elation to the depths of despair. He kept up his social obligations, meeting friends for dinner, going to parties and other entertainments. He savored every moment of his freedom to go and come as he chose. He was about to lose that freedom. And yet he looked forward to the challenge of learning all the things he needed to learn to become Ormahn. The truth was, other than training with his Elite Corps, other than planning for and going to war, he was somewhat bored with his life in Mattelmead. Going to Isofed, to oversee the army there, would have been challenging. But without this offer from Solagen, life would have become too routine, for Solagen had no plans to go to the Easternlands until the west was well consolidated under his rule and until his army was enlarged and trained. Two or three years at least. All he would have had as an obligation was his thrice-weekly training of the Elite Corps.

He wondered, had Solagen not offered him this incredible gift, if he might not have slipped away one day to seek out Lorenwile in Agavia—as he had thought of doing while still in Wildenfarr, as he had thought of doing while pondering Solagen's offer—and beg Lorenwile to accept him once again as a student. He tried to push away the sorrow of True-singing abandoned, of never seeing Meraleese again. But life demanded sacrifices, and those who would truly serve humankind had to make the largest sacrifices. By the end of the week Veldarr and Goredahl would be on their way to Isofed. Soon after that he would move into the palace. In six weeks or so, he would be adopted and declared heir to the throne of Mattelmead and of the United West.

The intensity of his emotions was more than he could handle, so a few days after his talk with Solagen he decided to go out hunting. He took with him his second in command, Roradahl, and a few other friends from the Elite Corps. There were woods half a dozen miles east of the city, set aside for the officers of the army to hunt in.

They had been out only a short time, perhaps an hour, moving stealthily through the trees, hoping to spot a deer. Suddenly an arrow shot past Auragole's face, causing Starwanderer to rear up and Auragole to shout loudly, "Hey!" In a moment the four men from the Elite Corps, their bows drawn, stood between Auragole and the direction from which the arrow had come.

"Wait, wait," a familiar voice called out. "Don't shoot. We thought you were deer." And out of the bushes came Goredahl, on foot, with five men.

"You almost killed Auragole, you fool," Roradahl shouted, too angry to care that it was Goredahl whom he was addressing.

"Peace, Roradahl," Goredahl smiled. "It was an error. We

must have fallen asleep here in the bushes and when we heard the sound of hooves, we assumed that it was deer. Sorry. But look, no damage done. Auragole is quite unharmed." He smiled a crooked smile at Auragole. But Auragole thought his eyes cold and filled with hate.

"Where are your horses?" Auragole said, his heart still pounding loudly in his chest.

"They're tethered a mile or so back." Goredahl motioned with his head. "We thought to make less noise on foot and not frighten the deer, which seem to be very scarce today."

Auragole looked at him calculatingly. "Well, go back to your bushes, then, but stay awake. You're not the only hunters out today." And he turned and rode off, his four companions following him.

When they were out of earshot of Goredahl and his friends, Auragole said, "I think I've had enough of hunting for today." He led his party out of the woods with no attempt at silence, and then turned toward Mattelmead.

He did not report the incident to Ormahn. Best let it slide. Goredahl would be gone soon and Auragole did not want to have his last few days of freedom curtailed by Solagen. He had no proof that the incident was other than an accident. Still, it was hard to believe that so skilled a soldier as Goredahl could not tell the difference between horses' hooves and deer hooves. Was it possible that Goredahl knew Solagen's plans? Or was this pure malevolence on the part of Goredahl? The king had said he would tell no one until his two nephews were out of the country and Auragole safely in the palace.

Goredahl and his Security Forces. If Auragole could do something about that when he was heir and close to Solagen, he would. Yes, he would definitely do something about that.

N

chapter twenty-one

THE NIGHT BEFORE the adoption ceremony, Auragole had a dream about his father.

Once again Auragole was in Wildenfarr-low-desert, sleeping at an oasis, on his way home to Mattelmead. Goloss, standing on the edge of the oasis, called his name, and Auragole rose up out of sleep and walked toward him. Once again his father led him away from the slight glow of the night fire toward an outcropping of rock. When Auragole caught up with him, his father turned and stared at him, a look of sorrow on his face. "So you are now going to be adopted by Ormahn of Mattelmead."

Auragole felt stricken. "Yes, but that doesn't mean that you will cease to be my father. . .my real father."

But the mournful look on his father's face did not change.

"It is more a political arrangement." Auragole wanted to reassure Goloss. "You see, Solagen wants me as heir to the throne, and in order to do this without causing legal battles or internal challenges he has to adopt me first."

The two men sat down on rocks facing each other. "Do you remember what I said to you the last time we talked?" Goloss asked.

"I think so."

"I warned you, son, of the difficult days to come."

"I remember."

"Yes, yes. . .difficult days." His father looked out at the vastness of the desert. "There is peace here," he said, "where few men are."

"A fierce war was fought for that peace, Father. Ormahn led the war, and I was one of his commanders."

Goloss turned to him. "You have become a soldier—even a courageous soldier. You will need that courage in the days to come."

"Father, what are you trying to tell me? Are you trying to warn me of something?"

His father's expression was still sad. "The challenging days will soon come. And I have not raised you to face them. How little I taught you. What an angry and selfish fool I was."

"Why a fool, Father? You gave me much. And since you've died I have also learned much. Surely I can face whatever troubles will come." He felt himself pleading for his father's affirmation.

Goloss stood up and turned to leave. "Remember," he said.

"Father," Auragole called to him. "Tell me that you approve of me. Tell me that I have made you proud. Tell me that I have helped give to the world what you yourself wanted for it—peace."

His father turned back to him and said, "Son, is this peace enough?"

"Tell me what is lacking, Father."

"You know." Goloss began walking into the desert night. "I love you, Auragole. I always have. Remember that when the hard times come."

Auragole woke up, his heart racing. He sat up in his bed in the palace. It was dark in his room. He didn't know what the hour was. He swung his feet over the edge of his bed and stood up. The floor was cold, even through the carpet. He walked over to the window and pulled aside the drapes. It was winter dark. Auragole stood shivering as he looked out at the blackness. What had that dream meant—if anything? Difficult times ahead? Well, of course there were difficult times ahead. When had there not been difficult times?

Was this peace enough? his father had once again asked. Auragole didn't have the answer to that one. But this he did know, peace came first. Of that he was certain. All else rested on that foundation.

But why had his father come to him? Why had he dreamt of his father just this night before the adoption ceremony? Perhaps, deep down, Auragole felt he was abandoning his birth father. That was probably it. But his father was dead. Auragole thought he had explained this well to Goloss—and to himself. This adoption was a political arrangement. He was fond of Solagen, admired Solagen, looked up to Solagen. But this was a legal arrangement so that Solagen could have whom he wanted as heir. And that happened to be Auragole. He was not deserting his real father. No need to feel this blame, and no need to worry about whatever difficulties might come. He was used to hard times. He had faced many since leaving his valley. Perhaps Goloss didn't know about these, didn't know how much Auragole had changed since his father had died. Auragole would manage the future and whatever came with it quite well. He wasn't afraid.

Auragole walked back to his bed, climbed in, and got under the covers. There were still a few hours of sleep left in the night. Tomorrow was a big day and he wanted to be rested. He fell asleep, and when he woke up the next morning he was far too busy to worry about that dream.

THE ENORMOUS GATES that gave access to the large outer courtyard of the palace were usually locked. That day they stood open wide. Beyond was the public park that surrounded the palace grounds. It was the third day of January—cold, sunny, the air crisp and dry. The snow had been swept clean from the courtyard where at least two hundred invited guests now waited, wrapped in their fine cloaks, hats or hoods covering their heads. Auragole watched them from the second-floor balcony outside the ceremonial hall of the palace. Then he glanced out at the park beyond the gates, where there seemed to be thousands of people.

Solagen stood next to him. Directly behind them were Oldwell and several pages. Auragole knew exactly where everyone on the balcony was placed—they had rehearsed it many times. There was an honor guard, carrying flags with a variety of coats of arms. The pages next to Oldwell held pillows on which items were arrayed for use in the ceremony. To the right of Ormahn, come down for this occasion from their country estate and seated on gilded chairs, were his wife and their three daughters, the youngest held by a nurse. They were dressed in their finest clothes under their warm capes. Jeweled combs adorned their hair under the loose hoods that covered their heads. To the left, seated on carved wooden chairs, were a harp player and a flute player. In the corners of the balcony, facing the public, were four guards with bows and arrows held loosely in their hands. His friend Roradahl, now Auragole's own personal guard, was one of them. Glancing at him, off to his right, he saw Roradahl studying the crowd below. Mixed in with the crowd on both sides of the palace gates were many soldiers, all well armed, all from his own Elite Corps.

Auragole and Solagen stood at the rail of the balcony, attired in the dress uniforms of the officers of the army of Mattelmead, lapis blue with elaborate gold braid. But for this occasion they wore no capes and no hats. Auragole looked out at the shouting crowd and did as Solagen did—he waved and smiled. They were chanting first "Solagen, Solagen," and then "Auragole, Auragole," and clapping their hands.

It had been little more than a week after Veldarr and Goredahl had left for Isofed that the order had come for Auragole to move into the palace. He was to bring only a few necessities. He was not to close down his house, nor say anything to the members of his household other than that he had been asked to stay at the palace for a time—something like that could not be kept secret. Semp and Lors had come with him then, as had Starwanderer. Auragole had taken some clothes and his harp, and nothing else. Even today his house was still his house, his servants still on full pay. Tomorrow, his house would be shut down and put up for sale, all his personal items would be brought to the palace, and most of his servants would be absorbed into the palace staff.

So this is it, Auragole thought, looking down at the cheering crowd. There's no turning back now.

For a month he had been living in the palace. For a month he had been dogging Ormahn's steps. Auragole had been in Solagen's office when he had received visitors, been at every one of Solagen's meetings, stood nearby when Ormahn sat on the throne of judgment and sentenced those who were said to be criminals or those who were said to be traitors. Auragole partook of every meal the king ate, and attended every state dinner that Solagen attended. The only times Auragole was not with the king were when either one used the toilet or bathed, or when they slept.

At night there were guards outside Auragole's bedchamber— men from the Elite Corps. As Auragole followed Solagen about the palace, Roradahl and two others discreetly followed him. What Roradahl thought about Auragole's stay in the palace, Auragole had often wondered. But he had offered no explanation, and Roradahl had not asked. The whole palace,

Auragole knew, had been astir with curiosity and rumor after Auragole had come to stay. He remembered the buzzing among the servants whenever he passed by. He had been in the palace four weeks now, and before yesterday rumors must have circulated around the city. To keep from fomenting trouble, it was not until the previous day that Solagen posted notices in every public place to inform the populace of today's momentous event. Invitations were hand delivered to nearly two hundred people—those who were now standing in the courtyard below him—inviting them to the ceremony, and to the luncheon that would follow.

Frankly, Auragole was numb. He hadn't allowed himself to think about the road he had set himself on. After he had made the decision to accept Solagen's offer, he had forced himself to stop evaluating and reevaluating what it was he had chosen to do. Only in that dream about Goloss had he felt his decision challenged. And in the clear light of day, that dream and that challenge seemed little more than a residue of unease because of the big step he was about to take.

He looked down at the crowd in the courtyard, searching their faces. He knew many of them, but not one of his old friends was there. How ironic that Meraleese's moving in with Sylvane and Donnadorr, so that she might help with the rearing of Glorr, meant that he would now be cut off from any direct contact with Don and Sylvie. And who was there, of the many people he had come to know in Mattelmead, that he could truly call a friend? Who among society's best could equal in friendship that of Sylvane and Donnadorr? What friendship was on a par with the friendship of Elarr, or Affredda, or even Lorenwile?

Of course, there was Roradahl, and Auragole was grateful for him. But Roradahl was his subordinate. As a captain of the Elite Corps, he was second only to Auragole, and devoted to him. But devotion wasn't what Auragole needed now that he had moved into the palace. Auragole was Roradahl's superior. Even though, before Auragole came to the palace, they had bantered and joked and gossiped over wine about the women they had romanced, Auragole had never shared his inner thoughts with Roradahl. Not the way Auragole had with Meraleese, or with Sylvie and Don, and earlier with Elarr and Affredda. And now, since coming into the palace, Roradahl had treated him with even more deference. Obviously he had suspected that something big was about to happen, something momentous, but it wasn't until just two days before, when rehearsals for this celebration began, that Roradahl had been taken into Solagen's confidence. Still, Auragole was glad that Roradahl was near. He was, at the very least, a man Auragole could depend on.

As Auragole stood there listening to the shouting crowd, listened to his name coupled with Solagen's, he felt utterly alone. But he had been warned about this. Solagen had warned him.

The king was raising his hands to quiet the crowd, and in a few moments utter stillness fell upon the people in the courtyard below. And then, like a slow-moving wave, the quiet rippled through the crowd watching from the park beyond the gates of the palace. Solagen gestured to Oldwell, who picked up a scroll and handed it to him with a slight bow. Solagen turned to the crowd and began to read.

"Hear ye, hear ye, hear ye. On this, the third day of January, I am taking as my lawful son Auragole of Mattelmead. I have done this in accordance with the adoption laws of Mattelmead. He is to be given all the privileges due the first son of a king, including the right of ascendancy to the throne when I am dead."

Murmuring riffled through the crowd.

Solagen continued. "He is now my son and heir to my throne, the throne of all the west. In token of this I mix my blood with his."

He handed the scroll to a page, then turned once again to Oldwell, who took a needle from the cushion held by one of the pages. Solagen and Auragole stepped back and each raised his right hand. Oldwell moved in front of them and pricked their middle fingers—first Solagen's, then Auragole's. He then moved away. The two men turned to face each other and, hands held high, they pressed their fingers together.

Again a murmuring, and then a hush. This was not part of the adoption ceremony as demanded by law. This was something new. The two men held their hands together for several utterly silent minutes.

Then Solagen turned to face the crowd and, with his hand still pressed against Auragole's, he said in a loud, ringing voice, "See, you who are gathered here, now my blood flows in Auragole's. Therefore, he is indeed a son of my blood and of my ancestors' blood."

A wave of mumbling again.

"My son will now be known as Auragole, prince of Mattelmead, and of the entire United West. All such deference and respect that are due a prince and a son of mine will be given to him by you." And then he removed his hand from Auragole's.

A page came up to them, bowed, then wiped their fingers with a damp cloth.

Oldwell turned to another page and took a large crown off the pillow he held, and placed it with great pomp on the head of Solagen. "This crown," Oldwell said hoarsely but loudly, "is a sign of the homage and respect due Solagen, Ormahn of Mattelmead, and now overking of the entire Westernlands." There was much shouting and applause.

Solagen stepped forward and held up his hands to quiet the crowd. "To remind you all of the high honor due my son, I myself shall place the crown of his authority upon his head." A page stepped forward, and Solagen took a crown only slightly less ornate than his own from the pillow the page held out to him and placed it slowly and with great deliberation on Auragole's head. Auragole could feel his knees shake and hoped it wasn't obvious to those who were watching him.

"I wish once again to inform all within the sound of my voice that when I die, the throne and the governance of all the United West will fall to my son, Auragole, prince of Mattelmead. Today I have sent out written proclamations to all the lands of the west to inform everyone under my rule that this is so."

Suddenly a voice called out from the crowd, "Auragole, Auragole, prince of Mattelmead, Auragole, Auragole, heir of Mattelmead." The chant was picked up by those nearby, and soon it had spread throughout the courtyard and finally into the park. A thousand voices shouted, "Auragole, Auragole, prince of Mattelmead, Auragole, Auragole, heir of Mattelmead."

Auragole stood there looking out at the sea of faces, and his heart swelled with pride. He thought it would burst, so excited did he feel. Yes, yes, he had made the right decision. Oh, yes. He smiled a huge smile and turned to look at the king. The king, seeing Auragole's smile of joy, reached out and gave him a warm hug. Now that was something that had not been rehearsed.

While the chanting went on, the king stepped back from Auragole. After a time, as had been rehearsed, he stepped forward again and faced Auragole. He put his hand on Auragole's emblems, an A and an M with a feather across both letters. These had been loosely sewn there, and Solagen pulled them off Auragole's jacket, then turned to the page, took his own emblem off the pillow—two crossed yellow feathers upright on a horizontal red sword—and pinned this on Auragole's jacket.

Once again Solagen turned to a page and took a sword off a pillow. It was a beautiful sword in a jeweled scabbard. He presented the sword to Auragole, who took it with a bow, pulled the sword out of its scabbard, and waved it in the air, then shouted, "In service to Solagen, Ormahn of Mattelmead and of the United West. In service to my father." Then Auragole knelt in front of the king, holding his sword out to him. Solagen took the sword, gave it to a page, and lifted Auragole up. Then the two, hand in hand, raised them and turned to the crowd, which began chanting, "Solagen, Solagen, Auragole, Auragole."

After several minutes of this, Solagen again motioned for silence. "Today just as written proclamations have gone out to all the leaders in all the countries under my rule informing them of the adoption of my son and heir, there will be posted all over the city copies of the adoption papers and of the new name and designation of my heir. In celebration of my happiness and joy, I have declared this day a holiday from work. Food and drink have been set up in tents in the park for all. It is my gift to the city in honor of my son and heir." Again there was much shouting. Solagen waved, then turned and, followed by Auragole, he left the balcony. Just as Auragole turned to follow Solagen, he caught sight of the gates of the courtyard swinging noisily shut while those inside the courtyard filed through a door into the palace. A small trickle of anxiety flowed momentarily through his joy. Shut in, he thought. Then he shook his head to clear it of the dark thought, and the moment passed.

DONNADORR STOOD AS close to the wide-open gates as he was able. He was frozen, more from shock than from the winter cold. He could hear the words spoken plainly. Could see Ormahn and Auragole as they stood there, both looking exceedingly regal. He wasn't able to see their features—that was impossible given the size of the courtyard. But he knew Auragole's face as well as he knew anyone's; they had been through so many adventures together. He could hardly believe what he was seeing, could hardly believe the words that sailed like birdsong, clearly, on the quiet, windless winter air. He wished Sylvane were with him. He imagined with pleasure the stunned look that would cross her face as he described this ceremony.

It was really only by chance that he was here on this particular day. He had come down to the city in a carriage along with two wagons to move Meraleese and her belongings to his estate. The request had come—hard to believe—from Ormahn himself. A messenger had arrived little more than a week ago with a letter on the imperial stationery asking him to take into his household the woman Meraleese, widow of Timorr, a priest who had died recently. Ormahn had suggested that she be given the job of nursemaid and governess to their adopted son, Glorr. Both he and Sylvane had been bewildered by the request. A royal request? Why should such a small matter be of interest to the overking?

"This is the work of Auragole," Sylvane said, after reading the epistle three times. "He is close to Ormahn. How else understand it?"

"You're probably right." Donnadorr looked at her across the small tea table at which they were sitting and held out his hand. She took it. "How do you feel about this, Sylvie?" His eyes explored her face.

"Oh, Don, how can I not feel glad in my heart to see Glorr united with his own mother? I love him. Shouldn't I want what is best for him?"

Donnadorr's breast swelled with caring, almost to bursting, for this wonderful woman he had been so lucky to wed.

"Aurie has been worried about Meraleese," Sylvane said, "ever since he learned that her husband had been imprisoned and executed and the child taken from her. Is this not a happy solution? Meraleese cared for and safe. And I don't think it will harm Glorr in the least to have two mothers who dote on him," she said firmly.

Don rose and came around the table, took her by the

shoulders, lifted her up out of her chair, and hugged her close.

"Besides," she said, when he released her, "I expect now we will see more of Aurie. I think he has feelings for this woman, don't you?"

Standing in the cold, outside the palace, Donnadorr put away those memories. He looked down at Meraleese, standing silently next to him. But her eyes were wide as she stared at the balcony on which this remarkable ceremony was taking place.

Donnadorr had arrived a few days earlier, opening up his own house for his short stay. He then arranged for the transport of Meraleese's belongings to his estate. When he had first met with her, she told him she had not seen Auragole nor heard from him in more than six weeks, though money and food had arrived regularly with no attribution. Don was sure where they had come from.

It was while they were eating a modest noon meal at Meraleese's home the day before this ceremony that a friend of hers had knocked on the door, entered, and told them some astonishing news. It seemed that notices of the adoption were going up all over the city, inviting everyone in the city to come to the park outside the palace the next day and witness the ceremony. The friend told them the news, to the bewilderment of both. Don and Meraleese had left their meal unfinished and had hurried out to the main street nearest Meraleese's house, and found the notice. The two had read it in silence. In silence they had returned to her house.

It wasn't until they were standing in front of the notice that Donnadorr remembered he carried a letter from Auragole to Meraleese that had been delivered to his country estate a few days before Don left for the city. Perhaps Auragole had thought that she had already moved. When Don and Meraleese returned to Meraleese's home, Donnadorr gave her the letter. She had excused herself and had gone to her room to read it.

My stars, Donnadorr thought, staring up at the balcony on

which his old friend stood. Our very own Auragole adopted by Ormahn and now heir to the throne, heir to the vast empire of the west. He could feel the tears sliding down his cheeks. He didn't care. He wanted to turn to his those who stood next to him and shout, "I know him. He is my good friend, and a very good man." Then he looked down and saw tears also streaming down Meraleese's face. But her expression was one not of pride but of loss.

AURAGOLE STOOD—IT seemed like hours—in a reception line, shaking hands. The crown sat heavily on his head, and he couldn't wait till this part of the celebration was over and he could remove it. As each man filed past Auragole and Solagen, he was instructed to sign a large scroll at a table overseen by Oldwell. It was a declaration of fealty to both father and son.

Afterward there was a long-lasting banquet at which many toasts were offered to the father and his new son. Auragole sat next to the king, sharing, on this occasion, the head of a table. Solagen's queen, without the children, sat at the head of another, some tables away. She had watched the ceremony, but had not taken part in it. She was not considered Auragole's mother. So Solagen had decided. Auragole was glad, because the queen was barely older than he.

MERALEESE SAT IN a corner of the carriage that was taking her to safety, and to her son, and once more read the letter Auragole had sent her.

"My dearest Meraleese,

"In a few days you will understand why I am writing this letter to you and saying what I am saying—what I have to say. I hope and pray, now that you are united with your son and living with the kindest and best people I know, that your life will be lifted out of the misery and the sorrow it has been in all these months, and you will find once again peace and even joy.

"It may be years before we can meet again. It is not my own wish but a promise I made. . . But for you, I think, the promise has resulted in happiness and security. And knowing this gives me great inner calm.

"Above all else I write this because I wish you to know that the silence that must now exist between us is not of my own choosing. I think you know that I have feelings for you. I know that you do not return these feelings. Having known, admired, and respected your late husband, I can accept that. He was a great man—far greater than I will ever be, despite the honor about to be bestowed on me that would have others believe differently. But you and I know the truth. So do not fret over my pain. It is pain I bear gladly—particularly now that I know you are reunited with your son, and living free from want with my dearest friends, whom I must also give up as part of my promise. . . You will understand all in a few days. Then you can explain this to Don and Sylvie, and tell them why it must be so.

"Let me just add these words, because I may never have the chance to say them to you in person. You have meant more to me than any woman I have ever met. I have lived more deeply in myself, known myself better, because of you—because of our talks and our wonderful few weeks together last summer. Though destiny has separated us now, I shall keep a special room in my heart for you always.

"Yours,

"Auragole"

Meraleese turned her face to stare out at the window. She didn't want Donnadorr—good, kind Donnadorr—to see the tears welling up in her eyes.

N

chapter twenty-two

VELDARR, SEATED AT his desk in the tent that was his headquarters, a mile from the North Gate of Isofed, heard the sound of horses' hooves outside. A man shouted at his groom, ordering him to attend to his mount. Veldarr waited. In moments, Goredahl thrust the flap back and strode into the tent. Dusty and grimy from a journey of more than two weeks in late-winter weather, Goredahl walked up to Veldarr's desk and, without so much as a greeting, removed his gloves, flung them on the desk, reached inside his cloak to the pouch on his belt, withdrew a few papers from it, and threw them before Veldarr.

"Have you seen these?" he demanded of Veldarr.

Without haste, Veldarr picked up the papers, looked at them perfunctorily, and dropped them back on the desk. "I've seen them, Goredahl. Old news. Sit down. I'll order you some wine."

Goredahl grabbed a chair and set it so that he was directly opposite Veldarr. "Well?" he said.

"Catch your breath. You've been on the road for weeks. We

will talk about this when you've had a drink, a chance to wash and change, and some dinner. Who has come with you?"

"A few of my men, that's all. I left Dorborr in charge at the East Gate. I trust him completely. It's quiet there."

"Good, then we will have time to talk. . .and to plan."

"Did you suspect this? Had you any idea? That sneaky bastard. All this time cozying up to Solagen, pretending indifference to the throne, pretending that there was nothing more that he wanted out of life than to sing. I knew it. I knew he was too good to be genuine. I wish I had killed. . ."

"Goredahl," Veldarr's tone was sharp. He motioned with his head to the young page coming toward them with a tray of wine and glasses. "We'll speak about this at dinner—when it will be just the two of us." He looked meaningfully at Goredahl.

Goredahl took a deep breath and gave Veldarr a curt nod. He took the glass from the tray and held it out, his face studiously blank, as the page poured the wine.

GLENELLE WAS WAITING for him in her formal drawing room. Two chairs were placed next to an open window. It was mid-June and a light breeze was blowing in from the garden, cooling the room. There was no table set with fine linen, china, and silver. No dinner would be served.

She was wearing the latest fashion. The collar on her blouse was high and cream colored, with ruffles setting off her long, elegant neck. Her silk skirt was narrow and just short enough to show off her slim ankles and her dainty feet, which were ensconced in matching silk-and-leather sandals. Her jewelry had been carefully selected. She had adorned herself with fine pieces, but nothing he had given her. Glenelle wanted to look beguiling, sensual—but subtly so. She wanted above all to look reserved, to show her disapproval, her anger. And she was angry.

Veldarr had been back from Isofed for nearly a month. He

had sent her a note a few days after arriving, saying he would come to her as soon as he had taken care of all the army and court business that had accumulated while he was away. He wrote that he needed some time with his wife before returning to his "old routine." He would let Glenelle know as soon as he could come. But a month had passed, and no word had arrived from him. She was furious. She disliked being treated so high-handedly. And she would make her feelings known, not by haranguing him like a commoner, but in this more subtle way. She would not receive him in her bedchamber for an intimate dinner as she had been wont to do in the past. There would be no dinner. Should he seem contrite, there might be a small repast that she could summon easily from the kitchen, and perhaps some wine. But she would wait and see.

Truth was, she wanted very much to know the gossip from the palace. More than six months had passed since Auragole had been adopted by Solagen and had moved into the palace. She had not been invited to the party given to celebrate Auragole's adoption. And she had too much pride to be one of hundreds standing in the January cold, watching from the park. But she had made Glenorr go. Glen was not at all concerned with society, with status—except of course in his own field, where he was making a name for himself in scientific research at the large hospital in Mattelmead. The opinions of his colleagues mattered very much. But not society. So Glen had gone to the ceremony and returned to tell her what he had seen. The news, when it had first been posted all over the city, had stunned her. And what Glen had told her had stunned her more. How would this affect her? Veldarr was away—and no longer a candidate to succeed Solagen to the throne. She wondered how he had taken it when he had heard the news. She could well imagine what Goredahl had felt.

But for Veldarr to stay away from her all this time with nothing other than that short note and the one that had arrived that morning saying he would come in the evening at about nine was, she decided, inexcusable. Yes, she was angry.

And so terribly curious about events in the palace.

"Who would have thought it of our Auragole?" Glen had said when he returned to her after the adoption ceremony. "He has more of the rogue in him than I had given him credit for. Imagine wheedling his way into Solagen's affections. Who would have imagined him so ambitious, or so devious? It is quite beyond me," he said, sipping the wine his sister had poured for him. "Our little country bumpkin rising so high. Did he seem that capable to you when you were seeing him here after he arrived in Mattelmead?"

"He had grown up some, of course. After all, he had traveled extensively by then," Glenelle said. "But I thought him still an innocent, without any sophistication, not at all cosmopolitan—not then. All in all, very sweet. He was quite overwhelmed by the city. And he definitely was a novice at lovemaking. I understand he's remedied that," and she smiled at her brother, knowing he paid little attention to the gossip of society. "Of course, he was singing beautifully. Well, why not? He was trained by Lorenwile. And he had gained great skills as a warrior. Luck had put him in the right place at the right time to save Solagen's life. But does he have the acumen, the intelligence, the mind for court politics? I never saw it in him. Perhaps I couldn't see past his tiresome adulation, the silly little love songs he wrote for me—quite puerile, really."

"You're just angry with him because he has kept you from much of society, especially that which whirls around the court."

"Well, isn't he being childish—especially after all these years? And especially after all the women he has been with since we. . . we stopped seeing each other? To hold a grudge for so many years. It seems so. . .well, so spiteful."

"Oh, yes," her brother said with a mirthless chuckle, "that trait I recognize in him. It was in the old Auragole. He did many things out of spite when we traveled together."

"You think so?"

"Think back, Glenelle. To mention one, waiting for Donnadorr knowing there was the danger of snow in the pass. That he did to spite me. And there were other times. . ."

"Hmmm," Glenelle said, taking a sip of wine, her eyes thoughtful.

"But Veldarr—surely he can take you wherever it is you want to go. Or while he's away, some other gentleman."

"Oh, Glen, you are so naive—all you think of is your work. Veldarr has a wife. There are—what shall I call them?— unwritten rules. It's his wife who goes with him to all the palace functions. I can meet him at parties. Occasionally we go out to dinner together at some restaurant where men don't usually bring their wives. I'm not complaining about that, Glen. I've made my choices. I'm content with my freedom. But before Auragole came, I was invited on my own account to many functions at the palace. I haven't been invited to the palace since In-tul-farr came for his visit. That's nearly two years ago."

"More than two years," Glenorr said, sipping his wine and watching his sister over the rim of his glass. "But why be concerned? You're healthy now, no more of those awful spells that made you so ill before we came to Mattelmead. And you're one of the most beautiful women in the city—as you well know. Your parties are huge successes. You're sought after by all kinds of men, many quite high up at court. You could marry well, if you wanted to. Why worry about Auragole?"

"But he will be Ormahn one day. Ormahn! Is that not something to be concerned about when he has taken such a dislike to me?"

"Oh, Ellie. Why are you worrying so needlessly? Solagen is a man in his prime. Only in his forties. It will be years before Auragole ascends to the throne. By then Auragole will be married, will probably have fathered several children, have a few mistresses of his own. He will surely not still harbor anger against you."

Glenelle came out of her reverie when a servant entered to announce the arrival of Veldarr. She stood up as he stepped into the room, moving with his light, easy gait. She did not rush to meet him as she used to do. She waited, well aware of what her posture was telling him. Let him come to her. If Veldarr noticed this intended slight, he didn't show it. He strode across the room toward her. As he neared her, she offered him her hand. He smiled at her, took it, kissed it, and looked with both affection and amusement at her. When he heard the door close, he took her in his arms. She held herself stiffly. He then held her at arm's length.

"You are looking well," he said, without a trace of discomfort. "Remarkably well. I can't tell you how much I've wanted to see you."

"Have you?" she said, then sat down in a chair near the window. She motioned Veldarr to a chair opposite her.

Veldarr sat in the proffered chair. Without waiting for Glenelle to speak, he said, "I've been at the palace almost every day, making endless reports to the king. Then I had to catch up with what has been going on with the army while I was away, and straighten out tangles and problems there. I've had to take care of my own personal affairs, and the affairs of my family. Had you heard that a son was born to me while I was away? Three sons now. There was much that needed my attention after I returned. Six months away is a long time."

"How is your wife?" Glenelle asked without a smile.

"Fine. Quite taken up with our newest family member. And I must say he is quite a specimen. He looks like me, same color hair, same eyes. He is already an armful. Their mother is doing a good job with my sons' education. But I needed to be a father for a time, to make sure all was going well with them. And with my wife."

"I see."

"So then, are you going to offer me some wine?" he asked, and smiled at her, still refusing to acknowledge her coolness.

Glenelle stood up and moved to the pull rope.

"Don't summon a servant. I can help myself." He rose and moved across the large room to the table on which stood an assortment of decanters. "Can I bring you something?" he offered.

"A glass of wine—whatever you are having."

He came back and handed her a glass of wine. "So what do you think of these new developments?" he asked, and resumed his seat opposite her.

"What developments?" she asked, raising her glass to her lips.

Veldarr seemed amused by her deliberate obtuseness. She held his eyes in what she hoped was her most innocent expression.

"Auragole becoming heir to Solagen. His adoption. He was at every meeting I had with Solagen, saying nothing, but following him about like his shadow."

"Oh, well the adoption is old news, at least for those of us who have been in the city all these months."

He nodded and peered out at her over the edge of the thin crystal wineglass, but said nothing.

After a moment, Glenelle said, "It seems to me that my opinions can mean little. It is you who have been affected most by this turn of events. And Goredahl."

"Ah, yes. Now he and I are no longer contenders and rivals for the throne." His tone was matter-of-fact.

"And how do you feel about that?"

"I must confess, I'm taking it much better than my cousin is taking it."

Glenelle was beginning to thaw, to feel less angry, glad to be once again with this man who was both lover and friend, one who always brought intimate news from the court. "How is

Goredahl taking it?" She bent a little toward him.

He in turn leaned toward her. "At first he was furious. When the letters arrived with the announcement at our respective camps, he rode for more than two weeks in the middle of March to see me—just to rail at Auragole's duplicity. That's how he sees it—Auragole as conniver, as one who wormed his way into Solagen's affections and stole the throne from him."

"From him? Were you not also in the running?"

Veldarr chuckled. "Not in Goredahl's mind. In his mind, he saw himself as better suited to governing than I. He has often accused me of not having the stomach for war or governing—despite my good showing on the battlefield. He doesn't understand one who is not so hungry for power as he is."

"Did he let Solagen know how he felt?"

Veldarr laughed. "Of course not. How could he? We came home to a situation that was already in place, or as you say, 'old news.' He arrived two weeks after I did, but I witnessed his reports to my uncle. What could Goredahl do but bow and scrape, and smile, and congratulate both Solagen and Auragole? But with me. . . Well, I have heard him vent his spleen more than once."

"What does he intend to do?"

"What can he do? He'll bide his time, scheming, no doubt. But my uncle is no fool. He's sending Goredahl to Thorensphere."

"To Thorensphere?"

"Yes, it's an unruly country, still not fully pacified. Solagen has offered him the chance, not just to go as a commander in the army, but to go as king. King of Thorensphere. A vassal king of course, but still, not a small consolation prize."

"Really!" Glenelle was fascinated by this bit of gossip not yet known to others in society. "And did Goredahl accept his offer?"

"Let's say that it was less of an offer and more of an order."

"I see."

"He will leave within the month. His whole family will follow shortly and take up their abode in the capital city as the royal family of Thorensphere. That should appease Goredahl somewhat. After all, he can do as he likes with that country—within reason, of course. Bringing order to Thorensphere should keep him busy for a while. When last I spoke to him, he said he intended to make the city of Thoren one to rival Mattelmead." Again Veldarr chuckled.

"Somehow I don't think he will be much missed in Mattelmead," Glenelle said. "Who will be in charge of the Security Forces after he leaves?"

"It's not decided yet."

"You?"

"Swords, no. Do you think I want that foul job? Actually, I was also offered a rather nice, new job."

"What is that?"

"To be king of Glovale."

"You're jesting."

"I'm not." He rose and took her half-full glass from her hands, walked back to the liquor table, and filled both glasses again. "I turned it down," he said as he poured the wine.

"You turned it down? You turned down the offer of a kingship?"

"I did." He came back and handed her the glass.

"Was it not an order?"

"Yes, in a way. But I took it as an offer, and then I asked Solagen not to press me to take on this new task. I tried to assure him that I was content to stay in Mattelmead, to keep my job as commander of his army. I told him I thought I would make a very poor king." Veldarr returned to his seat.

"You didn't."

"I did."

"And what did he say to that?"

"At first he just listened. Then I told him I didn't want to uproot my family. My wife is very attached to her parents and to her siblings, and all of them live in this city. I told him that I wanted my children raised in this most remarkable of cities, and not in some poor imitation. I told him that I thought he had chosen wisely when he had adopted Auragole and made him his heir. I swore fealty to both. And so he agreed."

Glenelle watched Veldarr, not sure what to make of this man whom she had known for so many years. Was he really so unambitious? Did being passed over as heir really bother him so little? She looked up to see his eyes watching her with that soft, hazy look of his. And suddenly she stopped thinking about the politics of the court. He was so terribly handsome, the most handsome of all her lovers. And the most ardent and skilled at lovemaking of all the men she knew.

He stood and held out his hand. She put her wineglass down on the table and rose.

"I can spend the night," he said to her as she came toward him, offering first her hand. "I made sure of that." And instead of taking her hand, he took her into his arms. "Shall we go up to your bedchamber?" he asked, his mouth close to her ear.

"Yes." Her voice was husky.

He let go of her then, and took her hand, and led the way into the hall and up the stairs.

N

chapter twenty-three

IT WAS LATE August when Lorenwile returned from Thorensphere to the Valley of the Agavi. He had departed from the city of Thoren only days after Goredahl had arrived in mid-July to begin his rule. The new king had brought with him a huge contingent of soldiers. Lorenwile was sure he knew some of the officers, and so he left. By then he had acquired much information. When he arrived at the outpost of Agavia's defenses, he encountered Elarr, who had been riding the mountain perimeters of the defense lines, checking on them as he did every few days.

"Come back with me to the school, if you can," Lorenwile said, offering only a quick greeting. "I have news you might want to hear, and after weeks on the road I don't want to repeat it endlessly."

So it was two men who arrived at the school in the hills above the Valley of the Agavi. Then within the hour it was four men, Lorenwile, Elarr, Meekelorr, and Pohl, who rode down the hill to the Lady Claregole's Great Mansion in a narrow horse-drawn wagon that was the common mode of transportation between the school and the valley. Claregole received them in her rooms. Her brother Galavi was sent for, and she ordered refreshments to be brought. While they waited for Galavi, Lorenwile's friends brought him up to date on what had been done to prepare for the Last Battle while he was away.

An hour later Galavi arrived. When all were seated around the table, Lorenwile began his account. Without preamble he said, "The entire west is under the control of Ormahn of Mattelmead."

"Including Isofed?" Meekelorr asked, leaning forward, his gray eyes thoughtful.

"Including Isofed. Including Wildenfarr-low-desert." Lorenwile sat back in his chair and watched without expression for the reactions.

Elarr emitted a low whistle.

"Tul-farr of the northern half of Wildenfarr-low-desert sided with Ormahn in the battle for Wildenfarr. And-ul-farr, of the south, was killed in that battle. And now Tul-farr, who had been ailing for years, has also died, and his son, In-tul-farr, has become vassal king there of a now united Wildenfarr."

"Auragole spoke highly of him," Meekelorr said. "Who are the other vassal kings?"

"There are no vassal kings, only army commanders who are in charge of overseeing each country. With the exception of one other country." He paused.

"Which country is that?" Elarr asked.

"Thorensphere. It now has a king of its own." Lorenwile leaned forward, picked up a small honey cake from a plate on the table, and popped it into his mouth.

"Poor Thorensphere," Elarr said with a shake of his head. "It has not been lucky with its kings. Why single out Thorensphere, of all countries, for a king? Who is this new king?"

"Ormahn's nephew, Goredahl."

"The man who was head of the Security Forces in Mattelmead?" Meekelorr asked, his gray eyes darkening.

"The one who was about to arrest you when you left Mattelmead City?" Elarr asked.

"The same." Lorenwile leaned back in his chair, and looked first at Elarr and then at Meekelorr through half-closed eyes.

"Is Goredahl then heir to Ormahn's throne?" Pohl asked.

"No," Lorenwile said.

"Then the heir must be his cousin, Veldarr," Pohl said, "and to ease the way, Ormahn has given Goredahl a country of his own as a consolation prize."

"A reasonable assumption. But a wrong one."

"Then who is Ormahn's heir?" Elarr asked. "Has he had a son since you left Mattelmead?"

"Three daughters, no sons." Lorenwile grinned and helped himself to another small cake.

"Then who?" Elarr asked again. "Come on, Lorenwile. You've had your fun. Who?"

Lorenwile sat chewing thoughtfully, then straightened his back, eyes wide open now, and looked around at the circle of expectant, puzzled faces. He said in a matter-of-fact voice, "Auragole." And he picked up his glass of wine and drank down its contents.

"Auragole? Our Auragole?" the Lady Claregole said, her face mirroring the astonishment that Lorenwile saw on the others around him.

"Correct. Our Auragole," Lorenwile said.

Pohl unexpectedly laughed. "Well, this must be a tale worth the telling and the hearing."

"It is a long tale, too long for this weary traveler to give the whole of it now. Let me give you at least the salient points. Point number one—Auragole's been adopted by Solagen."

"Adopted?" Elarr said. "Adopted?"

"Yes." Lorenwile turned to him. "It took place in a very public ceremony last January, at which time he was also made heir to the throne. That's point number two." Only stunned silence greeted him. "I heard it from a young, high-ranking officer, now assigned to Goredahl's army—one I didn't know from my days in Mattelmead. He was at the ceremony and at the celebration. I must confess he was rather drunk at the time we spoke—helped to that state by a kind stranger." He grinned at them. "But I trust his information. He told me that all the nobility and the commanders in the army were forced to sign a document at the adoption celebration, swearing fealty both to Ormahn and to the new prince, Prince Auragole."

"My stars!" Pohl said. "What are we to make of this? Is this something one could even have dreamed of? Almost outside one's imagination."

"Well, well," Meekelorr said, looking thoughtfully at Lorenwile. He stood up abruptly and walked to the tall windows opening onto the Lady's garden.

"Shall I tell you at least some of the tale?" Lorenwile asked, staring at Meekelorr's back.

"Please do, soul-friend, if you are not too weary," Claregole said. "Meekelorr?"

Meekelorr turned around to listen.

"It seems that not long after I left Mattelmead—let's see, that was about three and a half years ago—Auragole joined Ormahn's army and soon became head of a special unit, Ormahn's crack Elite Corps."

"Was that so unpredictable, my friend?" Meekelorr asked. "If he had become close to Ormahn, it would have been natural for him to join Ormahn in what has been Ormahn's greatest endeavor—uniting the west under his banner. And Auragole was always good with both bow and sword. He sat a horse well, and could shoot from a saddle as easily as he could on foot."

"But Auragole again and again told me he could never be part of anyone's army." Elarr's words revealed his bewilderment. "He said he could never endure the discipline, would never put himself under the command of another."

"Apparently he changed his mind," Lorenwile said, "or had it changed for him."

"You think it was a command of Ormahn?" Meekelorr asked.

"I don't know," Lorenwile said. "It seems Auragole acquitted himself extremely well in all the campaigns that have taken place in the west since I left."

"Well, Auragole always had courage, who would argue with that?" Elarr said. "But to join an army, even Ormahn's army? This sounds like an Auragole I wouldn't recognize. He must have been ordered to do so."

Lorenwile shrugged and went on. "Events seems to have moved quickly from the moment he left you and Meekelorr in the Sorren Heights. And why expect differently, considering the times, and considering that Auragole has some role to play in the affair that is soon coming to a head?" His eyes swept past both Elarr and Meekelorr. "You know that on leaving the Sorren Heights to join me in Mattelmead City, Auragole saved Ormahn's life after an attempted assassination by Ormahn's nephew Bendahl."

"So you told us," the Lady Claregole said, "when first you came."

"No accident, that meeting." Meekelorr's voice was hardly audible.

"In the right place at the right time, one could say," Lorenwile went on. "Well, he saved Ormahn's life once again on the battlefield—and that was before he joined Ormahn's army, when he had accompanied Ormahn only as a singer. Apparently Auragole could not sit aside while there was a fight going on. I'm sure that doesn't surprise you. However, what you may not know is that, in addition to his skills as a warrior, it seems Auragole possesses diplomatic skills. According to those I have spoken to in my travels, Auragole had taken a leading role in some of the negotiations with the conquered or threatened countries. I heard he was overseer of Wildenfarr for a time, then helped negotiate the peace treaty with Isofed, which made that difficult country a vassal holding of Mattelmead—no mean feat, that. Ormahn has taken quite a liking to him. Trusts him. I don't think he ever trusted his nephews. No doubt he was wary after his nephew and heir, Bendahl, had attempted to murder him. The gossip I've heard is that Ormahn never thought much of either of the surviving nephews, that he had grave doubts whether either would make a good overking for the west. Of course, these may be only surmises by some people after the fact of Auragole's ascension." He waited and stared from silent face to silent face.

Finally, Meekelorr said, "Go on."

"From my own experience and knowledge of Solagen's three nephews, Bendahl was by far the smartest and most capable. But Bendahl apparently became impatient, and when Ormahn was wounded in an ambush, Bendahl thought to finish the job and rise immediately to the throne. Of course, we will never know if Bendahl set up the ambush. However, if Auragole had not been on the road just at the right place after leaving the Sorren Heights, then Bendahl would no doubt be Ormahn of Mattelmead today. If he would also have had both the character and the battle skills to unite the Westernlands is a moot point."

"Destiny is working here," Galavi said. "How else see these events, my soul-friends, placing Auragole second only to Ormahn in the west?"

"Yes," Pohl said, "destiny is certainly at work here. But who could have predicted such an unexpected, one might even say wondrous, outcome?"

"Auragole is not the naive boy you knew when he was here six years ago, Pohl. Nor is he so unsophisticated as he was when I was with him in Mattelmead City. You should hear the stories

I have heard about him during my travels. I will tell these to you in the days to come—not today. Auragole has not only grown older but he's also become quite worldly-wise. If he was asleep when he first came here, he is wide-awake now."

"But," the Lady Claregole asked, "what does this mean for the Last Battle? When will it come? The west is united now. Does not that mean it could be soon—maybe in a matter of months? And what role will Auragole play? Will he willingly lead the Dark Breather here with an army bent on destroying us? Will he fight on the side of the Dark God?"

Meekelorr came and stood behind her chair, and she reached back to him. He took her hand. "Auragole has been led by destiny to where he is now, but he has also been left free. It is in his hands, out of whatever wisdom he now possesses, to fight on the side of the Dark Breather or not."

"So it must be, my heart-mate," Claregole said, with a sigh.

"But, my Lady, I agree that the event for which we all prepare draws near." Meekelorr's voice was soft and thoughtful. "Still, I doubt it will be in a few months. The entire west is under Ormahn's rule, but newly so. He must consolidate his hold throughout the Westernlands first. Then, no doubt, he will look toward the east, make plans for conquering the Easternlands. When that happens the Nethergod will make his move. A year or two—perhaps three. No more. We stand in the Dark Breather's way to conquering the Easternlands. Not because of geography, not because we are a great threat—for we are few—but because we are the Nethergod's destiny, as he is ours. For this he has incarnated—to attempt the conquest of the whole of the Grand Continent. We are the obstacle the Creative Gods have placed in his way, and he knows that. If he can succeed against us—and he needs human agents to stand with him in the attempt—then no human can ever stand in his way again. The Deep Earth will become his, and be lost to the Creative Gods forever."

"He will have to destroy us first," Elarr said, his countenance grim. "And we can overcome, no matter what Auragole chooses to do. Our fate is not completely in one person's hands."

"True, Elarr," Meekelorr said. "But if Auragole allies himself to the Nethergod, then it will be tenfold, no, a hundredfold more difficult for us to win out against him."

"It seems likely then that the Nethergod is Solagen, Ormahn of Mattelmead," the Lady Claregole said, her breath ragged as she pronounced the name.

"Not necessarily," Pohl said after a moment.

"Then how will his army come this way, if Ormahn doesn't order it to do so?" She turned to Pohl. "Would it not make better sense to any other commander of an army, if he is not the Nethergod, simply to bypass us and head directly for the east? It must be Ormahn."

"If he who is the Nethergod is someone influential," Pohl said, "someone who stands behind the throne, and if this person says that Agavia is opposed to Mattelmead and that the Agavians will harry Mattelmead's army in its march east, then undoubtedly Ormahn, thinking the overcoming of this small valley easy, will choose to come after us first, before he sets out for the east."

"Lorenwile." Claregole turned to him. "You know those high up in Mattelmead's hierarchy. And you have gathered much information on your travels. Who do you think the Dark Breather is? Is it Solagen? Is it Goredahl or his cousin, or that one everyone seems to like, the doctor?"

"Commander Oldwell," Pohl said.

Lorenwile eyed his friends, these colleagues on whom so much depended, and shook his head. All eyes were on him. "I have my idea, dear soul-friends, but I cannot bring myself to accuse anyone on speculation. I've told you this, but let me say it again. I believe the Dark Breather, our Nethergod, is likely someone at the court of Solagen. That's why I chose to live and work in Mattelmead's capital city. But in the time that I've been gone, someone I never knew, either from Mattelmead itself or from outside its borders, might have risen to a place of importance at the court. Frankly, it signifies little now who it is. What we know is that events are escalating rapidly, and therefore we must be ready when they descend upon us."

"You're right, Lorenwile, there's no use speculating." Pohl pushed back from the table and stood up. "We must move into the final stages of preparation."

"Yes," Meekelorr nodded. "So we must."

Elarr rose. "I cannot bring myself to believe that Auragole would turn against us all. He's been like a brother to me and to Affredda. We named our son after him. . ." And then he grinned, crookedly, and sighed. "Of course, I have been mistaken before in my judgments. Still. . . Well, whatever the truth is in all of this strangeness, we must prepare, must be ready for what we, and the Agavians, have been waiting for—the Last Battle. Thank the stars, we each know what our task is because this dream. . .no, this nightmare, will all too soon become a reality."

THAT NIGHT, IN the bedchamber of the rooms he and Affredda had been given in the Lady's mansion, Elarr said, "I feel out of my depths, Affredda." His lips brushed her hair. "I don't know how to think about this business with Auragole."

They had made love and for a while he had forgotten his troubles. He knew he should try to sleep. He had to rise early in the morning. Nevertheless he picked up the conversation he and Affredda were having at dinner, but had suspended so they could spend time with their son. They had read to him, tucked him into his bed, and watched him as he fell asleep.

Her head on his shoulder, Affredda lifted her chin a little. "My dearest," she murmured. "You are the bravest man I know. As courageous as anyone in the Companions of the Way. As courageous as Meekelorr himself."

"Courage is not what's needed here, my love. Good judgment is what's needed here."

She sat up then and turned so she could face him. "It won't do, you know, it simply won't do, Elarr. . .this doubting of yourself. Ever since that terrible night in the caves of Little Thoren. . ."

". . .when I went crazy and left Auragole tied in the cave, and followed, like an avenging God, the so-called Freedom Fighters of Little Thoren, and killed and killed. . ."

She put her finger gently on his lips. ". . .and came finally to your senses and went back to the cave looking for Auragole. . ."

". . .who was gone."

"Who was gone. But you had another encounter there. A profound, profound encounter. Can you forget that?"

"I know, I know." He drew her down then and kissed her gently on the mouth. "But to be forgiven, even by a God, doesn't mean one has suddenly acquired good judgment. Meekelorr knew I didn't have it when he imposed on me those long months of punishment and forced me to look over and over again at everything I had done. I accepted the punishment, but did I acquire good judgment? I tell you, Affredda, I don't know how to make sense of this. How to judge Auragole."

"And why should you judge him, Elarr? Why is that necessary? If he comes here, and you meet him, then you will judge, if need be."

"With what capacities?" his voice choked.

"Elarr, why this lack of faith in yourself? Have you not been restored to your previous position, a commander in the Companions of the Way? Second only to Meekelorr. Obviously Meekelorr trusts you. You will judge with the same capacities you used to bring us out of the children's village in the Ancient Woods through a land rife with war into the peaceful Woefuls, and then safely hundreds of miles to Agavia."

"Then I knew who the enemy was. Now. . .now I'm not sure."

"Auragole is not the enemy. You will see that, should he come here some day. The core of a man cannot change."

Elarr thought about his own descent into hate and hard-heartedness. "The core of a man," he finally said, "can be covered up long enough for him to do terrible, irreparable deeds in the world."

"Elarr." She rolled over and brought her face close to his. "Auragole will do the right thing. I feel it in my heart. Now sleep. And set worry aside."

BUT ELARR WAS unable to set worry aside. The next day when he returned from his rounds, he sought out Lorenwile in Lorenwile's room at the school in the hills above the Valley of the Agavi. It was half an hour before the noon meal. He found Lorenwile just rising from his bed.

"Come in," Lorenwile said when he heard the knock on his door.

"Did I wake you?" Elarr saw fatigue still heavy on Lorenwile's face.

"No."

How old is he, Elarr wondered? He had always seemed forty, certainly no older, but that couldn't be.

"True, I have been napping. I've been on the road a long time. I confess I'm footsore. I do miss my pony, Surefoot. I can't trust another horse to move as stealthily as my old pony, and there has been no time to train another. So, as you know, I went on foot and returned on foot." Lorenwile swung his legs off the bed and stared at his feet. "But you didn't wake me. I'm starved and I don't intend to miss the noon meal. Sit down and tell me why you've come, while I dress," and he motioned Elarr to a chair near the window. A pleasant August breeze was blowing off the mountains, causing the window curtains to move gracefully in the light.

Elarr sat. Lorenwile walked to the washstand and began

rinsing the sleep from his eyes and face.

"I've come to ask about Auragole," Elarr said.

"I know."

"I'm so confounded by this news. So much has happened since I saw him last. . . I realize it's been more than four years, but Auragole now sounds like a man I wouldn't recognize."

"I can only be certain of what I myself have seen at first hand, my friend. And those observations, while not so old as yours, are at least three years old. I told you about them when I first came here. What I've told you and the others is only gossip that I've picked up in my travels from soldiers or from merchants who journey throughout the Westernlands. What more do you think I can add to what I told you yesterday?" His words were gentle. "Or have you come to hear some of the gossip told about him?"

"Oh, yes, I'd like to hear some of the gossip. But not now. That's not why I came. I want something. . .something more concrete than gossip." Elarr sat looking at his hands. "When you've lived with someone as intimately as I have with Auragole, it's hard to imagine such changes. Since I've come to Agavia, I've learned from Pohl and Meekelorr that Auragole has some role to play that might decide the outcome of the Last Battle. They call him a wild card, though I must say I ardently dislike that designation."

"Not a flattering name."

How to explain? Elarr sighed. "Here is what I think—if it's worth anything, the way I see him—or saw him."

"Go on." Lorenwile was drying himself with a towel, but his eyes were on Elarr.

"Auragole possesses what all of us strive for—freedom, freedom of the will. I've seen little of that in the men and women I have known in my lifetime, even in the village of my childhood. Perhaps only at the school in Stahlowill. Seeing it in Auragole was, what can I say about it?. . ." Elarr rose from his chair, walked toward the open window, and tied back the curtains, ". . .was wonderfully refreshing." He stared out at the sun-drenched mountains. "I saw that freedom of will as a gift of the Prince. We who strive to know the Gods of the Creative World, strive mightily for that miraculous freedom. But it seemed to me then that Auragole had it naturally. Is that observation false or true?" He turned his back to the window and watched Lorenwile.

Lorenwile was slow to answer. "If he had it—naturally, as you put it—then it came as something he had won for himself in a past life. Then his upbringing in that isolated valley of his prepared the soil for it in this life."

"Yes, yes, that I can see. How else understand it?"

"But because it was a gift that he brought with him into this life, he didn't value it. Often the natural gifts you are born with seem like nothing special."

"But what about his refusal to join an army when he was with me and with Meekelorr? Wouldn't you say that was a conscious use of his own free will?"

"Was it? Was it free will, or willfulness—what one might even call stubbornness?"

"Stubbornness?"

"And if Auragole has this natural gift of free will," Lorenwile said, "why can't he put it in the service of whomever or whatever he chooses?"

Elarr came back from the window and sat once again in the chair opposite Lorenwile's bed. "You, and the others, actually believe he could or would put himself in service to the Nethergod? Should we overlook and deny all the good qualities Auragole possesses? The Auragole I knew was courageous, selfless, ready to do all, give all, for friendship. He saved my life twice, and attempted to save it a third time—and would have had not others restrained him at my request."

"You saw no arrogance in him, no unwillingness to forgive, in the months you were together?" Lorenwile's tone was casual. He sat down on the edge of his bed, his tourmaline eyes glinting red in the golden summer light drifting in from the windows.

Elarr hesitated, searching his memory.

But before he could answer Lorenwile went on. "I saw many of the same virtues you saw, Elarr. I would not deny Auragole his virtues. But I also saw how the riches of Mattelmead City, both cultural and material, had begun to entice him. I saw that when he was jilted in love, he was determinedly unforgiving. I saw that he took humiliation without humor and with ill will. I saw pride grow in him. You knew him as a callow boy, longing to be accepted and admired by others, willing to do almost anything for that admiration. What pains me most—and yes, my friend, I can feel pain—what pains me most is that he has, latent in him, an amazing gift. He could have become a True-singer, as fine as any there has ever been. But he turned it aside to follow the dream of another. That decision, sad as I may find it, may have been his last true act of freedom."

"Didn't you tell me yourself that Ormahn is charismatic, that he can inspire people with his vision for the west, for all the Grand Continent? The desire for peace is great in Auragole. He knew what the wars had done to the east. He knew the bitterness his father felt over the lack of peace in the world. He knew what the cost had been to his own family."

"The desire for peace is in all of us, Elarr. But Ormahn's peace? At what cost, this peace of Ormahn's? Auragole seemed unwilling to look at the toll on the individual that this peace of Ormahn's has taken. It is a peace without freedom—the very freedom once extolled, at least in words, by Auragole, the freedom his birth father tried to instill in him as an ideal, and that you think was his as a natural capacity," Lorenwile added. "Mattelmead's peace is a peace that is kept in place by a huge, well-trained, well-disciplined army—of which Auragole is a part. And by an insidious and secret part of the army called the Security Forces."

Lorenwile spoke quietly, almost languidly, almost as if he were describing a good meal he had eaten. But his eyes watched Elarr's face with hardly a blink. "Ormahn's word is law. And those who enforce Ormahn's laws are not to be challenged. The citizens of the new west are completely without rights. From Ormahn's law there is no appeal. Only prison and perhaps death. This limbless, this truncated peace is what Auragole has chosen as his life's work. True-singing, which could have led him into the heavens, into the presence of the Gods themselves, he sacrificed for Ormahn's dreams. Auragole chose to see these goals you and I treasure as useless on the Deep Earth, chose to see True-singing as too small a striving—no matter what he had heard and learned and even experienced of the Creative Gods and the Creative World. He worked hard at True-singing, I grant you that. And he learned. He learned much. More than I think even he realized. Yet he accepted this glorious gift without understanding the Creative World context in which it exists. That is his tragedy and his great flaw—at least as I see it."

Elarr thought about this, feeling a terrible sorrow. "You speak of someone I hardly recognize."

"Well, if I read destiny right, you will meet him again in the not-so-distant future. Then you can decide for yourself."

"Then may the meeting be one of joy and not of sorrow—for the Prince help me, I don't want to be his judge."

"No," Lorenwile said, standing and heading toward the door in a single fluid movement. "Now let us get down to the dining hall before all the food is gone. I'm as hungry as a wolf."

N

chapter twenty-four

IN LATE DECEMBER, though the snows were heavy on the ground, Sylvane and Donnadorr gave a dinner party for friends who lived nearby and could travel to their country house by horse and sleigh. Along with Don and Sylvie, there were six couples. Also present were Meraleese and a young man who was new to the neighborhood. Because Meraleese was no longer part of a couple, Sylvane had thoughtfully invited the young captain, who had recently acquired an estate not far from them—one that had been taken away from a couple she and Don had dined with who were said to be traitors. It had caused a terrible wave of anxiety throughout the area. Sylvane shook herself inwardly. She didn't want to think about that now. The estate had been given to this young captain as a reward for meritorious service in the army. What had happened to their acquaintances had nothing to do with him.

She looked down the table at the young man seated next to Meraleese. Sylvane was not matchmaking. It was just that she had not wanted Meraleese to feel uncomfortable without a partner at dinner. And it was natural to make the acquaintance of newcomers of their social class when they moved into the neighborhood. Roradahl, a captain in Mattelmead's Elite Corps, was second only to Auragole, who still commanded the Elite Corps. He was full of information about Auragole, which both she and Don were eager to hear. No doubt, so was Meraleese. Perhaps Auragole, in turn, would be told about Don and her, and about Meraleese and Glorr. Did Auragole still have time to wonder about them?

Roradahl was a young man, perhaps twenty-four or twenty-five, very handsome with his curly brown hair and brown eyes. He was about five feet ten inches, well built, with well-muscled arms and shoulders, and powerful legs. He had a happy, gregarious disposition and was enthusiastic about his work. He seemed bright and quick-witted and extremely loyal to Auragole—even a little in awe of him. Roradahl was entertaining the dinner guests with stories about the journey from which Auragole, Solagen, and their escorts had just returned. They had traveled through Glovale and into Wildenfarr-low-desert and back again. Solagen was showing off his new son and heir to the people in both countries. And Roradahl had been in the army contingent accompanying the royal party.

"Everyone was excited to see the king and prince. The roads through the Glovale countryside were lined with men and women cheering and waving. At every oasis in Wildenfarr, there were hundreds of people waiting to see us pass. One wonders how they knew just when we would cross through their oases." His smile was one of admiration and Sylvane thought him quite charming.

"Where did you stay? Whom did you visit?" Donnadorr asked him.

"In Glovale we traveled from manor house to mansion to

manor house, visiting everyone who is important. There are no towns to speak of in Glovale, and no cities, only small villages on the estates of the lords there."

An older man said, "No doubt, Solagen is showing his strength and is eliciting fealty from the Glovalians. They're a pretty easygoing lot, more interested in their farms, their grapevines, and their livestock than in stirring up war. I was in the battle for Glovale when I was in the army. The people there, if not the rulers at first, were quite willing to let Ormahn rule. He guaranteed them peace and rid them of the raiders out of the hills of the Sorren Heights. And he was true to his word." The ex-commander rose and raised his glass. "May I make a toast— to Ormahn, great king of Mattelmead and the United West." The other guests rose and the ex-soldier added, ". . .and to his new son and heir, Auragole, prince of Mattelmead."

"To Auragole, prince of Mattelmead," the others echoed.

"The Glovalians grow the finest grapes and make the best wine in all the west," Roradahl said as the guests sat again. "We sampled much of it while we were there. Auragole was a great success. You should have seen the ladies." He grinned. "Wherever we traveled, women leapt into the road and offered themselves to him—much to the displeasure of some of the husbands, I might add." And he laughed. "I mean the people couldn't take their eyes off him."

Sylvane looked up to see Meraleese staring down at her plate.

"But most important, he won the respect of the men," Roradahl went on. "At some of the larger houses there were contests—sword, bow and arrow, horse handling. Auragole bested most of the contestants. He's a very able fighter. Saved Ormahn's life, even before he was in the army. And we all know how smart he is." The young captain beamed with pleasure. "It's because of him that I've been given this estate. I mean, this particular estate. He said I would find the land lovely and the people here charming. I must say, he was right about that—as he is about most things." And he raised his glass to them.

A most agreeable young man, Sylvane thought, and here because of Auragole. Now that is something to ponder. And again she looked at Meraleese, who was still studying her plate as if it held some wonder she had just noticed. Sylvane had never seen her so quiet at a social gathering.

"What about Wildenfarr?" another man asked. "What's it like? How were you received?"

"We stayed with the chief there, In-tul-farr, in his palace. It's not a tent, as some have rumored, but a beautiful white stone manor house with dozens and dozens of rooms. It's near a large lake, an oasis in the midst of much sand and many rocky hills, with lovely buildings and homes, and strange trees with uncommon and rare fruit. In Wildenfarr all the men of importance came to us, to see their overking and the new prince. Day after day, people arrived. Most pitched their tents and stayed some days and then left. They are an unusual people, with their white hair and pale-blue eyes, and their very formal manner. It was fascinating. In-tul-farr and Auragole are old friends, and I think Auragole was especially happy to be there. But we didn't stay as long as I think Auragole would have liked. We had to return home—warm as it was in the desert—in enough time to avoid bad weather before we reached Mattelmead."

"How long will you be here at your estate?" one of the women asked.

"About two months. I'm due back in the city at the end of February. We will train hard for some weeks under Auragole, for he has not left off being commander of the Elite Corps. Then in April the royal party, and a contingent of the Elite Corps, I among them, will be off for a state visit through the northern hills of the Sorren Heights, then into Thorensphere, and a stop to visit Goredahl in Thoren City—I suppose one should call him King Goredahl now—then through the countryside and on to Noonbarr."

"That's a long journey," Donnadorr said.

"Yes, we probably won't be back until late fall or early winter of next year. Six to eight months is what I've been told."

"How is it going in Thorensphere?" one of the men asked. "I've heard that it is not an easy place to govern."

"There are still pockets of resistance there, but they say that Goredahl is pacifying those places. He doesn't tolerate dissent in his kingdom, so the story goes." Roradahl's voice was neutral.

No one spoke for a time. Finally, Roradahl continued, "Auragole will meet the woman he is betrothed to in Noonbarr. The engagement papers will be signed there; then she and some of her family will make the trip back to Mattelmead with our party. The wedding will take place next winter."

Sylvane's eyes widened in surprise, and she saw Meraleese's head jerk up and her eyes mirror Sylvane's.

"Well, that's news," Donnadorr breathed.

"You didn't know?" Roradahl looked from Donnadorr to Sylvane, who both shook their heads.

"Who is she?" Donnadorr asked.

Roradahl shrugged. "The daughter of an important lord and landholder there. I think Ormahn is going to offer him the kingship of Noonbarr. They haven't had a king there for centuries. It's a rural country, with large estates, many miles from each other. Lords with huge landholdings and armies of their own. Most of the large landholdings are self-sufficient. I hear that Noonbarr is not so—how shall I put it—not so civilized as, say, Glovale. Therefore its people were not so easy to conquer as those in other lands. But they've not caused trouble since the conquest."

"How does Auragole feel about this wedding?" Sylvane asked. She was trying to imagine Auragole accepting an arranged marriage.

"He doesn't say much about it. But that's what the noble families do. And since he has been adopted and is heir to the throne, it was to be expected that Solagen would arrange an advantageous marriage for him. This family alliance is Solagen's choice."

Again there was silence, until Donnadorr said, "And what about you, Roradahl? Is someone going to arrange a marriage for you?"

Roradahl chuckled. "No, not for me. I can choose whom I please, and since both my parents are dead and I have no siblings, there is no one to gainsay me. My position is only lowly captain. I serve, and I think I serve well, but I'm not so important as to have to marry where I do not fancy."

"Lucky boy," one man said under his breath, and his wife gave him a hard sideward glance.

THE DINNER PARTY was over. The guests had gone and Meraleese was finally in her room. She had first looked in on Glorr. There he was, safe, looking as untroubled as only children can in their sleep. Now she was slowly undressing, paying little attention to what her fingers were doing— unbuttoning her blouse, removing the hairpins from her hair, unlacing her silk boots. She was thinking about what she had heard that evening from Roradahl, wondering why the news of Auragole's pending betrothal so distracted her. No, distracted was not the correct word. Upset her. Yes, the news about Auragole had definitely upset her.

Aside from the adoption ceremony, Meraleese had not seen Auragole since that last visit to her house when he had, with a becoming delicacy, declared his love for her, though he had not used that word. It was Auragole who had decided that she could not return his love. It was Auragole who had decided that, after a man like Timorr, no one would ever measure up in Meraleese's heart. How could Auragole have thought otherwise, given her cool manner toward him? Meraleese wondered if he had heard her, at that last meeting, when she had said that people could love in different ways. Probably not. No doubt she had been too subtle. Given his agitation, he had nearly flown out of her house. The news he had brought her—his inability to keep seeing her—had certainly saddened her.

At first, she had thought she understood his reasons. It had become too dangerous for him. And for her too. What startled her was how bereft she felt after he left. And that bereavement had never totally gone away. Then finally there had been Auragole's letter delivered to her by Donnadorr—the last word from Auragole that she had ever received. When the announcements went up all over the city saying Auragole was to become prince of Mattelmead and heir to the throne of all the Westernlands, she understood why he had stopped visiting her. Auragole had purchased her safety and her freedom with a promise—a promise that Solagen must have exacted. Auragole had united her with her child, had seen to it that she had a stipend of her own. But Auragole was never to see her again—that much he had hinted at. He was never to have contact with her. She was the wife of a so-called traitor and Auragole was now royalty. Solagen could hardly have approved of their friendship.

But the security he had purchased for her had, to her sorrow, cost Auragole something else—his friendship with Sylvie and Don. Auragole could never visit them now that Meraleese was living with them, nor invite them to the palace to visit him. She wondered how many true friends Auragole had. After living with Sylvie and Don now for nearly a year, she was sure that there were few to match them for caring and good-heartedness.

She wondered if what Auragole had written to her in that last letter was still true. Had he kept a place in some corner of his heart where she still existed? She frankly doubted it. He was so busy now training to be king. She tried to imagine of what that training consisted. The little she knew came from visitors such as Roradahl who were either close to those at the palace or, in Roradahl's case, actually worked with Auragole. She was glad that he had a friend like Roradahl. He obviously cared for Auragole. But was it more hero worship than friendship? She wondered about Auragole's singing. Was he still singing? He had such a beautiful voice, an extraordinary voice. She should have asked Roradahl this. But she hadn't. She had been too shy to speak to him when she knew what his relationship with Auragole was, and too disturbed by the news he had conveyed. And there was something else. . .had Sylvie and Don thought of Roradahl as a match for her? Surely not. Well, it mattered little. He had shown only correct behavior toward her, and had spoken with as many of the others who had been at the party as he had with her—particularly to the men who had been in, or were still in, the army.

Meraleese put on her nightdress and climbed between the sheets that had been warmed by bricks the servants had placed there. She lay under the down quilts, trying to will herself to sleep, but she could not give up thinking of Auragole. Auragole was going to be married—and it unsettled her. Was she in love with Auragole?

It wasn't the first time she had allowed herself to ask that question. All these months since she had last seen Auragole, she had not been able to avoid thoughts of him. She had loved Timorr, and that love was special. Timorr was special. She had looked up to him, had admired his knowledge, his kindness, his loving care of Glorr and her. And she had done everything she could to support his work. She had lived for him and his work. He had been husband and friend and teacher. Yet she had known there were areas of his soul to which she had no access. He possessed such a lofty spirituality, and she could not follow him into those spheres where he was also at home. She could only listen, as others had, to what he had brought down from spiritual realms. Since his death, since coming to live with Sylvane and Donnadorr, she had thought often about her marriage. She wondered, not for the first time, if Timorr had been lonely because he could see and understand what no one around him could see and understand, not even she.

Her mind shifted to Auragole. With Auragole there was more equality. She could understand him, she was sure, in a way she had not been able to understand Timorr. Could Auragole understand her better than her dead husband had been able to? No question that Timorr had great insight, but in many ways he left her inwardly alone, left her to struggle through to her own thoughts and ideas, to her own sense of self. Auragole, in the conversations they had had together, was often challenging, argumentative, making her reach to explain, making her search for what she herself knew and not just what she had heard from Timorr. Also, Auragole had seen her as a woman, with a woman's needs. And his attentions had often seemed sexual, and, she had to admit, there was something thrilling about that. Not that Timorr was celibate. They had had Glorr, after all. But to Timorr she had been more than a woman, she had been first and foremost a human being, valued above all for her humanness and for her struggle to find her own individuality.

Auragole saw her, she was sure, first as a woman—as a man sees a woman—and then as an individual. Auragole would never deny her individuality. But, frankly, he was more sexual than Timorr had been. That was the truth of it. Good or bad, that was the truth of it. And, though she had protested his ever-so-subtle advances, she had inwardly been pleased by them. Meraleese had always thought of herself as one who loved truth. And the truth was she was in love with Auragole.

But it was all so hopeless now. It had always been hopeless. From the first Auragole had been told not to get involved with her. So what was the point of going on like this? She sighed. The point was to admit to herself the reality of her feelings. To live with them. To accept them. And to accept that she would never see him again. Life had always been full of losses, and this was another one.

She blew out the candle on her bedside table, and began the prayers she said every night. The prayers first for the dead. Then for the living—including a prayer for Auragole.

N

chapter twenty-five

AURAGOLE STOPPED ONLY once to look back at Goredahl's so-called palace. It had been built in the middle of what had once been a people's park in the center of the city of Thoren. Goredahl's new home had been constructed, Auragole understood, in a matter of months, using every carpenter, craftsman, and laborer for miles around. The entire public park had been closed down and turned into an estate for Goredahl. "It was filled with thieves and the dregs of humanity who had set up shacks there and preyed on law-abiding citizens. The crime was intolerable," Goredahl had told Solagen and Auragole, his face dark with disapproval. A large, high stone wall had been erected around the many acres surrounding the palace, the stones carried from mountains miles away. Auragole wondered how many laborers it had taken to drag those stones here. There were only two gates in those formidable walls opening onto the estate, and both were heavily guarded.

Auragole twisted in his saddle and looked back. The palace,

he thought, for all its size, was ugly—made of heavy timbers, three stories high. The striped wood, from the omroda trees, which grew in abundance in Thorensphere, was from the forests around the city. It gave the sprawling, unaesthetic structure an ominous, feline, even carnivorous look. Auragole shuddered as he glanced over his shoulder at the massive structure. Ah, well, Goredahl had never been known for his taste. Goredahl and his family were no longer standing on the portico to bid farewell to Solagen's party, which was now nearing the outer gate. But Auragole saw a barely visible figure in a third-story window, watching, as Solagen's party passed slowly through the thick, narrow front gate of the estate into the bustling city. Why that figure should have felt portentous to him, Auragole couldn't say.

Solagen's party, which consisted of a large contingent of Auragole's Elite Corps, was being escorted by an equally large number of Mattelmead soldiers now assigned to Goredahl's service. "They will accompany you all the way to the Noonbarr border," Goredahl had told Solagen, with what Auragole thought was a particularly obsequious smile. "This is for your own safety, Sire. A hundred members of the Elite Corps, no matter how well trained, are not force enough in Thorensphere—not yet," and he had smiled apologetically, looking first at Solagen and then at Auragole. But Auragole had seen the hardness in his eyes.

This is a man who will never forgive you for taking the throne from him, Auragole thought.

"As you yourself know, Sire," Goredahl went on, "Thorensphere is a hard land to subdue. There are still pockets of rebellion—and we cannot be sure which way some of our so-called loyal subjects lean. They will smile at you and bow to you in the day, and stab you in the back at night. We have had some terrible incidents, right here in the city. But I've already explained to you why we felt it was necessary to impose a night curfew on the city."

Auragole looked at Goredahl's soldiers to his right and to his left, who were causing Solagen's own troop to ride at their rear. It made Auragole uneasy. These soldiers assigned to Goredahl and Thorensphere were part of the huge army of Ormahn of Mattelmead. It was no longer necessary to travel with a large military escort anywhere in the west, because Ormahn's soldiers were everywhere—or so they had believed when they had started out. But to whom did this group of men accompanying them now feel first allegiance? It was a troublesome thought, and Auragole had been uneasy since they had arrived at Goredahl's palace five days earlier. If Solagen felt uneasy, he had not mentioned it nor shown it in his manner. But Solagen was hard to read. Even after all these months with him, Auragole could never be sure what Solagen was thinking.

"If you are going to be a diplomat, Auragole," he had once said, "and a king is always a diplomat, you must school your face and your body never to give away what you are really thinking and feeling. You, son, have learned to keep your facial expressions under control, but your body and its gestures still give away too much." That, Auragole knew, was a mild reprimand. Thereafter, he had tried to be aware of what his body was revealing.

Auragole's friend Roradahl had been apprehensive too in Goredahl's large palace, though he had said little. But it was Roradahl who had stood guard in front of Auragole's door at night—and had seen that a guard, from the Elite Corps, had been placed in front of Solagen's door each night also. How Roradahl had explained this need to Goredahl or his men, Auragole did not know, nor did he ask. If there was anyone he trusted, it was Roradahl. Words did not always have to be spoken between them.

Auragole would be glad when they were finally out of the narrow streets of the city and in the country. It had appalled him to see the citizens of Thoren City rush to get out of the way of the large party of mounted soldiers, appalled him to see how often Goredahl's men (for so he thought of them now) lashed out with their riding crops at those who did not move quickly enough, often pushing over their carts of fruits and vegetables and other merchandise. He wondered what Solagen thought, but Solagen was up ahead, and so far as Auragole could tell, had said nothing.

Riding now through the city, Auragole thought about a conversation that had taken place the night before at the dinner table. Solagen was seated on Goredahl's right and Auragole on Goredahl's left. There were a dozen or so people at the table—all men, mostly officers from the army assigned to Thorensphere, and therefore to Goredahl. Goredahl had spoken in detail about the measures he had taken to squelch the various rebellions in the country. Auragole found most of Goredahl's methods distasteful, and had listened with half an ear. But one remark made Auragole sit up and give Goredahl his full attention.

"As you know, Sire, that forest covers a great part of Thorensphere. It stands in the way of the most direct route to Mattelmead. You either have to go south practically into the Sorren Heights to get to Mattelmead or you have to go very far north, into Little Thoren, or north of it. That's foolish. The people are afraid of those woods," and he turned to give Auragole a piercing glance. "They say strange things happen there and that those who go in never come out again. I've sent in small troops of soldiers and they have not returned. It is my contention that there are rebellious gangs living there who have murdered my men. . .your men, Sire." Goredahl now directed his words to Solagen. "Can we have such a queer place in our country, one that gives free rein to the superstitions of the people? A place where no one wants to go, not even our soldiers, who have to be threatened with dire punishment before they enter?" He didn't wait for an answer. "So I have come up with a plan. The Ancient Woods are useless at present.

We can't harvest the trees for lumber if people will not go into the woods, nor can we build a road through them. They are, as it stands now, valueless."

"What is your plan?" Solagen asked.

Goredahl said, "Burn them down." He twisted in his seat and looked again at Auragole.

If Goredahl expected to see shock there, his expectation was rewarded. Auragole was appalled, and he showed it, much to his own annoyance. "But you are talking about hundreds, maybe thousands of acres," Auragole finally said.

"We have begun in the south and will slowly work the fire north."

"You've already begun?" Auragole could barely make his voice audible.

"Only days after your party passed south of it," Goredahl said with a smirk.

"But there are people living in that forest," Auragole said, and he looked across Goredahl at Solagen.

Solagen said, without hesitation, "The only kind of people who would live there, Auragole, are fugitives escaping the law. You heard. Our soldiers who enter are attacked and killed."

The look of satisfaction on Goredahl's face increased. But Auragole was thinking of the group of soldiers whose skeletons he, Elarr, and Affredda had passed by when they had crossed through the Ancient Woods. Their swords and bows had been lying near them. And no sign of a battle. Solagen went on, "A fire will probably drive them out. If you can control the fire, Goredahl, I cannot find fault with your plan. We cannot have this huge tract of land harboring criminals, and a forest that decent people cannot enter."

Auragole was quiet for the rest of the meal, aware that Goredahl had continued to talk, aware that he now and again glanced at Auragole with a look of triumph on his face. But Auragole's mind was miles away—in the Ancient Woods—

thinking of the community called the Guardians of the Flame, of the ancient temple to an unknown Goddess whose ruins graced a beautiful park. He was thinking about the remnants of the children's village that Affredda had worked in. Thank the stars, she and most of the villagers had left some time ago. But a few had remained to take in orphans from the war. Goredahl was a madman. If Auragole were king. . . But Auragole was not king. Solagen was king. And Solagen had not objected. In fact, he had given his approval to a scheme that seemed so preposterous that it took Auragole's breath away. A fire to burn down so many square miles of forest! May the Gods of that forest protect those who dwell there, he said inwardly over and over again.

Auragole turned his attention back to the streets through which they were traveling. Out in front, riding through this city of Goredahl's, was the overking of all the Westernlands, his adopted father, Solagen, the great peace bringer, seemingly unconcerned with the way the soldiers here in Thorensphere were treating the people, unconcerned about the burning of a huge forest where people lived. Was the fear that Auragole felt permeating this city something too small to concern Solagen? He knew he dare not bring up the subject of the Ancient Woods with Solagen. Solagen did not take kindly to complaints brought by Auragole. It was all right to offer his opinion when asked, but to challenge something to which Solagen had given his approval was not. Auragole's heart ached and his stomach was in knots as they moved through the sprawling and poor city of Thoren.

When they were finally in the countryside, the roads became wider and the army spread out a bit. Roradahl brought his horse alongside Auragole's. "Have you noticed," he said, quietly, "there are no people near the road to greet Solagen? This is not at all like Glovale where hundreds lined the roads, or even like Wildenfarr. This is not even like the Sorren Heights, which has fewer people than Thorensphere. Yet there are farms and houses all around us. Where are the people?"

"There are a few men up on top of the hills," Auragole said, motioning with his head.

"Are they so fearful that they will not even greet their overking?"

Auragole turned to his friend. "Goredahl calls these people a stiff-necked people—obdurate and rebellious. I met a few when I was younger and traveling through here, and I would have to say, from those I met, that they trust little. Why should they? For generations, they have been harshly dealt with by their kings."

Roradahl nodded, looking slowly around at the near-empty countryside they were traveling through.

"Or," Auragole said, "it could be something not caused by the past. It could simply be Goredahl."

THAT EVENING AND all the other evenings while they traveled through Thorensphere, they camped out in open meadows, and slept while Goredahl's men guarded them—and while some of the Elite Corps watched Goredahl's men. Roradahl trusted no one. And Auragole was glad of it.

"It is too risky for you to stay in any of the villages or manor houses along the way," Goredahl had said to Solagen. "I'm not sure of the loyalty of any of the nobility, and wouldn't want to trust your safety, Sire, to any but my own men—your men, really, for is not my army your army?" And he had smiled that smile that Auragole had come so to dislike. "Best to camp out, Sire. My men will guard you." Auragole was glad that Roradahl had not heard that particular remark of Goredahl's. "My men" indeed.

Auragole felt a sense of relief when they left the border of Thorensphere and entered Noonbarr. The soldiers assigned to Goredahl turned back as Solagen and Auragole were greeted by the nobleman who was soon to be his father-in-law, and by a small honor guard.

N

chapter twenty-six

THE DAY BEFORE there had been a threat of rain. But the rain had not come. Lucky, too, Roradahl thought, or where would the ceremony take place? Before leaving the walled courtyard on his way to making his final security rounds of the area, he turned back to look at the sprawling mansion of Lord Hameshall. It was a paltry affair, Roradahl thought, compared with the manor houses of Glovale, not to mention those of Mattelmead itself. But then nothing could compare to the grand houses of Mattelmead, he thought proudly. This one was made of rough wood, and inside the walls were covered with thick, craggy plaster. There were no decorations on the interior walls except some weavings, used more for protection against the inclement weather than for adornment. Well, the winds were fierce in this part of the country, coming off the Gandlese Mountains, which were visible in the east when the day was clear. The winds were strong even at the height of summer, and this was the height of summer—the last week in July. But today there was only a mild breeze. That too was lucky. He looked at the house and sighed. The sprawling structure was only one story—a nightmare for security. Roradahl had slept little the night before, rising frequently to make sure his men, stationed beneath every window, were awake and watchful.

Roradahl turned and walked through the first gate, then over the narrow bridge and through the second gate. The double walls were made of wood beams, sharpened to peaks, about ten feet high, one wall inside the other, and between them a rather scrawny moat, with water no more than three feet deep and three feet wide. These were all the defenses the lord here had built. The walls and moat surrounded the house and its courtyard, its outbuildings and barns. Thank the stars the barns were not attached to the house as they were on most of the farms, great or small, in Noonbarr. Except near the Gandlese Mountains, Noonbarr was fairly flat, with little stone or rock, but many small woods. It was excellent land for farming and the grazing of sheep. Auragole had told him that Noonbarr had been covered with forests centuries ago, but slowly the trees had been cut down and only small groves remained.

Hameshall's farm, located in the east near the Gandlese, and somewhat to the south, was said to be the largest holding in Noonbarr. Hameshall was also the largest employer of men and women in the country. There were five sizable villages on his land, and most of the villagers worked for Hameshall in some capacity or other. He still maintained a small personal army— his reward for having sided immediately with Ormahn when Ormahn had marched to conquer Noonbarr. Hameshall was a man in his early fifties, of medium height, stocky, powerfully built, with ruddy, coarse features and small, calculating eyes.

Roradahl had watched him with interest at dinner the previous night—the first celebratory dinner his duties had allowed him to attend since arriving. They were eating in the large and drafty hall of the house, which had two fireplaces that

Roradahl was certain did little to warm the place in winter. The main table was on a raised platform at one end of the hall. Hameshall sat at the center of the table, flanked by Solagen to his right and Auragole to his left. Next to Auragole sat the woman—a girl, really—who was to become his betrothed. She was Hameshall's youngest child. Next to her were her two sisters with their husbands, and on the other side of Solagen were Hameshall's two sons, big and brawny and rugged looking, neither of them married. Deeralee, Auragole's intended, in contrast to all her siblings, including her rather large sisters, was tiny, really quite petite, and not so plain as her sisters. She would have been rather pretty if her features had not seemed so pinched. But that was probably from fright. She was barely sixteen, after all. She picked at her food, hardly eating at all throughout the long dinner, which was filled with raucous conversation, much flowing wine, and many toasts. Every time Auragole directed some comment to her, she blushed, answered him in a few words, and then looked down at her plate.

From where Roradahl sat, at the back of the hall, he had wondered what Auragole was saying to her. Frankly, he felt sorry for the girl. She was trussed up like some prized livestock—well, that was a little unkind. She was wearing a red woolen dress cut so low that it barely covered her tiny breasts, with stiff ruffles all around the opening and with layer upon layer of skirts. The necklace of gold and jewels seemed too heavy for her thin, almost scrawny neck, and her bracelets slid noisily up and down her arm with each movement of her hand. There were enormous jeweled combs in her hair, which had been piled high on her head. He had to admit she had beautiful hair, golden and luxuriously thick.

They had been here on the Hameshall land for four days now, and Auragole and the girl had met several times—never alone, however. Roradahl had, in his role as personal guard to Auragole, been present at those meetings and had watched with interest Auragole's attempts to converse with her. Auragole had always had a way with the ladies. But this one could hardly compare with the sophisticated and worldly women Auragole had known and romanced in Mattelmead. Deeralee could barely speak when addressed by Auragole. Each time he spoke she shrank back from him as if he had made an indecent advance toward her. They guarded their women quite carefully in Noonbarr, Roradahl had quickly learned. Women were never allowed to be alone with a man not of their immediate family until the wedding night. Deeralee, for the most part, seemed in awe of Auragole. Yet as Roradahl watched him, he saw him treat the girl with kindness and deference. But she always looked terrified. Perhaps it was because she was a young, unworldly farm girl, about to be elevated to princess—and not only princess of Noonbarr, but princess of the entire west. That would have to be a shock, even to a pampered daughter of a wealthy father.

Roradahl was moving now around the platform where in a few hours two ceremonies would take place, and where workmen were putting the finishing touches on the decorations. For a time Roradahl had wondered why Ormahn had chosen to ally himself through the marriage of his adopted son to this particular family, out of all the families in the west. Finally he had ventured to ask Auragole one day as they were riding side by side past the grain fields of Noonbarr, still days from their final destination.

Auragole had said, "Hameshall's lands are large, the largest in this country, and they are situated in the southeast of Noonbarr as Mattelmead City is in the northwest. Between the two lie most of the Westernlands. Hameshall has proven to be as loyal a subject as any Solagen has. And Hameshall's no fool. He's adept at politics and knowledgeable about his own country as well as most of the countries in the west. By uniting the two families in marriage, by elevating Hameshall to the rank of king, by putting him in charge of all the sundry militia in Noonbarr, by assigning part of the army of Mattelmead to him, Ormahn will secure his own hold over the Westernlands." Auragole had recited this information without looking at Roradahl, without emotion in his voice, and with little expression on his face. It was, Roradahl thought, as if he had learned this explanation by heart and was merely giving it back by rote. Roradahl had been silent on the subject after that. But, he thought, Goredahl and Thorensphere will be nicely locked in between Hameshall and Solagen. Perhaps that was why Solagen had seemed so little worried in Thorensphere.

Roradahl looked out at the vast field just beyond the outer wall, used mostly for the training of soldiers, and had to admit that the setting up of colorful tents yesterday and the large platform in the center of the field did give this rather plain, grassless training ground a festive air. There were banners fluttering gaily from dozens of poles stuck into the ground. It was Roradahl's present task, and that of his men, to inspect every inch of the field where in a few hours hundreds of people would be standing. His job was to make sure no one with ill intent was hiding there. And his assignment was to make sure that all the workmen would be gone before the guests arrived. Many would return later in their best clothes to participate in the festivities. But for a while, Roradahl wanted the area totally empty of people so he could make his inspection with ease. The platform, where the ceremony was to take place, was still being worked on. The last of the decorative bunting was being attached to the sides of the platform. The foreman assured Roradahl that the workers would be done in half an hour. Roradahl looked underneath the platform. Empty of everything except a few vociferous insects. He waited until the workmen were finished and had finally taken their leave, searched under the platform one more time, and placed four guards on each side of it. He assigned locations in the field to twenty of his best men, then returned to the mansion to report to Solagen, and to dress for the ceremony.

LORENWILE STOOD AT the back of the crowd. Before he had ventured again into the Westernlands, he had blackened his hair and eyebrows; he had grown a beard and blackened that. He doubted if any of the soldiers of Mattelmead, though no doubt some had heard him sing at the Blue Heron, would recognize him. Still, he tried to stay concealed in the crowd while at the same time placing himself where he could see what was happening on the platform. The investiture of the new king of Noonbarr had just taken place and there had been loud and long cheering by the crowd. Apparently, Hameshall was a well-liked master, and the villagers who stood around Lorenwile in the back of the crowd seemed very proud of his elevation to king of Noonbarr, and through it a raising of their own importance as tenants of the new king.

Then came the announcement that Auragole, son of Ormahn, prince of Mattelmead, would now be betrothed to Deeralee, daughter of King Hameshall of Noonbarr. Papers were signed. Presents were exchanged between the two betrotheds, who stood next to their fathers. The two fathers shook hands and embraced each other. Then they led their offspring to opposite ends of the platform. This was an engagement ceremony, not a wedding. Solagen had insisted that the wedding take place at his palace in Mattelmead City. According to the villagers, with whom Lorenwile had spoken over drinks the previous night in the inn where he was staying, the father and daughter and some of the family would be making the trip back to Mattelmead with Ormahn's party. The wedding would be held not long after their arrival in the royal city. First, though, they would travel throughout Noonbarr, introducing the new king to the rich landowners and eliciting fealty from them. Then on to Thorensphere and back finally to Mattelmead.

Lorenwile watched with interest the young man who had once been his apprentice and who had sung with him in Mattelmead City. Auragole, who would be twenty-six at the end of September, had certainly filled out. His shoulders were wider and he seemed taller. But that might be because of his carriage. He indeed seemed royal, not haughty but noble. But then Auragole had always been comfortable in his own skin. His body had been a tool he had used well and with little concern. Lorenwile wondered how Auragole felt about this little mouse of a woman who was to be his wife. He could not make out the expression on Auragole's face nor the one on the girl's, but Lorenwile did notice that she stared at her boots for most of the ceremony. As for Auragole, he knew, and obviously accepted, that these unions were part of the life of members of the court. Marriage was a contract, an alliance between two important families. Love and amusement were sought elsewhere—long ago Auragole had learned that hard lesson.

The ceremony came to an end and those who had invitations headed into the mansion for a celebratory meal. The rest of the crowd entered the various tents where food had been set up for them and entertainment provided. Lorenwile decided to go back to the village and to the inn where he was staying, away from the Mattelmead soldiers who were watching the crowds along with Hameshall's militia. There was nothing more to learn. Lorenwile would have a meal, spend the night, and leave for the Gandlese at dawn. There would be little to tell those who prepared in Agavia for the coming of the Nethergod. Only that Auragole was to be wed and that Solagen with his adopted son and heir was traveling to every country under his domain save Isofed, carefully consolidating his control over the west.

THAT NIGHT, LORENWILE sat bolt upright in his bed. He had been asleep, probably dreaming—but that had faded from his memory the instant he awoke. What was left was an odd and troublesome feeling. He knew, with the intuition born of True-singing, that he should follow the army accompanying Auragole and Solagen and their entourage as they made their way slowly back to Mattelmead. There was trouble ahead, of that he was sure, and it would affect the entire Westernlands. And whatever affected the Westernlands would affect the nature and timing of the Last Battle. It was too soon to return to Agavia. That decided, he lay back on his bed and was soon fast asleep.

THE REASON FOR being on the road that Lorenwile gave to those who asked him at the inns in Noonbarr was that he was returning from a visit to his ailing mother and was on his way to the city of Thoren, where he lived. However, he had coins, gold and silver, and those spoke louder than words. He was generous with his money. He bought drinks for those who frequented the inns, and in turn they kept him informed about the journey of Ormahn and his entourage. Many worked in the manor houses where the royal party stayed on its leisurely tour through Noonbarr all that summer. They would enter Thorensphere at the end of September. Most of those he spoke to in Noonbarr were quite happy with Solagen's peace, and extremely proud not only that one of their leaders had been chosen king, but that his daughter would be married to Ormahn's adopted son and heir—a great honor for their country.

Occasionally, Lorenwile was able to talk to a soldier accompanying Ormahn. The soldiers usually camped outside some village near where the king was staying, and frequented the inn of that village when they had time off from their duties. They were proud of their status as members of the Elite Corps, and as guards to the king and his son. Lorenwile chose the younger soldiers to speak to, those who likely had not heard him sing in Mattelmead City. It had been four and a half years since he had left the great city. Though Lorenwile prided himself on his disguise, he didn't want to take unnecessary chances. From what he learned, the royal party was in high spirits. Everywhere they went in Noonbarr they were welcomed with excitement and joy. It was, all in all, a successful journey.

When Lorenwile tried to find out more about the young woman Auragole was to marry, he was told that she and the women who traveled with her kept to themselves, appearing only at the evening meal, which was usually a celebration. Otherwise, none of the soldiers had more than a glimpse of her. Sometimes she could be seen walking in the gardens or fields near a manor house, but always in the company of her women or her father. She was never seen with Auragole except at the dinners, where she was placed next to him. Auragole, Lorenwile was told, was in fine spirits. He was seldom far from the king, but would occasionally come out to train with his men or contest with the sons of noblemen in sword fighting or shooting. He lost only one competition, and when he did, he shook hands with his opponent, and with great grace complimented him to those who watched, and invited the young man to come to Mattelmead and join his Elite Corps. Ormahn seemed content and relaxed. In the weeks they traveled through Noonbarr, there was no hint of trouble.

The atmosphere changed when the king's party crossed into Thorensphere in September. Not far behind them came Lorenwile. Luckily, he had papers. It was only in Thorensphere that they were required. Lorenwile had his made years ago, in a false name, while still living in Mattelmead, for the emergencies he knew would come. So far, new papers had not been issued by Goredahl to his subjects. The papers he now had to show wherever he stopped for the night identified him as one Derikk, a maker of flutes, who came from the city of Thoren, and who had sold his flutes in Noonbarr and was attempting to sell them in Thorensphere as he headed home. Lorenwile heard that the reception of the royal party was different here in Thorensphere. He had overheard the grumbling of some members of the Elite Corps.

The royal party had been met at the border by a large contingent of the Mattelmead army now under Goredahl's command. The king's party no longer stayed at manor houses, but camped outdoors in large fields that were carefully guarded. The royal party was heading straight for the city of Thoren and for the palace of King Goredahl, one soldier told Lorenwile, as quickly as a large group could travel. A few days' rest with Goredahl in Thoren City, and then they would head north to Little Thoren, avoiding the Ancient Woods, which Goredahl had tried to burn down with little success. There they would cross over the new bridge that had been built just north of Little Thoren. It spanned the Thoren River, which divided Thorensphere from Mattelmead. Then the royal party would be in Mattelmead and on their way home.

Lorenwile had grayed his hair and beard before crossing into Thorensphere, and had changed the way he walked—a little stooped, now. He no longer displayed large amounts of silver and gold. He was now a poor itinerant flute maker. He no longer engaged in conversations with the Elite Corps. Often he sat in a dark corner with a drink, pretending to doze—but he listened with those ears that had been trained to acute sensitivity by True-singing. He was little noticed in his new guise. On the road, he carried in his pack almost two dozen flutes, which he had brought with him from Agavia in case of need. When he was stopped, and he was stopped often, he handed the guards his papers and allowed them to examine his pack. He tried to keep pace with Ormahn's party. That had been easy in Noonbarr. It had moved slowly and stayed three or four days at each stop. But since coming to Thorensphere, Ormahn's entourage had moved quickly, and it wasn't long before it had outstripped him. Lorenwile arrived, on foot, in the city of

Thoren three days after Ormahn and Auragole had arrived.

By then, it was too late.

RORADAHL LOOKED AT the folded papers that had been handed to him by a servant of Goredahl's. It was very late at night, and Roradahl was in his chamber preparing for bed. The papers had Ormahn's seal on them. He opened them and read them three times before he looked up. But the servant was not the person to ask about their contents. "This is a strange message," Roradahl said. He quickly dressed and grabbed his cloak. He walked through the long halls of the palace and up the stairs to the floor where Ormahn and Auragole had been staying in adjoining rooms. To his consternation, his own guards had been replaced by Goredahl's guards. Where had his own men gone? "I have to speak to the prince," he told the guard in front of Auragole's door.

"You can't, sir." The soldier grinned at him. "He has a woman with him and we have been given orders that he is not to be disturbed."

"A woman," Roradahl repeated. Well, that was not so unusual. There were often women. But could he follow the strange instructions that he held in his hand without first speaking to Auragole?

"It's his bride-to-be," the soldier told him, and winked. "It seems that neither of them can wait until the wedding." And he chuckled.

It would have to be Ormahn then. Roradahl was likely to get in trouble not following the king's orders and bothering him after he retired, but these orders were bewildering. He walked down the hall to Ormahn's door. "Where is my soldier who was assigned this task?" he asked the soldier standing guard.

Goredahl's man just raised his eyebrows and shrugged. "I don't know, sir. I was told to come and stand at the king's door, that your man had been given different instructions."

"I have to see the king," Roradahl said.

"But he has a woman with him, sir. I don't think we should intrude on him." The soldier looked genuinely terrified.

Roradahl stood there a moment, uncertain what to do. Then he asked, "Which is King Goredahl's bedchamber?"

"It's down the hall and to the left."

Roradahl started to go where the man had directed him, but he hadn't walked more than a few feet before the man called out after him. "But you won't find him there. He's in his office. It's. . ."

Roradahl wheeled around and headed for the stairs. "I know where it is," he said curtly.

In a few moments Roradahl was standing in front of Goredahl's desk. He handed him the papers with Ormahn's seal on them, and said, as politely as he could, "Can you tell me something about this order?"

Goredahl took the papers from him and read them carefully. "I think so. The king and I spoke about this after dinner. He seemed anxious that everything be ready for him when he returns to Mattelmead. He is most desirous for this wedding to take place immediately upon his arrival. Therefore he wants you and your men, all of them, to depart before dawn and make haste back to Mattelmead City and see to it that all is in readiness when he follows in two or three days. It's all in here. What's the problem?" He smiled as friendly a smile as Roradahl had ever seen on his face.

"But why did he not tell this to me in person? Why the need for so formal an instruction—a written instruction, when he sees me every day?"

Goredahl smiled. "Both he and Auragole had women waiting for them."

"Still. . ."

Goredahl raised his hand. "Wait," he said, and his tone was imperious. He gestured at the document Roradahl was clutching in his hand. "It is important that you have something more than just your words to give to Oldwell when you arrive in Mattelmead without the king and prince. And, as you can see, there is a message for Oldwell here as well."

Roradahl was quiet.

"I've sent the two guards you had placed at the king's and the prince's doors back to rouse your men, since I was privy to this information. They should be ready to leave as soon as you have packed up your own things. By then dawn will be breaking. There's nothing to be concerned about. Ormahn's party will follow in a few days. He will expect when he arrives in Mattelmead City to find everything ready for an immediate wedding. It's all in the documents you hold." And Goredahl pointed with one long-nailed finger at the papers. "I understand that an immediate wedding is necessary—if you get my meaning." And he leered at Roradahl. "No need to make the father of the bride unhappy at this point now that a good and necessary alliance has been made."

Had the girl been slipping into Auragole's rooms or tent on their march here? Roradahl hadn't thought it possible. But. . .

"Ormahn has a large army in Thorensphere. He will be well protected—no need to worry on that account. As will Auragole." Again Goredahl smiled. Roradahl had never liked his smile. "I don't think Ormahn will be too happy with you, Captain, if you disobey his orders," Goredahl said, but continued to smile.

Roradahl looked down at the seal. It was Ormahn's seal. There was no question about that. Well, if that was what Ormahn wanted, if there was a reason to hasten this wedding along, then he had better obey. Still, he was uneasy. "Thank you, sir," he said, inclined his head, and turned and walked out the door. He would obey the orders given him. He didn't really have a choice. Solagen didn't take kindly to those who disobeyed. Roradahl walked through the corridors to his room and quickly packed. At dawn he, and the entire Elite Corps traveling with him, left Thoren City, taking the southern route, which was the quickest way out of Thorensphere. He was miles away when the news broke in Thoren.

LORENWILE, ON FOOT, was nearly three days behind the king's party, arriving in the early evening. The inn he chose was close to the palace and, as he had anticipated, many of the servants who did not live at the palace often stopped there on their way home from their jobs.

After arriving Lorenwile washed, dressed quickly, then went down for his dinner. But no food was being served. The servants of the inn, the kitchen help, the customers were all standing in the dining hall talking quietly. On every face was a look of shock. Lorenwile moved into the shadows and listened. And the news he heard caused a tremor to ride up his spine.

Solagen, Ormahn of Mattelmead and overking of all the west, was dead. Murdered, it was said, by his adopted son and heir, Auragole. And the Elite Corps had deserted both king and prince and had either fled into the countryside or returned to Mattelmead.

The first thing Lorenwile did after he had heard the news—though it was already evening—was to buy a horse. He had not ridden one while traveling in the west. It was harder to stay inconspicuous on a horse, and he had traveled through Thorensphere as a not-too-wealthy tradesman. Now he desperately needed a horse. There was nothing he could do now in Thoren City. But there was something he must do in Mattelmead. The buying of the horse and the repacking took less than two hours. That same night he was on his way out of Thoren and heading northwest, first for Little Thoren and from there into Mattelmead. Pushing his horse to its limits, it would probably take Lorenwile three to four weeks to reach his goal. What would Goredahl do now? No doubt gather his army, then come to Mattelmead in full force as quickly as he was able. Still, that would take some time. And if Lorenwile was lucky he would get to Mattelmead, complete his mission, and get out of there before Goredahl's army arrived.

But would the news reach Mattelmead before him? News had a way of spreading quickly, more quickly than any army could move. What Lorenwile wanted to do, had to do, was keep ahead of the news.

He traveled mostly at night when the area was populated, and he spent little time resting. Lorenwile's excellent hearing kept him out of trouble on more than one occasion. He was heading, not to Mattelmead City, but north of there. He wanted to get to Donnadorr and his wife—he had become quite fond of the young man, this foster son of Aiku. As soon as the news spread to Mattelmead, Donnadorr and his wife would be in grave danger. He could not, in good conscience, return to Agavia without first trying to help them. The news Agavia needed to hear would wait—had to wait.

As he rode northwest, he wondered what had happened to Auragole. Was he alive or was he dead? It was days into his trip before the shock wore off. He bent his will to the task ahead. Too soon to mourn. Too soon to count Auragole out. Destiny. Once again it had taken a strange turn.

darkness and light

PART NINE OF AURAGOLE'S JOURNEY
AURAGOLE OF MATTELMEAD

N

preface

MERALEESE SAT BOLT upright in her bed, her heart pounding, drawn precipitously out of sleep. Something was wrong, she knew it—terribly, terribly wrong. It was not a dream that had caused her to wake. No, it was a feeling, a thought, some sort of warning. She needed to do something. But what? About what? It was still night. No light slipped around the edges of the drapes covering her windows. The fire that had been burning to take the chill off the late-September evening had gone out, leaving her bedchamber in total darkness. Not even an ember was glowing. She fumbled with the candle, managed to light it, and slipped quickly out of her bed. She did not stop to put on slippers or her robe, but, candle in hand, rushed to the door that divided her room from Glorr's and opened it. She hurried to his bed and looked down at the sleeping boy. He was lying on his back, his brown, curly hair framing his peaceful face, his slow breath quite audible in the stillness. She let out a sigh of relief. Her son was all right.

Meraleese returned to her room and closed the door behind her as quietly as she could. Setting the candle down beside her bed, she climbed in and drew the covers close around her. She was shivering. She couldn't dispel her feelings of fear, so she left the candle burning. Something dreadful had happened. She felt it in her bones. Thank the stars, it had nothing to do with her son. After a moment, she threw back the covers, put on her slippers and robe, took the candle, stepped out into the hall, and listened. Everything was quiet. Nothing seemed amiss in the country manor that was now her home. Surely if something dire had happened in the house, the servants and Don and Sylvie would be awake by now. Should she walk through the house? She did walk down the hall past Don and Sylvie's door, stopped there, and listened. Quiet. She went as far as the great staircase leading to the floor below. No sound from there. It couldn't be close to dawn or surely she would hear the servants moving about in the kitchen. Meraleese returned to her room and once more climbed into her bed. She lay back, telling herself that all was well in the mansion. Then why this sense of doom? For that was what it felt like.

Not in the house, Meraleese decided. Then where? Nearby? Had another of their acquaintances been torn away from his or her home in the middle of the night to be taken off to some unknown destination, never to be heard of again? She tried to come to grips with what she was feeling. When had she felt this way before?

After Timorr had been taken away. When she was uncertain whether he lived or died.

These were feelings, she decided, that came only when something bad had happened to someone you loved. But everyone she loved was right here. Except. . .except Auragole. And suddenly she was gripped with an overwhelming fear that something dreadful had happened to him. She couldn't stop the loud beating of her heart or her rapid breathing. Something had happened to Auragole. But what? He was still far away, traveling in the west—so the rumors went—on his unhurried journey back to Mattelmead with his bride-to-be. So how was it possible to find out anything about him?

Meraleese lay sleepless, struggling to stem the tide of panic. She glanced at the window. Surely it must be near dawn. She rose and pulled back the curtains. Still dark. She left the curtains open, returned to her bed, and stared at the window, willing the sun to rise, willing some sign that it was close to morning. After a time, she rose and dressed. Then she sat in a chair facing the window. At the first sign of dawn, she left her room and went down the back stairs to the hall that led to the kitchen. There were familiar noises that indicated the cook and his helpers were preparing breakfast. She entered the kitchen, startling the cook.

"What is it, Miss? Is something wrong?" he asked.

"I. . .I couldn't sleep, so I thought I would come down early and beg for a cup of tea."

"The water is in the kettle and should soon be at a boil. Come, Miss, and sit near the fire. You look pale. Bad when you don't get your sleep." He pulled a stool near to the fire and gestured her to it.

Meraleese sat down. After a few moments, she asked, "Is Rowbie in from the village yet?"

"No, Miss. He will be here soon to help with the cleanup from the breakfast. He's worth nothing, far as the cooking is concerned." The cook looked at her curiously.

But Meraleese remained silent, took the cup of tea when it was handed to her, and sipped it slowly and without interest. Her eyes were on the door to the kitchen. Finally, before half an hour had passed, the lad walked in. He was about sixteen and had a pleasant, freckled face and sandy hair. He seemed a little startled to see one of the household there in the kitchen.

The cook said to him, "Miss Meraleese has been waiting to speak to you, Rowbie." And he gestured with his head at

Meraleese, who was now standing.

"Me, sir? What have I done?"

The cook shrugged.

"Nothing," Meraleese said. "Nothing. Please don't be alarmed. I only wanted to ask you. . ." She paused, trying to find a way to phrase the question. ". . .about any news you might have heard in the village."

He looked at her, baffled. "I don't understand what it is you mean, Miss."

"I thought you might have heard if Ormahn's party has returned to Mattelmead."

"Oh." The boy's face lit up with understanding and relief. "Well, Miss, what they say in the village is that Ormahn's party is in Thorensphere, visiting with the new king there, and that they should be back sometime in November. But that's still nearly two months away," he added, as if she didn't know it was still September. And then he grinned at her. "Then, it's said, there'll be a grand wedding—for the prince that is, and for his betrothed." He looked at her expectantly.

"Ah," Meraleese said. "Thank you. Still with the new king of Thorensphere, you say?"

"Yes, Miss. That's what I heard."

Meraleese set down the cup on the large table the cook was working on, thanked him, and walked out of the room.

Two sets of puzzled eyes followed her.

chapter twenty-seven

"UNTIE HIM AND throw him back in his cell." That voice was Goredahl's. As Auragole tried to hang on to consciousness, two soldiers began to drag him from the room where he had been beaten. Goredahl stepped out in front of Auragole and grabbed his chin, so that Goredahl was looking into Auragole's bruised face. Goredahl's eyes were stone hard, and cold as the dungeon air. "No doubt you wonder why I keep you alive," he said, licking his lips and gloating. "Because dying is too good for you after what you've done. I want to keep you alive for as long as it pleases me. I want to tell you day by day what has been happening in the world you are no longer part of." He removed his hand and Auragole was once again staring at the earthen floor. Calling up strength from some unknown inner reservoir, he spat. It hit the floor near Goredahl's boots.

Goredahl struck Auragole hard across the face with his fist. "So you still have some fight in you, do you? We'll see how much fight there is left when you grow old in my prison, alone, unsought after, believed a villain of the worst kind. One who has slain a king—a king who loved you." And Goredahl laughed. The sound was brittle, like twigs under a horse's hooves. "The news I bring you, Auragole of the Cells, is this," and he bit down on each word. "Today I have wed your once bride-to-be. How do you feel about that? Well, of course, I had to marry her. She was promised a future king of the west, and now she has one."

Auragole could barely take in the words. He struggled through the fiery pain searing his back and face and attempted to recall what bride-to-be Goredahl was talking about.

"Her father has allied himself to me," Goredahl almost crooned the words, "and we will soon depart from here with the army of Thorensphere and that of Noonbarr behind us. When we enter Mattelmead in force, it should be easy to rally the army of Mattelmead to my banner. Take him away."

As the two guards dragged Auragole from the room where he had been beaten, Goredahl called after him, "Oh yes, one more thing. Except for a few of my most loyal men, everyone thinks you're dead—executed for murdering Solagen."

That was it! Oh, sweet Prince, Solagen was dead!

"So don't expect anyone to come rescue you. Did I tell you that your Elite Corps abandoned you? Yes, of course I did. We will 'talk' again tomorrow. Don't despair. I won't kill you. That would be too easy for you. No, you will be kept alive to grow old in my prison, your name despised by the world. You will be forgotten by all your friends—with the exception of me, of course. I have to leave you now. It is, after all, my wedding night." The last thing Auragole remembered was Goredahl's harsh, guttural laugh.

"WHAT DOES IT mean, Elarr?"

"It means, Auragole of the Way, that our punishment has begun."

He was drifting in and out of wakefulness, falling back into dream and fragments of memories that seemed to surround him like paintings in a gallery. He had lost count of the days.

Elarr rushed down the line of dead men when suddenly he stopped and stared up. Auragole's gaze followed Elarr's and he saw four distorted bodies, one next to the other, necks gaping in hideous grins, blood and rain washing down the white tunics with triangles on them.

Auragole was dragged time and again into a room where he was beaten. Each time when he awoke, back in his cell, the pain across his back, his arms, and his legs was so severe he willed himself to sleep.

Auragole caught up with Elarr just as Elarr fell to his knees and let out a cry of rage that sounded like nothing human.

Sleep was the only escape from a world so fraught with misery that he dared not stay there if he was to keep his sanity. But in sleep there were those terrible dreams. . .no, they were memories, fragments broken like the colored glass behind the altar in the temple at Adelmorr.

"Only in Agavia have I seen finer," Lorenwile said, coming up behind him. . . "Those fragments of glass on what's left of the windows. Incredible colors."

He was lying on a hard cot that irritated his wounds, no matter which way he lay. His shirt and trousers were wet with both blood and sweat. They stuck to his skin, and when he forgot and pulled at them, loud groans escaped from his lips. He was glad no one was there to hear. Mercifully, in the middle of the frequent beatings, with his arms twisted and tied awkwardly to a hook above his head, he lost consciousness, and dropped into oblivion.

Without thinking, Auragole lifted up his arm and hit Elarr hard across the side of his face with an open hand. Blood began to trickle from the corner of Elarr's mouth. Auragole was too angry to speak.

But then oblivion was not oblivion.

"Have you spoken to Glenelle?"

"Why should I speak to Glenelle? What can she say that will not add to my humiliation?"

There were those disconnected pictures from his life, as if time had been broken into thousands of pieces, and he could not gather them up in their right order, could not put them together in the pattern that was his life.

Meekelorr took a seat near Lorenwile and motioned to a stool opposite him. "Sit, Auragole."

But Auragole didn't move. Instead he plunged into speech, and his words were blunt. "Why did you break your promise? Why did you not come to the meeting place?"

He was sick and feverish.

"Glenorr. . .we can't go off and leave an injured man. We'll remain at this campsite until Donnadorr's ankle is healed."

"You would risk snow in the Northern Valley?" Glenorr asked, his mouth a rigid line.

"For a man's life, yes."

His hours, all his days were saturated with unbidden images that barely stayed for the watching, with beatings, and with blessed unconsciousness.

Meekelorr looked up and said, "I have given your request consideration. You may stay on until Lorenwile returns. Whether he takes you on as a student is Lorenwile's affair."

There were wounds that never healed—and something like a hot poker that seared through his shoulders. There was heat all around him and heat inside him.

Lorenwile said, "Can you be ready to leave in about a week?"

"What?" Auragole gulped.

"It will take all of the spring and summer and probably a good deal of the fall to make a fledgling True-singer out of you."

LORENWILE WAS TRAVELING mostly at night. The country of Thorensphere was alive with soldiers and army camps. How many young men had Goredahl conscripted since he had become king? It looked, from the number of camps and patrols Lorenwile observed as he traveled west, as if every young man between sixteen and thirty had been ordered into the army. Lorenwile wanted to avoid bumping into patrols that would ask to look at his papers, then ask where he was going and why. He had a legitimate excuse, of course, and that old safe-pass signed by Solagen. Still, the fewer people who remembered seeing him on the road, the better. So he avoided traveling by day. That made the going unhappily slow. But his hearing was keen, made so by years of True-singing. That saved him more than once.

Lorenwile wished he had his beloved pony, Surefoot, with him. But Surefoot was old and retired now to the pasturelands of Agavia in the warmer weather, and to the stables at the Last School in the colder months. Lorenwile had purchased as good a horse as was still available in the city of Thoren. But it was best to stay as far from the patrols as possible. With Surefoot he could have counted on the pony's silence. With this one, he had to dismount, hold tight to the reins, and stroke the horse's long nose until the danger had passed. With more than four hundred fifty miles to go until he reached his destination, and with the need to stay off the main road between the city of Thoren and the town of Little Thoren, it would take him at least three weeks to get to his goal, possibly longer. It was imperative that he be careful of his horse. He couldn't risk overtiring the animal, or worse, its going lame. Would he reach his goal in time, reach his friends before the terrible news arrived in Mattelmead? All he could do was try. Good people were in danger. He had not hesitated to go after them. Donnadorr and Sylvane had to leave Mattelmead as quickly as possible. If not, Lorenwile was sure, their lives would be forfeit, no matter who came into power now that Solagen was dead. Taking the news to Agavia—as important as it was—would have to wait.

AT SOME POINT the beatings stopped. Auragole wasn't

aware at first because he made no attempt to stay awake. But wakefulness came anyway.

He tried to think. But when he did, pictures from his past floated by. How many days since he had been dragged from his cell to that other one? How long since the punishment had stopped? How many days since Goredahl had come to watch and to gloat?

"Eleven of the thirty men I left with were killed." Meekelorr held Auragole's eyes.

"I'm sorry. It's hard to absorb. . .all this. . .this death."

His back, his chest, his legs were bruised, but there was little blood now.

"Fools," he remembered Goredahl screaming at the guards after an earlier beating. "I don't want him flayed alive. I want him punished, and severely. Yes, I want to see him suffer, but I want him kept alive, do you understand? I want to hear him cry for mercy. Oh, yes, that I want. But if any of you uses a whip on him again, I'll have the whip used on you. Use a leather strap."

Without thinking, Auragole lifted up his arm and hit Elarr hard across the side of his face with an open hand.

Auragole noticed—was it the same day?—that his shirt was in shreds and spotted brown with old blood.

Blood began to trickle from the corner of Elarr's mouth. Auragole was too angry to speak.

But none of his bones was broken. He touched his face. It was puffy. He saw that his wrists were raw, and his shoulders felt sprained, probably from the ropes that bound his hands and held them in an unnatural position high on a hook when he was beaten. No doubt the skin around his eyes was black and blue, for his eyes ached dully. His nose, though often bloody, was not broken. He found that remarkable. And, for a reason he could not fathom, amusing.

"I warn you, friend, do not endow me with qualities I do not

have. You'll only find disappointment."

A terrible thought occurred to him—which day was it? Had he cried for mercy when he had been flogged? He couldn't remember, but his jaw ached from clenching his teeth to keep from speaking or crying out loud. He had wanted more than anything not to give Goredahl that satisfaction. Better to become unconscious before the begging words fell involuntarily from his mouth, so during the beatings he purposely reached for senselessness.

Suddenly Goloss's hand flew out and struck Auragole hard across the cheek. Auragole was too stunned to cry out.

"I want you to remember that blow forever. There are no Gods. I didn't raise you so you could grow up foolish. There is nothing greater for a human being than freedom."

Only the pain was clear. Only Goredahl's face was clear. Auragole knew he had to think, had to understand why he was in this cell. He could tell now that many days and nights had come and gone because high up—perhaps twenty feet from the ground—was a small slit in the wall and through it came all the light there was, and all the air. But too often there was darkness, heavy and filled with threatening sounds. And always there was fever.

Goredahl pulled a drawer open and lifted a knife out and held it loosely in his hands. "You'd better leave now, Auragole. There are things I know about you that could cause you trouble if the king were told."

Sometimes he was asleep and awake and dreaming all at the same time—even after the beatings had stopped. The beatings had stopped. Why had they stopped?

In a daze, Auragole looked around at the cell and tried to take note of what there was around him in that dim light. There was a cot. There was a chamber pot. There was straw scattered about the earthen floor. There was a clay pitcher filled with water. That was all. His head hurt from the effort of observing. How large was this cell? Ten feet by ten feet was his best guess. It was cold, he suddenly realized. He looked at the blanket he had been given. It was worn and filled with holes. How long had he been here?

When the guard came with his food, Auragole would ask him. How often did he get food? Was it once or twice a day? Surely he had taken food, and water, or he would be dead now. Maybe he was dead. How many came into the room accompanying the one carrying the food tray? Think. Think, he ordered himself. But thinking hurt. Waking hurt. Two? Three? They carried drawn swords and clubs—that he remembered. They brought the food—some sort of soup, fairly thin, and a coarse piece of bread. And precious water.

"Oh, my dear friend, there is so much to tell. . . Can you imagine, in these difficult days to find love, to have love?"

Oh, my lovely friend, Affredda, have I failed you too? Had he ever told Affredda what his father had told him about love? Had he warned her?

But he couldn't have. He was in prison.

She lay on her bed as languidly as when he first saw her lying by that stream in the Gandlese Mountains, sleeping and ill.

Who was that?

She was not so pale now, not so thin.

Not Affredda. Glenelle. There she was, his poor lost Ellie. But wait, Glenelle was alive and loved by Goredahl. That must be why Goredahl was so angry with him. But Goredahl was keeping him alive, he had heard him say so. To what end? And why had Goredahl not been here for. . .how many days?

It was at a war conference, and suddenly Goredahl had said, "Haven't you had some dealings with that strange little people's army who call themselves the Companions of the Way?"

Auragole had looked up to see Goredahl watching him with unreadable eyes.

Auragole tried to sit up. It might have been a different day.

He felt nauseated and lay back down, then vomited over the side of the cot. Without warning, he began to feel panicky. It made him ashamed. A prince does not allow panic. His mother would be angry. But something terrible had happened, and it was best he didn't know about it.

And there coming toward the window was Ellie herself, in a flimsy negligee, her long hair billowing down past her shoulders. He stopped to look at her. Could she see him? Probably not.

He didn't want to think any more—not about this. He would sleep. But he couldn't sleep because of the fever. He was burning up. He felt the flames around him. He could die in this fire—that would make Goredahl angry.

"There are things I know about you. . ."

Auragole's mind wandered then, away from the conflagration.

"Peace is a noble gift to bring. What price does Ormahn ask for his peace?"

"Price!" Auragole's voice was hoarse. "Would it not be worth almost anything one could give to live in peace?"

"Almost anything."

"Is this peace enough?"

His thoughts felt now like whirling sand, and he lay unprotected in the middle of a sandstorm. It scoured his body.

"We are bringing a halt to the centuries of wars. We are bringing peace and prosperity to everyone, and giving work to all. Have we not accomplished much?"

There was a quality of boyish enthusiasm to his words and Auragole couldn't help but feel thrilled.

"Is this not a noble task, worth giving one's efforts to, even one's life?"

The guards finally came at night—how many days since he had been beaten? There were four guards. They had come to bring his meal. It had turned dark outside and in the cell. They came carrying a torch, and the unexpected light bruised his eyes.

"Awake, are you? Then stand over in that corner."

He somehow rose from his cot and moved away from the guards. He did, however, remember to ask his question.

"Where is Goredahl?"

A guard put the food down near the door. "He's gone," he said.

"Gone? Where? How long have I been here?"

But they didn't answer him. A guard exchanged the water pitcher, put down a chamber pot, and took the old one. Then they filed out and closed the door. Auragole returned to his cot, spent and confused. How long had he been here? He had no way of knowing. He wasn't sure he wanted to know. He wanted to sleep. That seemed best. He lay down and closed his eyes.

"Human, with this I charge you. Today you have rescued the future of the Seusadahhn. Let it be upon your head and the heads of your kind to make humanity a goal worthy of aspiration." . . .

"Father," Auragole called to him. *"Tell me that you approve of me. Tell me that I have made you proud. Tell me that I have helped give to the world what you yourself wanted for it—peace."*

"Son, is this peace enough?"

"Peace is a noble gift to bring. What price does Ormahn ask for his peace?"

Peace.

"Almost anything."

It was hours before Auragole crawled over to the tray and ate some of the soup, chewed a little of the bread, and drank some water.

chapter twenty-eight

SYLVANE LOOKED UP from her sewing as Meraleese hurried into the drawing room.

"I hope I'm not late," she said, looking around. "Where's Glorr?"

"He and Don are in their rooms, changing for lunch. He's turning into quite a good horseman, our little son," Sylvane said, and smiled. She noticed that though Meraleese's cheeks were flushed, the rest of her face looked pale. And her eyes had dark circles under them as if she had not slept. She had been looking unwell for more than a week now, picking at her food, distracted when addressed.

Often when they were together in the drawing room, Sylvane would glance her way, only to see Meraleese, embroidery in hand, staring off into space. What was wrong? Did Sylvane dare inquire? Meraleese was such a deep and private person, one who asked for little and never complained. And Sylvane didn't want to pry.

"Were you walking in the woods?" Sylvane finally asked. She

saw Meraleese struggle before answering.

"No, I walked into the village."

"Again?" Sylvane said, and immediately wished she could take her words back. Meraleese's face had reddened. "I'm sorry, I only meant that you were there yesterday." And the day before that and the day before that, Sylvane thought. Could there be a man Meraleese was meeting?

Meraleese hesitated, but only for a moment, and then said, "I wanted to find out if there was news yet of the king's return—or at least where they were on their journey home."

Auragole, Sylvane thought. It's Auragole who still concerns her. But surely she knew that this longing—or was it love?—for Auragole was hopeless. He was prince now, and would be wed come winter. Curious that she would pursue his whereabouts so persistently. Meraleese had always seemed to Sylvane someone who accepted her lot in life—with sorrow, perhaps, but without complaint. Auragole had been on other trips, and Meraleese had not gone searching after information about him.

"And was there news?" Sylvane asked.

"No," Meraleese answered, and stared at her lap. Then she looked toward the door and a smile lit up her face. Glorr and Don had come into the room. Glorr hurried first to Meraleese and gave her a kiss, and then to Sylvane and gave her a kiss.

"I jumped a fence today," he said, looking proud.

"He certainly did," Don said, with an approving nod. "And didn't fall off his horse."

IT WAS LATE at night, but the rider was ushered into Veldarr's study, dirty and sweaty, still panting from the exertion of his long ride, from meals gone without and sleep missed. Two weeks on the road, and two horses ruined. Surely that must be some sort of record. The young soldier felt he was about to pass out. But he mustn't.

"Get us some wine, quickly," Veldarr ordered the servant

who had brought the young man in. "And then some food."

The servant hurried to obey, going to a table with several bottles and glasses on it.

"Sit, man, and catch your breath. Your message can wait a few minutes longer."

The young man did as he was bid, inhaling and exhaling deeply. In only moments the servant served both men the wine. "I'll go order the food now, sir," the servant said, and he bowed and left the room.

Veldarr motioned to the glass the young man was holding. "Drink that down, Korr, all of it."

Korr drank the wine down quickly and then looked up at Veldarr, waiting to be instructed.

Veldarr sat down across from him. "Now, can you tell me the news you bring?"

"Yes, yes," Korr gulped. "It's terrible news, sir. Shocking news."

"I can see that."

"Ormahn is dead, stabbed to death in his sleep." Korr's lips quivered. "And Prince Auragole is accused of his murder."

Veldarr leapt to his feet, and with quick steps moved to the fireplace. He turned to the young man. "What details can you give me?"

"I didn't want to wait too many days before I left, but I waited long enough, I think, to be able to bring a full account. You said to come as quickly as I was able should there be something to report that might affect the nation."

"Yes. Go on."

"First, the Elite Corps that had accompanied Ormahn and the prince was ordered to leave the country by night. They know nothing of. . .of what happened."

"Well, you certainly made good time. They've not yet arrived."

The young man smiled. "I did ride awfully fast. Your safe-pass got me through all the army posts without a problem and even got me two fresh mounts."

"Good. Tell me, who ordered the Elite Corps to leave so precipitously?" Veldarr returned to sit opposite Korr once more.

"The order was signed and stamped with Ormahn's seal, but they say that it really came from Auragole. He and the king had adjoining rooms, and it is said that in the night—fifteen or sixteen days ago now—Auragole entered and murdered the king while he slept. Goredahl arrested the prince."

"Where is Auragole now? Was he alive when you left?"

"That I don't know, sir. But this much I know. Goredahl is gathering his army and intends to march on Mattelmead to claim the throne—so rumor had it before I left. It is said that he will come with a great force drawn both from Thorensphere, which has a very large army now, and from Noonbarr."

"Noonbarr?"

Korr nodded. "Hameshall, newly anointed king of Noonbarr, will march alongside him. He is the father of Goredahl's new wife, Deeralee."

"The bride who was intended for Auragole?"

Korr nodded.

"Goredahl put aside his first wife?"

"Put her aside the very morning after the murder was discovered. The wedding took place immediately after the divorce—that very day—even before Solagen was buried!"

"Before the. . .unconscionable! So Goredahl married Auragole's intended." Then Veldarr chuckled. "He does have gall, you have to give him that."

"Yes, sir. Now he is allied with the lawful king of Noonbarr by marriage. It was then I left. I hope I did right."

"You acted exactly as I knew you would, Korr. That's why you, of all the soldiers still loyal to Mattelmead, were chosen. I won't forget your faithfulness. You can be certain of that." Veldarr smiled at Korr, rose, and came toward him. "You've done well. However, this terrible news, this very shocking news, must be kept secret for now—we certainly don't want riots in the streets."

"No, sir."

"Come."

Korr stood up.

Veldarr put his arm around the boy's shoulder and began walking with him to the door. "Let our beloved city be without sadness and fear for a few more days—we won't be able to keep it from the people for long. Stay here at my home. I want your presence kept secret. And I see that you need a rest after your arduous ride. Let me provide for your comforts. As I promised you when you left to serve in Goredahl's army, you will be well rewarded—say, an officer's commission in Mattelmead's army? Yes, I think you will make a very good leader of men. You think clearly and make decisions quickly and with good judgment."

"Thank you, sir, that is indeed generous." Korr's eyes shone with pleasure.

"You understand, I need a period of secrecy so that I can prepare to meet Goredahl. He is claiming a right that doesn't belong to him. You have seen him, seen how he governs. He would make a terrible Ormahn, don't you agree?"

"Yes, sir."

"Good. Now let me call my servant and have you taken to one of the guest bedrooms. The meal I ordered will be sent to you there. Your task, for the time being, is done. Mine is about to begin." He let go of the boy's shoulder and gave him a dazzling smile. Then he walked to the bell rope and summoned a servant to take the young soldier to his room.

LORENWILE CROSSED THE recently built bridge over the Thoren River north of Little Thoren into Mattelmead. He presented his safe-pass, then moved along the new road, which had been built with great difficulty through the marshes and with much loss of life. He rode through many miles of wetlands on the new but always soggy road until, a day away from the swamps, there was good hard Mattelmead soil beneath his horse's hooves. This part of Mattelmead was sparsely settled, as was much of the northeast, for the land was poor. But now there was a decent road, and he was making good time. However, when he saw a small village not far off the road, he decided he would risk the time and look for its tavern. Every village had a tavern. Lorenwile wanted a hot meal, and whatever news he could get from the villagers. He was not overly concerned about being recognized in this part of the country. There were as yet no grand estates here, merely small farms whose owners eked out a paltry living on the substandard land. Besides, he thought his disguise quite a good one. So he turned his horse off the main road and trotted the half mile to the village, which contained a dozen or so shacks, a general store, and the expected tavern. The sun was high. With luck there would be a few people in the tavern from whom he could get some information.

It was a poorly made structure: wood walls that barely kept the wind out, and a dirt floor. The roof was made of old beams and thatch. There was a fireplace, with a meager fire. There were four or five rough wooden tables with stools beside them.

When Lorenwile walked in, half a dozen pairs of eyes turned his way. The man who stood behind the bar came out and greeted him. His look was cautious, but not unfriendly.

"I'm lucky to have found this place," Lorenwile said in a jovial voice. "I thought I'd have to travel all the way to Mattelmead City without ever getting a hot meal. I can get a hot meal here, I hope," and he jangled the coins he carried in his pocket.

The proprietor gave him a quick nod. "That you can, if you like mutton stew, for that's what we have today."

"Good, good," Lorenwile said. The proprietor didn't move, so Lorenwile waited.

"And what takes you to Mattelmead City?" the proprietor finally asked.

"Why, that's my home. I've just come from the city of Thoren," Lorenwile said, gesturing broadly. "This is the first time I've used the bridge north of Little Thoren instead of going south around that impassable woods. I must say it's a much shorter route. I'm a maker of flutes, and I go sometimes to Glovale, sometimes into Thorensphere to sell them—now that peace has come."

"Ah. Well, sit, sit." The proprietor motioned to one of the tables. "I'll just tell my wife in the kitchen and get you your bowl of stew."

While Lorenwile was eating, one of the men sitting at the bar ventured a question.

"What news out of Thorensphere?" he asked.

What news indeed, Lorenwile thought.

"He means," another man piped up, "what news is there of the king and his party? We heard tell that he is on his way home, passing through Thorensphere, and bringing back with him a bride for Prince Auragole."

"We're hoping they'll pass this way," another added. "We're hoping many people will pass this way in the future."

"That would fatten our purses," a third man added with a nod.

So they knew nothing. Lorenwile felt relieved.

"Last I heard, Ormahn and his party were in the city of Thoren visiting the new king there. And, yes, in Ormahn's party is a bride for the prince—all the way from Noonbarr."

"From Noonbarr, hmmm," one muttered with no comprehension.

"Ah, Thoren City," the proprietor said, entering the room in time to hear this last exchange. "That be a far distance. You've gone all that way?"

Lorenwile shrugged. "If you want to make a business out of selling flutes, you have to be prepared to travel great distances. But I tell you true, I will be happy to see my home again, and my wife and children."

He spent another half hour regaling the men with stories of his adventures in Thorensphere—most of them lies—and then left. The terrible news had not yet reached this part of Mattelmead, and, he hoped, not where he was heading either.

THE BEATINGS BEGAN again. Goredahl was back and he came and watched. Auragole saw the look of pure pleasure on Goredahl's face, and the cold, steely glint in his eye. "Don't break any bones. Be careful of his face. I have a very good use for him, and I want him looking moderately well when the time comes." When they dragged Auragole back to his cell, Goredahl said, "Give him another blanket. He looks feverish, and I don't want him dying on us. And clean up this cell. The stench is dreadful."

Before Auragole cursed in pain, before he lost consciousness that first day after Goredahl returned, he thought, I've done something dreadful. What have I done? His whole body was on fire. Was it from the beatings or the fever? The same fever? A different fever?

Someone had hit him in the face. Was it Goredahl? Was it his father?

In his entire life, his father had struck him in the face only once. Why was he being beaten? What had he done? What was wrong with asking about the Gods? Is that why he was being beaten?

They had made camp near a lively stream. The day had been a fruitful one.

Auragole was observing the scene—his father and his younger self, sitting around the campfire, sipping the hot, strong senta tea. Auragole sat down on the ground and watched the two. How old was he then? Eleven? Ten? What had they been speaking about? Goloss's own father, yes, that was it. And Goloss looked happy then, as if lost in some pleasant memory.

Auragole hadn't planned it, but the words were out of his mouth before he even thought them.

"Why do you hate the Gods?"

His father looked up at Auragole without expression, but his blue eyes became dark. "What Gods?" he finally asked.

"I don't know," Auragole said. "Any God."

The Creative Gods, the watching Auragole thought. You know, Father, you were once a priest of the King God. Why did you never tell me? Why did you hide all knowledge of the Gods from me?

"There are no Gods. There is the earth, the plants, the animals, and humans. That's all."

"But how did we come to be, the earth and humanity?"

You have always been stubborn and willful, he told his younger self.

Suddenly Goloss's hand flew out and struck Auragole hard across the cheek. Auragole was too stunned to cry out.

"I want you to remember that blow forever. There are no Gods. I didn't raise you so you could grow up foolish. There is nothing greater for a human being than freedom."

You shouldn't have done that, he told his father. That was a terrible mistake. I didn't cry. But I remembered. Oh, yes, I remembered.

But this beating was not because his father was angry. This was something else—what? Something more terrible—what? Auragole was struck hard across the face and could taste the blood on his lip.

"I want you to remember that blow forever, king-killer."

He opened his eyes for a moment. He was being held by two soldiers, and Goredahl was staring into his face with a hideous grin and a look of satisfaction. Auragole wanted to tell him that he shouldn't have done that because he did remember the Gods. Had he told Goredahl about the Lady of the Lake or the Guardians of the Flame? Shhh. Don't tell Goredahl about them. He will try to burn down the Ancient Woods.

"Auragole, of the Mountains and of the Way, you are a seeker after spiritual knowledge. But you do not know it yet. You think

380

in these woods you have found an answer to the existence of the
Gods. But I tell you, child, before very long the certainty will
leave you, and all that you experienced near the lake and with
the Lady who was once worshipped there will recede into dream.
It will have no substance for you. And you will end up uncertain,
even bereft.”

"Never," he cried, and then blacked out.

RORADAHL STOOD IN the grand foyer of Veldarr's
mansion, waiting to be taken into Veldarr's study. It was the
second such request from the commander of the army since
Roradahl had arrived in Mattelmead City less than three days
earlier. It was just after the evening meal that the summons had
come. Roradahl had acquiesced, he hoped with good grace, but
he was extremely tired and had planned on an early night. It had
been a long ride from Thoren. The Elite Corps had not ridden
alone through the Thorensphere countryside. They had been
escorted by what Roradahl now referred to as Goredahl's army,
guided by it along the southern route that skirted the Ancient
Woods. He was certain that, left alone, they could have traveled
faster. However, their escort had not left them until the Elite
Corps had reached the Mattelmead border. There had been no
stops at army camps, or at any of the village inns for
refreshment. They had stopped only to rest the horses, usually
in some farm field or other.

It had been a great irritation to Roradahl, this escort, and he
hadn't always hidden his displeasure. But the leader of the
Thorensphere army escort outranked him, and so Roradahl had
swallowed his vexation and said nothing. What had Goredahl
expected, that a captain of the Elite Corps would disobey
Ormahn's orders? How Roradahl detested Thorensphere's new
king. But on that score, better to keep silent.

He liked Veldarr. While Ormahn and Auragole were out of
Mattelmead, Roradahl would naturally take his instructions

from the commander of the army—and from Oldwell, who was in charge of the country in Solagen's absence.

Roradahl was mildly curious about why he had been called yet again. As soon as he had arrived in Mattelmead City he had reported first to Oldwell, then to Veldarr. Roradahl was still bone weary. After the prince's wedding, he would give leave and a much-needed rest to those of the Elite Corps who had traveled with him as escort to Ormahn's party. Then he would go up to his country house. He was wondering if the wedding party was arriving even sooner than expected when he was ushered into the commander's study.

Roradahl entered the room and stood at attention just inside the door. Veldarr, sitting at his desk, looked up as Roradahl entered. He motioned Roradahl to a chair placed directly in front of the desk. Roradahl moved quickly to it, sat down, back erect, and waited to hear what the commander of Mattelmead's army wanted.

He was a little surprised when Veldarr said, "Tell me about that last night—your last night in Thoren City."

He had given this information to Veldarr, as he had to Oldwell. "I don't understand, sir," he said. "I told you everything about that night just two days ago."

"I know, but I want you to tell it to me again. Sit back, be at ease. And tell me again."

So Roradahl did.

"And you never corroborated those, to say the least, rather unusual instructions with either Solagen or Auragole?"

Roradahl reddened and began to feel uneasy. Something was wrong. "I told you, they both had women with them. It would have been unthinkable to disturb them. . .but I assure you both orders came written on the king's paper with his unbroken seal upon it. I've seen that paper and that seal often. If you doubt my word, I've given those written instructions to Commander Oldwell, those addressed to me and those addressed to him. If you want to see the documents, I'm sure he'll show them to you." Roradahl was feeling a little put out.

"I don't doubt your word, Roradahl. Just answer the question, please—with whom did you corroborate those orders?"

Roradahl took a deep breath and said, "Since neither the king nor the prince was available, I sought out Goredahl, who assured me that he knew about the orders, that they were genuine, and that I was to follow them without any hesitation on my part. And so I did. Why? Is something amiss?" Of course there was. He could feel his heart pounding.

Veldarr looked at him, his eyes hooded. When he spoke it was barely above a whisper. "King Solagen is dead, murdered, I've been told, by Auragole. What do you know of this?"

Shock reverberated through Roradahl's body, and he leapt from his chair. "What are you saying! The king dead?"

"Murdered."

"It's not possible. It must be some joke, some horrible joke. Or a rumor."

"I assure you it is not. Ormahn is dead. Murdered."

"It can't be true!"

"But it is."

"Not by Auragole. Never. Never. It was not in him. He adored the king."

"Murdered the very night you were sent away—sent, it is said, by Auragole and not by Ormahn." Veldarr's words were measured.

"Oh my stars!" And Roradahl sat down hard, too stunned to think or to speak. It was cold, but sweat was pouring down his face and neck. Suddenly he looked up. "What's happened to Auragole? Where is he? Is he also dead?" The thought caused his throat to constrict.

"We don't know yet what has happened to Auragole. But if he was accused by Goredahl, I have little hope that he survived that night, unless. . ."

"Unless what?"

"Unless Goredahl has some use for him."

"Oh my stars. I should have been there. I should have been there." Roradahl could feel the tears stinging his eyes. "I sensed it was a strange request—but it had the king's seal on it, you see. The king's seal—the one he wears on his finger and never takes off. Oh, stars, I should have been there."

Veldarr stood up and went to a table. He poured some brandy into a glass, returned, and gave it to Roradahl, who swallowed it in one gulp.

"There's something else," Veldarr said, seating himself at his desk opposite Roradahl.

Roradahl's eyes widened in alarm. "Something else? What?"

"I think Goredahl's intention is to claim the throne of Mattelmead—and therefore of all the west—and to back up his claim by force."

"Claim the throne?"

"Goredahl is gathering the army assigned to him, which I understand has become quite sizable, since he has conscripted all eligible young men in Thorensphere."

"Yes, all that is true."

"He plans to march on Mattelmead when he has everything in readiness. He is allied now with Hameshall, who is probably gathering his own army from Noonbarr. Goredahl has put aside his wife of twelve years and is now married to Auragole's intended, Hameshall's daughter."

"What?"

"That is confirmed." Veldarr's tone was matter-of-fact.

"Goredahl took Auragole's bride-to-be and now wants to become Ormahn? Preposterous! Unthinkable!" And then Roradahl glanced at Veldarr. Had he said the wrong thing? But it was all too much to take in. Surely Veldarr was not in favor of Goredahl's ascension to Solagen's throne. Veldarr himself had been a rival for the throne until Auragole had been named heir.

Suddenly Veldarr looked irate. Was it at him?

Veldarr rose and began pacing about the room, but his eyes never left Roradahl's face. "You say it's unthinkable. But it is very thinkable—unless Goredahl is stopped. I intend to stop him. Goredahl has always wanted the throne, you know that, but he would be a disaster for the country—not only for the country, but for the whole of the west."

No, not at him.

"He's a vain, cruel, stupid, yet extremely devious man—with no vision, but a mighty lust for power. All that my uncle worked for the whole of his life would go to ruin." Roradahl could hear the anger in Veldarr's voice. "Goredahl is a dangerous and vicious tyrant. And he must not be allowed to claim the throne. As he isn't the heir, he has no true claim, no more than. . ." Veldarr paused, then came and stood behind the desk, watching Roradahl with an unreadable expression on his face.

Roradahl held his gaze, and waited.

"I know of what Auragole stands accused," Veldarr continued, "but knowing him as you do. . .as I do, can you even entertain for a minute that it was he who wielded the knife? To believe Auragole guilty is to believe Auragole stupid. And both you and I know Auragole is not stupid." Veldarr's voice became soft with sorrow. "However, my friend, I doubt whether Auragole survived the night."

Tears spilled down Roradahl's cheeks as the likely truth of what Veldarr was saying hit him. "I should have listened to my heart and stayed there."

"No doubt the king was already dead when you received your orders."

"I should have. . .I should have listened to my heart." Roradahl shook his head from side to side.

"Roradahl, are you with me?" Suddenly, Veldarr's words were harsh, bringing Roradahl out of his musings. Veldarr was leaning across the desk, his face close to Roradahl's.

"What?"

"I agree with you, my friend. Auragole is surely innocent of these charges."

"Yes. Yes."

"I imagine you would want to avenge him, to clear his name, to clear the name of the Elite Corps, who have been accused of running away."

That brought Roradahl to his feet. "What?"

"Sit, sit, Roradahl." Veldarr also sat. "If it wasn't Auragole who killed Solagen—and we know it wasn't—then we know who did."

The heat drained from Roradahl's face as the reality of Veldarr's words hit him.

"The Elite Corps is now yours to command, if you want it, Roradahl. As head of the army I can give you that power. They are the best soldiers we have, and they adored Auragole. I doubt if any in Goredahl's army can equal them in skill. I can't believe that there is one man among them who would believe Auragole guilty of this heinous crime. Roradahl, I want you and your men with me. Listen to me. I want to gather the army that is still in Mattelmead, and the countries to the south, and meet Goredahl when he crosses into Mattelmead."

"But when will that be? And where? Will he enter from the south of Thorensphere, skirting the Ancient Woods—which he failed to burn down—or. . ."

". . .or come across from the north of Little Thoren on the new bridge and head directly west to Mattelmead City, thus cutting off many miles."

"Impossible," Roradahl said. "A whole army cross over on a single, narrow bridge and a single bad road surrounded by bogs. . ."

"It takes little to build rafts—and no doubt Goredahl will assume that we expect him to come from the south, and that we will send our entire army south, thus leaving the north wide open. However, if Hameshall is with him, Goredahl might split his army and come at us from two directions."

"Hmmm."

"Right now we have the advantage. He doesn't know that we are already aware of the king's death. My guess is Goredahl will want to cut us off from Glovale and Wildenfarr and any help we might get from there. We have many soldiers in those two countries. And no doubt Goredahl believes that he still has time on his side."

"Then for a certainty he will send an army to the south of Mattelmead," Roradahl agreed. "But you also think he will attempt a crossing near Little Thoren?"

"The Thoren River is wide but it can be crossed slowly—if there is no visible army waiting on the other side. A beach has been cleared for a mile on either side of the bridge. We can't afford to turn our backs on the crossing at Little Thoren. I know his mind, which is not hard to read, and I'm sure what Goredahl is expecting us to do is bring all our men south."

"And to discount the north because of the swamps and the narrow bridge."

"Exactly, and because there is only one passable road through the swamps. In some ways he is right. If we tried to meet him at the river's edge, we would be forced to fight in the dangerous swamps, or cross over and fight him in Little Thoren. So I won't meet him at the river. I have a different plan. I will send men to the north. And wait twenty miles in, where the bogs end. I want as much of Goredahl's army as possible within Mattelmead before we begin our own assault. But first I must, in all haste, bring our army back from the southern countries. Emissaries are even now on their way. I intend to call up immediately all the troops who are on leave, even those who have retired from the army. This is an emergency and we will need everyone we can get, since a great part of the army is spread over the entire west, including, unfortunately, in Thorensphere. But if those soldiers assigned to Thorensphere believe Auragole killed the king, they will fight for Goredahl. I tell you, Roradahl, in my heart of hearts I feel that it was Goredahl who killed the king, and has put the blame on Auragole. I know my cousin all too well."

"Yes, yes, I can well believe Goredahl capable of that!"

"It is not in Auragole's nature, as you say, to become an assassin. But, my friend, sadly, it is too late to help Auragole now. Would Goredahl allow him to live if Goredahl were the true murderer? Think, friend, what would Auragole want you to do now? Surely he would want you to avenge him, to avenge Solagen, to avenge the Elite Corps. Are you with me?"

Roradahl could feel the blood rising hot in his veins. The king dead. His friend dead, his Elite Corps accused of cowardice. Roradahl's sentimental sorrow slid away. He would have vengeance. He stood. "Tell me what you want me to do, Veldarr, and I will do it."

HOW BEAUTIFUL SHE was when he first saw her lying near the stream close to the rapidly moving water with its healing forces. Her face looked pale, almost translucent. Her golden hair lay around her face like a halo of light.

He had fallen in love with Ellie then.

But there was no such thing as love—he knew that, didn't he? After all, that's what his father had told him on his deathbed.

Auragole shook his head. "My father warned me."

"About what?"

"He said there was no such thing as love. That love was merely an illusion, a bodily need. That it would entrap you, take away your freedom."

He had been beaten for the willful things a child does, but those beatings were not like those inflicted on him now. . . Whom was he talking to? Ah, yes, Lorenwile.

"Do you believe that, friend?"

"Why should I believe differently? I feel like a fool. And right

now I think I hate her as much as I've ever hated anyone. What else does she deserve from me?". . .

"*Let me speak, Auragole, for I cannot fight the blackness much longer. Everyone will speak to you of love and sing its praises.* . . *They will all lie.* . . *Don't succumb and you will be free, free.*" *Then the flaming eyes saw no more.*

"*I was too angry in life, and that anger made me selfish. I never said this to you when I was alive, Auragole—I love you. I know it is not adequate for the hard days ahead. But it is all I have to give you.*". . . *And he looked sorrowfully at Auragole, rose, and walked away into the desert.*

"*Is this peace enough?*" Auragole heard from the periphery of his dreaming.

"Enough. Enough. Let's not damage him too much. I have use for him." But that was not his father's voice.

chapter twenty-nine

LORENWILE WAS NOT challenged by anyone in Mattelmead as he cantered openly and in broad daylight toward his destination. The land he was now moving through was fertile land and beautiful, much of it woodland, but in the clearings there were large farms and grand estates. The marshes and the arid land were days behind him.

It was the middle of October. He had left the bridge over the Thoren River a week earlier, hurrying to reach the country estate that belonged to Donnadorr and Sylvane. It was now three weeks since Solagen had been killed, and Auragole accused. Once past the marshlands, Lorenwile had pushed his horse as hard as he dared, since he had to make up for the nearly two weeks it had taken to get out of Thorensphere.

He was hailed by field hands and gardeners as he rode through Donnadorr's lands, but no one challenged him. Solagen's peace still reigned here. A groom came to take his horse and, noticing the mud and Lorenwile's wrinkled and dirty clothes, said, "You must have ridden a long way, sir."

"I have. Indeed I have. But I must see your master and your mistress immediately. Are they in residence?"

"Yes they are. Just knock on that door, sir, and someone will fetch them for you."

Lorenwile felt an immense sense of relief as he headed for the large house. It had been a calculated risk to assume that Sylvane and Donnadorr would be here and not in Mattelmead City, which they cared little for. If the couple had been in the city, getting them out of that populated place would have been ten times as dangerous—were it even possible. More worrisome, he might have been too late to help them. Surely the dreadful news would have arrived in the city by now, with the accusation against Auragole at the center of the terrible tidings. Would any of Auragole's friends be safe?

As Lorenwile reached the portico of the mansion, he noticed a woman and a child walking toward the house from the gardens. She was a well, if somewhat simply, dressed woman in her early thirties, with a pleasant face. It was animated now as she spoke to the boy walking along beside her. Had Sylvane finally given birth to the child she and Don longed for? His mind did a careful calculation. This child was too old—about eight, he thought—to be Sylvane's. The woman, catching sight of him, came toward him, smiling.

"Hello," she said. "May I help you? Are you looking for someone?"

"I am," he said. "I'm looking for the master and mistress of this house. Tell them, if you would, that Lorenwile of the Songs is here and that he has ridden a long way to bring them important news."

The woman's expression lost its easiness, and her hazel eyes, almost golden in the afternoon sun, became wide with concern. "Lorenwile of the Songs. Can that be so? Auragole's teacher?"

"None other, and who might you be?" he asked, looking at

her with mounting curiosity. Her face paled beneath his gaze, and not, he surmised, out of shyness.

"My name is Meraleese. And this is my son, Glorr. Shake hands with the gentleman, Glorr," she said, but her eyes never left Lorenwile's.

Glorr did as he was bidden, staring at Lorenwile gravely.

The names were unfamiliar to Lorenwile.

"Come inside," Meraleese said. "Let me take you to a place where you can wash the travel dust from your face and hands and refresh yourself. I will look for Sylvie and Don and order you some food. Sylvie might be resting. She's pregnant, you know. But how would you know that? Where is it you come from? No wait, no need to tell your story more than once."

What is this all about? he wondered. The woman was speaking rapidly, almost anxiously. Who was she? For a brief moment Meraleese searched his face before she led him down the hall into a room where there was a washstand, a tub, pitchers of water, and a chamber pot.

"I'll find Sylvie and Don and come back for you."

As he was washing, he wondered if indeed the news of the king's death had reached this far north. Well, he would find out in a few minutes.

In half an hour he was brought to the drawing room, where Sylvane and Donnadorr were waiting. Donnadorr rushed toward him, a look of pure delight and welcome on his face.

"What a wonderful surprise. I can't believe it's really you." He clasped Lorenwile's hands and pounded his back, talking all the time as he pulled him to where Sylvane sat, her fingers resting on her slightly rounded belly. "I certainly never thought to see you in Mattelmead again. What has brought you all the way from Agavia to my door? But wait, we shall hear your story when you've had some refreshment. What a sight for sore eyes you are, Lorenwile. Look, Sylvie, isn't he a sight for sore eyes? But how is it you have gray hair and a gray beard? Of course, you're traveling in disguise. But maybe it's no longer necessary, since Goredahl is no longer head of the Security Forces. He's been made king of Thorensphere. But you probably knew that."

"Don, stop going on and on," Sylvane chided with a gentle smile. "Offer Lorenwile a chair and give him a chance to speak."

"Of course I'll give him a chance to speak." He grinned at Lorenwile as he escorted him to a chair. "You must have stories to tell far more interesting than what we country bumpkins can tell you. And I have a hundred questions to ask you, first about those I knew in Agavia. . ."

"Don. . ."

"I know, I know, first the food," he said, glancing sideways at his wife, then back at Lorenwile. "Sit, sit. It should be here in a moment. In the meantime let me give you a glass of wine—from Glovale, the kind you like. I haven't forgotten." Donnadorr hurried to a cabinet where there were assorted bottles, and poured from one. "I take it you've met our friend Meraleese," and he gestured toward Meraleese, who had entered the room behind him, "and her son and our foster son, Glorr. Well, that's a story worth a night's telling."

No doubt, Lorenwile thought with interest, turning once again to the woman and child.

Meraleese came toward the group and sat on the sofa, her son next to her. Her hands, lying in her lap, were twisting a handkerchief, and her eyes, Lorenwile observed, were wide with worry.

Donnadorr was back now with a glass of wine. He handed it to Lorenwile, who watched the redheaded, red-bearded man with fondness, but also with concern. This was not going to be easy, he thought, glancing around at the lovely room. Their estate was certainly splendid. It would be hard for them to give it up. Particularly now with a baby on the way. He hadn't counted on that. Well, no use worrying. One played the cards as they fell. Give it up they must, if they hoped to stay alive. There would be no safety in Mattelmead for present or former friends of Auragole now that Auragole had been accused of regicide. No matter who took the throne—Goredahl, or Veldarr, or even Oldwell—the lives and property of Auragole's friends would be forfeit. Thank the Creative World Lorenwile had arrived in time, before the terrible news had spread into this part of Mattelmead. Then he glanced again at Meraleese. She knows something, he thought. Or suspects something. Well, there would be time to find out about her after a good meal, and he saw by what was being wheeled in that this was indeed going to be a good meal. Then, after their stories were exchanged, they would have to make plans to leave for the Valley of the Agavi, as quickly as possible.

MERALEESE BARELY MADE it to her room before the tears began to fall. Somehow she had sat through Lorenwile's terrible tale, had managed to ask a question or two, but had let Don take the lead in the questioning. When she knew what she needed to know, what she feared to know, she excused herself, saying she was not hungry and therefore would not take a late dinner with them that evening. She went first to say goodnight to her son, who had not been allowed to stay for the news Lorenwile had brought. His nurse had come to fetch him for his own dinner. He had finished his dinner and bath, and was waiting in his bed, when Meraleese arrived. She had kept calm while she listened to her son reading from his storybook, had kissed him, tucked the covers around him, and then had gone into her room. She locked the door between Glorr's room and her own— something she had never done before. She locked the door to the hall, then dropped into the chair near the fireplace and wept, the tears coming in a flood of stifled sobs. She held her hands tight against her mouth to still the sounds.

All these weeks she had sensed that something terrible had

happened to Auragole. How she knew, she couldn't have explained to another. How does one explain that the heart can know things the mind cannot? Auragole. In prison. Or more likely, dead. Why would Goredahl keep him alive? He hadn't kept Timorr alive. Yet another loss. She didn't think she could bear it. She wept now as she had when Timorr had been torn from her, and then again when she knew for a certainty that he was dead.

Meraleese had not wept in front of Glorr when his father had been taken away, nor had she wept at that heart-stopping moment when the soldiers had dragged Glorr from her. He kept calling her name, and she had heard that little bereft voice long after he was gone and out of earshot. But afterward, finally, she had wept, alone in her empty house. And when Auragole had found her son, and taken her to him, she had not wept when she parted from him. But later, yes, later, she had been unable to control the tears. Timorr gone, and now Auragole. How many loves must she lose? Her parents had died, but in their right time. Her brothers now lived far from her in Glovale, and her sister and her brother-in-law had moved to the south. There had been no answer to the letters she had written them since Timorr had been arrested. She suspected it was fear that had caused their silence, caused them to flee the city. Eventually she had stopped writing. Perhaps they needed protecting. But she had felt like an orphan then, except for a few kind friends.

She had listened to her son's prayers nightly after coming to this haven, but had not prayed herself, except the prayer for the dead she said twice daily for Timorr. She knew she was angry. The Gods seemed so indifferent to the suffering of humanity, to her suffering. Her mind understood their distance—no, not their distance, their waiting. She had been taught well by Timorr, but she couldn't help it, she was angry—desperately, horribly angry. And unwilling to give it up. Tonight it welled up in her and flooded out of her eyes in what felt like a torrent.

Must humankind's road be such a cruel one, so filled with suffering? Oh, yes, she could answer that in the abstract. But this was not the abstract. And there was no Timorr to help her overcome her anger.

She could have borne it had Auragole married and served the country as prince. She could have borne it if she were kept from him the rest of her life. But this. . .this she couldn't bear. Auragole accused of a murder he was not capable of committing, killed, or else locked in a cell and tortured. Who that Auragole knew would gainsay Goredahl now and stand against him? Who had that power? She couldn't bear the thought—Auragole dead, or alone in a cell without any comfort, without ever knowing that she. . . But how could she have told him? She hadn't known herself until it was too late. Even if she had, she would have kept silent. He had been forbidden to see her, and she had not wanted to cause him trouble. Well, with or without her, trouble had come. And so she wept. Just tonight, she promised herself. Let me have this one night of weeping. Tomorrow, I must rise and help in the preparations. We must leave here. Lorenwile had been clear on that point. And no one had argued. This home was no longer a haven.

Hands over her face, she bent forward across her knees and cried until there were no more tears left in her. Then she undressed and crawled into her bed, unlocking her doors first. For weeks she had known that something terrible had befallen Auragole. She had been right. The worry had become reality. But tomorrow there would be work to do. Exhausted, she fell into a deep sleep and did not stir until the servant came with morning tea, and drew back the drapes to let the October sun in.

"I'VE TOLD YOU never to contact me at my home." Veldarr stood in Glenelle's drawing room, his blue eyes flashing. He had not given his cloak, hat, or riding crop to the servant who had opened the door.

Glenelle's hand flew to her throat. "I'm sorry. But what choice did I have? I left a message also at your club, but I wasn't sure when you would go there. So much is going on—and you haven't come in a long time."

"You worry too much for your safety, Glenelle. By now you should know that I'll take care of you, see that you are protected. You should have trusted me more."

"Glenorr, too?"

"Of course, Glenorr."

"But what's going on? Are the rumors true? Everyone I know is in such a state, not knowing whether to run from the city or stay. . ."

Veldarr's eyes lost their hardness and his voice was less cold. "I don't know what you've heard, but I tell you this—you are safe in the city. Let me dispel the rumors by telling you what is true. Yes, Solagen is dead. Yes, Auragole stands accused. No, I don't know if he's still alive. And yes, Goredahl is coming to claim the throne. But I don't intend to let him near the city."

"Is he coming with an army?" Glenelle's hand had moved from her throat and she was now wringing her hands.

"Of course, with an army," he laughed. "How else back up his 'legitimate' claim? But I think Goredahl would make a terrible king, don't you?"

She nodded.

"We must do all we can to prevent it. You see that, yes?"

"Yes." Her voice was hardly above a whisper.

"Therefore, you must understand how busy I am. I intend to meet Goredahl on the battlefield long before he makes it to the city. Just stay comfortably at home, my pet, and let those whose task it is, see to dealing with these troubles."

Again she nodded.

"I have to go. I have a meeting with Oldwell and the leaders of the city and the commanders of the army, and I'm already late."

"Oldwell is with you?"

"He is."

Glenelle walked him to the door.

As it stood open, Veldarr said, "Don't send a note to my house again, Glenelle. It upsets my wife—and I have enough to deal with at present." He took her chin in his hand and kissed her lightly on the nose. "Don't worry, my beauty. As always, you are under my protection," and with that he turned and hurried down the steps, calling for his horse.

"I'D LIKE TO adopt you, Auragole. That would make everything legal, make you legally my son."

He was riding in a cart filled with the smell of overripe apples.

"You will give up visiting that woman—the wife of that priest—yes, yes, I know all about that."

Where were they taking him? But he couldn't stay awake long enough to see, or to ask. He kept sinking into dream.

"I've come to return your horse, which I took without permission, and. . ."

"And?"

"And to say I'm sorry."

Meekelorr looked up and said, "I have given your request consideration. You may stay on until Lorenwile returns. Whether he takes you on as a student is Lorenwile's affair."

Why did he want to be awake when there was so much agony and confusion there?

Because there was agony in his dreaming also.

The wagon was bouncing hard on the road and he felt tossed about like the sacks of apples he knew he was lying on.

"I see a flame burning in you, child of the mountains, but it will not sustain itself in the harsh world, in a world that belongs to the Gods of Adversary. If this flame is extinguished, you could become an enemy of the Gods, could become allied to the Dark Force."

It hurt to be tossed about so. Maybe it was he who was dead. Yes, that must be right.

He was standing again on the shore of the radiant lake . . . "Too soon, my child," the Beautiful One said. His voice was all around Auragole, gentle as mist.

"Find me with what is most yourself, then you will never lose me again."

Look, he's touching my face, Auragole thought, and light and quiet rest drifted through him.

"Drink this water."

"No." The water was poison. He knew he mustn't die. He had been told so by the Sweet One.

"Drink!" and a hand struck Auragole's face.

"I must go back," Auragole said.

Did he drink? He must have, because the Sweet One was gone.

"It's hard to absorb. . .all this. . .this death."

". . .you could become an enemy of the Gods, could become allied to the Dark Force."

THEY HAD BEEN on the road for nearly a week, heading north. Despite the danger they were moving at a slow pace because of Sylvane's condition. And, too, they wanted to give the appearance of a leisurely autumn camping expedition. That was the story they had told their servants, who were trusting and compliant souls.

By now the shock had worn off, but not the sorrow. Ormahn of Mattelmead was dead. Auragole stood accused of his murder and was also presumed dead. The pain Donnadorr felt every time that thought arose was one he could not set aside. Now the fate of the country of Mattelmead was in doubt. No, not only Mattelmead; the fate of all of the west. It had not taken Donnadorr much convincing to realize that those who were close, or had been close, to Auragole would be under a cloud of suspicion, persecuted with no questions asked, no matter who was in charge now. For Don to give up his wonderful and beautiful estate had been less difficult than he had expected. But to lose Auragole, that had been a terrible blow. That first night after Lorenwile arrived, Donnadorr had a hard time consoling Sylvane. Don had been glad for the dark as the two lay entwined in each other's arms, for his eyes too were wet with tears.

After a childhood and youth of hardship and poverty, Don had at first enjoyed his life of luxury and privilege. But in these last few years it had seemed less and less rewarding. His life, which had once been full of adventures of every imaginable kind before he had arrived in Mattelmead nearly seven years before, had soon become one of routine, even trivial routine. Frankly, Don was bored with his life, had been bored for a long time, though he had hardly wanted to admit it, even to himself. Where was gratitude, after all? Because of the leg injury he had sustained on his journey to Mattelmead, he had not been allowed to buy a commission in the Mattelmead army, and that still rankled. Donnadorr had longed to be part of Ormahn's peace-bringing movement. For years he had thought that he was far too young to be doing so little in a world undergoing such vast changes. He had longed to be part of those changes. At least until recent times.

Recently he had become uneasy over what was occurring in Mattelmead—not its great goals, but some of the methods employed to achieve those goals. Too many of the people he and Sylvie had known, both in the city and in the country, had been taken away in the night, never to be heard from again. After a while their property had been given to someone else—usually to young officers who had been of outstanding service to Ormahn. But Donnadorr had never found out what had happened to those acquaintances. And then there was Meraleese's terrible and sad story. So he had become more and more cautious about whom he spoke to, and about what he said.

Because of the jewels he and Sylvie had brought from Agavia, Donnadorr and Sylvane had lived a life of comfort and privilege, but in more-recent times they had also lived in fear. It was a fear they had not been eager to talk about together. That hadn't been necessary. They always knew what was going on in each other's mind.

Now they were on their way to Agavia, and who knew what interesting adventures lay ahead? Being on the road again—this time not on foot but on a good horse—filled him with an excitement he was ashamed to give voice to. Donnadorr had only three worries. One was how well Sylvane could take this trip, since she was more than five months pregnant. The second was the weather this time of year. It was past mid-October, though admittedly still fairly warm. His third concern was the long route Lorenwile had decided on—almost six hundred miles to the beginning of the Gandlese Mountains. And once in the Gandlese, Don had no idea how much farther it was to the Valley of the Agavi. But Lorenwile had a plan. Because of the danger, Lorenwile was leading them due north away from Mattelmead City. They would eventually cut through a forest in which few dwelled and head toward the rugged, barren hills that divided Mattelmead from the Northern Desolation. It was said that these hills were as sick as the Northern Desolation on the other side. It was said that the air in the hills was unfit to breathe. Therefore, it was said that no one lived in those hills.

When Don had first voiced his concern, Lorenwile had answered, "Let us hope that the rumors about the hills are false. However, let us also hope that those stories are still believed, and that no one lives in or travels through those hills— especially no soldiers. Personally I doubt the accuracy of those rumors."

Don knew that he had looked dubious, because Lorenwile had spread a map of the Westernlands out on the table in Donnadorr's study the night before they left.

"Look carefully, my friend," Lorenwile said as he pointed at the map. "There's no other way that we can travel without running into various armies. In the countries west of us the news of Solagen's murder will be known by the time we try to pass through."

"What about traveling east through these woods?" Don pointed at the forest south of the Northern Desolation.

"True, those woods are sparsely settled, but there are army camps there. And the woods end not long after we enter Thorensphere." Don stared at the map, following where Lorenwile pointed. "If we try to go another route through Thorensphere, or even venture south into the Sorren Heights," Lorenwile went on, "what will we find—chaos, anarchy, out-and-out war? Do you have any doubt, Don, that the two cousins will go at it, each claiming his right to the throne?"

"No doubt whatsoever, Lorenwile."

"Then there is Oldwell. He's a pleasant enough fellow, but also a strong and smart commander. And not without a little ambition of his own. In these circumstances, many, not caring for the other two choices, might decide to rally behind his banner, should Oldwell choose to raise it in his own name. But that's not all of it. What will stop petty leaders all over the Westernlands from disdaining to follow any of them? What will stop ambitious leaders from laying claim to parts of the kingdom for themselves?"

"You think the west will so quickly fall apart?" Donnadorr asked. "That Ormahn's United West will so easily disintegrate?" That was a terrible thought.

"I do," Lorenwile said. "Therefore, five people, obviously well-to-do and traveling west through settled lands and on very good horses, would not make it many miles without harassment. Likely we would not even get out of Mattelmead."

Donnadorr shook his head in consternation.

"And, my friend, if you and Sylvie are being consciously

sought, if there's a price on your head. . ." He did not finish that thought. "We will be conspicuous anywhere we travel. But with one pregnant woman and one child in our party, I am not willing to give up the horses, even though they make it more difficult for us to travel unobserved." Lorenwile must have seen the worried look on Donnadorr's face, for he said, "This is the best plan I can devise, Don. If we get into those unpopulated hills and they are passable, we can travel through them all the way to the Gandlese, and likely meet no one. If it's the Northern Desolation you are worried about, there is no need to descend there. I know our route is not the most direct way, that traveling through hills is hard, and that it is late in the year. But, my friend, it's by far the safest way. And safety is paramount now," Lorenwile said, and then folded up the map.

And so it had been decided. Donnadorr and Sylvane had told their servants only that they were going on a camping trip to look at the autumn foliage—thank the stars it had been a warm autumn and the leaves were only now turning. They said they would then head to Mattelmead City, where they would spend the winter months and where Sylvane would deliver her baby. If such a camping trip at this time of the year seemed peculiar, no one said anything. They were servants, and Donnadorr and Sylvane were good masters. Besides, the rich were known to be peculiar. Luckily, the news of Solagen's death had not yet arrived in this part of the country—but it would come soon, Lorenwile had made that clear. Don had, on the day they left, sent a servant to Mattelmead City to tell the servants in their city house to prepare for their arrival in a few weeks. It was important to keep everyone from knowing that they were indeed fleeing the country. The less the servants knew, the better.

The night before they left, after the household was asleep, the adults returned to the kitchen and packed additional food, water, and supplies, adding to what had already been prepared by the cook and kitchen maid. Meraleese fetched extra blankets from the upstairs cupboard. Donnadorr had then taken these added supplies out into the woods of his estate and hidden them. The travelers would pick them up in the morning as they headed out on their journey. Before the kitchen staff noticed that there was less food in the house than they had supposed, the travelers would be long gone.

Glorr had been told what the servants had been told. He was excited about this trip because he had seldom been taken far from the estate. When they reached the hills, they would tell him the truth.

Most of Donnadorr's and Sylvane's fine clothes had not been taken—they had been sent with a servant to their city home. But money and jewels they had taken, and Donnadorr's harp, his precious Agavian harp. The servants would be fine, he had assured Sylvie. In all likelihood they would simply stay where they were, waiting for their masters to return. Don had left the servants wages for a year, saying he and the others would return to the country as soon as the baby was strong enough to travel. If the property should in the future be confiscated, no doubt the servants would stay on to serve the new owners, as had happened at other estates.

Before the four adults returned to their rooms that last night, Sylvane spoke up. In a voice fraught with emotion, she said, "I'm worried about Glenelle and Glenorr. Can I. . .can we just go off without a word even of warning?" She had addressed her words to her husband. Donnadorr had turned to Lorenwile.

"Glenelle will be protected by Veldarr," Lorenwile said. "And if not by him, then by Goredahl. I don't think you need worry about your foster sister and brother, Sylvie. They will survive whatever comes." His spoke with assurance, and after a moment Sylvane nodded and allowed her husband to lead her to their bedchamber.

They left two days after Lorenwile's arrival. Five people and six horses, the extra horse to carry supplies.

A day's journey north the land was sparsely inhabited, so they met hardly any people as they traveled. Where there were few or no trees, the earth was too poor to farm. There were sheep here, and some goats. The land became more inhospitable and colder as they made their way north toward the forest. In this northern region, there were few estates, only an occasional homestead or a small village—a few huts with a tavern and a general store, where they bought more provisions. They would hunt and fish when they could. And perhaps in the woods there would be wild apples or pears that ripened far into the late autumn.

The people in the small villages they came across seemed barely interested in them. Caught up in concerns for their own survival, they asked no questions. They were obviously glad for the money that was spent on supplies in their stores. If news of Ormahn's death had finally reached Mattelmead City, it had not yet reached this less populated part of the country.

Three days into their trip they came to the forest, and three days later the forest ended and the land beyond was barren. There was no sign of human habitation, no sign of army camps. As they rode through this inhospitable land, Donnadorr looked again and again at the approaching hills. Finally, he rode up to Lorenwile. "Those hills look as lifeless as the hills surrounding Wildenfarr-low-desert." Donnadorr gestured with his head toward the approaching range. "Let us hope you are right and they are passable, but also that they are not empty of game and water. Perhaps they'll become greener farther west."

"Hmmm," was all Lorenwile said.

By the afternoon they had come to hills. No gradually rising land, no rolling foothills. Suddenly there the hills were, shooting up from the brown flat lands and looming over them. Not terribly tall, but oh, so desolate looking.

Sylvane gasped.

Donnadorr was by her side in a moment. "Are you all right?"

She nodded, but her expression was somber. "I think the realization that we are not out on a fall camping trip but leaving Mattelmead forever is only now hitting me." She pointed to the hills. "And our way to safety is through that."

"I'm so sorry, Sylvie."

"No, no," and she gave Donnadorr a bright smile. "The thought of returning to Agavia surpasses any sense of loss—except. . ." her voice trailed off.

"Except Auragole?" He could hear her swallow and try to gain control.

"Except Aurie, and also Ellie and Glen."

"Ellie and Glen will come to no harm. You heard Lorenwile. You know they are very well connected. And that they have not been friends with Auragole for years now." He looked past her and saw the naked sadness on Meraleese's face. It's Auragole, he thought, not the leaving of Mattelmead, where her life has never been easy. She was very fond of him.

At that moment, Lorenwile came over to Don. "Make camp under that large maple. I'm going to ride into the hills and see what they are like. I'll be back in time for supper," he said, and grinned. "I wouldn't want to miss that."

chapter thirty

AURAGOLE OPENED HIS eyes, but there was no light, and the apple-scented air was stifling yet cold. He was aware that he had lost something, something valuable. Oh, yes, he had been dreaming of Meraleese. They were at his country estate, the time he had brought her there. Shhh. That was a secret. Solagen would be angry if he knew.

"You will give up visiting that woman—the wife of that priest—yes, yes, I know all about that."

But look, how beautiful the woods were. There they were, the two of them, walking. He longed for woods, for the endless sea stretching away from his property. . .to where? He longed for the company of Meraleese.

Meraleese laughed and started down the path once again. "Well, I don't think he meant your beautiful clothes, or your handsome face, or your well-made body." And then she blushed, and hurried a little ahead of him.

Seeing Meraleese brought a sense of warmth to his freezing

body. It wasn't Ellie he loved—how strange he had forgotten that. It was Meraleese.

"Auragole, when you think of me, think this. There are many ways to love. Not just one. Each relationship creates its own unique bond of love."

But he was forbidden to see her—and besides, there was no such thing as love; his father had told him so. Which father was that? Was he also forbidden to think about her? What had he done that Meraleese had been taken from him? Oh yes, he had become prince.

"Go, with the guidance of the Prince. I will miss you greatly."

But that was a different prince, that was the Prince Meraleese had spoken about, and Elarr—Elarr, who had studied to be a priest of the Prince God, and had turned away to become a soldier so that he could look for the Dark Breather.

But Auragole, too, had become a soldier. Was he also looking for the Dark Breather? But he didn't want to be a soldier. He wanted to be a singer.

"Auragole, you have made a good beginning with True-singing. You have learned much and on what you have learned you can build. I say only this to you, the self that can True-sing must someday also be the self that leads you in this life."

How had he become a soldier? He had never wanted to follow the discipline and give up his freedom. There must have been a reason he had agreed to something so drastic.

"Freedom comes—at least for the Companions—in choosing to join or refusing to join."

That was Pohl speaking.

"But what if the leaders are foolish or ill-advised?"

"Then it is an ill day for all who follow or who lead."

"I was taught that a grown man's freedom is his most precious possession, that his own judgment is a thing to be valued, and that he should never give himself over to another's rule."

His father, Goloss, had taught him that.

But he had become a soldier.

"I fear for the Westernlands, Auragole."

"Now take my two nephews. They are good commanders, good soldiers. But does either have vision?"

Ah, yes, it was his other father, Solagen, who had asked him to become a soldier. Was it so he could fight the Adversary God? Where was he now, this Dark Breather? The Agavians knew. Auragole was suddenly agitated and tried to sit up, but he couldn't. His hands were tied, and so were his feet. Had he become a prisoner of the Adversary God? Oh, stars in the sky! The Dark Breather, the Adversary God will come and destroy Agavia, perhaps the whole world. It's up to me to do something. Isn't that why I had joined the Companions of the Way?

But no, that wasn't right. It wasn't the Companions he had joined, it was Ormahn's army. The invincible army of Mattelmead. He struggled against his bonds.

The sight was grisly. Each village was charred, had been burned to the ground. The sound that came from every village was near unbearable—as if the earth and the wind both had joined in the sorrow, wailing and sobbing. Sitting on the ground, their bodies blackened by the fire and ash, dozens of people sat staring at him. Auragole could see their large, hollow eyes beseeching him silently. He became frightened. What did they want from him? What could he give them? He thought of running to get away from the eyes and the sound, but he couldn't move his legs.

"No, no," Auragole cried out in a loud voice. "Who will save them now?"

"Drug him again and stuff something in his mouth," a voice said. "He'll wake the dead, and we were told to get him to Little Thoren without anyone knowing."

But wait, it isn't I who must fight the Dark Breather, it's Solagen, Ormahn of Mattelmead, peace bringer, overking of all the west. Yes, Solagen will see to that task. For a moment Auragole felt immense relief—until he remembered that something had happened to Solagen. Something terrible. What was it? Why could he not remember?

Water was forced down Auragole's throat, and a rag was stuffed into his mouth. Then he received a ringing blow against the side of his head.

"Human, with this I charge you. Today you have rescued the future of the Seusadahhn. Let it be upon your head and the heads of your kind to make humanity a goal worthy of aspiration."

And then the blessed darkness again.

TOWARD THE END of October, Grohl, the steward who was in charge of Donnadorr's estate, was awoken in the middle of the night by a loud pounding. In great agitation, he put on his robe and hurried down two flights of stairs.

"Who is it?" he called.

"Open up, by order of the army of Mattelmead."

Trembling, Grohl unlocked the door, opened it a crack, then fell back in terror as an army commander pushed it wide. He strode into the foyer of the house with half a dozen men behind him. Behind the troop, Grohl could see a large contingent of soldiers on horseback.

"Get your master," the commander ordered.

It took Grohl a minute to find his voice. "He's not here, sir. He's been gone a week now."

"Then get his wife."

"She's gone too."

"Where? Where have they gone?"

"On a camping trip."

"A camping trip, at this time of year?" The commander's eyes were piercing and full of disbelief.

"That's what we were told. To look at the autumn foliage, they said."

"And just who went with them?" The officer strode up and down the large vestibule, throwing open doors and peering into rooms.

"Besides the master and mistress, there was their adopted son and his governess. And the guest who was staying with them."

The commander turned on his heel and walked back to where Grohl, visibly shaking, was standing. "And just who was that?"

"Someone I had never seen before. His name was Lorenwile."

"Lorenwile!" The man obviously recognized the name. "And when did he arrive here?"

"A day or two before they all left."

The commander motioned to the men who had come into the mansion with him. "Search the house."

They spread out, carrying lanterns, some heading up the stairs, others going into the rooms on the first floor.

"What has happened?" Grohl asked, his alarm making him bold.

"Who said anything has happened?" the commander said, and stared hard at Grohl.

Grohl didn't answer.

"When are they expected to return?"

"I don't know, sir. They were going to camp out for a while, and then journey down to Mattelmead City, where the mistress intends to deliver her baby."

"Your master and mistress decided to take a camping trip even though the lady was pregnant?" The commander's tone was incredulous. "And at the end of October?"

"That's what we were told. It isn't for me or the other servants to question those we work for."

The commander grimaced. "No, you wouldn't do that."

"One of our boys went down to the city the day they left, with some trunks, and to tell the servants there to prepare the house for their arrival."

"Yes, we know that already."

The soldiers who were searching the house returned to report that they had found no one except the servants.

"I think we will just have a look around the grounds." The commander turned and walked out of the house to give instructions to his men there.

An hour later, after the commander and his troop had finished their search, he returned to the house. By this time all the servants were in the foyer, wide-eyed with anxiety.

"You were telling the truth. That's to your credit. I will leave some of my soldiers in the nearby village. When or if your master and mistress return, you will let the soldiers know immediately. In the meantime, go on doing what you've been instructed to do."

Grohl nodded. "But we don't expect them to return here until after the child is born and able to travel."

"Nevertheless, please do as I have asked, if you value your own safety and freedom."

"Yes, sir," Grohl said.

"And that goes for the rest of you." The commander raised his voice and looked at the group standing ill at ease in the hall. "If they return, I want to hear about it. Do you understand?"

"Yes, sir," a chorus of voices answered.

"Good." The commander turned on his heels and walked out the door, followed by his soldiers.

The servants waited until the sounds of horses' hooves died down in the distance before huddling together to discuss this strange and frightening turn of events.

"WE CAN'T GO on like this," Donnadorr said to Lorenwile, his voice anxious and grim. They had been riding in rough hills for almost a week. There seemed to be no paths to travel on other than goat trails. "Sylvie will lose the child if we keep on as we are. Perhaps we can rest a few days."

Lorenwile had been choosing the way carefully, but it seemed to Don that they were moving mostly up and down and around and around rather than forward. Often Lorenwile and the others dismounted so Lorenwile could lead the travelers and the horses single file over the more-treacherous terrain.

Lorenwile must have seen Donnadorr's stricken face, for he said, "We'll stop for the day. Let me see if I can come up with a solution. Rest easy, friend." He put his hand on Donnadorr's arm. "Sylvane will not lose her child."

Donnadorr woke that night to hear an exquisite singing. Aiku, he thought, coming slowly out of sleep. He was remembering the man who had taken him under his wing when Don was a child, orphaned and wandering the war-torn Easternlands, as had many children. He sat up. Sylvane was lying close to the fire for warmth. Donnadorr had lain away from her so as not to disturb her sleep. Lorenwile was sitting on the ground beside Don's wife, with Donnadorr's harp in his hands, playing and singing. But it was a kind of singing Don had never heard before, other than that one time, a time he had never forgotten—a time when, as a child, he had followed Aiku on one of his journeys after Aiku had expressly ordered him not to. Don had kept that disobedience hidden from Aiku. But it was then that he had heard a similar kind of singing—a beautiful, almost otherworldly singing. And here was Lorenwile singing in a way that reminded him of Aiku. But why not? Lorenwile had been a student of Aiku's.

Meraleese and Glorr were also sitting up. She was holding her son close to her, but he was motionless, looking too enthralled to move or speak. Donnadorr turned his head again to watch Lorenwile. He listened and tried to follow the words. What was Lorenwile doing? He was singing about Sylvane, about Sylvane healthy and Sylvane happy and Sylvane at ease in her mind and in her body. She didn't wake, but from the way her hand was flung out, he knew she heard him in her sleep and was at peace. Then Lorenwile began to sing about the child in her, how she

413

had looked for Sylvane, searching throughout the whole of the Deep Earth, how the child had come to her because she had already loved Sylvane and Donnadorr in the Creative World, where they had been together before this life. Lorenwile sang about that love and how the child was ready to endure whatever hardship and whatever fate might come to her so that she could be with just these parents on the Deep Earth. Lorenwile was singing strength into the child. He was singing strength into Sylvane. And the song was, Donnadorr was sure, the most beautiful melody he had ever heard. Tears were rolling down his cheeks. There was a sound coming out of Lorenwile's throat that Don would never adequately be able to describe.

After a while, Lorenwile stopped singing and rose. He walked to where his blankets lay and, without glancing at anyone, placed the harp gently on the ground, and crawled between the blankets. In only moments, there was a gentle snoring emanating from where he slept. Donnadorr lay back down. I must ask him about that singing in the morning, he thought, feeling a wonderful sense of ease. Now he believed his wife, and yes, his daughter, would both be well, and so he too fell quickly asleep and did not dream.

In the morning, Lorenwile told them that they would descend to the Northern Desolation, whose land was flat, and that they would stay in the Northern Desolation until they came to the Gandlese Mountains.

Donnadorr did not question Lorenwile's judgment.

And the singing was not mentioned by anyone.

ELARR CAME BACK from his watch a few miles west of Agavia, overlooking a large, flat valley where they expected the first attack of the Last Battle would take place. He was somewhat disheartened. His eyes had turned again and again to the mountains on the far side, hoping to see Lorenwile appear, willing Lorenwile to appear. He should have returned in

August, and here it was a week into November. Lorenwile had planned to go only as far as the nearest eastern villages in Noonbarr, gather as much information as he could, and then return to Agavia. What had happened to delay him this long?

Elarr once again voiced his concern to Pohl when he returned from his watch. Elarr had found Pohl eating dinner in the dining room of the Last School. Elarr helped himself to food and went to sit across from him.

"I wouldn't fret." Pohl's words were mild. "Lorenwile is like a cat. He has nine lives."

"But how many has he used up?" Elarr asked, his teeth tearing at the thick chunk of bread in his hand. "Great stars, Pohl, it's going on three months since he should have returned."

"What a worrier you've turned into since you've arrived in Agavia. You know that Meekelorr has sent a man into Noonbarr to see if he can get word of Lorenwile. I'm sure we will have news soon."

"Not soon enough."

"You've been like a caged animal this past month, Elarr. Yes, yes, indeed, you have. You want the battle to start and get the thing over with, correct?"

"Have I become a worrier? Don't let my men hear you say so." Elarr grinned and then he shrugged. "Perhaps I have become a worrier. It's fathering a child, I think. Young Auragole. I have a personal stake in this world now and in its future in a way I never felt before—and a loving and wonderful woman. Much to live for. So, yes, I do think I would like to see this battle fought soon and its outcome decided once and for all. Let us perish, or begin to live the way the Gods have wanted us to live." He paused and his expression changed.

"What else is bothering you?" Pohl looked up from his bowl of soup.

Elarr drummed his fingers on the table. "Auragole. Not mine. Our Auragole. I can't understand what has happened to alter him so, or if the outside circumstances can have changed the inner man to the degree that some here in the school fear has happened. How did his life manage to take such a curious, and rather remarkable, course? But most of all I can't understand how Auragole, according to you and others, might turn out to be our most formidable foe, second only to the Nethergod himself. I simply can't believe it—will not believe it."

"Life has its great and small mysteries."

"So it seems. But I'm not content with that answer."

"No, for it isn't really an answer. Are you spending the night at the school?"

"No, it's late, but I think I will go down to the valley to be with my wife. He looks like her, you know, my Auragole," Elarr said, finally dipping his spoon into his own soup. "Hair that beautiful red, and he has such a lovable nature." He grinned. "But I fear he also has my stubbornness. Though come to think of it, Affredda can be pretty stubborn herself."

The two were silent as they finished their food.

Finally, Elarr stood. "Enough food. Something more nourishing awaits me in the valley. My two loves will ease my restlessness, I think. See you in the morning."

"In the morning then, Elarr. And don't be concerned about Lorenwile. He'll get here with some sort of interesting news that will need a week's telling, I wager."

"May the Prince see that you are right," Elarr answered solemnly, and turned and strode out the door.

Amen, thought Pohl.

IT WAS NIGHT and the others were asleep. But Lorenwile was awake, exhausted past sleeping. They had left the hills for the Northern Desolation almost a week earlier, and he knew they couldn't go on this way, not at this pace. He needed another plan. Moving at the rate they were going, what with a pregnant woman, a child, and a man with a bad leg, and his own steadily diminishing energy, it would take them weeks and weeks to get to the Valley of the Agavi—maybe twice the time it would have taken had the situation been different.

It was True-singing health into the Northern Desolation as they traveled that was responsible for his fatigue—though without question, the singing was doing what was necessary. At least where and while they traveled, the land became restored before them with no sign of noxious air, and some green returning where they walked and for a few miles ahead of them. Luckily the land was flat. That meant they could ride on their horses—better for the boy and better for Donnadorr. And it seemed to be causing no harm to Sylvane, so long as they rested frequently and did not travel long hours.

But this singing was taking a toll on Lorenwile's strength. He had never before True-sung for such an extended period. As he True-sang, the land before them was healed, for a time. But he couldn't keep it up. He felt his forces ebbing from him like snowmelt slipping down a mountain. And still to come were the Gandlese. When they finally arrived in those formidable hills—no doubt in the worst part of the winter—he would not be able to True-sing away the cold or the snow. And he certainly could not make the mountainous land flat. He was good, but not that good. Nor would it have been proper for him to have changed the nature of the earth's terrain, even if it were within his power. There were some things one did not do with True-singing. What he was doing to the Northern Desolation was not changing it, only singing back to it that which it had once been.

His companions were taking this gift of his quite well. At first, they had appeared dumbfounded at what must have seemed to them a magical power. Well, in a sense it was—but one open to all who had a good ear and a gift for singing, and a great desire, a willingness, and the patience to go through the training. He had explained True-singing to them after that first day in the Northern Desolation when he had True-sung a path for them. There was no reason to hide this gift as he had done when he lived in the Westernlands. He was taking these people to Agavia, after all. If he didn't trust them he wouldn't have gone back after Donnadorr and his wife, and found there Meraleese of the sad face and the beautiful eyes, and a child whose very depths gave Lorenwile hope for the future. Often after he had sung, he caught Donnadorr watching him with both pleasure and longing. Could he be another one, Lorenwile wondered, this foster son of Aiku? Had that been Aiku's plan before he met with whatever had caused his death?

While they were traveling in comparative ease in Mattelmead, he had heard Meraleese's story. What she told him of her dead husband's beliefs comforted Lorenwile greatly. Yes, she would be of interest to the council at the Last School when they finally reached Agavia, and she would feel at home there. Lorenwile had known of the little church dedicated to the Prince God while he was living, performing, and playing the buffoon in Mattelmead City. But he had never dared go there. Interesting that Auragole had gone there. Interesting that Auragole had tried to help the woman after her husband had been imprisoned and killed by the very regime Auragole served. It was because of Auragole, he was told, that the woman had been reunited with her son. From Meraleese and from Donnadorr, he had pieced together much of what had taken place in Auragole's life since Lorenwile had left Mattelmead until these recent days.

Events had certainly moved quickly after Lorenwile had left Mattelmead more than four years earlier. And now Solagen was dead, and Auragole, his adopted son and heir, stood accused. No doubt the Nethergod was preparing inexorably to consolidate his power in the still-unruly west. Too soon for the Adversary to worry about Agavia. First the battle for the west would have to be fought between the two cousins, and then against whichever fractious lords might want to withdraw from the United West. Would the Nethergod wait until the

Westernlands was completely reunited before he turned his attention to Agavia? But armies move slowly. There should be more than enough time for Lorenwile to guide his troop to safety.

What disturbed Lorenwile was two—no, three things. First, what had happened to Auragole? Was he alive or dead? Could he be dead if Auragole had a part to play in the Last Battle? Could he be dead if he was the wild card that had been foretold? Surely the events that had taken place in Auragole's life since Lorenwile had left the west only corroborated the assumption that he had a part to play in the battle against the Adversary God. Perhaps Lorenwile and the others hadn't understood what that meant. Perhaps Auragole's part in these crucial events was now over. Had his becoming prince and heir to the west been the catalyst that had caused the Nethergod to begin his activity—first with the murder of Solagen? Yes, that made sense. Still, it didn't mean Auragole was dead, and deep in his bones Lorenwile didn't think he was. No. True-singing had created a bond between them. If Auragole was dead, Lorenwile was sure he would sense it. But if Auragole had been kept alive by Goredahl, to what purpose—and in what condition?

The second thing that bothered him was that he had not been able to let friends in Agavia know about these latest events. They could know nothing about the death of Ormahn of Mattelmead and the accusation against Auragole. No doubt they would be worried about Lorenwile, since it was long past the time he had been expected.

The third thing that disturbed him, and that was his most immediate concern, was how was he going to get this little troop to the end of this long journey—part of it in the dead of the Gandlese winter—before their supplies or his strength ran out? As he asked himself that question, an idea began forming in his mind. At ease at last, he closed his eyes and fell asleep.

The next morning, just after they had mounted their horses,

Glorr came up to Lorenwile. He rode alongside him for only a moment before he spoke.

"My father said I was to give you a message," the boy said, his face solemn, his dark eyes serious.

"Oh," Lorenwile said, knowing that he didn't mean Donnadorr. "When did you speak to him?"

"This morning. Just as I was waking up I saw him. He was sitting on the ground next to me, watching over me as he often does."

Lorenwile nodded. "And what was the message he asked you to give me?"

Two little lines furrowed Glorr's forehead as he tried to remember his father's exact words. "My father said that you were not to worry so about the True-singing. He said he will send you strength for your singing, with whatever power lies within him to do so."

"Your father said that?"

The boy nodded.

"Well, when next you speak to him, give him my thanks, and tell him I would very much appreciate the help."

"I will," Glorr said, and then dropped back to ride next to Meraleese.

N

chapter thirty-one

"AURAGOLE, WAKE UP! You've been here two days. It is time." The voice was a woman's.

"What?" Auragole sat up on the straw that was his bed. "Who spoke to me?" He had distinctly heard a voice, one that caused him to wake suddenly. But he was alone, and in a new cell. Because of the dim light that filtered in from the skylight above him, he could see into every corner of this new cell. No one was there save himself.

I must have been dreaming, he decided. Strange. I thought I heard my mother speak.

Where was he? Frankly, at that moment he could remember little of how he had arrived here. When had it been? Two days, the voice had said. And before that? He tried to think. He had a vague recollection of having been on the road in some sort of wagon. He could recall the smell of overripe apples. His captors had kept him unconscious most of the trip—drugged, probably. Or maybe he had been sick with fever again. He had tried to

refuse most of the food his captors forced on him, but the water
. . . After a while he couldn't bear it without water, and so he
drank, and drifted into a half sleep peopled by memories.

Auragole looked about him. This prison cell was larger than
the cell he had been in before. But there was no cot here, only a
pile of straw, on which he now sat, and a blanket. There were
the usual necessities, a chamber pot and a clay jar with water.
When his hands touched his face, he realized that he had a full
beard. How much time had passed? He knew he had been in
Thoren City—that was clear. But he had been moved from
there. To where? As he tried to recall how long he had been on
the road, he heard a door slide open. No, not a door but a
shallow panel in the bottom of the door.

"Do you hear me?" a muffled voice called to him.

"Yes."

"Pass out the chamber pot and the water jar."

Auragole rose slowly. He was too shaky to stand, so he
crawled to the chamber pot and began dragging it toward the
opening. Had he done this before? Or had they entered the cell
when he was too drugged to hear?

"Hurry up," the voice said, "or you won't get any dinner."

Auragole made it to the door and pushed the pot through.

"Where's the water jug?" the man asked in an irritated voice.

"I'll get it," Auragole answered. "Wait, please."

He crawled as fast as he could to where the jug stood and then
back again to the door and pushed the jug through. In a moment
a tray with food was pushed into his cell, and a jug of water, and
an empty chamber pot. The opening in the door started to slide
shut.

"Wait," Auragole called. "Where am I?" But there was no
answer. The door closed and Auragole was left with a bowl of
some thin, tepid cereal and bread, and the water. He suddenly
realized how hungry and thirsty he was. Auragole sat back on
the dirt floor and ate all the cereal and drank half the water.

Better be careful with the water, he thought. How often did they bring water or food? He would watch and see.

AT THE BEGINNING of the second week of November, Meekelorr sought out Pohl in Pohl's rooms. It was late. Though Pohl was in his nightclothes, he hadn't been able to fall asleep. There were embers still glowing in the fireplace and he had been lying in bed staring at them for what seemed like hours. He was thinking—no, worrying was the better word—about Lorenwile, wondering why he had not returned to Agavia after all these months. This was one individual they couldn't afford to lose. Lorenwile was, so far as Pohl knew, the last True-singer on the Deep Earth. If something had happened to him, that would be a great loss for the earth.

And they needed him at the Last Battle.

Meekelorr knocked loudly. Doors were not locked in the Last School, but few came into a room without an invitation. However, this evening Meekelorr didn't wait for an answering call. He entered Pohl's room without an apology. He was still dressed in his battle clothes and a sword still hung from his side.

"Is there trouble?" Pohl sat bolt upright, ready to jump into his own garments.

"No, no, stay put," and Meekelorr flung himself into a chair near the hearth. "Just some information I want to share with you."

"What information?" Pohl's legs still hung over the side of his bed.

"The young man I sent into Noonbarr to see what he could find out in the way of news. . ."

"Yes?" Pohl felt a rush of excitement.

"He's just returned."

They had sent a young soldier less than a month before into the nearest village in Noonbarr. It was usually a four-week journey through rugged mountains most of the way. He had done it in less time.

"And does he have news?"

"He does indeed. Remarkable news. It may have something to do with Lorenwile's absence. Whether it augers good or ill for our friend, I'm not sure."

"Well, what is it, man?"

Meekelorr rose in one fluid movement and came to stand at the foot of Pohl's heavily carved bed. "Solagen, Ormahn of Mattelmead, is dead. Murdered. And Auragole stands accused."

"My stars! You can't be serious!" Pohl leapt from his bed. "Murdered? And Auragole accused?"

Meekelorr nodded. "It happened at the end of September when the king and Auragole were returning to Mattelmead through Thorensphere, with the newly anointed king of Noonbarr and his daughter, Auragole's intended bride. The murder happened while they were staying in Goredahl's palace in Thoren City. It seemed the king and prince had adjoining rooms there, and Auragole is alleged to have gone into the king's room at night and to have stabbed him to death."

"No! Can such a story be true?" Pohl moved toward the fireplace and sat down in a chair there.

"That Ormahn is dead is certainly true," Meekelorr said and followed him, taking the chair opposite him. "That it was Auragole who killed him is, I think, uncertain, even unlikely. A foolish place to perpetrate such a deed—in Goredahl's palace. If Auragole wanted Solagen dead surely there would have been a better time and place in which to commit such a deed, one that would not point so obviously at himself. I can't imagine Auragole such a fool. But he stands accused by Goredahl, the king of Thorensphere—a man Lorenwile called a devious bastard."

"What news of Auragole? Is he still alive?"

"No one knows. If he is alive he is likely in Goredahl's prison."

"Why would Goredahl keep him alive?" The room was cold, made more so by this strange turn of events. Pohl rose and threw a log on the embers. "Surely Auragole is a danger to Goredahl if he is innocent and would, if he escaped, proclaim his innocence, and perhaps get the backing of Mattelmead's Elite Corps, which he commands. It makes no sense to keep him alive."

"Goredahl would keep Auragole alive if the Nethergod wants Auragole alive," Meekelorr said.

"Swords!" said Pohl, sitting back down again.

"But there is more."

"More? What more can there be?"

Meekelorr rose and began to pace about the room. Pohl followed him with his eyes. "Goredahl has allied himself with Hameshall, who was newly anointed king of Noonbarr by Ormahn. Goredahl set aside his first wife and married Hameshall's daughter, Auragole's intended, the day after the murder. The two kings are now mustering the armies of both Noonbarr and Thorensphere. Goredahl intends to march into Mattelmead as soon as he has gathered enough men, and claim Ormahn's throne." Meekelorr stopped and stood behind the chair opposite Pohl and stared at him.

"Well, well," Pohl said.

"Well, well, indeed."

"Events are certainly moving rapidly."

"They are."

"But what about Solagen's other nephew, Veldarr? Won't he oppose Goredahl's claim? After all, he has as much right to the throne as Goredahl."

"If Veldarr does, there will be all-out war, once the news spreads. Then members of the army and the citizens of the west will have to take sides." Meekelorr returned to his seat and leaned toward Pohl, his arms resting on his thighs. "The whole United West could come apart in a matter of weeks, Pohl—it may have already. It is six or seven weeks since Solagen was killed. There are many once-independent landholders who would be glad to see the two cousins fight it out while they lay claim to the parts of the west that they want."

"Anarchy," Pohl said.

"Yes, anarchy—a return to the days before Solagen came to power. And some time during that anarchy I think the Nethergod will turn his attention to us." Meekelorr leaned back in his chair and watched his friend.

"Before he unites the west?"

"Does he want to unite the west?"

"Is the Nethergod not supposed to come as the great bringer of peace?"

"Oh, yes, but perhaps he will claim there are people in the Gandlese who are the greatest threat to peace and stability of anyone in the west."

Pohl was silent for only a moment before he asked, "So you think this news is connected in some way with Lorenwile's absence?"

"It's a possibility. He might be attempting to gather as much news as possible. Let's hope that's the explanation." He rose. "I'll see you in the morning. Go back to bed. There will be much to discuss and many plans to make." And with that he strode out the door.

Pohl returned to the warmth of his bed, so shocked that he fell immediately into a restless sleep.

EARLY THE NEXT morning, Meekelorr came again to Pohl, this time pounding on his door and waiting to be invited in.

"Come," Pohl said, sitting up, instantly alert.

Meekelorr strode in. "Dress quickly. We must ride down to the Lady's mansion."

Pohl was already out of his bed before Meekelorr completed his request. Pohl was drawing on his trousers when he asked,

"What's happened? Has the time arrived. . ."

"No, not this soon, friend. But there is something we must do. . .something we must at least try," Meekelorr said, and began pacing around Pohl's room.

"Have you been to bed at all?" Pohl asked, buttoning his shirt.

Meekelorr simply waved away the question.

"What's this about?" Pohl asked, tucking his shirt in his trousers.

"Lorenwile. I have an idea. Hurry."

In less than an hour they were in the Lady Claregole's private sitting room in front of a fire, with a light breakfast on the table around which they sat.

Meekelorr had just finished explaining his request.

The Lady Claregole, her black hair still down around her shoulders, looked thoughtful. "I will certainly ask her. But dear heart-friends, although Binta's gift is great, it is rare that it can reach beyond our valley or its surrounding hills. And if you think that Lorenwile is still somewhere in the Westernlands, that is indeed a long distance to ask of her far-seeing. And, too, Lorenwile is not Agavian."

"But Lorenwile is a True-singer," Meekelorr said, "and for those who have sight, his heart, usually closed to most, is open and readable. It might not work, I understand that. But if Binta is willing, I would ask her to try. I've even brought Lorenwile's harp for her to hold while she makes the attempt."

"You sense that he is in some sort of trouble."

Meekelorr hesitated, but only for a moment, then answered her. "I've told you the news out of the west. If not trouble, at least danger."

Both the Lady and Pohl knew there was something other than mere thinking here. Meekelorr's gifts were considerable, greater than many who knew him were aware of, Pohl thought. To his soldiers he was the tough commander of the Companions of the Way, and to the Agavians consort prince to the Lady Claregole. But Pohl knew that Meekelorr had been trained at the Last School in the Easternlands before he had become a soldier, and had developed gifts of the spirit that few have.

"Then I shall call her and put the request to her," the Lady Claregole said.

THE THREE SAT watching the old woman, who was help-mate to Claregole, but also the best far-seer in all of Agavia. She was seated now in a chair, holding Lorenwile's harp against her knees. Her eyes were closed and her body very still. Only her fingers moved, now and then making strange gestures in the air. She had been silent for nearly ten minutes. Pohl was afraid to breathe too loudly lest he disturb her concentration.

"I do see him, Lady, yes." Binta suddenly spoke, but her eyes remained closed.

Alive, Pohl thought with a sense of relief.

"I see him riding a horse leading a small group of people on mounted horses behind him. There is a man, a boy, and two women. One of the women is pregnant, and the man with him has an injured leg."

Stars in the heavens, thought Pohl.

"Can you tell us who they are, dear help-friend? Are they those who have been here before?" the Lady asked her.

"I cannot say. I cannot see their faces clearly—only Lorenwile's. But I can describe the land they are passing through—that I can do."

"Yes, please, Binta." The words were Meekelorr's.

"It is a very flat land, very gray and empty of people. I see. . . feel that the land is ill. But where they walk the land is green. It is very strange, that green. To one side are barren hills, to the other are great ruins. All that is gray is lifeless, and the air above it is suffused with poison. Yet where the troop of riders goes, the land is green and lush, as if it were summer, with no poison in the air they pass through. And here is another strangeness. Not long after the troop passes, the land where their horses have trodden turns brown and sick again."

"I see," Meekelorr said, sitting erect. His gray eyes looked like roiling clouds. "Tell me, dear Binta, can you say more of Lorenwile?"

She was silent for a time. "Yes. Lorenwile is singing. As they travel he sings and sings—songs like our singers here sing. I think he is calling forth health into a sick land."

"I see," Meekelorr said again.

Pohl looked first at Meekelorr, and then at Binta, and back again at Meekelorr. Meekelorr knows something, Pohl thought.

"But, my dear Lady, my dear friends, Lorenwile is tiring."

Pohl turned to Binta in alarm.

"I can feel his great forces diminishing. I fear he will not be able to sing much longer." Binta suddenly opened her eyes. "I'm sorry. I am old. My own strength is not what it used to be. I'm not able to hold onto the picture any longer."

The Lady Claregole came to her, drew her out of her seat, and gave her a hug. "You have done well, my help-friend, very, very well."

The old woman's pale eyes lit up. "Then this far-seeing is of use?"

"It is for a certainty," Claregole said. "Go now and rest, dear Binta."

After the woman left, Meekelorr walked to the window. "Lorenwile is leading some people out of the Westernlands through the Northern Desolation—no doubt bringing them here," he said, turning to look at them. But there was a troubled expression on his face. "They must be people Lorenwile very much cares about, to take such a risk. How far west did he go to find them—all the way to Mattelmead?"

"Surely not such a long distance," Pohl said.

"The Northern Desolation," the Lady said. "But why

through such an ill place?"

"Undoubtedly the west is in chaos, and travel through the countries there is unsafe," Meekelorr said. "The description of one of the people he is guiding I think I recognize, the one with the injured leg. That must be Donnadorr—one of the Easterners who was here years ago with Auragole. Lorenwile befriended him in Mattelmead. If my guess is correct, then one of the women must be Donnadorr's wife, Sylvane. But which one? The pregnant woman or the other woman? And the child, to whom does he belong?"

"Could the second woman be Glenelle?" Pohl asked.

"But if it was Glenelle," Meekelorr said, "where is her twin brother? Hard to imagine her leaving Glenorr behind—they were so close."

"More important than who they are, or why Lorenwile went back for them," Pohl said, perturbed, "is how can he keep up what he is doing? Even a True-singer can't sing hour after hour with little rest."

"He would attempt it, to save the lives of his companions," Meekelorr said. "To many people he may seem like an indifferent friend. But we know that once he cares for you, you are indeed a lucky one, for he will never forget you, no matter how long the parting."

"But this is madness. How long can he keep up what he is doing?" Pohl said. "How far west are they, I wonder, traveling above Mattelmead, above Thorensphere, above Noonbarr?"

Meekelorr shook his head.

"We must devise a way to help Lorenwile," Claregole said.

All eyes turned to Meekelorr. He stood with head bowed, a thoughtful look on his face.

"WE HAVE TO go after him. There's no other way. He's too important to lose before the Last Battle," Elarr said, stomping around Meekelorr's private quarters, until he finally flung himself into a chair.

Meekelorr stood near the window, gazing out at the snow. Eventually, he turned back to look at his second in command. He had been listening to Elarr for ten minutes without interruption, and here was a familiar argument. One they had had before, one that had caused a terrible rift between them once—and had almost lost Elarr his life. Nevertheless, Elarr was an exceptional leader of men, respected and adored by those he led. He was good at war strategy and brave in battle. But occasionally his hot temper overrode his good judgment.

"No." Meekelorr said it quietly.

"No?" Elarr rose. "You can't mean that. Surely that old rule of not sending soldiers out to rescue captured Companions doesn't apply here."

"I'm not saying it does, Elarr. I'm saying it makes no sense. We don't know where they are exactly—how far west. I can't send men into the Northern Desolation. The air is not fit to breathe, the water. . ."

"But he is in trouble, man, can we just sit by and let him get sicker and sicker, and not attempt to help? We need him."

"There is no man we need more, Elarr. But I can't risk the men we have on what could be a fool's errand."

"I'll go."

"No."

"You intend just to sit by while Lorenwile is in trouble and not lift a finger to help?" Elarr's cheeks were red with choler. He was glaring at Meekelorr.

"Lorenwile has gifts you and I, both trained at the Last School, can barely imagine. We must trust—at least for the time being—in his own innate abilities, and the help he might receive from the Creative World."

Elarr glared at Meekelorr, then turned and walked briskly to the door.

"Elarr!" The sharpness of Meekelorr's words stopped him.

"Don't go off and attempt a rescue on your own."

Elarr didn't turn back to look at him. "Is that an order?"

"That's an order."

THAT NIGHT WHEN Elarr returned from his duties, he complained bitterly to Affredda about Meekelorr's stubbornness. "I cannot bear that icy hard-heartedness that comes upon him sometimes. This is Lorenwile, after all. Meekelorr just stood there and gave me all those cold, reasonable excuses for doing nothing."

"And no doubt," Affredda said, going to him and moving into his arms, "Meekelorr cannot bear the fiery irrationality of your hotheaded temper that comes over you sometimes." She stood on her toes and kissed him.

He stepped away from her and scowled. But when he saw her sweet smile, he laughed. "No doubt."

"No going against orders this time?"

"No. Meekelorr's reasoning is right, damn him. Even if he were willing to let one of us go, where would we even begin to look for Lorenwile?"

"And how withstand the Northern Desolation, since you can't True-sing?"

He hugged her. "I sometimes resent it—often resent it—but Meekelorr is right as usual. But oh, how I hate doing nothing."

"I know, but the time of action will soon be upon us," she said, and this time her words were melancholy.

"Then let's make the most of the time given us," he said, and he took her by the hand and led her to their bedchamber.

chapter thirty-two

MERALEESE, RIDING THROUGH the narrow path of health that Lorenwile was singing them, had long ago stopped wondering at the glorious and otherworldly power of True-singing. It was mid-November, but there was no snow on the greensward where they were traveling, and none on the gray, flat landscape to their left and north, or on the hills south and to their right. She knew they were now traveling above Thorensphere with three hundred, or maybe four hundred, miles still to go before they came to the Gandlese Mountains. Meraleese kept her eye on her son and on Sylvane for any signs of difficulty in traveling. The land where their horses were walking was fairly flat, and that kept Sylvane from the bouncing that was so dangerous to her. That she and the child she was carrying were able survive such a rough journey, Meraleese knew, was due to the miracle of Lorenwile's singing. Many a night, after he had sung most of the day—it was more than two weeks now that they had been traveling in the Desolation—

Meraleese would wake in the dark to hear Lorenwile singing health into Sylvane and into Sylvane's child. After that first time when he had explained True-singing to them, Lorenwile hadn't spoken about it again. She knew Lorenwile's gift was a godly gift, though he rarely spoke about the Gods. But when she had told him about what was taught in Timorr's little church dedicated to the Prince God, she knew he understood it all—no, more than understood, he was familiar with it all—and that gave her a sense of, if not well-being, then affirmation. Watching Lorenwile day after day, her own anger at the Gods abated somewhat. How often had Timorr said that human beings were no longer children, and the Gods would not guide them as if they were?

Meraleese was watching Lorenwile now and listening as the land changed in front of them, but she was worried. She knew he was growing more tired—even though Glorr had told her that his father was helping Lorenwile from the Creative World. Obviously it wasn't enough, because they were traveling shorter and shorter distances each day. If Lorenwile needed the rest, or if Sylvane did, then they stopped and made camp. That was a deep concern to Meraleese, given the rapidly approaching winter. She knew that when they finally reached the Gandlese Mountains— the Prince willing—it would be winter and there would be snow. Then what? How far must they travel in the Gandlese before they reached their destination? Well, they would face that problem when they got to it. Surely Lorenwile had some plan.

In the meantime, to distract herself, Meraleese allowed herself to become interested in the land they were moving through— the Northern Desolation. She knew that it had been uninhabited for many, many centuries. But she hadn't realized that at one time—perhaps before the wars, perhaps even before the Golden Century—it had been a land with many cities, towns, and farms, a prosperous and populated land. Often there were ruins in the distance off to the north—gray stone buildings still looming tall in the sunless landscape, empty and roofless. Sometimes the stones seemed to move with them for miles, and she knew that a large city had once been there, perhaps as large as Mattelmead City itself. What had happened to all the people? If their party rode over to look, would they find a city of bones, a city of the dead, unburied and unprayed for? The northern horizon, filled with so many sights of a once-thriving civilization, amazed and saddened her. Humanity had built great things. It must have taken centuries to raise up such cities, but they had all been destroyed, and by that same humanity—a humanity gone mad. She spoke about this occasionally with Donnadorr as they rested or as they camped for the night, after both Sylvane and Lorenwile had fallen asleep. Don too was caught up in the wonders they were passing. He told her he had seen the ruins of towns in the Easternlands when he had wandered there as an orphan of war, and then as a youth. But he had never seen any town or city as large as those they were passing, almost on a daily basis.

"I had always thought the Desolation a land too cold for people to dwell in," Donnadorr told her one evening.

"But it's not cold. It's unusually warm. Perhaps the climate has always been this way," she answered.

"Perhaps, but I have heard that there were many climatic changes—not during the wars, but during the Golden Century—due not to the Gods, but to humankind itself."

Meraleese had merely nodded.

Today, she was watching the landscape and speculating about its past when she heard Lorenwile falter in his singing. It was early in the afternoon. They had been on the road for only an hour after their stop for lunch and a rest. Suddenly the singing ceased altogether. She saw Lorenwile slump in his saddle. Donnadorr was at Lorenwile's side seconds before her.

"We'd better make camp," Donnadorr told her, his voice tight with concern.

"No, not here." Lorenwile opened his eyes for a moment. "Get back to the hills," he whispered. "I can no longer keep the poison from this place. Hurry, go directly south. It shouldn't take more than an hour to reach the hills and be free of this foulness. Hurry." And he closed his eyes and fell forward over his horse's neck.

"You attend Sylvane, Don," Meraleese said. "I will lead Lorenwile's horse into the hills. Glorr, you follow me."

And the small party, anxious now for their leader, moved as quickly as they could into the hills in the increasingly colorless day.

SEVERAL DAYS AFTER Binta's far-seeing, the Lady Claregole sent for Meekelorr and Pohl. Pohl was in the Healing Tower attending the sick when the message came, and he sent a rider to bring Meekelorr back from where he was training with his men. It was almost two hours after the message had been delivered that the two men arrived at the Lady's apartment in her mansion.

Claregole ushered them in, and barely had they closed the door when she said, "Binta has had another far-seeing." Then she motioned the men to the table near the fireplace, where food and drink waited.

When all three were seated, and the Lady had poured the hot tea, she said, "Lorenwile and his friends are no longer walking in the Northern Desolation."

"Where are they, then?" Pohl asked.

"It seems they have returned to the hills. Barren hills, Binta described them."

"They must still be above the Westernlands," Meekelorr said. "That description does not fit the Gandlese."

"But where?" Pohl asked. "Above Mattelmead? Above Thorensphere? Noonbarr? If he started from Mattelmead, that could be a trip of more than five hundred miles."

"There is more." Claregole's voice was low. Pohl could hear

the concern in it. "Lorenwile is ill and rests now in a cave in the hills."

"Stars!" Pohl exclaimed. "Is he too sick to go on? Is this illness a serious one?"

"She couldn't say," Claregole answered, and watched as Meekelorr rose and began pacing about the room.

"Now what?" Pohl directed his question to Meekelorr's back. When he didn't answer, Pohl turned to Claregole. "Do you think Binta could pinpoint the location of that cave? If she can we might now think of sending out a rescue team."

"She hasn't been able to do that, Pohl. That's asking much even for a far-seer as good as Binta."

"What do you think, Meekelorr? Pohl asked. "I've never known Lorenwile to be sick before. And do they have remedies with them, or food? Is there something we should be doing?"

Finally, Meekelorr returned to his seat. The lines in his face were etched with concern, but he said, "We wait. There's nothing else we can do if we don't know where they are. We wait and pray."

THEY WERE RESTING. Donnadorr had taken them into the hills, as far south from the Desolation as was possible with a sick man and a pregnant woman in tow. All his old traveling skills seemed to have returned, and he had managed to find a cave, a shallow affair—no more than ten feet deep—but one that at least afforded them some shelter against a northern wind. It was mid-November, and still there was no snow. They had been on the road about a month and still had some four hundred miles to go just to get to the Gandlese. How far then to Agavia, he had no idea. Its location was on none of the maps Lorenwile had shown them. Lorenwile was unconscious, and if he didn't regain consciousness, it would be up to Donnadorr to lead the group—but to where? Surely Lorenwile would regain consciousness. Though he had not spoken nor opened his eyes since they had brought him to this cave, his breathing was regular, and that was a good sign. Lorenwile was merely sleeping deeply—both Donnadorr and Meraleese had agreed—overcome with a weariness they could only guess at. No need to worry yet about Lorenwile leaving them. Don looked over at his wife. Though Sylvane had not complained about the journey, she, too, seemed glad for the rest.

Donnadorr had a more immediate concern. Their supplies were getting low. They had moved much more slowly than any of them had anticipated, even with a pregnant woman and a boy to take into consideration, though Donnadorr had to admit Glorr had managed much better than Don had expected. He was a fine boy, with an inner strength not often found in the young.

Now they were back in these almost treeless hills, treeless probably until they finally reached the Gandlese. Don looked at the sleeping singer. Obviously, Lorenwile had used too much of his strength True-singing them a path through the poison of the Northern Desolation. Donnadorr's leg, which bothered him little as long as he was astride a horse, would do less well if he had to walk many miles a day. And it looked as if they would have to do much walking, leading their horses, through these increasingly higher hills. He would have to manage it. Grin and bear it. He was not going to lose his child because of a game leg.

How long would it take them, he wondered, to get to the Gandlese? At least a month, probably longer, once they got started again. But the Gandlese were hills also, no, mountains, and there winter would have already taken hold. When he had asked Lorenwile about this some time ago, Lorenwile had said he had a plan for their journey in the Gandlese that should keep them out of the worst of the snows. But he hadn't elaborated. Would Lorenwile be able to put his plan into effect? That was a big question. How would they move forward now, not only with a child and a pregnant woman, but with a sick man? He did not include himself in that group of people with unique needs. He couldn't afford to worry about himself. He could and would do whatever was necessary.

Once again, Donnadorr looked over at the unconscious man. Do not worry about tomorrow or the day after, he warned himself. Surely that is one lesson from your earlier life that you have not forgotten.

After he was certain that all the travelers were settled into their small cave, he kissed his wife, took his bow and arrow, and went out to hunt. Luck was with him, for within the hour, bad leg notwithstanding, he had tracked and killed a mountain goat. The hills may have had few trees, but there was grass now, and low bushes. The travelers would have meat for several days.

THE NIGHT BEFORE Lorenwile returned fully to consciousness—two days after Donnadorr had found the cave— Lorenwile had a dream. In it he saw Aiku, his teacher, and behind him a man he somehow knew to be Timorr. Aiku said to Lorenwile, "You must stay in the hills north of the border of Thorensphere and then of Noonbarr. There are no people brave enough to return to live in the hills, for they do not yet trust that the hills are well. Since the sickness has left them, and since the animals and plants have returned, you need not True-sing these hills. There will be animals for hunting, and you will find water.

"However, each night you must sing health into the woman who carries a child. I will help you. I will add my voice to yours though no one on your side of the threshold will hear it. Do not travel too quickly. Do not tire yourself. Walk now, and lead the horses—at least most of the way. It will be difficult for Donnadorr because of his leg injury. But my heart-son will not complain, since it will be better for the woman who carries his child to walk now.

"You are correct in your thinking. When you arrive in the Gandlese, you must not try to come through the Northern

Valley. There is snow there and it is now impassable. But that is not the worst of the dangers. Soldiers out of Noonbarr guard the entrance to the Northern Valley—at the behest of their leader, Hameshall. What his purpose is in all of this remains unclear. Keep north of the valley. When you reach the Gandlese, do as you had planned. True-sing the mountains and you will be shown a network of tunnels that will lead you most of the way to Agavia. I will help you also in that singing. Do not worry about food. Let Donnadorr hunt. He is still very apt, and will find enough meat to see you through the hills and into the tunnels for a time. You can eat of the fruit of the trees in the hills, which will become more numerous as you travel. The warmth has kept the fruit ripe. Increasingly as you move east, you will find rivulets with fresh, unsullied water trickling down from the Gandlese, and even fish. Once in the tunnels, if your supplies become low, return to the surface for a day or two and hunt. Though in the Gandlese it is already winter, there is game. You and Donnadorr will find it. Rest two days more, leave on the third, my friend, then go on your way in peace. I and others are with you."

And Lorenwile woke up. The first thing he said was, "I'm hungry."

CLAREGOLE KEPT HER eyes on Meekelorr, who was standing behind a chair watching Binta. His intense gray eyes looked black and shadowed with worry. Every evening since they had first heard that Lorenwile was unconscious and in a cave in the hills above the Northern Desolation, Meekelorr had come, no matter how late, no matter how tired he was, to request that Binta try to far-see Lorenwile once again. But for two nights she had not had any success.

This evening Binta was again sitting in a chair. Lorenwile's harp was leaning on her knees, her eyes were shut, and her hands were making those peculiar gestures in the air. "I see

440

them, Lady. I see them, Prince."

"Where are they, soul-friend?" Claregole asked. "Can you describe where they are?"

"They are still in that cave, Lady."

Claregole heard Meekelorr's deep inhalation of breath. "Still in the cave," he murmured.

"But, wait, something has changed, Lady."

"What has changed, Binta?" It was Meekelorr who spoke.

"Lorenwile." Claregole gasped.

"What about Lorenwile?" Meekelorr asked.

"He is awake—and eating."

"And eating!"

Claregole could hear the triumph in Meekelorr's voice.

Binta opened up her eyes. "Is this good, Prince, Lady?" Her eyes moved from Meekelorr to Claregole.

"This is very good, my soul-friend," Claregole said. "Go now and rest. Once more you have done well."

Binta rose with a smile of pleasure and left the room.

Meekelorr pulled Claregole to her feet and took her in his arms. She gently pushed his chestnut-colored hair from his brow. There was no need to say anything. Lorenwile was awake and eating, and on his way, no doubt, to recovery. The rest would be up to Lorenwile, and to the Gods and humans in the Creative World who guided him.

NO ONE HAD come to visit Auragole, to talk to him, to beat him since his arrival in this new place. Little by little his wounds were healing and the bruises and swelling on his face and body were disappearing. His mind was slowly clearing. The fever that had clouded his thoughts had finally abated. He still didn't know where he was. Whenever his food was delivered to him through the panel in the bottom of his cell door, he asked, but there was no answer. One day he had been given a warm blanket, and a clean shirt and clean trousers to take the place of the ones he had been wearing that were in shreds. He used some of his precious water to clean himself. His beard itched, but he had no tools with which to cut it or shave it. He didn't know precisely how long he had been in this cell, but it was at least two weeks—probably longer, because he didn't know how many days it had taken him to come to this degree of wakefulness. But as soon as he was able to think, he began to mark off the days that were passing, by scratching on the stone-and-dirt walls with a spoon.

He knew it was late fall or perhaps even winter because at times there was snow on the skylight above him. Often it blocked the light so that he lay in grayness most of the day. It had taken a long time before he felt capable of trying to think sequentially. There had been so much pain and then a long illness with fever—perhaps more than one illness—and no remedies, only water. Sometimes he could hear himself saying over and over, "Dear Prince." Just that. "Dear Prince." Pleading for something. What? Oblivion, or to be awake? At first being awake had caused him too much anxiety and he had begged for merciful sleep. But there was no stopping it; with healing came wakefulness. Without the beatings he was more and more alert. However, he couldn't remember why he was in prison. At first he had thought it had something to do with helping Meraleese. He knew that wasn't right. Yet he had been accused of something. Somehow he had made Solagen angry, so angry that he had thrown Auragole in prison and had him beaten repeatedly. But he couldn't remember the occurrence. What had he done? He lay on the straw and tried desperately to remember. The effort caused his stomach to twist into knots so tight that they made him vomit.

How could he lie there not knowing? And no one would tell him. No one would come to talk to him. So he decided he had to take some action. He was weak. His body was very weak. You can't think clearly if your body is weak, he told himself. He had to do something about that. He was being given two meals a day. Cereal in the morning, and then, toward evening, soup and bread. Sometimes cheese. He knew that he had eaten little in the weeks that had passed. He had lost a great deal of weight and muscle. His cheeks felt hollow beneath his beard, and his ribs beneath the bruises protruded more than they had when he was a youth. That wasn't good. He decided that he would eat every morsel of what he was given. He couldn't gain strength if he didn't eat. Then he needed to do something to regain muscle. He would begin to pace about the cell, pace for as long as he could, as long as his legs held out. He wouldn't try to force his mind to remember why he was here. Not yet.

And so he began. He ate. He walked. He did some of the exercises he had learned and practiced in Solagen's army. After a few days he decided that he needed something else. What he was doing was not enough to fill up his days. And when he lay down after exerting himself walking and exercising, the panic would begin to build. If it got out of hand he would throw up or have a bout of diarrhea, and that would make him weak again. It's this not knowing, he decided, that caused the anxiety. So he devised a plan. He would eat. He would walk. He would exercise. And he would go through his life in memory, starting from his childhood, as far as he could until he hit the stone wall that blocked out the event that had caused his imprisonment. Perhaps, just perhaps, by doing that, the stone wall would crumble and he would remember what transgression had caused him to be thrown in jail. Yes, this was a good idea. He would lie on the straw, close his eyes, and picture as many events from his life as he could. If nothing else, it would help him while away the time.

He began with his mother's face.

Auragole was standing in the kitchen of the house he had been born in, looking at the scene. There he was, perhaps eight years old, seated at the table. His mother was standing at the sink, her long black hair braided and piled high on her head. She is very beautiful, he thought, gazing in surprise at her, and not very old, still in her twenties, close to his own present age. It was a startling thought. Itina was tall and full figured, with a straight back and huge dark eyes, much like his own. Had he known when he was a child that she was beautiful and still a young woman? But how could he? He had never seen a woman other than his mother until after he had left his valley. His mother was drying the dishes after their dinner. He didn't remember where his father was, or their friend, Spehn. But his mother was talking.

"You will not grow up like a wild animal—I won't have it. That is not what your father means when he says he wants you to be truly free. Just because we are here in the wilderness of the Gandlese, without anyone near us as neighbors, does not mean that it will always be so. When you are older your father will have to accompany you back to the east to find you a. . . Therefore, you will learn manners, deference, respectful behavior of every kind, if I have to correct you every time we are together."

"Yes, Mother."

"When you go out into the world, as you must one day, it is important that you know exactly how to behave among people, how to treat your elders, and how to treat your peers."

"Yes, Mother. Spehn is teaching me how to fight with a sword," he told her with enthusiasm. *"That will be useful."*

She sighed. "Yes, I suppose that must be so."

"And father has taught me how to shoot with a bow and arrow and how to make both. I'm quite good, I think." He smiled proudly.

"That is altogether different. We need meat. You have to know how to track animals for food to put on this table. A sword is something quite different."

"I know," he said, and his dark eyes were solemn. *"I know the difference."*

"Good. But, Auragole, I'm a little put out with you."

He looked at her, feeling uncertain and guilty. What had he done this time?

"You have been neglecting your lessons."

"But I'd rather sing and hear your stories and Spehn's—those too are full of words."

"Singing and storytelling are important. But you must also learn your numbers and to read."

"For what purpose?" he asked.

"Oh, Auragole." She put down her towel and came and stood opposite him at the table. She placed her hands down on its surface and leaned toward him. "Must I repeat this over and over again?" Her tone was one of exasperation. "Very well then. Because you must become a man of culture, principle, and virtue. You must not grow up wild, simply because we are out here in these uninhabited mountains. I will not have you looked upon as a fool. You must learn the skills that will make you an educated and civilized human being."

"Father says it's civilization that has caused all the trouble in the east."

"Father says. . ." She nearly spat out the words. "What your father means by civilized and what I mean by civilized are two different things. We haven't many books—thank the stars I was able to bring some with us, though I had to argue with your father to do so. They are few, but enough for you to learn to read and to acquire a decent vocabulary. Books are precious. . .almost all were burned in the wars. Now please bring the book we are working on. You may not go out to play until we have spent at least an hour reading."

He got up from the table.

"Yes, Mother," he said, and he fetched the book from the cupboard where she kept it.

AURAGOLE WAS WORKING through his life in sweeping panoramas, without any attempt to assess it, to judge it. For the most part he was looking at it without excessive emotion. Even the learning of True-singing with Lorenwile caused him only a twinge of regret, knowing he had given it up to become a soldier for Solagen. But this first look was only a beginning. Once he had reached that hard wall where memory stopped, and had finally gone through it, he would begin at the beginning again and look at everything in much more detail. Then there would be time to assess. Then there would be time to judge.

He had worked through his life until the day of his adoption by Solagen and the declaration that Auragole was now heir to the throne of all the west. And then he stopped. He couldn't go on. He didn't want to go on. He could feel the panic he thought he had overcome rising up again. Why? Had he betrayed his vow somehow?

Or was it remembering his last painful visit to Meraleese that made it so hard to continue? From the moment he had recalled his first visit to the little temple, he could not drive her face from his mind. He felt haunted by her. And she was lost to him. Earthly attachment brings only agony, he thought. Only grief and loss. After that fiasco with Glenelle, he had been involved with many women—many whose faces he could no longer recall. Those romances were light, hardly romances at all. Their endings, no loss. And certainly no anguish.

But those people he had truly cared about had all been taken from him, either by death, as was the case with his mother and father and Spehn, or by circumstances he could not control, or by his own naiveté, or by direct order. The last had lost him Meraleese, and consequently Don and Sylvie. Had his father been right? His father had told him not to believe in the reality of love. Was it because his father had wanted to spare him pain?

Enough. Enough remembering. He would wait. Do something else for a while. And lying in that cell, he suddenly had the urge to sing. He had no flute. He had no harp. But he still had his voice. He opened his mouth to try to sing, but a harsh croak came out. There was only a hoarse rasp. For a moment fear paralyzed him. What did he have left except his voice, his singing? Had the beatings taken that away, too? Then he realized he had barely spoken in weeks, maybe months. The thought calmed him down.

"You have to begin to talk out loud," he told himself. He decided he would begin to exercise his voice along with the other activities he was doing. He would begin to recite all the poems his mother had taught him. Surely he had not forgotten those. And so slowly he began to speak, to recite, to use his voice. After a few days of this, he began to sing—songs he had sung with Donnadorr and songs he had sung with Lorenwile, and songs he had created and sung alone.

chapter thirty-three

SYLVANE FELT SURPRISINGLY well. She was six months pregnant, but her small rounded belly had not yet made walking difficult. She was glad to be off her horse. After the first few days on the road her old traveling strength had come back. They were moving slowly, not only because of her and Glorr, but also because of Don. He was limping a little more than usual. But he insisted that he was not in pain. She watched him carefully. However, even when she saw the lines tighten at his mouth or furrows crease his brow, she kept silent. In every way her husband was a man, and she did not want to treat him like an invalid. If the walking became too difficult, it would be up to Don to speak. But she knew that Lorenwile was also aware of it.

Lorenwile, too, seemed better, far more robust than he had been when he was in the Northern Desolation and singing the land clean. What a marvelous talent the man had. She had heard him sing several times in Mattelmead City and knew he had a glorious voice, but the singing he called True-singing was indescribable. She could hear him sometimes while she slept, True-singing health into her and the daughter she carried, and was grateful. When she woke the morning after such singing, she felt refreshed and full of energy. Surely once one had heard True-singing one would have to believe in the Gods. Where else could such a gift have come from? She wished that Glenorr could hear him. She and Glen had argued incessantly about the Gods while they traveled to Mattelmead, all those years ago. She tried not to be concerned about Glenelle and Glenorr, but that worry too was difficult to set aside. Sylvane had been raised with the twins, and she had cared for them for so many years. If they had not seen much of each other during their stay in Mattelmead, it mattered little. The love was still there. But surely Lorenwile was right. Veldarr was fond of Glenelle; therefore, she and Glenorr should be safe. And if the gossip was true, the twins should also be safe if Goredahl came to power. Sylvane shuddered at the thought of Goredahl as Ormahn. She would not have wanted to be in Mattelmead then.

One time when Sylvane had tried to thank Lorenwile for his help, he had said, "It is I who should thank you for the privilege. I've never before sung to a child circling through the stars on its way to the Deep Earth." Then with a dismissive shrug, he said, "Let's eat. I'm starved and that goat stew smells delicious," and he went off and was soon fishing food out of the pot with great concentration, leaving her gaping at him.

Once in a while, Sylvane let Auragole drift through her thoughts. She could not believe, would not believe, that he had killed the king. Granted, Auragole had changed much from the shy country boy he had been when he had guided them through the Easternlands, the country boy she had loved before she had loved Donnadorr. But hadn't they all changed? Hadn't they all grown up? Yes, that was true. However she would never believe Auragole guilty of so odious a crime as regicide. Was he dead or alive? She longed to know that answer.

It troubled Meraleese, too, though Meraleese never spoke about it. Meraleese loved Auragole—no, was *in* love with Auragole—that had become more obvious as Sylvie had watched Meraleese's reactions to news of Auragole once Meraleese had come to live with her and Don. Without a doubt Auragole had once felt the same for Meraleese. Sylvane had noticed it when Auragole and Meraleese had come that first time to visit Glorr. Sylvane had seen the way Auragole looked at Meraleese. But at that time Meraleese was newly widowed, traumatically widowed, so Auragole must have felt his love unrequited. Despite the danger to himself, despite feeling Meraleese did not love him, Auragole had arranged for Meraleese to live with Sylvie and Don so Meraleese could be united with her son. That showed something great in his character, Sylvane thought, a kind of nobility as well as gallantry.

Sylvane remembered how Meraleese had listened when Auragole's name was mentioned in a conversation, or if at a dinner party a bit of news about him came their way. Somehow Sylvie had been less surprised by Auragole's adoption than either Don or Meraleese had. Compared to Veldarr and Goredahl, Auragole was by far the superior man, and Solagen, whatever else could be said about him, was no fool. Sylvie would not let go of the hope that Auragole was still alive.

Sylvane had felt few qualms about leaving the grand estate that had been their home for nearly seven years, particularly now that Solagen was dead. They had lived in luxury, yes, and she had enjoyed it. She didn't fool herself about that. But in recent years, she and Don had become more uneasy about what was happening in Mattelmead—and perhaps, deep in her heart, she had always known that someday they would have to leave. Too many friends had been taken away in the night and no one knew why. In the past few years there had been an ever-increasing anxiety about the future in their circle of acquaintances. To live under a cloud of uncertainty was no great way to live. No luxury had made up for the fear that was growing almost daily.

Sylvane, with effort, forced herself to look to the future. She loved the Valley of the Agavi. To see again the Lady Claregole and Pohl, Meekelorr and Galavi, that was an exciting prospect. How precious the memories were of those months she and the others had spent there. She had never felt fear in Agavia, never felt anything but warmth and caring from everyone she had met, and always an indescribable peace that seemed part of the very air of Agavia. She was glad to be going back there, back to a haven where they would not be hunted. And in her heart she blessed Lorenwile daily for turning back for them, for bringing them out of Mattelmead before the battle between the two cousins began, for giving the child she carried a chance for life.

She felt someone come up and take her hand. It was Glorr. "I think you need a little help along this path," he told her, a serious look on his face.

"Why thank you, Glorr. I think I do." And they walked together following Lorenwile, who was moving through the hills, whistling.

A WEEK AFTER Auragole had begun the reciting and the singing, something happened that shook him to his core. It was so traumatic that the wall blocking his memory simply crumbled, like a structure built of loose stones.

Goredahl came to visit him.

It was the first time Auragole had seen the large iron door to his cell open. It did so, making a grinding, spine-grating sound. He had been napping and the loud moaning of the door as it pushed slowly into his quiet cell caused him to open his eyes and leap to his feet almost at the same time. First, six heavily armed guards came in, and then Goredahl. The shock of seeing Goredahl brought back vividly to his mind the early days of his imprisonment in Thoren City. Goredahl was dressed in full battle uniform. He strode in, stopped just inside the door, and stared at Auragole with a calculating look.

"So you are recovering, are you? Good. Good. But still a bit thin. That won't do." He turned to the officer of the guards. "He is getting two meals a day? See that he gets three. And see that there is meat in at least one of the meals. I want him to fill out a bit. In the days to come I will have use for him, and I want him looking healthy and well treated. I want the people to see what a benefactor I will be for them."

He looked Auragole up and down, then at the cell. "Bring a cot in here, and another blanket." When he turned back to Auragole, he said, "Not the comforts of the palace in Mattelmead, but then why should you expect anything better than this after what you have done?"

Auragole did not reply.

"You know what you have done?" Goredahl's eyes were cold and dark, like frozen mud puddles.

Again Auragole remained silent.

"Be insolent with me, Auragole, and I will have you beaten again. You know what you have done?"

"You told me that I killed the king," Auragole answered carefully.

"Good. And that's why you are here. That you are not dead is because I have use for you yet. That you have food and drink you owe to my generosity."

"Where am I?" Auragole asked, his eyes finally meeting Goredahl's.

"You don't know? Well, why shouldn't you?" Goredahl gave him a mirthless smile. "You are in the fort at Little Thoren. It's the last week of November. Two months since you killed Solagen. The armies of Noonbarr and Thorensphere are gathering here and also in the south. And then when we are in full force, we will move into Mattelmead to claim the throne. If my cousin chooses to contest me, then there will be a battle or two, which I believe I will win easily. Frankly, I think Veldarr has little stomach for kingship—he turned down Glovale, after all—and little stomach for battle. I think the lazy fellow will easily offer me fealty. After I lay claim to the throne, then you will be of use to me."

"How?"

"Why, for a public confession and a very public trial. Then you will hang for the murder of Solagen. No heir can claim the throne who has killed to achieve it. In the meantime, enjoy my hospitality while you can." He started toward the door, then looked back at Auragole. "I'm sorry I can't leave you the tools with which to shave. But rest assured, before I present you to the public, you will be cleanly shaven, so there will be no doubt as to your identity." And with a cold smile, he left. The guards followed, and the door grated shut.

Auragole stood a moment, transfixed, staring at the locked door. At the sight of Goredahl's face, the memories had come flooding back to him. They were so powerful he had barely taken in what Goredahl was saying. Auragole flung himself on the straw and thought about them. It was not because Solagen was angry with him that he had been imprisoned. Not because of Meraleese, or some terrible infraction of Solagen's rules. No. Solagen was dead. Dear Prince! Solagen was dead! The king was dead. He had been murdered. He had been murdered while Solagen and his party were visiting Goredahl's palace in Thoren City. What exactly had happened while Auragole had slept so soundly in the room next to him? One thing Auragole knew— it wasn't he who had killed Solagen. Solagen was his adopted father. He had great affection for the man who had wanted him as heir, who had given him everything.

He wept then for Solagen. Had he wept for him before, and then forgotten the terrible event? Auragole began to recite the prayer for the dead that Meraleese had taught him. Then he tried to recall that fateful night.

He had been dragged that night from his bed, still foggy with the sleep that must have been drug induced, and thrust into Goredahl's dungeons. He had been beaten, told over and over again that he had killed the king. Had he in his agony and confusion, in his pain and then his illness, believed that? He must have, because the whole incident, one too terrible to contemplate, had disappeared from his mind after the beatings, after the sickness, after the ensuing anguish, the drugs, and the travel.

He had even forgotten, as the pain and fever-filled days had tumbled one upon the other, that it had been Goredahl who had imprisoned him. He had forgotten that it was Goredahl who had accused him of murder, who had first had him beaten and then, with no explanation, had stopped the beatings. Goredahl, like a bad dream, had slipped from his mind.

At some point Auragole had been brought from the capital of Thorensphere all the way to the town of Little Thoren. It must have taken weeks to get him here, to the town that was close to the Mattelmead border. He vaguely remembered the smell of apples and riding in a cart.

So he was in the fort at Little Thoren—the very fort that Elarr's men had been taken to years ago. The same fort that Auragole had seen from the outside when he had accompanied Elarr in a vain attempt at rescuing the four Companions of the Way who had been held prisoner here. The town lay next to the Thoren River, the river that divided Thorensphere from Mattelmead. When he was here with Elarr, seven or eight years ago, there had been no bridge across the river. A nearly impassable swamp lay on the Mattelmead side. Now there was both a bridge north of the town and a road that ran through the swamp. The waterfront had also been cleared for a mile on each side of the road. Many men had died of the fever, building that road and that beach—dispensable men, Solagen had assured him. That thought caused a knot in his stomach. Had Auragole acquiesced to this brutal assessment, and simply turned his attention elsewhere? Dispensable men. So now it was he who was imprisoned in this despicable fort that was next to the river, he who would soon be dispensable if he could not find a way to get out. He must find a way out. Think, he told himself.

He remembered that the large public square in front of the fort had been used daily as a marketplace—or as a place to hang malefactors, as had happened to Elarr's men. But what was important, and this caused him some excitement, was that near the fort, perhaps even underneath it, was a honeycomb of caves and caverns, some leading to the river. Many of those entrances were hidden beneath various buildings around the town—some in the back yards of houses. He had never spoken about that trip he had made with Elarr and Affredda to Little Thoren to anyone in Mattelmead—unless it had been to Glenelle. He tried to remember if he had told her, but couldn't. So those various caverns leading to the river might still be secret. Surely this would come in handy when he escaped. He had to escape.

His thoughts turned in another direction. Solagen had been murdered in Goredahl's house. Auragole had no doubt who had committed the murder, or why it was Auragole who stood accused. Solagen, usually so astute in his assessment of men and their motives, had made a fatal error. He assumed that giving Goredahl a kingdom of his own would appease him for not making him Solagen's heir. But Goredahl, his eyes still on the throne of the entire west, had amassed a great army in Thorensphere. It was drawn in part from the Mattelmead regulars assigned to Thorensphere, in part from those recruited in Thorensphere itself. Here, too, Solagen had made an error. Had the Mattelmead army assigned to Thorensphere changed its allegiance? Placed under Goredahl's command, had the soldiers thought first of Thorensphere and second of Mattelmead? Auragole had certainly not trusted that army when he had traveled through the country, first on the way to Noonbarr and then on the way back. Had Solagen not noticed this change in his army?

And now Noonbarr, too, was allied with Goredahl. The very day of Solagen's death, without even a decent period of mourning, Goredahl had taken as his wife Auragole's intended, Deeralee, the daughter of the newly crowned king of Noonbarr. She was a poor specimen of womanhood, but no doubt a worthwhile price for Goredahl to pay for Hameshall's alliance. Solagen, too, had thought so when he had arranged a marriage between Auragole and Deeralee. When the armies of Thorensphere and Noonbarr marched into Mattelmead, would the army stationed in Mattelmead and in the south accept his claim and follow Goredahl?

And what was Veldarr doing all this time? Mattelmead must certainly know about the king's death by now—and that Auragole stood accused. From his earlier conversations with Veldarr, Auragole knew Veldarr would not sit idly by while his cousin tried to take over the west. There would be war. Of that Auragole was certain.

He glanced up at the window. It was late November, Goredahl had told him. For two long months he had been in a stupor caused by the beatings, the drugs, the fever, and his consequent loss of memory. Two months. Two months! No question that Goredahl had used the time to gather his forces. When would Goredahl make his move? It would certainly be soon. That was why Goredahl had made his headquarters in Little Thoren. It bordered on Mattelmead. That was why Auragole had been brought here. But what had happened to Roradahl and the Elite Corps the night of the murder? Goredahl had told him that they had deserted him. Auragole didn't believe it. Somehow Goredahl had gotten rid of the king's men. What ruse had he used? It must have been something powerfully convincing to send Roradahl away. Roradahl disliked Goredahl, of that Auragole was sure.

What was going on outside these walls? Did everyone believe him a slayer of the king? Was there no one out there who believed him impossible of such a deed? And what had happened to his friends in Mattelmead, and to Meraleese and Glorr, to Sylvane and Donnadorr, once the terrible news was known? If Veldarr stood ready to oppose Goredahl, would he protect Auragole's friends? Perhaps Glenelle and Glenorr. But the others? Auragole had to know, had to get out of this prison somehow and defend his friends and clear himself. But how could he? How could he? And after all these weeks, would it not be too late? That thought weighed like a stone on his heart.

He didn't get up when the six heavily armed soldiers returned with two porters carrying a cot and a dish of food that looked like some sort of stew. He didn't say a word. Just watched as they left and heard several bolts slide through the locks on the other side. He knew he needed his strength if he was to get out of there, so after a while he got up and ate the stew. Then he lay down again, so worn out with these sudden recollections that he slept soundly that night.

The next day he woke up filled with rage. He began pacing about the cell, kicking at everything that got in his way. By what authority did Goredahl keep him prisoner? Auragole, not Goredahl, not Veldarr, was rightful heir to the west. How dare Goredahl keep him locked up and accused of a murder he had not committed? Auragole could feel the blood hot in his face. He cursed and railed against Goredahl. When the lower door opened and a dish of food was pushed through, he looked at it without appetite. He pushed through his chamber pot and his water jug, and got an empty chamber pot and water in return. But he barely touched the food that day. Nor did he eat much the next day, nor the next. He was too angry to sit still or lie down. He paced around the small cell, feeling a rage that would not dissipate. He neither sang nor exercised. He hardly slept.

How dare Goredahl and his men keep him locked up? He was by rights, by legal decree, Ormahn now. How dare Goredahl marry his intended bride? How dare he ally himself with Hameshall? How dare he spread lies to the army and carry those lies to Mattelmead? The throne was rightfully Auragole's. That had been Solagen's wish and Auragole had given up much for that inheritance. He had given up True-singing. He had given up his personal freedom. He had given up friendships. And now was he to be denied the prize for which he had sacrificed and then worked so hard—a prize he had earned? Day after day he could feel the bile inside him and the anger consume him. He sent back tray after tray of barely eaten food.

On the fourth day of his rage, the large door creaked open and six soldiers entered with another—not Goredahl, someone he had never seen before, but someone who was obviously in command.

"How dare you keep me here?" Auragole shouted. "Do you know who I am?"

"I know who you are. You are the murderer of Solagen."

"It's a lie," Auragole barked.

"So you say," the commander said. "You will have your day before the throne. I have not come to judge your innocence or your guilt."

"Why then have you come? Where is that sneak and that coward, Goredahl?"

The commander hit him so hard across his face that Auragole staggered and almost lost his footing. "Don't speak of the new Ormahn in that way, king-killer. I have come for a reason. And you had better listen well. You are not eating. For three days you have sent back your food barely touched. My instructions are that you be given three meals a day, and to see that you eat them."

"And how do you propose to do that? Force food down my throat until I choke, because Goredahl wants to fatten me up like a pig for the slaughter? I don't have to cooperate."

"Hold him," the commander ordered. And four men held his arms and legs.

The commander came up to him and struck Auragole four times hard across his face. His nose and his lip began to bleed, but the man's hand had been open. Auragole had not cried out. At that moment he was so angry, he was beyond pain.

"Now you listen to me, if you value your life, king-killer— what time is still left to you. I have orders that you are to eat three meals a day. You will do that. If you do not, I will see that you are beaten daily as you were in Thoren City. You can enjoy the days left to you in comfort free of torture, or you can end them in beatings and misery. The choice is yours."

The tray was placed on the floor. The water and chamber pots were exchanged.

Auragole was flung onto the straw in the corner. A man held a bow with an arrow directed at him until the commander and his men exited; then he backed out, and the door closed noisily behind them. Auragole lay back, all the fury leaving him. His face smarted and his nose was bleeding. He tilted his head back to stop the flow of blood. What had he accomplished in his days of rage? What had he achieved by refusing food? He had lost weight, he could feel it. He needed his energy. He needed his strength. If he was ever going to get out of there, he would need all his wits, and his physical as well as mental capacities. He would eat—everything that he was given. He would let them think that they had him cowed. But he would bide his time. He would think of some way to get out of this rat hole. He crawled over to where the tray sat on the dusty floor, picked up the spoon, and forced down every morsel of his dinner.

For a week Auragole ate, walked, exercised, and recited poems and stories he had learned from his mother and Spehn, and from Glenelle and Donnadorr. He sang song after song. His determination to get well, to be prepared to get out of his cell, sustained him for most of the week. At night he tried to think of ways to escape, tried to formulate plans, tried to think who might come and rescue him.

But as the week passed and a new one began, he had formulated no plan. He asked his captors questions through the small door when his food was given him. He asked about what was happening outside these walls. Had Goredahl marched into Mattelmead? Was there war between the cousins? If so, who was winning? His questions were met with silence. Gradually, barely felt at first, he began to slide into melancholia. As the second week passed, he exercised less, recited less, sang less. He lay on his cot, getting up only to eat what was given him. He wanted, at all cost, to avoid the beatings he was sure to get if he didn't comply with that order.

Yet his despair grew and by the end of the second week he had stopped all activity except forcing down the food delivered to him thrice daily. He lay on his cot, too miserable to think about anything except that he had been forgotten, that those who once thought well of him now despised him, that his friends were likely dead, that he was going to die in this prison, or else in time be paraded in front of a mob howling for his blood. Then hanged for a murder he had not committed. All anger and frustration seemed to drain like melting snow into a river of terrible black hopelessness, and all he wanted to do was sleep and not think.

chapter thirty-four

IT WAS THE end of the third week of December, and there were at least two inches of snow on the ground. Two armies faced each other over the large plain and awaited the instructions of their commanders. The breath of the horses looked like escaping steam, and they pranced restlessly, snorting in place. There were several rows of mounted men. Over their uniforms they wore leather tunics. With their leather gloves, they held tight to the reins of their mounts. In front of them, the men on foot blew on their hands to keep them warm, their woolen mittens helping little in the cold air. They were silent, carrying their swords or spears, or in the front rows, bows and arrows. They hoped they would be able to hear what the two parties who were riding out to meet each other were about to say. Some hoped the battle would be averted. Some did not—their blood was up and they wanted a good fight, stories to tell to grandchildren when they were old. The two leaders were fast approaching each other. Each held the white flag that meant a parley. Behind each of the two were a dozen men with bows drawn and arrows ready if there should be any subterfuge.

When they were twenty yards apart, the accompanying horse-soldiers stopped, but kept their bows aimed and ready, and the two leaders, in full battle gear, moved forward to meet each other.

They stopped only feet apart.

It was Veldarr who spoke first. "You called this parley, cousin. What is it you wish to say?"

"I want to give you a chance to surrender, cousin," Goredahl said, "and spare your soldiers their lives. There doesn't have to be bloodshed between us. Just acknowledge me as rightful heir to the throne, and you can have as a reward any of the western kingdoms you choose."

"You think I want to be king of some small country? Had I wanted that I would have accepted Solagen's offer long ago."

Goredahl gave Veldarr a friendly smile. "I've always known that you didn't have it in you—no, let me rephrase that, that you never wanted to be Ormahn, never wanted to take on the responsibility of governing. Swear fealty to me and keep your present job, commander of the army."

Veldarr smiled in return. "You misunderstand me, cousin. I have no wish to be commander of the army. . ."

"Then. . ."

Veldarr raised his hand. "Hear me out. I don't want to be king of some vassal country in the west, nor commander of your army. . ."

"Then what *do* you want?" Goredahl's brows drew together, and he looked more intently at his cousin's face.

"I thought you understood. I want it all."

"You want it. . ."

". . .all. Mattelmead, Thorensphere, Glovale, Wildenfarr, Noonbarr. . ."

"You mean to fight me for the throne?"

"I do."

Goredahl stared at him, almost blankly, for a few minutes. Then he said, "You can't win. Your forces are too small."

"Are they? You forget the forces of Glovale and Wildenfarr, and our troops that have kept watch on Isofed."

Goredahl laughed. "I wouldn't count on them. Why should they join you and not me? Besides, they are cut off. Hameshall, with the army of Noonbarr, is at the border near Glovale ready to bar anyone from approaching out of the south."

"Too late."

"What?"

"It's too late. Those soldiers have long ago entered Mattelmead. And no doubt Hameshall has already felt the brunt of their attack, not from the south but from the north and the west and the east."

"But how could they have mustered so quickly? It's a lie. A ruse. An attempt to trick me into giving up this battle."

"Oh, no, cousin. Not at all. I have no intention of suggesting you give up this battle. I think you and I should decide the question of who should be Ormahn right now, today." Veldarr turned his horse and began moving back toward the men who had come with him. Their arrows were still aimed at Goredahl and his men. When Veldarr reached them, he turned to face his cousin, who had not moved. "If you think that the men you see arrayed on this field are all the men I have here," he shouted, "you are mistaken. In the woods behind us and to the north of us is as large a contingent as the one you see on the field. Now I think you'd better return to your soldiers, because the moment I get back to my own lines, the combat will begin."

At these words Goredahl turned his horse and began racing back to his lines, with his men after him.

HE WAS NOT sure how many days of despair had gone by— perhaps ten—before he had the dream.

He was in the kitchen of the cabin in the valley where he had grown up, standing at the table. Only he was not the child who had once lived there, nor the youth who had left there eight years earlier. He was himself, as he was now, twenty-six years old and a man.

His mother, still young, still in her twenties, was standing across the table from him, with her arms folded. She was frowning at him, her beautiful face expressing her disapproval.

"What have I done wrong this time?" Even to his own ears, his words sounded petulant—like the child he had been when he had done something to call down upon his head his mother's displeasure.

"I'm ashamed of you," she said, her lips forming a tight line after the words were uttered.

He glared at her, but she met his eyes unwaveringly. Abruptly, he sat down at the table and said, "Are you going to tell me what I've done?"

"You sit in your cell and feel sorry for yourself. That is not how I raised you. I tried to instill in you the virtues of courage, endurance, and steadfastness. I tried to teach you that suffering should be felt for others, not for oneself."

"And just how did you do that?" he asked, knowing he was being argumentative. He was challenging her in a way he had never done as a child. He even began to laugh. "What in my years growing up required true courage in the service of another, or steadfastness, or any of your so-called virtues? When did I need to worry about someone else's suffering— except at your dying? What great difficulty did I have to endure in my eighteen years with you except your constant harping and disapproval? You and Father raised me in total isolation. Did you expect that all those virtues you were constantly drumming into my head would be enough to stem the tide of ignorance that swept over my early life?"

Itina sat now, her hands together on the table, her head held high. If his words had hurt, she didn't show it by so much as a quiver of her lips. "Why do you think I told you all those stories, Aurie, filled with the courage and the nobility of the human being? Or sang you all those songs about valor and fearlessness and the overcoming of great obstacles? Did you think I did that only to entertain you?"

"Stories are not life," he said.

"No, but they show the ideal, show the integrity to which one should aspire. They educate the heart." Her eyes never left his face, but her features had softened and so had her tone.

He exhaled one long breath. "I'm in prison, Mother. What can your stories tell me about that?"

"You have given up, Aurie. That makes me ashamed."

He looked away from her probing gaze. "Why should I feel any optimism?" he finally asked her.

"Because," she said, "you are still alive. And you cannot know the end of your story—even though you have thought through to an ending that is as likely to be false as to be true."

"What would you have me do, then?"

"Live."

"Live?"

"Live each day as if it were a gift. It is a gift, you know. And prepare yourself to be strong in body and strong in soul and strong in spirit. Do that and you will be ready for the next chapter of your earthly story, whatever that chapter may be and whenever that chapter may come—even if it's the final chapter."

He sat there, head bowed, thinking. Finally, he raised his head and said, "You are asking me to have hope."

"Yes. The first ingredient one needs to face each new day. Lose hope and they win."

"Who, Mother?"

"You know."

And he woke up.

ABOUT A MONTH after Lorenwile and company had resumed their journey, they reached higher hills. There was snow now on the ground, and the sounds of winter birds in the trees.

"We've come at last to the Gandlese," Lorenwile told them, a satisfied look on his face. "We need to find a place to camp."

"This looks to be hard going, friend." Donnadorr came up to him. He motioned toward the even-taller peaks in the distance.

Meraleese looked about her. Somehow taking one step after another had brought them to these tall and rather forbidding mountains. She marveled at Lorenwile's easy manner. He seemed genuinely happy finally to have arrived here—not at all concerned or worried. But there must be many miles to go before they reached the Valley of the Agavi, and the trail now would be treacherous with snow and ice. She glanced at Donnadorr, at his face, pale with the pain he tried to conceal, then at Sylvane, carrying a little life inside her, and then at Glorr, who walked with his short legs as fast as he could, and never complained.

Lorenwile was looking about him slowly, cocking his head the way he did sometimes when he was listening. No question, he had very keen hearing.

"Follow me," he said, and started on his way. Glorr came up and took his mother's hand. "Isn't this wonderful?" he said, gesturing at the snow-covered mountains with his head.

"Do you think so, darling?"

"Oh, yes. Things are going to be fine from now on. Father told me so."

I pray you are right, Meraleese thought, and smiled reassuringly at her son.

They had not been walking more than fifteen minutes when they came upon the entrance to a cave.

"The Gandlese is riddled with caves," Lorenwile said. "We'll camp here tonight. Bring in the horses."

The horses, tied each to each and led by Donnadorr, were brought into the spacious cave.

"Set up the camp," Lorenwile instructed the troop. "There is something I need to do. I'll be back in an hour or two." And out he went before anyone had a chance to question him.

They had begun unloading the horses, and were about to make a fire, when Meraleese suddenly heard an unusual singing. The others heard it too, and came to stand at the entrance of the cave. What a curious song. It had in it something of the hardness of rock, and something of the height of these hills, and something indefinable. The sound was craggy, and sometimes hollow. They couldn't hear the words. But there were words.

"Lorenwile is True-singing these mountains," Glorr said.

"But why?" Sylvane asked.

No one answered her. They stood there for a long time, loath to leave the incredible sounds they were hearing.

Finally Donnadorr said, "We'd better finish setting up for the night, and get the fire lit and food ready. Lorenwile will be hungry when he returns."

The sun was beginning to set when Lorenwile returned. "Something smells good," he said, and walked over to the fire and looked at the pot hanging over it. "May we eat?"

Meraleese hurried to serve him, and they all ate in silence, waiting to hear what Lorenwile would tell them.

But after he ate, he lay back and fell asleep. Sylvane covered him with his blankets and they all, not daring to speak and wake him, went to their own sleeping places.

Before retiring, Donnadorr added some wood to the fire. Yes, Meraleese thought, let's keep Lorenwile warm.

The next morning, as they sat at their breakfast, Lorenwile spoke. "We will stay in this cave one more day. Don and I will go out hunting." He looked at Donnadorr. "We can take two of the horses. We need food and water for two weeks' traveling, which we will do through the many tunnels and caves that honeycomb these mountains. That will keep us out of the snow and cold. If our hunting is poor today, we can return to the surface for another hunt another day. The beginning of our underground path is no more than half a day's march from here. While in the caves we can ride the horses most of the way."

Meraleese was relieved. She had marveled at Don's stalwartness, but she could see how often his leg hurt him, and how much greater his limp had become.

"Did you True-sing the mountains to find an underground path, Lorenwile?" It was Glorr who asked.

Lorenwile gave him a smile. "I did indeed, Glorr. And the mountains were very accommodating. If I can picture in my mind's eye what I saw while singing, then I can lead us under these mountains to within a week of Agavia."

"True-singing is the best magic in the whole world," Glorr said.

"I think you are right, young friend."

"I should like to learn to do it," Glorr said with conviction.

"Would you?"

"Yes."

"Well, then first we shall have to hear you sing. You do sing, don't you?"

The boy's smile was enthusiastic. "Donnadorr taught me. He is a very good singer."

Don reddened with pleasure.

"Then you shall sing with me in the tunnels, which are dark and gloomy places. That will help pass the time and will certainly cheer up all your parents," and Lorenwile's eyes twinkled.

"I would like that," Glorr said.

Lorenwile patted Glorr on his head, rose gracefully to his feet, and said, "Come, Don, we have work to do." Then he turned to Glorr. "You must help your mothers," he said. "There is much hard work here, and we wouldn't want to leave the hardest work to your mothers, would we?"

"No, I shall certainly help them."

While the women and Glorr worked to clean the campsite and to make the main meal, Meraleese thought about the singing she had heard the day before. This trip had been so full of miracles her heart could barely contain them. To know that there were others on the Deep Earth who knew what Timorr had known filled her with gladness. Sylvane, too, looked thoughtful—no doubt thinking about that singing. But the two women didn't speak about it. What was there to say? Lorenwile had guided them out of Mattelmead and into the Gandlese, all with True-singing. And surely he had saved Sylvane's baby with his songs. Meraleese would have been happy and completely at ease, cooking dinner there in that isolated cave in the Gandlese, if she didn't feel the rush of sorrow, like a swift river in her blood, whenever Auragole came to her mind.

But she would not lose hope. How could the Gods help humanity if human beings didn't give them the substance of hope with which to work? Meraleese had turned away from anger long ago. She would keep her hope ignited, like a small, unquenchable flame, in her heart.

The two men returned a few hours later with a deer. They cleaned and carved the animal and packed it in snow.

"This should last us a while," Donnadorr said.

"It was Don's shot that brought it down," Lorenwile said. "We shan't go hungry under these mountains, so let's have a grand feast tonight."

And they did.

N

chapter thirty-five

WHEN HE AWOKE from the dream about his mother, Auragole was angry. She had always demanded much of him, had pushed and prodded him, had taught him things that he had as a child thought useless. But he had obeyed. Oh yes, he had obeyed. Had he not, he would have brought down the wrath of his father. One thing his father would not have tolerated from him, had never tolerated from him, was impertinence toward his mother—even if Goloss himself thought some of what Auragole was asked to learn useless or even foolish. Civility, his mother had called all those things she had taught him. Virtues. Good manners and the proper behavior toward others. Cordiality. Kindness. Deference. And she had insisted he learn to read and to write and do his numbers. Goloss had rolled his eyes, but agreed that at least knowing his numbers would be important. And Itina had demanded he learn words, many, many words. *"A good vocabulary is a sign of a proper upbringing and is especially necessary if one is going to be able to think clearly,"* she had said in a tone that brooked no argument.

As he paced about his cell, his anger began to drain away. Hadn't her teaching helped him on his journeys? Surely his interaction with others, clumsy as it had been in the beginning, had been made easier by how he had been instructed. His ability to think and to speak, even though in his earlier travels he had been more taciturn, had helped him come into the society of people in a much easier way than if he had been taught only the use of sword and bow. He had to admit, in all fairness, that he had learned much from his mother, that he owed her much. She had been hard on him, had been demanding, and he had often been recalcitrant. But how would he have fared without what he had learned from her? He had been an innocent when he first came into the society of people, but he had not been coarse, had not been primitive. And if she had not taught him song and story, would True-singing have come into his life? Yes, he owed a lot to that woman, who had been stern, uncompromising, and exacting. She had bestowed her approval only seldom. But what sunshine had been created in his soul when some word of praise fell from her lips.

His mother was right; he must not now give way to despair, must not give up hope. By midday Auragole had decided to resume his exercising, his speaking and singing. He decided also to return to the retrospective of his life, this time going over it in backward order—last event to the earliest he could remember. This time he would judge, as coolly as he could, his life, his deeds, his attitudes, his words, even his thoughts and feelings if he could remember them.

And so he began again.

Somehow going backward helped him see how one event had often been propelled by an event that had happened before. That was to be expected. But sometimes an incident had occurred that had merely welled up out of, what?—his character, his destiny? Something took place that had nothing to do with what had come before. It broke into the flow of days, a dam bursting, unanticipated, changing everything in its path— such as being asked by Solagen to become his adopted son and heir. Or before that, being asked to become a commander in Mattelmead's army when he had no conscious wish to be a soldier. Or before that, rescuing Solagen in the Sorren Heights when Solagen had been wounded, or meeting Lorenwile. Or losing his first companions on the Noonbarr River, or finding Sylvane when he was eighteen, only days away from his valley in the Gandlese, and alone for the first time in his life. There were many of these incisions. Meekelorr and the beast from the cave, and the stone Auragole threw to divert the beast. And Agavia. All of Agavia—and what he had been offered there, and what he had rejected so he could accompany his friends west.

But what were these incidents, each of which had changed his life so irrevocably? They were events he could not have predicted by noting only what had come before.

"You cannot know the end of your story—even though you have thought through to an ending that is as likely to be false as to be true," his mother had said.

All those unpredictable events had helped create the pattern that was his life up to this time, had helped create his destiny— a destiny that was partly formed by him, but also in part brought about by another force. Had he not been told, by those who believed in the Creative World, that destiny in these times happened in just this way? Certain events or people had been brought to him and would be brought to him, but how he handled those events, or what he did with those people, was up to him, up to the freedom he chose to exercise. Could this be true?

As easily true as not, he thought.

"You can cooperate in your destiny, or you can become a victim of it."

Who had said that to him? Was it Pohl? Or Meekelorr? Or

had he heard it from Timorr when he had sat in the back of the little temple, sent as a spy by Solagen, but caught up in the greatness of what he was hearing there?

Auragole observed his life now as if he were watching an actor in a play, and saw in himself selfishness, often indifference to the feelings of others, an ability to manipulate the truth, to hold at bay any sense of wrongdoing, to blame others for his actions. He saw his growing lust for power—from the days of his confrontation with Glenorr over rescuing Donnadorr to the day he was imprisoned. He saw his love of battle, which he had once so smugly denounced, saw his willingness to turn away from what he had once considered his ideals for the sake of fame, of popularity, of being well regarded.

He saw too what had been offered him that he had turned his back on, from the chance to study the Gods at the Last School to—but surely most important of all—True-singing, a glory that few on the Deep Earth had been offered, or had achieved. He saw, in his pride over being Solagen's man, how he had denigrated the Companions of the Way who were determined to help those who were persecuted by terrible tyrants such as Goredahl. And perhaps tyrants such as Solagen? That thought grieved him terribly. He had, in his years in Mattelmead's Elite Corps, inwardly scoffed at the small army of Companions who searched for the Nethergod incarnate on the earth. The Nethergod who had as opponents only the Companions—at best a few thousand strong—and with them, Pohl, Lorenwile, and a peace-loving people called the Agavians. These people were willing against all odds to fight the Dark Breather for the soul of the Deep Earth, even if all the rest of the world was asleep to the danger, even if all the rest of the world denied that there was another world called the Creative World, denied that such a being called the Nethergod existed. And was he among those unbelievers? Or a "now and then" believer? Was it convenience, and the desire for comfort, that made him vacillate between belief and non-belief?

He saw how he had looked in the other direction when freedom was eschewed in favor of peace. What kind of peace was that? his father had asked him in dream after dream. A peace without freedom, Auragole realized, was a peace without honor. What had happened to him on his journey from childhood to manhood? Had he ever been a man, or even a child, who had valued honor, let alone possessed it, despite his mother's prodding? Had he turned away from the integrity he had been taught in order to wield power—or had he never had integrity even though he proclaimed its importance? He thought of those he knew who were willing to make sacrifices for something larger than themselves and their own self-promotion. He thought with shame of the priest Timorr, who had died because he had pursued his own understanding of truth, risking all to speak to those who had ears to hear his words.

"I approve that you are making the effort to assess your actions, but Auragole, you carry it too far," his mother told him in another dream. "You see only the faults in your character and none of the good you have done."

Again they were sitting at the table in the kitchen of their old house in the Gandlese. "All humans do ill in their lives, Auragole. Do not, in your attempt to see your failings, become prideful." His mother's hands were clasped tightly together and resting in her lap. Her back was ramrod straight.

He was sitting opposite her in what had always been his chair, watching her with a fondness he had not felt in a long time.

"All humans have much to regret," she said. "We are not yet Gods, Aurie. Even the Gods are not perfect and still strive."

He smiled at her then. "You speak to me now of the Gods. You never spoke to me of the Gods except that one time when I was a child. You made Goloss angry then."

"Did I?"

"Don't you remember?"

"I remember. We are talking about you, Aurie, not about me. It can be an arrogance to beat your chest and decide you are the most evil human being on the Deep Earth."

"No need to worry on my account, Mother. That much importance I don't give to myself," he said. "But I must look at what I have done and whom I have become, or else how am I to change? And change seems crucial to me now, even if I remain in a cell the rest of my life."

"Then, my child," and her hand reached toward his, but did not touch it, "balance it with looking as coldly and candidly at the good you have done, just as you have done with the bad. For you have done good."

"Have I?"

She rose as if to leave.

"Mother," he said.

She had started to walk away, but she turned back. "What is it?"

He wanted to say, "I love you." Wanted her to say, "I love you." But he didn't. And she didn't.

"Nothing. Just thank you for coming."

She nodded and looked at him for a long moment with those incredibly large, dark eyes. My, he thought, she is beautiful—I never knew. Then she turned and walked away.

And he woke up and lay on his cot, thinking about his mother. Why couldn't he tell her he loved her? Why couldn't she say the words—even now? Why couldn't he? Did he really know anything about love, that he could lay claim to it? Was there truly such a thing as love? Godly love, yes, but so-called human love, was it real? Wasn't human love just longing, loneliness, instinct—or attraction and lust? He wasn't sure. He would look again at the issue of love as soon as he was finished with his retrospective.

But he took his mother's advice and began also to look at what he had done in his life to be proud of. If there wasn't pure unadulterated sacrifice, there were outcomes at least that were good.

"You see in your good deeds a mixture of motives," his mother said. "You should see also in that which now seems ill in you a mixture of motives."

AS THEY JOURNEYED through the tunnels and caves under the mountains, riding their animals when they could, Lorenwile sang, and with him sang Glorr. It wasn't True-singing, it was plain song. Funny songs and children's songs and songs about nature and even songs about love. Somehow, Sylvane thought, Lorenwile has managed to take us through tunnels that are roomy enough for us to ride our horses in, and she was grateful for Don's sake. These tunnels were not like those they had traveled through after they had left Agavia for the east all those years ago. Those had been difficult tunnels, narrow, twisting, and climbing. And there had been that monstrous tunnel where they had almost lost Ellie, the Cave of Terrors. Sylvane wondered then if there had been some purpose behind that arduous way as there seemed to be some purpose behind this way.

Lorenwile never showed any indecision when there was more than one tunnel to choose from. He, with hardly a moment's hesitation, chose the one they were to go through. It was dark and they carried only one torch. Still Sylvane felt no uneasiness. Nor did the others, as far as she could tell. Lorenwile led the group, with Glorr at his side or just behind him. Then came Meraleese, and Sylvane behind Meraleese. Donnadorr was last, with the packhorse tied to his saddle.

BEFORE MEEKELORR RETURNED from the Lady Claregole's mansion to the school two miles up the mountains, he decided to ride through a part of the Valley of the Agavi. It was early morning, the first day of January, with snow lying like a clean blanket on the ground. It would be months before it would begin to melt and early spring flowers break out of the ground, and the lush green grass that was so beautiful in the valley finally appear. But what else would the spring bring, or the summer? He felt sure he knew, and decided to look at the fortifications once again, but also to ride around simply to enjoy this unique valley.

He had left Claregole at dawn, had saddled his beloved horse, Sunflight, declining the offer of the Lady's groom who was just rising from sleep. Climbing into his saddle, Meekelorr had directed his horse away from the path that led to the school. Down the snow-swept lanes from the mansion, then through the long valley he rode. He passed few people. Most were still at home eating their breakfasts or feeding their livestock. He glanced up at the sky and knew the day would be clear, the sun would shine with little concern for fortifications or coming battles. Meekelorr looked toward the east, where a coral glow now glimmered through the mountains. There it was, about to make an appearance, the ever-constant and predictable sun. But nothing else in the days ahead was predictable.

He came to Claregole as often as he could now. Claregole was his beloved, though he knew, with a tinge of sadness, she would never become his wife. This coupling between two Agavians, before any ceremony that united the two before the Gods, was the custom. But, according to that same custom, only those couples living together who produced a child would wed. It was not the lack of a marriage ceremony that he felt as a sorrow— Claregole could not be more wife to him than she already was. The ache he felt for Claregole was that she would never bear a child. There would be no children—no girl child to pass on the leadership of the Agavians, as Claregole's mother had passed it on to her. Claregole was the last leader of the Agavians. As Claregole would never become a mother, he would never become a father. It was a loss that he would silently share with Claregole, for she would accept no pity from him. Nor he from her. Even now few Agavian couples were bearing children. That too was one of the signs that announced to the Agavians that the Last Battle was near.

Claregole and Meekelorr each had difficult tasks in these world days. These tasks had often drawn them apart for months, even for years. But their love for each other, through all the arduous times, had never wavered. Meekelorr had long been accepted as the Lady's consort when he was in Agavia, just as his long absences had been accepted.

He turned his attention to the valley he was riding through. He, of course, knew what he would see—ugly walls around the large mansions and manor houses, all built in the past seven years. There were no true villages in the Valley of the Agavi. The smaller homes were scattered around the greater ones. Should the defenses in the mountains fail, then the Agavians and the Companions would retreat behind the wooden fences surrounding these larger homes for their last stand.

Agavians, as had been true for all of humanity in an older time, were born into their circumstances, and were content. There were no poor; no one ever went hungry. The Agavi simply accepted their status in life with grace and confidence. There were those who led and those who followed, those who served and those who were served. But all were cared for and cared about. Each accepted his or her responsibility without question and with all seriousness. And each was an artist in some field or other—that was one of the unique qualities of the Agavians. Sometimes the greatest artist came from the most humble circumstances, and that too was accepted. Their Gods ordered all things in their lives, now as before. And they had always been, and were even now, content. Even as they prepared to be the last of their people, even as they prepared to do what no other Agavian before them had done—go to battle—they were accepting and content.

At first, after returning from the Sorren Heights, Meekelorr had thought the walls and fences abominations—wounds cut across the body of the old valley he had come to love. But he had grown used to them, and now could see past the necessary defenses to the still indomitable charm of the land. After all, it was for the battle soon to come that the Agavi had lived in this valley for thousands of years.

Why was he riding past what he already knew he would find? Was it the sadness he had seen in Claregole's face as she lay sleeping the night before, and he, elbow on the pillow, head resting on his hand, his arm about her slim waist, watching her? The awaited days were growing ever closer. Solagen's murder, the chaos in the west as the two cousins fought each other for control, Auragole possibly alive but likely in prison, all these signified. When would the Nethergod's army come? In the spring? The summer? Would this be the last winter in the Valley of the Agavi? He thought it likely.

He rode past one of the memory signs—a tall, intricately carved stone of hoary age—and stopped to bow his head. But Meekelorr had no gift to read the signs. These gifts were gifts for the Agavi alone. He knew Claregole's brother, Galavi, came often now—not to read the future, for there were no future thoughts contained in these signs dotting the valley. Only the past resided in them for one who could read them. The past had always guided the Agavi people—until now. All the signs could do was to remind Galavi and all the Agavians that it was for these days that they had been created and guided by their Gods.

Meekelorr rode from mansion to manor house, from memory stone to memory stone. At last, he turned Sunflight toward the mountain and the Last School. Time to be at his own task. There was training to be done, and his soldiers would be waiting for him.

"I CAN'T UNDERSTAND how you come to your beliefs, frankly, Meekelorr. You have one set of beliefs, the Agavians

another, the people of Wildenfarr-low-desert another—no, each tribe there has a different set of beliefs and they fight each other over them. Why is your belief better than others? Or more true? How do any of you know that there are Gods at all?"

"Do you believe only what you can touch with your hands and see with your eyes?"

Auragole sighed and looked out at the dead city. "No, I can easily believe that there are hidden things, hidden forces, things we can't see. I believe that because I've experienced such things. Strange ailments in the Deep Forest, for instance, and strange Beings behind the wind, for so I experienced it in the Deep. Not only myself, but Don and Ellie and Sylvie and. . .well, I'm not sure about Glen. But that only gives me a. . .a. . ." Auragole paused and couldn't go on.

"A sense of something behind the visible?"

"Yes, a sense. But that is not the same as knowing. There may well be Gods, Meekelorr. But you say that there are good Gods, whom you call the Creative Gods. And you say that there are evil Gods called Adversary Gods, led by someone called the Nethergod. You say he is on earth right now, that it is your task and the Companions' and the Agavians' to find him and do battle with him. And to that you devote your life. But what I don't understand is how you know all of this. Pohl told me that there is a path to the Gods, but I don't understand how that can be." His voice cracked with intensity. "I don't understand how you can claim to know something in its reality, its true reality, if it is hidden."

"Well, young Auragole, how do you know anything?"

Auragole answered without hesitation. "I know something if I have experienced it."

"Good," Meekelorr said. "That's a beginning. And someday you will have to tell me what you mean by experience.*" And he rose in a fluid, graceful gesture and whistled for Sunflight.*

Auragole, too, stood up. His head hurt slightly and he rubbed his temples. Wasn't it clear what experience meant? He would have to ponder that.

Auragole had gone through his life backward, and was now examining portions of it again, portions that troubled him. It seemed to his current observation that he had, when presumably free, moved through much of his life in a kind of dream, pushed and pulled by the winds of chance or fate. It was only in Mattelmead that he had finally woken up—after Glenelle had betrayed his trust. Had coming out of the dream of childhood and youth in so brutal a fashion been a good awakening? He wasn't sure. But it was an awakening. Yet out of knowledge and out of hurt he had become more selfish, more interested in doing what pleased and fed his pride. Yes, he had courage. Yes, he was a capable soldier. Yes, he was good at negotiations, even a good leader of men. Yes, he had good ideas, and he had never been a lover of cruelty or the harsh treatment of others. But he had looked away when Goredahl and his Security Forces had rampaged through the country and the west, arresting people on rumor and throwing them, without a hearing, into prison. And Solagen, whom he had so admired, had also turned away—too busy with the larger issues of war and peace and governing to pay attention to "a few individuals." Solagen had loved peace, but had not valued freedom or individuality, and Auragole had been unwilling to see anything untoward in Solagen's attitude. Was it Solagen's eloquence, his willingness to sacrifice for the future, that had prompted Auragole to say, first, yes to joining the army, and then yes to becoming his heir?

"Think carefully on what we are doing here—we privileged few. We are uniting all the west... Is this not a noble task, worth giving one's efforts to, even one's life? And the army—my army—is the instrument that is bringing it about. Because of this army, there will be schools and hospitals, scientific academies and theaters, concert halls, and galleries for art all over the west, not

just in Mattelmead City. There will be cities like our city in every country in the Westernlands. Just imagine it, Auragole! And all because of the army and what it's accomplishing. . . You sing exquisitely, Auragole, and give pleasure to all who hear you. I respect and value your talent. Believe that I do. But lift your eyes a little higher, son. Be part of this inexorable movement that is bringing peace and order to the Grand Continent, that is making it possible for singers like you to fulfill your private dreams. But for now, give something greater to the world than a song."

But there had been a flaw in Solagen's dream—one Auragole had refused to look at clearly until these days in prison. His two fathers shared something: a love of peace. However, only one of them loved freedom. This dichotomy troubled him for many days.

Then there was True-singing. He had gone through that period in his life as he had gone through all the other events in his life. Somehow those glorious months, learning from Lorenwile, were suspended above all else, and judgments of good or evil didn't seem to apply there. Had he been more awake when True-singing, or less awake? Lorenwile had taken off months from his own pursuits to become his teacher. Why had Auragole never seen that as a great gift given to him by Lorenwile? How had he taken so much for granted?

"I have regrets," he told his mother, "for roads not taken."

"That is useless," she said, her dark eyes so deep he had to pull back from looking too long at them. "A life is not like a story that can be told, then retold in a different way, changing details to suit your likes. A life is a road—one way. You can look back at where your feet have trod, and learn, but you cannot change the steps you have taken. Do not waste time in vain regrets, Auragole. That does nothing. Remember, yes. Then look to the future, to the road ahead on which your feet have not yet walked. All change is there."

Auragole was growing stronger, eating, exercising, singing,

speaking, and going over his life like a judge. He was dreaming frequently of his mother. He tried once to tell her how little what had once seemed important in his life seemed important to him now. She was important, and his father—but he couldn't say that to her. His friends—and they must still live, for any other thought was unbearable—were important. True-singing was important, but lost to him. What else? If he were suddenly to find himself free, what would he seek, what would he want to do? But other than True-singing, what else would he desire? To make sure his friends were safe. And to find Meraleese. Yes, he would look the world over for her if he were free.

"Why don't you think through again all you have heard about the Gods," his mother said unexpectedly.

"You *do* know about the Gods!" he exclaimed.

She didn't answer.

But she must, he thought, being where she is. Why won't she speak about them? "It's true, I have heard much," he said then. "Stories told me by Don and Glenelle on our travels. Stories in Wildenfarr. Stories in Agavia. Many things told me by Pohl and Meekelorr and Elarr. Less from Lorenwile, but something."

"And from the priest, Timorr?" she said.

"Yes. Do you know him? Do you know if Meraleese still lives? And Don and Sylvie and Glorr?"

She didn't answer his questions but said instead, "It seems there is much you can think about and recall."

"Yes," he said. "Why not recollect what I have heard about the Gods?" And so he did. For many days he went through everything he could remember that had been told to him about the Creative World.

But there was something else on his mind. And this he didn't bring to his mother. Not this question—he couldn't. His concerns about the nature of love. What was love? A bodily need? A feeling? A force? Was he the only person in the world who didn't know? Did it indeed exist as a thing in itself? Or was it all illusion, as his father had told him on his deathbed? If love were real, had Auragole ever experienced it? He knew love as instinct—for that was surely much of what had bound him to his parents, still bound him. He knew at first hand about lust and obsession. But what about. . .something else? Was there something else? Something not bound so tightly to the body?

It was said that the Prince God had come to the Deep Earth to quicken the possibility for individuality in the human being. First individuality, then freedom, finally love freely given. That was in everything that he had learned from Elarr and Meekelorr in those months they had been together in the Woeful Peaks. And wasn't that what Timorr had taught in his little temple, hundreds of miles from Elarr and Meekelorr, and with no knowledge of either? If this quickening of the individuality was why the Prince God had come to the Deep Earth all those centuries ago, why wasn't that something known to all those who claimed to worship the Prince? In-tul-farr of Wildenfarr-low-desert worshipped the Prince, as had his vanquished enemy, And-ul-farr. But neither of them had spoken of this quickening of individuality in humanity. The tribe was still all in all to them. And their different ways of worshipping the Prince God had brought only enmity, not love. And what about the Agavians who worshipped not the Prince but earlier Gods? They surely were loving. Born loving, Galavi had told him once. But was that kind of love, beautiful as it was to behold, freely given, since an Agavian was born with it?

And what about the Guardians of the Flame, who had isolated themselves in a community in the Ancient Woods? They were more concerned with wisdom than with love. They claimed they worshipped all Gods, but no particular mention had been made of the Prince God whom Timorr said was the source of all earthly creation. The Guardians did not see the Prince as Creator God, but believed an evil God had created the Deep Earth.

Nor did the priests in the great temple dedicated to the Prince in Mattelmead City speak of the Prince God as the bringer of love to the Deep Earth, nor the necessity of developing individuality and freedom as its precursor. They saw him only as one God in a pantheon of Gods.

Did Auragole know anything about this unique kind of love that the Prince was supposed to have brought to earth through his own being? Had Auragole ever experienced it? Was he capable? It was this idea of love that agonized him the most. Perhaps if he had ever truly understood it, he wouldn't have been so willing to give up freedom for Solagen's single and narrow goal of peace. It troubled him, and Auragole spent hours examining it as he paced about his cell, but he couldn't resolve it. He had too easily turned away from the goal of freedom his birth father had set before him, in order that he might accept the goal that his adopted father had placed before him—peace. Did that mean he was incapable of experiencing real love, since he had eschewed freedom, had eschewed individuality, for all his pretending he was unique? Somewhere in his time in Mattelmead, he had given up expecting to experience that ephemeral thing called love.

Then what was it he felt for Meraleese? If it wasn't love, then he had no name for it.

From individuality to freedom to love. The question of love loomed in his mind as an insoluble problem.

N

chapter thirty-six

THE LADY CLAREGOLE had sent a message up to the school for Meekelorr. It asked that he come down to the mansion at once. If he was not available, would Pohl please come?

It was Pohl who was ushered into the Lady Claregole's rooms. When he entered, he found the Lady Claregole and her help-mate Binta deep in conversation.

"I'm sorry, but Meekelorr is out on the battle plain," Pohl said, "and since this seemed of some urgency, I didn't wait. Is my coming in his stead acceptable?"

"More than acceptable. I'm happy to see you, Pohl. No need to pull Meekelorr away from his duties. You can send a message to him when you return to the school."

"Willingly. What is your message, dear soul-friend?"

"Binta has had another far-seeing. Sit, my soul-friend."

As Pohl took his seat, he looked over at Binta sitting upright in her chair.

"This came of its own, dear doctor," she said. "I did not call it forth."

"I shouldn't wonder," Pohl said, "since you have been keeping such a good eye on their progress. What did you see, dear Binta?"

"Lorenwile and his troop have left the tunnels, and are now trying to make their way through the mountains."

"Do you know how far they are?"

"I think. . .but I cannot say for a certainty, I think they are about a week away from Agavia."

"But that is good news," Pohl said. "Yes, yes, indeed, very good news!"

"Yes." Binta hesitated. "Yes, but I think the traveling is very hard. They must lead their horses. There is snow. One of the two women is heavy with child. There is a boy of eight or nine with them. And the other man has a bad limp. I think they might need some help, for only two of the five are in sound health, and all are exhausted from weeks of traveling. The mountains can be treacherous at this time of the year."

"Stars in the heavens!" Pohl said. He rose quickly. "I must take this news to Meekelorr. A rescue party must be sent out at once." He started to hurry to the door when the Lady stopped him.

"Pohl, be calm and wait a moment longer. First try to ascertain from Binta which path they are traveling on."

Pohl struck his forehead with the palm of his hand. "Dear Lady, sometimes I fear I am getting too old to think clearly." And he resumed his seat.

IT WAS DEEP winter now. Auragole had made many marks on the wall. He had spent his days making himself physically stronger, and had taken an inner journey he had never thought to take, nor knew that he could take. He had not had another visit from Goredahl. What was happening on the outside? What would he actually do if he were suddenly to find himself outside these walls? Other than longing to find those who had been his friends, he longed most of all for True-singing—the gift he had given up to become Ormahn's man.

"Why don't you practice True-singing in your cell?" his mother asked him.

"What?"

"Practice what you know of True-singing."

"You know about True-singing? How?"

She did not answer him, so he then asked, almost amused, "But what would I True-sing? My cot? My meals? My chamber pot? The prison walls with their terrible memories?"

"Sing what you remember. After all, you have had much practice remembering."

"What a curious idea." But he thought about what she had suggested.

"The walls are so thick in your cell, what unworthy person would hear you?"

The idea intrigued him. He spent some days thinking about it. And one day, he just began.

"DO YOU THINK six men besides you are enough?" Pohl asked Elarr, as Elarr was in the kitchen at the school packing provisions for the trip.

"One person for each of Lorenwile's party, including Lorenwile, one to guide the horses. Too many people will only increase our chances for an accident."

"Agreed. Don't forget the remedies."

"I have already packed them, Pohl."

"What about extra clothing?"

Elarr crossed his arms and looked at his friend. "Perhaps you would rather go in my stead. Then you could stop worrying like an old woman."

"Am I?"

Elarr just lifted his eyebrows and smiled. "Aren't we all? It's Last Battle fever. We're getting so close. Surely by late spring or early summer. And we want Lorenwile by our side, safe and well."

"Indeed, yes."

"Perhaps Lorenwile brings us the news we need," Elarr said.

"Perhaps. But he's been on the road a long time."

"Do you have any idea whom he is bringing with him?"

"The lame one could be Donnadorr," Pohl said. "If so, one of the others must be Sylvane."

"I know that's what Meekelorr thinks. But could not the injured man be Auragole?"

"I doubt that," Pohl said. "But I cannot say for a certainty."

"Two women—one pregnant, a child, and a lame man. Intriguing."

"Well, if all goes well, you should have the answers to all these speculations in less than a week."

"Yes. Now if you're done interrogating me, I'll go gather my men and get under way."

"No more questions." Pohl reached out his hand. "Good fortune, my friend."

"Thank you—may the Gods will it."

"Yes, yes, indeed."

AURAGOLE BEGAN SLOWLY—first only *thinking* about True-singing and about his teacher, Lorenwile, and their wonderful learning journey in the Woeful Peaks of the Sorren Heights. When he started to sing, he began with single objects from nature—a rock, a tree, a river, a mountain. He sang what he saw in his mind's eye, and was amazed that, after all these years, he could do it. He was True-singing the simple things he had started with, and all from memory. The joy of this discovery made him forget for hours at a time that he was in a cell, awaiting a fate that would probably end in his death. He sang, and what came flooding back to him was the fierce joy with which True-singing had filled him. In those days traveling through the Woeful Peaks, he had been unconcerned with war or peace, with Adversary Gods or Creative Gods, with anything but the world whose hidden depths he was plumbing. If he had shut out everything else at that time, it had been all right. Lorenwile had let it happen, had even encouraged it to happen. Auragole remembered, too, how Lorenwile had saved him from that creature, half bird, half animal—an abomination of the Golden Century—that had grabbed Auragole and had soared into the sky with him, carrying him high above a deep ravine. Lorenwile, with a still unimaginable kind of True-singing, had entered the bird beast and had coaxed it to bring its prey back to the path. Auragole remembered how he had first encountered his horse, Starwanderer, roaming wild with a herd, and how Lorenwile had encouraged him to True-sing the colt to him.

One day, from his cell, Auragole attempted to sing to his beloved horse, Starwanderer, whom he had last seen in the city of Thoren in the stables at Goredahl's palace. He had thought of his stallion often in the weeks since he had been in prison and had wondered if Goredahl had killed him too. But he could not imagine Goredahl not coveting a horse as grand as Starwanderer. So Auragole attempted to sing to Starwanderer. In his singing, he directed the horse to go to Agavia, and sang the path to him that Elarr had once drawn for him so many years ago. Auragole wanted Starwanderer in Agavia. If Starwanderer was going to be pressed into battle, let it be on the side of the Agavians. And so for hours that day he sang to his horse and hoped beyond hope that somehow his words would be sensed and that his marvelous stallion would break free from wherever he was and find his way to Agavia.

In the days that followed, Auragole recalled again the few days he and Lorenwile had spent with the Starmaster, how one night Auragole had drifted up out of sleep to hear singing coming from the plateau above him. Singing that he could only describe as the most exquisite he had ever heard. Out of some inner, never-doubted intuition, Auragole knew that Lorenwile had been True-singing the stars. And another voice had joined him—but not the Starmaster's. Who it was and what had become of this second singer after that night, Auragole never found out. He had never been able, no, had never dared ask Lorenwile.

Auragole thought about the one time he had sung, against all warnings, into the will of a human, attempting to direct it. No, that was not quite right. . .a half-human, because Kaynadahhn was half horse, half man, a son of the Seusadahhn, the legendary horse-men of the Woeful Peaks. The Seusadahhn were awaiting the coming of their human stage. On Auragole's conscience still was the death of Kaynadahhn, who had sired the Awaited One, who would lead them to their hearts' desire. Auragole had saved the two-legged child, and because of it had lost the father. When Kaynadahhn returned the child to the arms of Auragole, he left Auragole with one admonition before he leapt, in angry passion, to his death.

"Human, with this I charge you. Today you have rescued the future of the Seusadahhn. Let it be upon your head and the heads of your kind to make humanity a goal worthy of aspiration. As for me, I cannot bear the thought of the future. Already I feel it too much in me. The others do not know yet the loss it requires, a bitter loss for the Seusadahhn that I, alone, have tasted." He trotted back from the ledge. Auragole watched him, frozen. "I will not participate in what comes, though I lose all eternity," he shouted. Then, with a cry of exaltation, Auragole saw Kaynadahhn race back to the edge of the overhang, saw him leap, with a loud horse whinny, gracefully into the air. Auragole half expected him to fly. But he did not.

Remembering it now shook Auragole—for had he not forgotten? Had he not broken his word to Kaynadahhn?

Then and there, in his cell, he decided to try to put into song—the first he had written in years—his and Lorenwile's adventures with the Seusadahhn. It was a precious story, a strange and unearthly encounter that no other human had ever experienced. Yes, he would make a song, a new song. He would begin first with a poem, then try to See-sing it. And then he would try to go further— if he could. In his mind he first wrote then recited these words:

This is a tale of the Seusadahhn
the horse-men of the Woeful Peaks
and I, Auragole, tell you it as seen
in the mist-filled mirror of my mind.

Ride, ride, you creatures of the wind
while four legs are still left to you
four legs and a measure of suspended time.

I cannot sing them as Lorenwile sang them
that fire-brilliant day, while I stood naked
on our rock, flustered and awed, drunk
on their beauty, drawn to their innocence.

Lorenwile's song was the Seusadahhn's
own song found where all True-songs
are found. Their bodies trembled
in the brilliant sun, while great gold eyes

watched and heard and understood.
Lorenwile's song was tier upon tier of single
tone. And rhythm, rhyme and rhythm
rolling, rolling wild out of his throat.

From their human breasts he called
it forth, a story lush as the carpet
of grass that grew without season
in their color-saturated glade.

Ride, ride, I say, creatures of the wind.
The days are passing, passing, passing.

I want to tell you what my eyes
once saw—glory and madness
wonder and agony, all carved now
into the hardness of my bones

as Kaynadahhn's death weaves
in the flow of my blood, though
I forgot, forgot, living as I did
for years in arrogance and pride.

Beloved of the Gods, I thought
them and watched as they rode
like a hundred breezes rushing
through the thighs of the mountains

like light galloping out of the night
that nurses it. Night and darkness
madness and innocence bound them
yes, as surely as this cell binds me.

I know this now and weep—the glorious
horse-men of the Woeful Peaks
will soon be gone. The future cannot
hold them, will not hold them back.

So ride, ride, my legendary friends
and do not hasten yet into our war-
weary world even though the Child

has come. The Awaited One. After
years without number, years
without change the Father has granted
you your wish. You will become us—

two puny legs and hate in the heart.
Another fable lost to a world
that cannot raise its eyes
from the pebbles beneath its boots.

So ride still ride until you
must leave at last the Mother
for leaving is all your longing.

Anger and love are twisted tightly
in human souls. We will not unwind the strands.
But the horse-men of the Woeful Peaks
are sometimes light, sometimes shadow

sometimes love, sometimes rage
with never a bridge between. And it dug
in them a misery I could not understand
until I sang Kaynadahhn to his death.

To become was all their yearning
for in the days we call the First Days
they rushed to earth too soon, plunging
and falling out of the Creative World

into bodies not yet right
for the housing of humanity.
And so they lived unaltered and unalterable
in the bosom of the Mother and longed

for change and mourned, were good
and mad in turn until Lorenwile and I
were with them. Then the Father, whom we call
the King, took pity, and the two-legged child

was born. They will in a few generations
become wholly human and I am charged
with this—by him whose death I caused
that I make of humanity a worthy goal.

It was the central meaning of my life—
until I forgot. That forgetting is all my misery.
Ride. Ride. Oh, won't you ride.

Come, please come, those of you who will
and let me tell you a tale of the Seusadahhn,
the marvelous horse-men of the Woeful Peaks.
Let us remember before the wonder blows away

and dissipates on the thin breeze
of our forgetfulness. From the stars
in the heavens may the Gods
whose decree it is, weep.

Let he who wills to hear it, hear.

ELARR AND HIS men might have passed the cave where
Lorenwile and company were resting if it had not been for
Lorenwile's uncanny hearing. The cave was hidden behind
snow-covered whackle bushes and set some thirty feet above
the path Elarr had been following. A small, almost invisible trail
led to the cave where Lorenwile's troop had stopped for lunch
and a rest.

Lorenwile came to the entrance of the cave, but did not step out into full view. However, he called, "What heavy-footed group of incautious men is tramping so noisily past our resting place? What? No fear as yet in the Gandlese? Can you be sure the Nethergod is not hard at my heels even now?"

Elarr stopped in his tracks and tried to locate the familiar voice that was echoing off the mountains.

"Where the stars are you?" he finally asked in mingled pleasure and exasperation.

Lorenwile stepped out from behind the bushes. "Look up, my friends, but watch your footing. The trail you are on is a narrow one indeed."

"There he is," one of Elarr's soldiers said, and pointed.

Lorenwile put his fingers behind his ears and wiggled them at the men below. From behind him Elarr could see a child's face peeking out.

"You all had better come up—can you see the path?" Lorenwile said, "and tell me how you come to be on just this trail a few days away from the Valley of the Agavi. Looking for the Nethergod, are you?"

"Looking for you, you tardy old fool," Elarr said as he spotted the track to the cave and motioned his men to follow him.

How had they managed to get this far? Elarr wondered, when they were all under way again. The path was narrow, and treacherous with ice. The mountain was to their left, a steep decline was to their right. He was glad that he had brought one man to guide each traveler. It had taken them a day longer than he had expected to meet up with the company. He had begun to fear that they had passed Lorenwile by, or that they were on the wrong trail altogether, or, the Prince forbid, that some harm had come to them. Another day and he would have turned back for the valley.

If Elarr had been disappointed that the man was not Auragole, he quickly set that aside. He had heard of Donnadorr and Sylvane from Auragole when he and Affredda had traveled with him to Little Thoren in search of Elarr's captured men. Pohl had been right in his thinking. Two of the travelers with Lorenwile were indeed Donnadorr and his wife, Sylvane. Lorenwile had mentioned that he had befriended the two of them in Mattelmead City. It was from Pohl that he had learned that Donnadorr had once been foster parented by the great True-singer Aiku. Was it this connection to his own teacher that had caused Lorenwile to go hundreds of miles out of his way to rescue them? Or was it simply his own attachment to the couple? Elarr had never thought of Lorenwile as particularly sentimental. That, Elarr was sure, was his own lack of perception. One need not display emotion in order to love. Well, Lorenwile knew what he was about. For all his seeming nonchalance, he was probably the best judge of character that Elarr knew. If Lorenwile said that Donnadorr and Sylvane would have been captured, imprisoned, and possibly killed, then it was no doubt true. The other woman and her child were also friends of Auragole, found at Donnadorr's estate when Lorenwile arrived there.

Though not actually beautiful, Meraleese had a serene manner that Elarr found attractive—quite the opposite of his own tempestuous and self-assured wife. But this one was probably quite self-assured, too, and no doubt courageous. And the child, with his huge, dark, knowing eyes, watching and listening and thinking, was not so willful as many an eight-year-old boy can be, but cooperative and sensitive to the needs of those around him. That was not so easily found in the children Elarr knew, the orphans out of Little Thoren that he and Affredda had brought with them to Agavia. Glorr seemed more like the Agavian children, whose instincts made them sympathetic to the members of the group—as Agavians had been from time immemorial. Yet what lived in this child, Glorr, was something different. Children who had incarnated many times on the Deep

Earth often carried as a natural capacity some deep-seated wisdom—if their early years hadn't ruined those faculties. He had seen it in his own child of five, and had marveled.

Elarr had placed one of his soldiers in front of each of the travelers. The one leading the horses followed in the rear. Lorenwile led the group, with Elarr behind him. Lorenwile kept Elarr to a slow pace, and when he looked back at the pregnant woman, Elarr understood why. The path was dangerous. What was not needed was a fall and a premature birth. The thought of Sylvane giving birth on this narrow, icy trail kept Elarr at the unhurried pace Lorenwile had set. Elarr turned often to watch the progress of his companions. Donnadorr was limping badly, and his mouth was white and drawn into a thin line. But he never complained, nor did he disdain the hand that was often offered him when the path narrowed and was particularly insecure.

More than once that first day, Elarr wondered how on earth they had come this far. These people had been on the road for months. Lorenwile seemed healthy enough, but thinner than Elarr had ever seen him. Only the woman, Meraleese, seemed strong and untouched by the weeks and weeks of traveling. She walked with a careful yet easy grace, turning often to watch the progress of her son behind her, or to observe Sylvane's progress before her. Elarr wondered about Meraleese, how she had come to be living with Sylvane and Donnadorr. But there would be little stamina left for conversation at the end of these next four or five days. All stories would have to wait until they reached Agavia. Stopping for rest meant just that, and stopping for dinner meant also an early sleep. They exchanged only a few necessary words as they set up camp.

To Elarr's disappointment, Lorenwile knew no more than Elarr about what was going on in the west. He had kept his small band to the north, away from the habitations of humans. Lorenwile assumed that war and chaos filled the west now, just

as did Elarr and the commanders of the Companions of the Way
and the teachers at the school. Elarr wasn't sure what
Lorenwile's friends knew about the Nethergod, so he remained
silent on that subject. But he felt sorry for this troop of
wanderers, refugees from the bloodshed in the west. If they had
hoped to come at last to a safe haven, hidden from the world's
troubles, they would be sadly disappointed. There was no place
on the Deep Earth that was safe now.

It was late afternoon of the second day when the accident
happened. They had been walking in a single file led by Elarr,
who now walked behind the horses. Suddenly there was a
roaring sound, followed by a loud "Oh, dear Prince." He
turned to see that part of the path had collapsed, leaving their
group on either side of a path that had been cleft in two.
Meraleese, on his side of the cleft, was about to descend the
fairly steep snow and rocky slope.

"Stop," he commanded. "Don't move. I'll go after him."

He knew it had to be Glorr who had been swept down the
mountainside. One glance had told all. The soldier who had
been walking with Glorr was standing on a narrow ledge about
ten inches wide up against the side of the mountain. The path in
front of him was gone. As Elarr looked down, all he could see
was a ball of snow tumbling and rolling, and in it a little red
piece of cloth sticking out that had been Glorr's scarf.

Those on both sides of the broken path stood silently, the
women with their hands pressed against their mouths.

"Lorenwile, Dorr, Meraleese, Speel," he addressed those who
were on his side of the divide as he dropped his pack and
searched for his rope. "You will have to hold the end of the
rope. Tie it to Dorr, and you others hold on to him. There is
nowhere else to tie this rope." He tossed the rope to Dorr, who
tied it around his waist and sat down. Tying the other end to his
own waist, Elarr held the rest of the rope coil loosely in his
hands. He then sat down, pushed himself off the edge of the

path, and began sliding down the side of the mountain as slowly as he could, keeping his eye on the little red scarf and letting go more and more of the rope as he descended. The ball of snow had come to a stop some one hundred feet down, possibly on a ledge.

"Glorr," Elarr called as he drew near. "If you can hear me, listen carefully to what I am saying. First of all do not move, not a muscle. That might send you tumbling even farther. I am coming after you with a rope, and with the help of all your friends, we will get you back to the path. Don't move. Don't try to speak. I'm not far away." Elarr kept talking, hoping the boy was conscious, hoping he wasn't dead, hoping that his words would keep the boy calm and still until he got to him. When Elarr was finally next to the snow mass that covered the child, he called to those above to pull up the slack.

"Glorr, I'm here, next to you." The mass of snow that held Glorr had indeed stopped on a narrow shelf. Elarr sat down beside him. "I'm just going to remove this snow from you very carefully. When you see my hand, catch hold of it. But otherwise don't move." Elarr began pushing the snow away a little at a time. He didn't want to send the boy flying down the long mountain. He prayed the ledge they were on would not give way. There was no movement under that snow. Dear Prince, let me find this child alive, Elarr prayed as he brushed snow away.

It took no more than five minutes, though it seemed an eternity to Elarr, and no doubt to the group who waited above him, to find the boy's head and remove the snow that lay loosely on the boy's face. Glorr had his eyes closed and lay huddled on his side, one arm covering his head, leaving a pocket of air near his mouth and nose, the other arm held loosely at his side.

"Glorr, can you hear me? It's all right to speak now."

"Yes," came the quavering reply.

"Before I move you, tell me what hurts. Where are you injured?"

"I'm all right—except my arm."

Elarr brushed the snow away and looked at the arm. Broken, he thought.

"Well, we'll be careful of that. Let me clear enough snow from around you and then I will need you to help. Can you do that?"

"Yes."

Elarr dug carefully around the boy, freeing him a little more from the snow. "Now I'm going to take hold of you around the waist and I'm going to pull. As soon as you can, with your good arm, grab me around the neck." Elarr knew this was going to hurt because the injured arm lay just where Elarr needed to take hold of the boy. Glorr let out a small cry as Elarr slipped his arm around the boy's waist, jarring the broken arm. But as soon as Elarr had hold of the boy's waist, he yanked and the boy thrust his good arm around Elarr's neck. At that moment the shelf they had been on gave way. The two were dangling over the side of a mountain whose bottom was yards and yards below. There were shouts of alarm from above.

"It's all right. I have him," Elarr called. "Pull us up. I'll help as best I can with my feet. But I'm holding the boy with my arms. Just don't any of you come sliding down. Hang on to each other."

The group of three had sat down behind Dorr, each hanging on to the one in front, and slowly they pulled the two up.

"Be careful," Elarr warned Meraleese as they came over the ledge and she was about to embrace her son. "His left arm is broken, I think. Glorr, sit on the path with your mother. We need to get those on the far side of this split in the path onto our side. Lucky the horses were ahead of us."

The young man who had stood on the now ten-inch path had come over to their side.

"Hang on to the rope," Elarr told the men. "I'm taking it over to the other side and one by one I'll send the others, tied to the rope, across that narrow bit of a path." And he did. In half an hour all were gathered on the appropriate side of the broken path.

"There is a cave no more than half an hour from here," Lorenwile informed them.

No one asked how he knew.

"Then let's get there," Elarr said, "and then we can attend to Glorr's arm."

It wasn't until sometime late in the night, as Elarr tried in vain to sleep, that he began to feel all his own scrapes and bruises.

But somehow or other, before the last week of January, Elarr and Lorenwile brought the group safely to Agavia.

Mission accomplished.

chapter thirty-seven

AURAGOLE WOKE UP from sleep. He felt reluctant to start the day. It was yet another night without a dream about his mother—he had not dreamed of her since she had suggested he True-sing. It was more than two weeks since they had met in the night. He dreamt sometimes of Meraleese—that they were making love. But when he awoke from those dreams, he knew they were only dreams, dreams of wish and need. What he had shared with his mother seemed like something else. And now she was gone. Why, as the weeks in prison grew into months, had she suddenly abandoned him? He needed something to sustain him, someone to encourage him. Why did she not come to him? He hadn't realized how much those dream-meetings, real or imagined, had meant to him, hadn't realized how much he had actually enjoyed their contesting, their arguing, and finally their quiet talks. What did it mean, that he could no longer bring her into his dream consciousness? She had become so much a part of what he did in prison, and now there was no one to share anything with.

He began to wonder, and yes, to worry again about what was happening on the outside. Without the distractions and comfort of those dreams he began again to feel anxious for his old friends. Were they alive? Don, Sylvie, Meraleese, and Glorr. And what had happened to the Westernlands—the United West that rightly belonged to him as heir of Solagen? Had Goredahl finally achieved his illegal desire? Was he now Ormahn of all the west? And where was he? It was two months since Goredahl had visited him. If the west was now his, wouldn't he have brought Auragole to trial? Or had he forgotten about him? And if the west was now his, was Goredahl about to turn his attention toward Agavia? Or had he already? If there was such a being as the Nethergod, had the Nethergod in the form of Goredahl finally attacked that peaceful valley and overcome it? Not so soon. Surely not so soon.

Auragole sat up. He mustn't allow such thoughts to overwhelm him. There was no way he could know if any of his worries were true. No reason yet to fear the worst. He believed in the Nethergod and disbelieved at the same time. But he was growing used to these contradictions in his soul. Auragole had managed to hang on to his calm and his sanity for weeks, managed to keep anxiety at bay. When the meetings with his mother had stopped, he had tried to pray. He remembered how Elarr had an encounter with the Prince at a time of great despair. It had changed Elarr's life. But here in prison, surely the most difficult time he had ever faced, Auragole had experienced no encounter with any God. Did the Gods despise him? Had they turned from him? Did they exist?

It was hard to reason himself into starting his day of exercise, the now-familiar retrospective of his life, the singing. He forced himself to begin. But all calm was gone. When had it slid away, to be replaced by these fears? He managed to walk, managed to exercise, but when he tried to look back at his life again, he failed. A different kind of mental exercise was what he needed. So he tried to think about love and its meaning in the world, but it all seemed like an exercise in futility. He tried to sing, but he could not keep his mind on even plain singing, let alone True-singing.

Finally, Auragole lay down again. He would rest a while and try again later. He fell asleep. When he awoke, he tried once more to think—about anything—but could not muster the interest. He tried to sing. But it was of no use. He was filled with anxiety over the fate of his friends, over the Valley of the Agavi, over the west that he had worked so hard to unite.

He began to pace about the room, but after only a few minutes, he lay down again. It took too much energy to move about. It did nothing to decrease his growing panic. When the food came, he forced that down. It took great effort to eat when his stomach was churning so. Still, he wanted to avoid becoming weak again, avoid the beatings that would surely come if he did not eat. When the last meal was over, he lay down again and, hoping to dream of his mother, fell asleep.

MERALEESE WAS LYING in bed in the Lady Claregole's mansion, thinking about Agavia. The door between her room and Glorr's was slightly ajar and in the quiet she could hear his rhythmic breathing. Down the hall were the rooms that Donnadorr and Sylvane had been given, and not far from those rooms were the rooms occupied by Affredda and Elarr, two new friends. She and Affredda had immediately taken to each other. Often the men stayed up at the school overnight. On those occasions, the three women would get together in the evening to talk.

Meraleese had learned much from Affredda, who had been in Agavia for about five years. Of course, Auragole had also spoken to Meraleese about this wondrous land. He had even spoken to her about the Last Battle. She wondered what he would have thought of the fences and walls built around the manor houses and mansions in the valley, or the fortifications in the hills Don spoke about when he came home for the night. As Don and Sylvie had never mentioned the Last Battle to her in their years together, Meraleese had not said anything to them about what she had learned from Auragole. But now they talked about it, the three women—and sometimes the men.

Meraleese would have liked to tell Auragole about the Feast of Aa that she had witnessed a few nights earlier, just days after their arrival in Agavia. She would have liked to tell him that she had heard the old storyteller, the same one, she had been told, that Auragole had heard at the Feast of Aa. He was very old, but his voice was still strong and mellifluous. The feast had been a wonder, a true wonder. But then, all of Agavia seemed a wonder to her. How she wished Timorr had lived to see this place. When she had been invited to the school to meet the teachers and had been questioned about Timorr's beliefs, and her own, she had so wished that it could have been Timorr himself who had given the report of his investigations into the Creative World. But perhaps he had been there, because she knew she had spoken eloquently about what he had given as knowledge to those who had attended his temple—and to her. The teachers had been delighted and amazed, and, she thought, heartened. Perhaps there were other pockets of knowledge on the Grand Continent. Perhaps they were not so alone.

Her thoughts turned from Timorr to Auragole without any sense of guilt. It was with Auragole that she would have liked to have shared the celebration. The Feast of Aa. The King God, Timorr would have called him. And in the spring Meraleese would participate in the celebration of the Feast of Demeda, Goddess of growing things. Meraleese was to sing in a chorus at that celebration.

Eight days she and the others had been there. Only eight days. And so much had happened. Despite the preparation for war—the significant Last Battle, which the Agavians and the Companions of the Way would wage for the soul of the Deep Earth—a remarkable peace seemed to pervade the Valley of the Agavi. The calmness with which the Agavians met the possibility of battle in the coming spring or summer amazed her. But she too felt calm. Surely goodness would win out. She had to believe that. And the way the Agavians went about their daily tasks, as if there were nothing to be afraid of, added to her sense of tranquility.

Whatever would happen, this was a good place to live in—or to die in, if it came to that.

What had happened to Auragole? Somehow she couldn't think of him as dead. Somehow she felt she would know if he were gone—the same way she had known in her heart when Timorr was dead. And if Auragole was alive, they would meet again, of that she was sure. Besides, Affredda had said to her, with a belief that was unquestionable, that if Auragole was alive, somehow he would find his way to Agavia. Meraleese hung on to that thought. And she hung on to the afterglow of the strange and lovely Feast of Aa.

HE DIDN'T REMEMBER it, but Auragole must have stopped eating, because one day the great door opened and in came six armed men and the commander who had threatened him with beatings long ago.

"Why are you not eating?" the commander asked him. "Have I not told you what would befall you if you stopped eating? Stand up when I am talking to you."

Auragole tried to stand, but sank back on the bed. "I. . .I can't. I think I'm sick."

The commander came closer. He stared at Auragole, then backed away. "He is ill again. See to it that he has clear soups and fruit juice for a week before he is given solid food again. He looks feverish. And clean this cell. I have orders to keep him alive, and I intend to do that. If he dies, you will all pay. Bring him another blanket."

When he turned to leave, Auragole called out, "Wait, what has happened in the war? Does Goredahl hold the west?"

The commander turned at the door. "All you need to know is that you are to eat all that is given you or, sick or not, you will be beaten." And he left, his men following him.

POHL GLANCED AROUND with interest at the room that Meekelorr occupied at the school, as he always did when invited there. By Agavian standards it was austere. A bed in a corner, a desk, a chest for clothes, a table in front of the fireplace with four chairs. Even at the school, most of the teachers and longtime students had adapted to some of the ways of the Agavians. The Agavians loved the ornate. Every piece of their furniture was exquisitely carved, their walls covered with hangings. There were carpets on the floor with intricate designs, sculptures on every available surface. Though ornate, nothing made by the Agavians was garish. They had a love of detail, yet they could be exquisitely subtle.

Meekelorr's room was his retreat; few were invited. It was furnished in part like the cabins of his soldiers who dwelled in the large camp on the sloping field north of the school. There had been no time to make the kind of furniture the Agavians would have liked to make for the Companions. The Companions of the Way had come, in these last years, in such large numbers that the need for housing for protection against the winter had precluded the slow making of buildings and furniture that was the Agavian way. The soldiers' camp was temporary and meant to be temporary. When the Agavians made something, it was made to last hundreds of years. Whatever the outcome of the Last Battle would be, the barracks with all their furniture would not remain after the conclusion of the battle.

The Companions had not built their structures out of the Agavi wood that grew only in the hills above the Valley of the Agavi. Whether it would have been a desecration or not to use the Agavi wood, Meekelorr had decided that the pine trees that grew not far from the school were good enough. They were fast growing, common in the Gandlese, and not sacred, he had explained.

Meekelorr had taken into his large room at the school some of the pine furniture that his soldiers were also using. Only the desk in his room was of Agavi wood, beautifully made and carved by Galavi himself. And there was that large and glorious tapestry hanging on the widest of Meekelorr's walls. This had been stitched over many years, and it depicted one of the creation stories of the Agavi. The simplicity of everything else in the room drew one's eyes again and again to the desk or to the tapestry. The Lady Claregole was purported to be the most skilled of the Agavian tapestry weavers, and she had made this one. She had recently taken Meraleese under her wing and was attempting to teach her this ancient Agavian art—as if they had nothing but time and no war was imminent, as if the end of the Agavian way of life was not almost upon them.

Pohl was sitting at the table in front of the fireplace, warming his feet. It was early February and very cold in the mountains. The rituals for the Feast of Aa would go on for at least ten more days. And in these rituals the Lady Claregole led. Meekelorr had not gone down to the valley except briefly while she was thus engaged. He was pacing now, as was his wont when something was on his mind. They were waiting for Elarr and Lorenwile. It was unusual for meetings to be held in Meekelorr's room. There were enough conference rooms in the school, and if the talk concerned battle plans, there was Meekelorr's office down at the camp where they could have met, with maps of every sort. This gathering must be about something quite private, something that did not have to do with battle strategies.

The tea and cakes had been brought. The kettle of hot water was hanging on a hook over the fire. Meekelorr was silent, walking, walking. Meekelorr often seemed restless, but Pohl knew it was Meekelorr's way of thinking. "Getting some muscle behind my thoughts," he had once explained to Pohl, who, after watching this activity many years ago, had implored, "Sit down, please. You're making me dizzy." But now he watched and waited and wondered what was on his friend's mind.

Elarr and Lorenwile arrived together. After quick greetings, and after Meekelorr had served the tea, Meekelorr began by asking Lorenwile, "How are the newcomers adjusting now that they've been here two weeks?"

Surely, Pohl thought, the Lady Claregole had given him a full report, as all were staying in her mansion.

But Lorenwile did not seem baffled by the question. He popped a small cake into his mouth, leaned back in his chair, and stretched out his legs. "In my opinion, they are doing very well. I thought they took the news of the expected coming of the Nethergod with little perturbation, didn't you?"

"But Don and Sylvie had heard about the Last Battle when they were in Agavia seven years ago," Pohl said. "Surely it is not news to them."

"Yes, but that it is imminent, that caused an initial surprise," Lorenwile said. "They are a sturdy group. They took it in with remarkable equanimity. The Gods for them have always had some basis in reality. Did you know that Meraleese, too, knew about the Last Battle? It seems Auragole told her about it before he became heir to Mattelmead. She also knew about the incarnation of the Nethergod—that from her husband, the priest who was executed."

"An interesting lady, that one. Indeed, yes," Pohl said.

"Very interesting," Lorenwile said.

"The story of that little church. . ." Pohl said. "Sad and yet heartening. To know that there are people here and there who can out of their own capacities still find their way into the Creative World and bring back knowledge. . ."

"Far too few, I'm afraid," Lorenwile said. "And of course, Don is very happy since you have allowed him to join the Companions." Then he paused and looked questioningly at Meekelorr.

Pohl too turned to Meekelorr. They had not been called to this private meeting to discuss how well the newcomers were adjusting.

"You spent a great deal of time with Auragole, Lorenwile," Meekelorr said. "Did you ever tell him how to find his way back to Agavia?"

Lorenwile raised his eyebrows. But his answer came quickly and unequivocally. "No."

Meekelorr watched him, his gray eyes black in the firelight. Lorenwile met Meekelorr's gaze. If Lorenwile said "No," Pohl thought, it was "No."

Next Meekelorr turned to Pohl. Pohl looked back at him in surprise. "Are you asking me that same question?" But Meekelorr waited in silence. So Pohl said, "After taking the whole crew of them through the Cave of Terrors all those years ago just so none of them would ever find their way back here, or lead anyone back here, after almost losing Glenelle in those confounded caves, do you think I would cancel out the whole experience and tell any of them how to return here?" His tone was mild, but his eyes blazed and he was certain Meekelorr saw it.

"When I didn't show up for the rendezvous," Meekelorr said, "and after you had directed the Easterners west toward Mattelmead on a most dangerous path, different from the one we had intended for them. . ."

"There were bandits in the hills. No possibility of going north as planned."

"I know all that, Pohl. I just wondered if, in your concern for their safety, you might have told Auragole how to return here if they could not make it through."

"I see," Pohl said, and his anger dissolved. "I could have done. I might have done. But I did not. The fate of Agavia loomed too large in my mind to take the chance. It seemed a cruelty then, but I told him nothing."

All eyes turned to Elarr. The color had risen in his cheeks. That's not from the heat of the fire, Pohl thought. Elarr had sat unmoving during this last exchange, arms resting on his knees, leaning slightly forward and staring at his hands.

"Yes," he said, his voice barely audible.

No one spoke.

So Elarr went on. "It was years ago." He finally lifted his eyes to Meekelorr's. "It was when Auragole and I were returning to the Doldarr Valley, after our vain attempt to rescue my men from the fort in Little Thoren. I was going back, as honor finally dictated, to report to you—to report, among other things, the death of the rebel leader Boreen, and to take the punishment due me for my disobedience. And Auragole accompanied me." He turned to the others. "He had taken a horse from Meekelorr without permission and wanted to return it. And," he looked now at Lorenwile, "he wanted to wait for you to return from the east." He glanced around at the others. "But I think you all know that story."

"Why did you feel it was necessary to tell him the way to Agavia?" Meekelorr asked, his expression unreadable.

"I didn't know what might happen to me, you see. And Affredda had remained at the children's village in the Ancient Woods in war-torn Thorensphere. Just before we arrived at the Doldarr Valley, I requested of Auragole that should something befall me that would make me unable to get back to her, to find Affredda, and bring her and the community to safety in Agavia."

"How did you explain the way here?"

"I drew him a map—on the ground—showing him the way

through the Northern Valley, and from there to what is now the Battle Valley. He memorized it and then I erased it."

"I see."

"But that was years ago. I doubt if he would remember it today."

Meekelorr rose from his chair. He walked to the fire and began poking it.

"Is it important? Frankly, if he's alive and able, I hope he finds his way to Agavia. Is there a problem here?" Elarr's last words were a little defiant.

Meekelorr straightened his back, turned, and looked at Elarr. "There's only a problem, Elarr, if he has told anyone else how to get here."

THE SMALL DOOR opened unexpectedly in the middle of the night. But the sound woke Auragole. He sat up.

"Prince Auragole, can you come to the door?" The voice outside sounded young and urgent.

Auragole rose up and, shaking off sleep, knelt down at the door. "I'm here. What is it?" No one had ever spoken to him before when bringing food or retrieving things. And it was the middle of the night.

"Listen, I can't talk. But here, I've brought you three pitchers of water. Take them quickly. If I get caught. . . And here are two loaves of bread." The stranger shoved the items through the small door as quickly as he could. "Make them last. I don't know when you will receive food or drink again."

"Why? What's happened?" Auragole's mind was racing and the blood was rushing through his veins.

"I can't tell you. There's no time. And this is dangerous. Be well. I hope they find you," and then the door slid closed and Auragole heard no more. He stood up and looked at what had been pushed into his cell: two medium-sized loaves of bread and three jugs of water. He placed them against a wall and sat down on the bed. His heart was beating rapidly. What was going on? What was happening in the fort or in the town? Was the fort under attack? Or was Goredahl simply abandoning the fort and moving on, leaving his prisoners to their fate? Who was the kind young soldier who had given him water and bread? "Make them last," he had been told.

Auragole felt torn between excitement and fear. Perhaps Goredahl was not succeeding in his attempt to take over the west and Solagen's throne. Perhaps Goredahl was on the run. But who knew that he, Auragole, was here in this prison? And if the fort was under attack, was it by someone who was also Auragole's enemy? Was it by some group who would be as glad as Goredahl to see him dead, and the throne up for the grabbing? He could be rescued, or forgotten. If rescued, would it be by friend or foe?

He stared at the bread and at the jugs of water. "Make them last." How long could he make them last? The water was by far the most important. He could go a long time without food, but without water. . . He lay back down and tried to assess his plight. Either he would be rescued, or he would die here, a slow death by starvation and dehydration. Not a pleasant way to go.

Well, he thought, at least something has changed after so many monotonous weeks. I'd better figure out how long I can manage to stay alive on what provisions I have. And so he began to calculate in his mind how many days he could make the food and water last.

HE WAS STANDING in the middle of the room. It was immense. He was facing two tables.

This is not quite like the room where the elders of the Guardians of the Flame sat in council, Auragole thought. But this was some sort of council.

The lower table was on his level. It was the larger of the two. The smaller table was above the other on a platform. This enabled Auragole to see all the individuals at both tables at once. At the upper table, seated in the middle, was Biehmar, and arrayed on both sides of him were the other six teachers who made up the council of the Last School in Agavia: Gewdril; Alumbra, the only female teacher; Sandrofil; Fllordon; Mondrief, the eldest; and Stor.

At the lower table, starting on Auragole's left, sat Sylvane, Donnadorr, Affredda, Elarr, Galavi, Meekelorr, the Lady Claregole, Pohl, Lorenwile, and at the far right end, Meraleese. Their hands were folded and they rested them on the tables. All eyes were on Auragole. Cool eyes, Auragole thought.

What did they want with him? Why was he here?

Biehmar rose and said, "Auragole of Mattelmead, this is your trial. What are the charges?"

"I don't understand," Auragole said, puzzling over Biehmar's words. "If I am on trial here, surely someone has brought charges against me."

"That is correct," Biehmar said. "So I ask again, what are the charges you have brought against yourself?"

Auragole looked at him in astonishment, then at each face staring back at him. No one was smiling—only watching, waiting.

"In truth, sir," Auragole finally said, looking up at Biehmar, "I don't remember."

Fllordon rose. "That is not an acceptable answer, Auragole, son of Solagen."

"It won't do, you know, Auragole," Affredda said from where she sat. "It simply won't do."

He turned to her. "Is it that I've been adopted by Solagen? Is that the charge?"

"Do you accuse yourself of that?" Biehmar said.

"I don't know. I'm not sure what I'm supposed to say." He turned to Elarr. "Is it because I joined the army of Mattelmead, when I said I would never give up my freedom to be in anyone's army, that I stand accused?"

"I remember that you said that, Auragole. You were quite adamant," Elarr answered.

Auragole turned from him in confusion. He tried to remember. What had he come here for? Biehmar said he had come with an accusation against himself. An idea occurred to him then. He looked now at Meekelorr.

"Is it because I didn't look for the Nethergod, believing instead that Solagen would find him and destroy him?"

Meekelorr only stared at him, and Auragole turned to the Lady Claregole. "Is it because I have not come to the aid of the Agavians in the Last Battle, even though I am mother-kin to you and Galavi?" He looked now at Galavi. "But perhaps the Nethergod is dead and you wait for him in vain."

"He is not dead," Galavi answered. "He will come, and soon. For this we have prepared thousands of years. It is our destiny."

"But is it mine?" Auragole was shocked at his own words, and once again he turned to the Lady Claregole. "Is it?"

"You choose, Auragole," she said.

"Pohl, you risked your life for me and my friends. Is it that I have not repaid you in some way?"

"A deed freely done incurs no debt," Pohl said.

Auragole walked toward Donnadorr and Sylvane. "I endangered you, didn't I? When I became prince, I endangered you. My enemies became enemies to you."

"You gave us Glorr," Sylvane said.

"And Meraleese," Don added.

Auragole hurried down the table to its far end, where Meraleese sat. She looked up but there was no welcoming smile on her face.

"It must be because I came as a spy to your temple and brought disaster to you and your family that I stand accused."

"Is that what you think, Auragole?" she said. "Has your mind become so closed and your thoughts so withered and lifeless?"

Stricken, Auragole's eyes brushed across Lorenwile's face. "It's the True-singing, isn't it? I deserted you and gave up the chance to become a True-singer in favor of becoming Solagen's man. That's it, isn't it?"

"This is your trial and your story, Auragole," Lorenwile said.

Auragole slowly walked back to the center of the room. "My trial and my story," he mumbled. He turned to face those who waited for him to speak. All eyes were on him.

Suddenly, behind the upper table vague shapes began to appear. Shadowy, transparent figures, but quite clear to his vision. There were his mother and father and Spehn. There were Solagen and Kaynadahhn. There were Quill and Antine, who had gone with him to rescue Elarr back those years ago and were killed. There were several Companions of the Way whom he had known, Companions who had died in battle, and there were many members of the army of Mattelmead who had also fallen in the wars.

And there was a host of ephemeral figures he could not quite make out—light-filled figures, yet human in form.

"I failed to find the Gods," Auragole cried, "to believe in the Gods. I failed to find the meaning of love, to honor my commitment to make of humanity a species worthy of taking into our ranks the glorious Seusadahhn. I failed to believe what I did not want to believe, yet knew in my heart."

And then he was in his prison cell again. Awake. Or perhaps this cell was the dream.

THE BREAD HAD been gone for many days. He didn't remember how many. He had finished the last of the water— was it yesterday? He had no strength left other than to lie on his bed and wait for death. Auragole had long ago given up the walking and the exercise. He had stopped wrestling with memories or questions. He had even stopped praying. Some weeks earlier, he had called and called on the Gods, but none had come. He had received no vision of the Prince, as Elarr had when he was in such misery and despair. Auragole had no dreams like the one he had had after he had been burned by the beast's poison in the Cave of Books before he had been taken to Agavia. Over and over again, sitting in his cell, he had begged the Gods to come, to give him a sign of their caring, to give him something. But none had come. If they came in his dreams, he did not remember.

He vaguely remembered some sort of trial.

Auragole slept more and more as the food and water diminished. He could no longer tell the difference between his dreams and reality. His mother came and sat by him and watched him, but said nothing. His father came and said to him, "Victorious are those who believe, son, even when they do not believe." Auragole didn't try to answer. He was too tired, had no voice. Yet he understood that he was dying and that they were waiting for him, those two who had given him life. He wasn't afraid. What was dying? he wondered. Either endless sleep or a crossing over to another reality. It didn't matter much now. He wondered if he had learned anything in his short life. "Only love matters," his father answered. "All else is chimera." His mother said nothing, just sat in her rocking chair, the one his father had made for her, and watched him as she had through many childhood illnesses and injuries. Love, the big question, Auragole thought. The unanswered question. I shall bring that question with me like a bone in my throat wherever I go. "It is not how much you are loved that matters, my son," his father said. "It is how much you have loved others."

Once he saw Solagen walk by his bed with a sorrowful look on his face. His step seemed heavy, and he didn't look at Auragole as he passed by. Auragole tried to call out to him. His father said, "He is blind here, and deaf. He cannot hear you, nor anyone. Yet he is conscious of being—and is very confused."

How pitiful, thought Auragole. Will I be blind? Will I be deaf?

"No," his father said to him. "You have thought about the Gods and they have come to you, though you were unaware, and through you they looked out onto the world and saw with your eyes and heard with your ears. You, my son, will see and hear with whatever capacities you made yours on the Deep Earth."

I am not afraid, he thought.

"No," his father said, and his mother just rocked and rocked and watched him with interested eyes.

Was it the next day, or the next? Auragole heard a key in the door and that terrible grating sound when the door was pushed open. He saw his mother rise from her rocking chair, come toward him, and stroke his head. "You will live," she said. "Remember."

"Remember, son," his father said. And they both disappeared.

"Stars in the heavens," someone was saying, "it's Prince Auragole. Bring me water as fast as you can. And a litter."